WRITTEN IN RED

ALSO BY ANNE BISHOP

THE BLACK JEWELS SERIES

Daughter of the Blood

Heir to the Shadows

Queen of the Darkness

The Invisible Ring

Dreams Made Flesh

Tangled Webs

The Shadow Queen

Shalador's Lady

Twilight's Dawn

THE EPHEMERA SERIES

Sebastian

Belladonna

Bridge of Dreams

THE TIR ALAINN TRILOGY

The Pillars of the World

Shadows and Light

The House of Gaian

WRITTEN IN RED

A NOVEL OF THE OTHERS

ANNE BISHOP

A ROC BOOK

ROC
Published by New American Library,
a division of Penguin Group (USA) Inc.,
375 Hudson Street, New York, New York 10014, USA
Penguin Group (Canada), 90 Eglinton Avenue East, Suite 700, Toronto,
Ontario M4P 2Y3, Canada (a division of Pearson Penguin Canada Inc.)
Penguin Books Ltd., 80 Strand, London WC2R 0RL, England
Penguin Ireland, 25 St. Stephen's Green, Dublin 2,
Ireland (a division of Penguin Books Ltd.)
Penguin Group (Australia), 250 Camberwell Road, Camberwell,
Victoria 3124, Australia (a division of Pearson Australia Group Pty. Ltd.)
Penguin Books India Pvt. Ltd., 11 Community Centre,
Panchsheel Park, New Delhi - 110 017, India
Penguin Group (NZ), 67 Apollo Drive, Rosedale, Auckland 0632,
New Zealand (a division of Pearson New Zealand Ltd.)
Penguin Books (South Africa) (Pty.) Ltd., 24 Sturdee Avenue,
Rosebank, Johannesburg 2196, South Africa

Penguin Books Ltd., Registered Offices:
80 Strand, London WC2R 0RL, England

First published by Roc, an imprint of New American Library,
a division of Penguin Group (USA) Inc.

First Printing, March 2013
1 3 5 7 9 10 8 6 4 2

LIBRARY OF CONGRESS CATALOGING-IN-PUBLICATION DATA:
Bishop, Anne.
Written in red: a novel of the Others/Anne Bishop.
p. cm.
ISBN 978-0-451-46496-5
1. Fantasy fiction. I. Title.
PS3552.I7594W75 2013
813'.54—dc23 2012036432

Set in Albertina MT • Designed by Elke Sigal

Printed in the United States of America

For Blair

ACKNOWLEDGMENTS

My thanks to Blair Boone for continuing to be my first reader and for all the information about animals and other things that I absorbed and transformed to suit the Others' world, to Debra Dixon for being second reader, to Doranna Durgin for maintaining the Web site and for information about cow tongues, to Adrienne Roehrich for running the official fan page on Facebook, to Julie Green for telling me about Bully Sticks, to Jennifer Crow for her role as enabler when I talked about the Others Etiquette column, to Nadine Fallacaro for information about things medical, to Douglas Burke for answering questions about police (and for not asking what I would do with the information), and to Pat Feidner for her support and encouragement. Thanks to Kristen Britain, Starr Corcoran, Julie Czerneda, Claire Eamer, Lorne Kates, and Paula Lieberman for their input about stores for the Market Square and the surrounding neighborhood.

A special thanks to the following people who loaned their names to characters, knowing that the name would be the only connection between reality and fiction: Elizabeth Bennefeld, Blair Boone, Douglas Burke, Starr Corcoran, Jennifer Crow, Lorna MacDonald Czarnota, Julie Czerneda, Roger Czerneda, Merri Lee Debany, Michael Debany, Chris Fallacaro, Dan Fallacaro, Mike Fallacaro, Nadine Fallacaro, Mantovani "Monty" Gay, Julie Green, Lois Gresh, Ann Hergott, Danielle Hilborn, Heather Houghton, Lorne Kates, Allison King, and John Wulf.

GEOGRAPHY

NAMID—THE WORLD

CONTINENTS/LAND MASSES (so far)

Afrikah
Cel-Romano/Cel-Romano Alliance of Nations
Felidae
Fingerbone Islands
Storm Islands
Thaisia
Tokhar-Chin
Brittania/Wild Brittania

Great Lakes—Superior, Tala, Honon, Etu, and Tahki
Other lakes—Feather Lakes/Finger Lakes
River—Talulah/Talulah Falls
Cities or villages—Hubb NE (aka Hubbney), Jerzy, Lakeside, Podunk, Sparkletown, Talulah Falls, Toland

DAYS OF THE WEEK

Earthday
Moonsday
Sunsday
Windsday
Thaisday
Firesday
Watersday

LAKESIDE

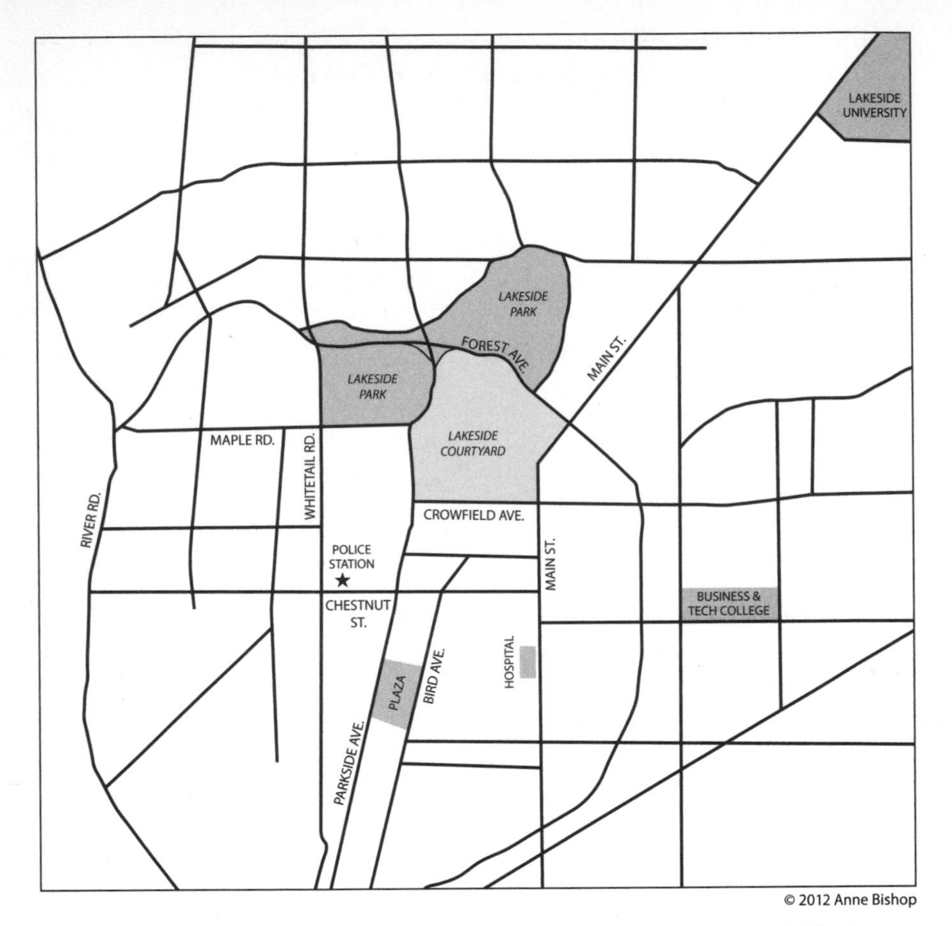

This map was created by a geographically challenged author who put in only the bits she needed for the story.

LAKESIDE COURTYARD

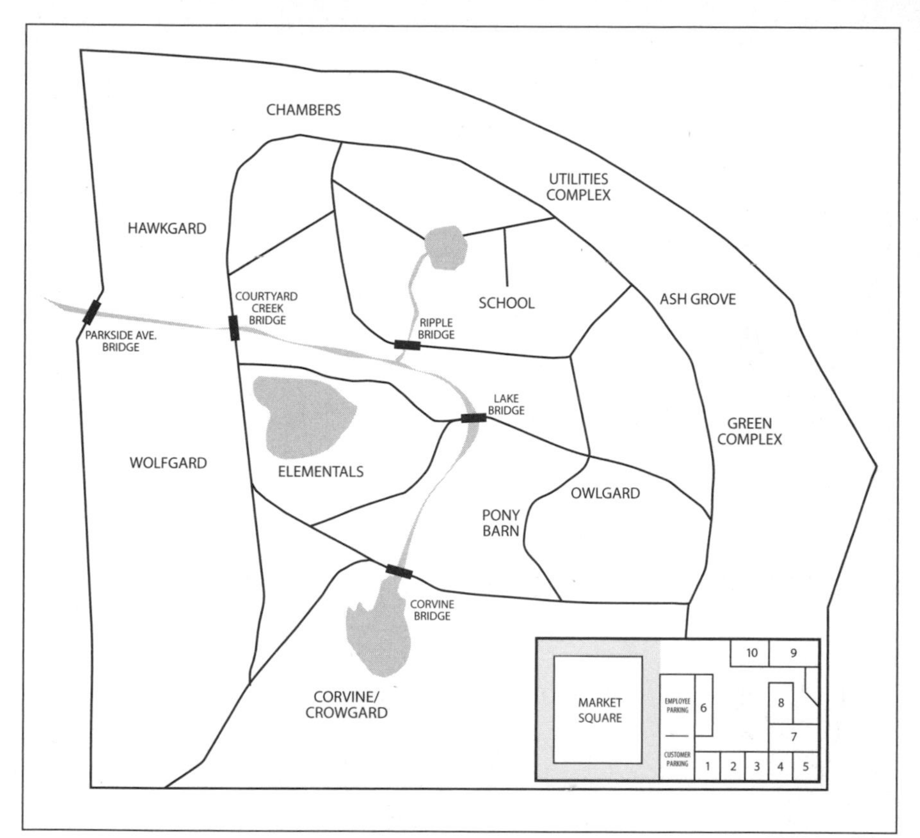

1. Seamstress/Tailor & efficiency apartments
2. A Little Bite
3. Howling Good Reads
4. Run & Thump
5. Social Center
6. Garages
7. Earth Native & Henry's Studio
8. Liaison's Office
9. Consulate
10. Three Ps

A Brief History of the World

Long ago, Namid gave birth to all kinds of life, including the beings known as humans. She gave the humans fertile pieces of herself, and she gave them good water. Understanding their nature and the nature of her other offspring, she also gave them enough isolation that they would have a chance to survive and grow. And they did.

They learned to build fires and shelters. They learned to farm and build cities. They built boats and fished in the Mediterran and Black seas. They bred and spread throughout their pieces of the world until they pushed into the wild places. That's when they discovered that Namid's other offspring already claimed the rest of the world.

The Others looked at humans and did not see conquerors. They saw a new kind of meat.

Wars were fought to possess the wild places. Sometimes the humans won and spread their seed a little farther. More often, pieces of civilization disappeared, and fearful survivors tried not to shiver when a howl went up in the night or a man, wandering too far from the safety of stout doors and light, was found the next morning drained of blood.

Centuries passed, and the humans built larger ships and sailed across the Atlantik Ocean. When they found virgin land, they built a settlement near the shore. Then they discovered that this land was also claimed by the *terra indigene*, the earth natives. The Others.

The *terra indigene* who ruled the continent called Thaisia became angry when the humans cut down trees and put a plow to land that was not theirs. So the Others ate the settlers and learned the shape of this particular meat, just as they had done many times in the past.

The second wave of explorers and settlers found the abandoned settlement and, once more, tried to claim the land as their own.

The Others ate them too.

The third wave of settlers had a leader who was smarter than his predecessors. He offered the Others warm blankets and lengths of cloth for clothes and interesting bits of shiny in exchange for being allowed to live in the settlement and have enough land to grow crops. The Others thought this was a fair exchange and walked off the boundaries of the land that the humans could use. More gifts were exchanged for hunting and fishing privileges. This arrangement satisfied both sides, even if one side regarded its new neighbors with snarling tolerance and the other side swallowed fear and made sure its people were safely inside the settlement's walls before nightfall.

Years passed and more settlers arrived. Many died, but enough humans prospered. Settlements grew into villages, which grew into towns, which grew into cities. Little by little, humans moved across Thaisia, spreading out as much as they could on the land they were allowed to use.

Centuries passed. Humans were smart. So were the Others. Humans invented electricity and plumbing. The Others controlled all the rivers that could power the generators and all the lakes that supplied fresh drinking water. Humans invented steam engines and central heating. The Others controlled all the fuel needed to run the engines and heat the buildings. Humans invented and manufactured products. The Others controlled all the natural resources, thereby deciding what would and wouldn't be made in their part of the world.

There were collisions, of course, and some places became dark memorials for the dead. Those memorials finally made it clear to human government that the *terra indigene* ruled Thaisia, and nothing short of the end of the world would change that.

So it comes to this current age. Small human villages exist within vast tracks of land that belong to the Others. And in larger human cities, there are fenced parks called Courtyards that are inhabited by the Others who have the task of keeping watch over the city's residents and enforcing the agreements the humans made with the *terra indigene*.

There is still sharp-toothed tolerance on one side and fear of what walks in the dark on the other. But if they are careful, the humans survive.

Most of the time, they survive.

Half blinded by the storm, she stumbled into the open area between two buildings. Hoping to hide from whomever was hunting for her as well as get some relief from the snow and wind, she followed an angled wall and ducked around the corner. Her socks and sneakers were soaked, and her feet were so cold she couldn't feel them. She knew that wasn't good, wasn't safe, but she had taken the clothing available just as she had taken the opportunity to run.

No sound of footsteps that would confirm she was being followed, but that didn't mean anything. Blocked by the wall, even the sounds of the slow-moving traffic were muted.

She had to find shelter. It was too cold to be out here tonight. As part of her training, she'd been shown pictures of people who had frozen to death, so she knew she couldn't stay out here much longer. But the city shelters that provided a place for the homeless would be the first places the hunters would look for her.

Was she going to die tonight? Was this the storm that was the beginning of the end? No. She wouldn't consider that possibility. She hadn't done this much and come this far for it all to end before she had a chance to begin. Besides, she hadn't seen other parts of the prophecy yet. She hadn't seen the dark-haired man wearing a green pullover sweater. She didn't have to worry about dying until she saw *him*.

That didn't mean she could afford to be stupid.

The building at the back of the open area drew her attention, mostly because it provided the only light. Peeking around the corner to reassure herself that she was still alone, she hurried toward it. Maybe she could figure out an excuse to stay inside for a few minutes—just long enough for her feet to thaw.

But the light, which had seemed so bright and hopeful a moment before, was merely the overnight lighting. The place was closed. Still, there was enough light for her to see the sign above the glass door—a sign that would have chilled her more than the snow and wind if she hadn't felt so desperate.

LAKESIDE COURTYARD

H.L.D.N.A.

Human Law Does Not Apply. She was standing on land that belonged to the Others. She might be momentarily safe from human predators, but if she was caught here, she was at the mercy of beings that only looked human, and even someone who had lived a confined life knew what happened to humans who were imprudent in their encounters with the *terra indigene.*

A second sign was taped to the inside of the door. She stared at it for a long time, despite her numb feet and the freezing temperature.

WANTED:

HUMAN LIAISON

APPLY AT HOWLING GOOD READS

(AROUND THE CORNER)

A job. A way to earn money for food and lodging. A place where she could hide for a while. A place where, even if she was found, the hunters couldn't take her back because human law did not apply.

Howling Good Reads. It sounded like a name for an Others store.

She could die here. Most people who tangled with the Others died, one way or another. But based on what she had seen in the prophecy, she was going to die anyway, so for once in her life, what happened to her would be on her terms.

That much decided, she tromped back to the sidewalk and hurried to the corner. When she turned right on Crowfield Avenue, she saw two people walk out of a store. Lights and life. She headed toward both.

Taking his place behind the checkout counter, Simon Wolfgard glanced at the clock on the wall, then said, <Now.>

The howl from the back of the bookstore produced the expected female squeals and more manly grunts of surprise.

Raising his voice to be heard by the humans within sight, he said, "Ten minutes to closing."

Not that they didn't know that. The howl was the ten-minute warning—just as the Wolf who took up a position at the door was the bookstore's own brand of security. A would-be shoplifter having his hand bitten off instilled a strong sense of honesty in the rest of the humans who came to Howling Good Reads. Having to walk over the blood—and walk past the Wolf who was still crunching on a couple of fingers—left a lasting impression, not to mention a few nightmares.

Didn't stop the monkeys from coming back the next day to stare at the bloodstains and whisper to one another as they browsed the contents of the store. The thrill of rounding a shelving unit and coming face-to-face with one of the Others in its animal form—and the more chilling thrill of sometimes seeing swift and terrible violence—tended to increase the sale of horror and thriller novels and helped the bookstore maintain an acceptable profit.

Not that any store in the Courtyard needed a profit to stay in business. The stores were run for the convenience of the *terra indigene* who lived in the Courtyard and provided a way for the rest of the Others to receive the human-made goods they wanted. It was more his own desire to understand the way businesses were run—and test the honesty of the human companies he dealt with—that gave Simon the push to keep his store in the black every month.

But Howling Good Reads didn't follow human retail practices when it came to hours of operation. HGR closed promptly at nine p.m. on the evenings it was open to humans, and some of the staff didn't hesitate to shift shapes and nip lingering customers who thought the store's listed closing was a suggestion rather than a firm time.

He rang up a few sales, more than he'd expected on a night when the sensible would have been tucked in at home to avoid subzero wind chills and wind-whipped snow that had as much bite as any Wolf. Of course, some of the monkeys lived nearby and used the bookstore and adjoining coffee shop, A Little

Bite, as their social gathering places when they didn't want to spend an evening drinking at the taverns on Main Street.

Humans, Simon reminded himself. He adjusted the wire-rimmed glasses that he didn't need for vision but thought made him look a little gawky and more approachable. *Call them* humans *when you're in the store. That way you're less likely to use the slur when talking to an employee. It's hard enough to find help we can tolerate. No sense driving away the ones we have by insulting them.*

The word had traveled across the ocean from Afrikah, where the Liongard referred to humans as hairless, gibbering monkeys. After the *terra indigene* in Thaisia saw pictures of monkeys, they adopted the word because it fit so many of the humans they encountered. But he was a member of the Business Association that ran the integrated stores and Courtyard shops, as well as being the leader of the Lakeside Courtyard, so he tried not to be insulting—at least not out loud.

"Simon."

He turned toward the voice that sounded like warm syrup as the woman shrugged into a hooded parka. The movement lifted the bottom of her short sweater, revealing a couple of inches of toned belly that still looked softly bitable.

Plenty of human females came sniffing around the store, hoping to be invited for a walk on the wild side, but there was something about this one that made him want to sink his fangs into her throat instead of nibble on her belly.

"Asia." He tipped his head, a gesture that was both greeting and dismissal.

She didn't take the hint. She never did. Asia Crane had set her sights on him from the first day she walked into Howling Good Reads. That was part of the reason he didn't like her. The harder she pushed to get close to him, the more he felt like a challenge to be conquered and the less he wanted her around. But she never pushed so hard that he could justify attacking her for being in his store.

A couple more people were shrugging into winter coats and scarves, but there was no one else by the register.

Giving him a *Bite me, I like it* smile, she said, "Come on, Simon. It's been over a week, and you *promised* to think about it."

"I didn't promise anything," he said as he straightened up the counter space around the register.

She had blond hair and brown eyes, and he'd been told by a couple of human males who worked in the Courtyard that she was beautiful. But there were things about Asia that bothered him. He couldn't point a paw at any particular thing, besides her pursuing him when he'd made it clear he wasn't interested, but that feeling was the reason he'd refused to give her a job at HGR when she'd first come around. It was also the reason he wouldn't let her rent one of the four efficiency apartments that the Courtyard sometimes made available to human employees. Now she wanted to be the Human Liaison, a job that would give her access to the Courtyard itself. He'd eat her before he gave her *that* job. And Vladimir Sanguinati, who was the store's other manager, had offered to help more than once if Simon looked at Asia some night and felt peckish. A fair arrangement, since Vlad preferred the blood while Simon liked ripping off chunks of fresh meat.

"We're closed, Asia. Go home," he said.

She let out a theatrical sigh. "I'd really like the job, Simon. The one I've got barely pays the rent and it's *boring*."

Now he didn't even try to sound friendly. "We're closed."

Another sigh, followed by a pouty look as she zipped up her parka, pulled on gloves, and finally left.

John, another member of the Wolfgard, left his spot by the door to do a check for any stragglers. So Simon was alone in the front of the store when the door opened again, letting in a blast of cold air that he found refreshing after all the scents humans used.

"We're—" He glanced toward the door and swallowed the word *closed*.

The woman looked half frozen. She wore sneakers—*sneakers,* for pity's sake—and her jeans were soaked up to the knees. The denim jacket was a light covering suitable for a summer night, and she was wearing a T-shirt under it.

She looked so painfully cold he didn't have the automatic consideration of whether she'd be edible.

"Is there something I can do for you?" he asked.

She stared at him as if she'd seen him before, and whatever had happened made her afraid. Problem was, he didn't recognize her. Not by sight or smell.

Then she took a couple of steps toward the counter. He suspected that was to get farther into the store, where it was warmer, than to get closer to him.

"I s-saw the sign," she stammered. "A-about the job."

Not a stutter, he decided. Her teeth were beginning to chatter. How long had she been out in that weather? It was a natural storm, coming off the lake. The first one of the new year. Being a natural storm didn't mean it wasn't a bitch.

"What sign?"

"H-human Liaison," she chattered. "The sign said to apply here."

Moments ticked by. She lowered her eyes. Probably not brazen enough to meet his stare now that she'd said what she wanted.

Something about her troubled him, but it wasn't the same feeling he had when he was around Asia Crane. Until he figured out what that something was, he didn't want to kick her back out in the snow. And except for Asia, this was the first human to ask about the job. That was reason enough to give her a few minutes of his time.

Movement at the edge of his peripheral vision. John, now in human form and dressed in a sweater and jeans, tipped his head by way of asking, *What now?*

Simon tipped his head slightly in turn and looked at the cash register.

"Want me to close up?" John asked, giving the shivering woman a smile as he approached.

"Yes." He looked at the woman. "Let's go next door and have a cup of coffee while we discuss the job."

She turned toward the outer door and hesitated.

"No, this way." He took a couple of steps past the counter and pointed to an opening in the wall.

The archway between had a lattice door that could be latched when one store was closed and the other was still open to customers. On the wall beside the door was a sign that read, PAY FOR THE BOOKS BEFORE ENTERING A LITTLE BITE, OR WE'LL TAKE A BITE OUT OF YOU.

The sign on the other side of the door read, SURE, YOU CAN TAKE THAT MUG. WE'LL JUST KEEP YOUR HAND IN EXCHANGE.

He didn't think the woman's brain was thawed enough to take in the words. After the first jolt of seeing him, he didn't think she had taken in anything.

Tess was wiping down the glass display case when he walked in. The friendly smile she started to give him shifted to guarded when she noticed his companion.

"Could we have some coffee?" he asked as he took a seat at a table closest to the counter—and away from the door and the pocket of cold that seemed to settle around the tables close to the windows.

"There's still some left in the pot," she replied, giving the woman a sharper look now.

Simon leaned back in his chair, resting one ankle over his other knee. "I'm Simon Wolfgard. What's your name?"

"Meg Corbyn."

He heard the breath of hesitation that told him it wasn't a name she was used to. Which meant it wasn't a name she'd had for long. He didn't like liars. Humans who lied about small things tended to lie about a lot of other things as well.

And a name wasn't all that small a thing when all was said and done.

But when Tess brought the mugs of coffee to the table and he saw the way Meg cupped the mug to warm her hands, he let it go.

He thanked Tess, then turned his attention back to Meg Corbyn. "You know what being a Human Liaison entails?"

"No," she said.

"So you don't have any experience with a job like this?"

"No. But I can learn. I *want* to learn."

He didn't doubt the sincerity of her words, but he did wonder if she wouldn't die of pneumonia or something else before she had a chance to learn anything.

Suddenly he remembered the scarred old woman sitting in the sun, offering to read her cards and tell people their fortunes. But she didn't use her cards that day, not for him. What she had done was the reason her words had whispered through his thoughts for the past twenty years. And now her words rang in his memory as clear as if he'd heard them yesterday.

Be a leader for your people. Be the voice that decides who lives and who dies within your Courtyard. The day will come when a life you save will, in turn, save someone dear to you.

His being the leader of the Lakeside Courtyard hadn't saved his sister, Daphne, two years ago. But thinking about the old woman when this shivering young woman was waiting for his decision made him uneasy.

Tess set one of her earthenware soup bowls on the table, along with some crackers.

"Last bowl in the pot," Tess said.

"Thank you, but I can't pay for it." Meg's voice was barely above a whisper—and full of longing as she stared at the food.

Giving Simon a hostile look, Tess said, "On the house."

"Eat it," Simon said when Tess resumed her cleanup. "It's hearty and will warm you up."

He turned his head and drank his coffee while he watched Tess go through her closing routine, giving Meg a little time to concentrate on the food in front of her.

Tess was a worry. Tess was always a worry, because there was too fine a line between her being amused by humans and being unwilling to tolerate their existence. He didn't know what she was, only that she was *terra indigene*—and she was so dangerous even other species of *terra indigene* feared her. But when she arrived at the Lakeside Courtyard a few years ago, there was something in her eyes that made him certain that if she didn't get some kind of companionship, she would become an enemy of everything that lived.

Inviting her to stay had been his first official decision as the new leader of the Lakeside Courtyard. Watching her change from a brittle loner to an individual capable of running a public business, he'd never regretted that decision.

That didn't mean he always trusted her.

"What does a Human Liaison do?" Meg asked.

Simon glanced at the bowl. Half gone. He wasn't sure if her question meant she couldn't eat anymore or just needed to pause.

"By the agreements established between humans and the *terra indigene,* every city in Thaisia has a Courtyard, a tract of land where the Others reside. These Courtyards are also places where products manufactured by humans can be acquired. But humans don't trust the Others, and we don't trust humans. A lot of the products are delivered by humans, and there were enough incidents early on to convince the human government and our leaders that it was prudent to have someone receiving the mail and packages who was not inclined to eat the messenger. So a receiving area was built at each Courtyard and is manned by someone who acts as the liaison between the humans and the Others. Each Courtyard's Business Association decides on the pay and perks. By the agreements, the human government is required to penalize any delivery service that refuses to deliver merchandise to a Courtyard. On the other hand, there is a limited window of time when the position of Human Liaison can be unoccupied before companies can refuse to enter our land without penalty. Those kinds of interruptions tend to fray the tolerance each side has for the other—and when tolerance frays, people tend to die. Sometimes a lot of people die."

Meg ate another spoonful of soup. "Is that why you allow humans to shop in your store? To build up the tolerance between humans and the Others?"

Smart woman. Her conclusion wasn't accurate—most *terra indigene* weren't interested in being tolerant of humans—but it did indicate an understanding of why a Liaison was needed. "The Lakeside Courtyard is a kind of experiment. While the shops in our Market Square are exclusively for our own people and our human employees, the businesses facing Crowfield Avenue have hours when they're open to humans in general. The bookstore and coffee shop are two of those businesses. There is also a fitness center that has a few memberships available to humans, the seamstress/tailor shop, and a gallery on Main Street, which is open to anyone when it's open at all."

"But human law doesn't apply in those stores?"

"That's right." Simon studied her. He didn't trust Asia Crane. His reaction to Meg wasn't that simple. Because of that, he decided to hire her. It wouldn't hurt the Courtyard to have her around for a few days, especially if someone kept an eye on what she was doing, and it would give him time to figure out why she made him uneasy. But before he told Meg, he needed to say one more thing. "Human law does not apply. Do you understand what that means?"

She nodded. He didn't believe her, but he let it go.

"If you want the job, it's yours."

She looked at him with eyes that were the clear gray of a Wolf, except she wasn't a Wolf. The pale skin blushed with a hint of rose on the cheeks. And now that it was drying, he realized her hair was a weird shade of red—and it *stank*.

They would have to do something about that.

"I can have the job?" Meg asked, her voice lifted by something he would have called hope.

He nodded. "It's a basic hourly wage—and you're responsible for keeping a log of your hours. You also get the use of one of the efficiency apartments above the seamstress/tailor shop, and you can purchase items at any store in the Market Square."

Tess returned and dropped a ring of keys on the table. "I'll fetch a few basics from our stores while you show Meg the apartment. Leave the dishes on the table. I'll take care of them later." She left as quickly as she'd arrived.

Meg ate one more spoonful of soup and drained the coffee mug. "Is she angry with me?"

"You? No." With him? Sometimes it was hard to tell with Tess. Other times it was all too easy to see the warning signs.

He held up the keys. "We have rules, Meg, and we enforce them. Access to the Courtyard is restricted. You don't bring guests to your apartment without us knowing about it first. If we smell a stranger, we'll kill him. We aren't interested in excuses, and we don't give second chances. The storefront on the corner is the place where humans and Others can socialize without needing a leader's permission. You can bring guests there. Is that understood?"

She bobbed her head.

"All right. Come on. We'll go out through the bookstore."

He led her back through HGR, picking up his winter coat, which John had left on the counter for him. Shrugging into it, he pushed open the door, holding it against the wind until Meg slipped out. Then he locked the door, took a grip on her arm to keep her from slipping, and walked her past A Little Bite to a glass door in the seamstress/tailor's building.

"First key is for the street door." He pulled out the ring of keys and slipped the first key into the lock. He opened the door, nudged her into the small entry, then locked the door behind him. Remembering that humans didn't have the same night vision as Wolves, he flipped on the light switch, revealing the stairs that went up to the second floor.

She went up the stairs, then stopped on the landing to wait for him.

He went ahead of her, checked the apartment number on the key, and made an almost soundless grunt of surprise. Tess had given him the key for the front apartment that was farthest from the Crowfield Avenue door—and closer to the stairway that led into the Courtyard.

He opened the apartment door and flicked the switch for the overhead light, automatically toeing off his wet boots and leaving them in the hallway. While he waited for Meg to wrestle her feet out of the wet sneakers, he looked around. Clean and basic. Bathroom and closet at one end. A kitchen area that held a half fridge, a wave-cooker, a small counter and sink, and minimal cupboards for storage. A single bed and a dresser. A small rectangular table and two straight back chairs. A stuffed chair and hassock and a reading lamp next to an empty bookcase.

"There should be a set of towels in the bathroom," he said. "You look like you need a hot shower."

"Thank you," Meg whispered.

"Bathroom's over there." Simon pointed.

She was shivering so hard, he wondered if she'd be able to get out of those wet clothes. But he had no intention of helping her.

The bathroom door closed. Couldn't hide much from animal-sharp hearing, but he ignored the sounds. While he located the extra blankets in the dresser's bottom drawer, the toilet flushed. A moment later, the shower turned on.

He was staring out the window, watching the still-falling snow, when Tess walked in carrying two big zippered bags.

"I put it all on your account," she said. Her hair, usually brown and straight, now curled wildly and had green streaks—a sign that Tess wasn't feeling calm. At least the streaks weren't red, the indication that she was angry.

When her hair turned black, people died.

"Put what on my account?" he asked.

"Two sets of clothes, sleepwear, toiletries, a winter coat and boots, and some food."

The coat was a bright red, which was a color that attracted a lot of the Courtyard's residents because it usually signified downed prey. Since that was the most likely reason no one had bought it, he wondered why Tess would bring it for Meg.

"I thought we could offer the midday meal as part of her pay," he said.

"You might want to discuss this with the rest of the Business Association before you make so many decisions, especially since you just hired a new Liaison without talking to the rest of us," Tess replied with a bite in her voice.

"You brought me the apartment keys before I asked for them, so you must have made a decision too," Simon countered.

She didn't respond. She just set one of the bags on the bed, then took the other into the kitchen area. After putting the food away, she joined him by the window. "You're not in the habit of taking in strays, Simon. Especially not stray monkeys."

"Couldn't leave her out in the cold."

"Yes, you could. You've left other humans to fend for themselves. Why is this one different?"

He shrugged, not wanting to talk about the scarred old woman whose words had shaped so many of his choices.

"We need a Liaison, Tess."

"A fool's idea, if you ask me. The only humans that want the job are thieves who think they can steal from us or ones hiding from their own law. The last one you threw out for being a lazy bag of shit, and the one before that . . . the Wolves *ate* the one before that."

"We weren't the only ones who ate him," Simon muttered.

But he had to admit that Tess had a point. Liaisons barely had time to learn the job—if they even bothered to learn the job—before a replacement needed to be found for one reason or another. Humans always had a reason for wanting the job that had nothing to do with the job. Wasn't that one of the reasons he wouldn't give it to Asia? Wanting the Liaison job was just her next attempt to make him notice her. He didn't need her sniffing around him more than she already was.

"What is Meg Corbyn running from?" Tess asked. "She didn't start out around here. Not with the clothes she was wearing."

He didn't respond because he didn't disagree. Meg might as well have *runaway* stamped on her forehead.

The green streaks faded from Tess's hair. She sighed. "Maybe she'll stay long enough to clear out some of the backlog of mail and packages."

"Maybe," he said. He didn't think Meg Corbyn, or whoever she really was, would stay beyond receiving her first paycheck. But she had said she wanted to learn, and none of the other humans had said that. Not even Asia.

An awkward silence.

"You should go," Tess said. "Naked girl in the shower. Strange man. I read these kinds of stories in books the humans write."

Simon hesitated, but Tess was right. "Tell Meg I'll meet her at the Liaison's Office at eight thirty tomorrow morning. That will give me time to go over a few things with her before deliveries start at nine."

"You're the boss."

Setting the keys on the table, he left the apartment—and wondered if, by leaving Meg alone with Tess, he'd just murdered the girl.

The hot water pouring over her hurt, and it felt wonderful. She used the shampoo and soap that was in the shower rack, then just stood there with one hand braced on the wall.

Safe for now. The wind and snow would have scoured her tracks away. She would be seen by humans, and that was a danger, but as long as she stayed within the boundaries of the Courtyard, no one could touch her. Not even . . .

Shaking, she held out both arms. Thin, straight scars marched down the tops of both arms from shoulder to elbow, one-quarter inch apart. The same kind of scars marched down the top of her left thigh and on the outside of her right thigh. There was a line of them down the left side of her back—precise in their execution. They had to be precise or the cut was worth less—or even worthless. Except for punishment.

Ignoring the crosshatch of scars on the upper part of her left arm, she studied the three scabbed lines on that forearm. Those scars she wouldn't regret. The visions she'd seen when she made those cuts had bought her freedom. And had shown her a vision of her death.

A white room. A narrow bed with metal railings. She was trapped in that room, in that bed, feeling so cold her lungs couldn't draw in a breath. And Simon Wolfgard, the dark-haired man she'd seen in the prophecy, was there, pacing and snarling.

She turned off the water and opened the shower stall door.

A moment later, someone tapped on the bathroom door.

"Meg? It's Tess. I'm going to open the door and leave some pajamas for you. Okay?"

"Yes. Thank you."

Meg grabbed a towel and held it in front of her, glad the mirror had steamed up so that no one would see the scars the towel didn't hide.

When Tess closed the door again, Meg got out of the shower, dried off as quickly as she could, and dove into the pajamas. Wiping the condensation off the mirror, she double-checked to be sure she wasn't showing any scars, then opened the door and stepped into the rest of the apartment.

"Give me your wet clothes," Tess said. "I'll get them dry for you."

Nodding, Meg fetched the clothes she'd left in the bathroom and handed them to Tess.

"There's a bit of food in the cupboards and fridge," Tess said. "And two sets of clothes. I guessed at the sizes, so you can exchange them at the shop if they don't fit. Simon will meet you at the Liaison's Office at eight thirty tomorrow morning to go over your duties."

"All right," Meg said. Now that she was warm, staying awake was almost painful.

"Keys are on the table." Tess headed for the door.

"You've been very kind. Thank you."

Tess turned and stared at her. "Get some sleep."

Meg counted to ten before she hurried to the door. She wasn't sure it was possible to hear anything by pressing her ear against the wood like people did in movies, but she did it anyway. Hearing nothing, she locked the door and switched off the overhead light. The streetlights on Crowfield Avenue provided enough light for her to make her way to the windows. She pulled the heavy drapes over one window, then hesitated and left the second window uncovered. Feeling her way to the bed, she got in and lay shivering until the sheets warmed from her own heat.

Death waited for her somewhere in the Courtyard. But it wasn't coming for her tonight. No one was coming for her tonight.

Breathing out a sigh of relief, Meg closed her eyes and fell asleep.

Simon shook himself to fluff out his fur. Wouldn't want to be out here in his human skin, but the snow had stopped falling and, as a Wolf, he didn't mind the cold—especially when some of the Wolves were heading out for a romp and run through the Courtyard.

Spending too much time in human form made him edgy. Yes, he had volunteered to run this Courtyard and had been the one to push for opening up a few stores to humans as another way of keeping an eye on them. But that didn't make him less edgy about being around them or wearing that skin for so many hours when he was in Howling Good Reads. He needed time in *this* skin, needed to run.

Elliot trotted up to him. Simon was the dominant Wolf at Lakeside, but his sire was the Courtyard's official face. Elliot had no interest in running businesses and wasn't comfortable dealing with the other *terra indigene*, especially the Elementals and the Sanguinati, but he had a knack for dealing with human government and was the one among them who could talk for hours with the city mayor or other officials and not bite anyone.

So Simon was often thought of as the business leader, while the more social and sophisticated Elliot was mistaken for being *the* leader of the Lakeside Courtyard. And that suited Simon just fine. His sire could shake hands and attend dinners and have his photograph taken. And if the mayor and his buddies were very lucky, they would never discover that Elliot's sophistication really was only skin deep.

Seven more Wolves joined them. Pleased with the company, Simon headed up the snowy road. Each species of *terra indigene* that lived in the Courtyard had a section that was respected as its home territory, but the rest of the land was shared by all of them. Once Simon and his friends crossed the Courtyard Creek Bridge, they would be in the Hawkgard area, so they would take the first road that led into the interior for their romp and run.

Wolf, he thought as they all settled into an easy trot to warm up their muscles. Maybe wolves had looked like them when the world was young, but the *terra indigene*— swift, strong, and lethal—had kept the larger, more primal form. Now the animal humans called wolf was to the *terra indigene* Wolf what a bobcat was to a tiger.

They trotted over a couple of inches of snow on the road; the rest of this evening's snowfall was artfully drifted on either side. He'd have to remember to thank the girls at the lake for that.

Muscles warmed up, Simon stretched into a run, leading the pack over the bridge. Good to run. Good to feel the clean bite of weather. Good to taste . . .

The wind shifted. An Owl, one of the Courtyard's nighttime sentinels, flew overhead, calling a warning. <Intruders!>

There shouldn't be anyone out on the road that wound between Lakeside Park and the Courtyard except for the snowplows that would rumble through the night to clear the roads for all the humans heading to work the next day. If a city worker *had* to come into the Courtyard, *especially* at night, a government official would have called Elliot beforehand. So no human had a reason to be here tonight.

Catching the scent, Simon turned onto a narrow service road that ran close to the Courtyard's fence, pushing for all the speed he could get.

No howl, no sound, no warning. Just black, white, and gray shapes blending with the snow and the night as they raced toward the enemy.

A danger if the humans brought weapons, since the deeper snow on the service road was slowing the Wolves down enough that the intruders might get off a shot or two. But the humans had to break a trail through that snow too, so even if they wounded a couple of Wolves, they still wouldn't get away.

<There,> Simon said.

Three humans slogging through the snow, heading away from the black wrought-iron fence that served as the Courtyard's boundary.

<Rifle,> Elliot said.

<I see it,> Simon replied. Only one coming into their land with a weapon? Not likely. Just because he couldn't see other weapons didn't mean they weren't there.

He caught sight of the black smoke moving just above the snow, rushing toward the intruders. Ignoring the smoke, he focused on the man with the rifle. The fool wasn't paying attention and didn't see him or the other Wolves coming until the third man looked around and shouted a warning.

The rifle swung in Simon's direction.

They wouldn't reach the enemy fast enough. The shot was going to hit one of them.

The black smoke suddenly surrounded the man with the rifle. Some of the smoke changed into hands that jerked the rifle skyward just as the man pulled the trigger.

Simon raced past the smoke and leaped, hitting the second man so hard they both lifted out of the broken trail and landed in fresh snow. His teeth closed over the thick scarf wrapped around the man's neck, and the crushing power of Wolf jaws slowly strangled the prey while other Wolves clamped down on the man's wrists, preventing him from fighting back.

The man engulfed in the smoke screamed.

Simon held on to his prey until it stopped struggling. Releasing the throat, he raised his head and sniffed the man's face. Just unconscious.

Perfect.

Blood spread on the snow from the throat of the third man as the Wolves ripped open the clothes to get at the meat.

The smoke around the first man condensed until it became a black-haired man dressed in a black turtleneck and jeans. His arms were around the human; his hands were still clamped over the hands holding the rifle.

In their smoke form, the Sanguinati engulfed their prey and drew blood out through the skin. Not much skin was exposed in this weather, but the man's face was sweating beads of blood that froze almost instantly.

<Vlad,> Simon said.

Vladimir smiled, revealing elongated canines. "I'll take this one back to the Chambers. Grandfather is watching some of his old movies and will appreciate a fresh snack."

Simon dipped his head in acknowledgment.

"Nyx and I will come by later to sort out whatever might be useful and dispose of the rest." Still smiling, Vlad ripped the rifle out of the man's grip, got a good hold of the heavy winter coat, and headed back to the Sanguinati's part of the Courtyard, running easily as he dragged his prey.

Following the trail the humans left, Simon studied the broken junipers that had been planted as a screen to keep the Courtyard private from cars driving by—and from unwelcome eyes that might be watching from the park on the other side of the road. Standing on his hind legs, he shouldered between two bushes.

The trail led from a car parked on the shoulder of Parkside Avenue, its flashers blinking. The car would be reported when the next snowplow went by, but no one would come asking questions until morning—if anyone came by at all.

He trotted back to his prey.

Several Wolves were happily ripping the other body apart. Elliot waited near the unconscious man. When Simon approached, Elliot looked in the direction Vlad had gone.

<That was our prey,> Elliot growled.

<His too,> Simon growled back, showing his teeth. <We share.>

<Waste of meat.>

<Not a waste.> True, the Sanguinati didn't use the meat, but after Vlad's family had dined, he would call Boone Hawkgard, the Courtyard's butcher. Tomorrow there would be a discreet sign in the shop's window informing the *terra indigene* that special meat was available.

A change in the man's breathing indicated a return to consciousness. Now it was time to eat.

Front toes elongated into strong, furry fingers with heavy claws. Simon and Elliot tore open the winter coat, ripped off the scarf, flannel shirt, and T-shirt, and shredded the jeans and long johns from thighs to ankles.

A gasping breath. The man opened his eyes.

Baring his teeth, Simon bit into the belly while Elliot tore out the throat, cutting off the man's scream.

Rip. Tear. Gulp the hot, fresh meat. Simon pulled out the liver and gleefully devoured it, leaving the heart for Elliot. He ate his fill, then moved away, shrinking his front toes back to Wolf form as he rolled in fresh snow to clean his fur. When his friends had eaten their fill, Simon howled the Song of Prey. Any other Wolves who were out running tonight would swing by for a bite or two.

We share, he thought, looking at the arm he'd torn off the body at some point during the feeding. He picked it up and retraced his steps back to the Courtyard's main road. Then he trotted off. He crossed over the Courtyard Creek Bridge and passed the Wolfgard land, finally leaving the arm in the Corvine part of the Courtyard. The Crows would appreciate an easy breakfast tomorrow.

A minute later, Elliot caught up to him, lugging part of a ribcage. His sire might not like sharing a kill, but when they had moved to Lakeside, Elliot had agreed to follow Simon's lead.

Yes, the Crows would eat well in the morning. And by the time everyone else had had their share, there wouldn't be much left of the monkeys to burn and bury.

CHAPTER 2

This is a car, this is a train, this is a bus. . . . Skull and crossbones means poison. . . . Shh. Be quiet. This is another lesson. . . . Pay attention, cs759. Watch what happens to someone who is poisoned. . . . This is a dog, this is a cat. . . . This video shows a woman riding a horse. . . . This is a child, this is a hammer. This is what happens to a face when . . .

A rumbling sound jerked Meg out of a restless sleep. Heart pounding, she stared at dark shapes defined by gray light, trying to remember where she was while she listened for footsteps in the corridor that would indicate the Walking Names were coming to begin the day's spirit-breaking "pampering" and lessons.

The caretakers and other staff in their white uniforms with nametags pinned above the breast pocket. The men in white coats who poked and prodded and decided what the girls needed to stay in prime condition. And cs747 screaming at them that she had a name too, her name was Jean, and just because she didn't have her name pinned to her shirt didn't make it less true.

Jean had been restrained for weeks after she stole one of those name tags and used the pin to carve her name in big letters across her belly, ruining all that expensive skin. After that, the uniforms had the names sewn on with thread. And when Jean returned to the training sessions, she referred to everyone who worked in the compound as a Walking Name, refusing to give them so much as a distinct designation.

The Walking Names hated Jean. But Meg had listened to the older girl's ravings and dim memories of a different kind of life, and had yearned for something she had glimpsed only through the images that made up the lessons. Thinking of herself as Meg instead of cs759 had been her first silent act of rebellion.

Another sound, more a steady crunch than a rumble.

She wasn't in the compound anymore. Wasn't within reach of the Walking Names or the Controller who ran the place. She was in the Lakeside Courtyard . . . within reach of the *terra indigene.*

Slipping out of bed, Meg crept to the side of the window where she could look out without being seen.

Another rumble as a big truck came down the street, its heavy blade clearing the snow in its path.

Snowplow. The ones she'd seen in training videos hadn't made a sound, but that was typical. Identifying sounds was a different lesson from identifying images. Except when the girls were being shown video clips, sounds and images weren't often used together.

Steady crunch.

She shifted to see more of the street.

Car moving down the street. The crunching was the sound of its tires on the snow. Her feet had made that same sound last night. Snow and bitter cold. Now she had a sound to go with what she'd seen and felt—a memory image rather than a training image.

Shivering, she got back into bed and huddled under the covers until she warmed up again.

She'd escaped and she'd run. She wasn't sure where the compound was located—she'd been focused on where she needed to go and not where she had been—but it felt like she was a long way from the place where the Controller had kept his girls. He would send someone to find her. Even if she'd been used up enough for him to write her off as a loss, he couldn't allow her escape to be successful. More girls might try to get away, and that was something the Controller couldn't afford.

But for now, she had a job—and an employer who was a Wolf in his other form. That's what his last name meant. Anyone named Wolfgard was a *terra indigene* who could change into a Wolf. Or maybe it was a Wolf who could change into a human. Even the Controller, with all his spies searching for information, couldn't find out much about the Others that wasn't known by almost everyone.

She thought about the snow and cold. She thought about staying snuggled in bed for a day.

Then she thought of being dismissed on her first day of work and being out there alone. So she got up and took another long, hot shower, because there was no one to tell her she couldn't. Bundled in her robe, she rubbed her hair dry while she considered the clothes Tess had left for her. Not much variety. A pair of black jeans and a pair of dark blue jeans. Two heavy pullover sweaters—one black; the other a medium blue. Two cream-colored turtleneck tops.

The black seemed too solemn for her first day, so she chose the blue outfit. Relieved that everything fit, from the underwear to the shoes that looked clunky but were surprisingly comfortable, she went into the kitchen alcove, opening cupboards and drawers. She identified a small coffeemaker, which she didn't know how to use, and a wave-cooker, which she didn't know how to use. She found instruction manuals in one of the kitchen drawers, but a glance at the clock discouraged her from trying to understand either appliance. Her head was full of images, but they were pictures or snips of a complete action—enough for her to identify something, but not enough to figure out how to do anything for herself.

The cuts she had endured as punishment for lies and defiance had almost driven her insane, but they had also connected many previous images that she must have seen in prophecies, suddenly putting them into a useful context. If she hadn't been punished, she wouldn't have learned how to escape.

Not sure how long the food was supposed to last, she settled for a half glass of orange juice, two bites of a sharp yellow cheese, and one chunk of cooked chicken. Still hungry, she rummaged in the cupboards and found a box of dry cereal and a package of chocolate cookies.

She tore open the package and ate two cookies so quickly, she barely tasted them. Taking one more cookie, she ate it slowly, savoring the flavor. Then she put the package back in the cupboard and firmly shut the door.

Training image. Bugs crawling over open packages of food left in a cupboard.

Meg opened the cupboard and pulled out the package of cookies. It wouldn't seal properly, so she rummaged through the other cupboards until she found small, glass-covered dishes in the storage unit under the wave-cooker. But none of them were big enough to fit the package—unless she ate more cookies.

She reached for another cookie, then shook her head and went back to searching the cupboards. She found a pot that was big enough and had a lid. A glance at the clock above the cooker warned her that she'd used up her time, so the pot would have to do.

She pulled on the boots, then tucked her shoes in one of the large zippered bags Tess had left. She'd have to see about getting a purse for any small personal things she needed to carry with her.

What things did women carry with them?

She walked toward the door, completely focused on recalling every training image of purses and their contents. A quiet knock made her squeak as she stumbled away from the door, her heart pounding. The second knock, louder and impatient, sounded more reassuring, in a scary way.

She turned the lock and pulled the door open enough to look out.

Simon Wolfgard stared back at her.

"Mr. Wolfgard." She pulled the door open. "I wasn't expecting you."

"Weren't you?" He stepped over the threshold, forcing her to back up. "Since you hadn't done this kind of work before, I thought you'd like an explanation of your duties. And I thought you'd like to see the shortcut to the Liaison's Office instead of walking on the street."

How did he know she wanted to avoid being outside their territory as much as possible? Did he know who she really was? *What* she was?

He watched her. The wire-rimmed glasses he wore didn't hide the amber predator eyes the way they did last night. But he wasn't doing anything except watching her . . . because he was waiting for her to get her coat so he could show her to the Liaison's Office before he went on to his own work.

In some movie clips she'd seen, people said "Duh" or smacked a hand against their foreheads to indicate a brainless moment. She had a feeling he already thought she was pretty brainless, and she didn't want to confirm it.

She fetched the red coat from the closet.

"Hat, gloves, and scarf," he said, looking around the room as if checking for differences between what he'd seen last night and now.

She found those items on the stacked shelves built into one side of the closet. She wrapped the scarf around her neck and pulled on the hat as she hurried toward him.

"Keys," he said.

She spotted the keys on the table. She looked around much as he had and wondered if there was anything else a normal person would remember to do before leaving their domicile.

"Ready?" he asked.

Was that a trick question? She had so many questions. There were so many things she didn't know. But he was her employer, so it didn't seem smart to ask him about anything that didn't involve her job.

He stepped into the hallway and watched her fumble through locking her door. She put the ring of keys in the coat pocket, relieved when she realized the pocket had a zipper. People were always losing keys. She had scars on her toes to prove it.

Just a few steps away from her door was another hallway that went to the back of the building and ended at a glass and wood door.

Simon turned the lock. "This is the third key on the ring. You don't need a key to get out, but you do need one to get back in."

"Third key," she repeated. She followed him outside and felt her lungs freeze. "It's *cold*."

"You're in the northeast and it's winter. It's supposed to be cold. Be careful on these steps. They were swept this morning, but they can be slippery."

In contrast to his own warning, he bounded down the stairs. Meg kept a firm grip on the handrail with one hand while she clutched the zippered bag in the other.

Simon pointed to a building catercorner from where they stood. "That's the back of the Liaison's Office. We'll go there in a minute. First . . ." He strode past a one-story building with large doors. "Garages. A couple of them hold vehicles; the others are used for storage."

"Garages," she muttered, struggling to keep up with his longer stride.

He turned left, and they walked past an empty space enclosed by walls on three sides.

"Employee parking lot," he said. He paused a moment and pointed to a door in the back wall. "That leads to the customer parking lot. It's locked and used only when we're doing maintenance." He passed the parking lot and went through an archway.

Meg looked at the buildings that surrounded an open space. The buildings on three sides were three stories tall. The side that had two larger archways was two stories.

"This is the Market Square," Simon said. "There are steps leading down to the open area, but you can't see them now, so stick close to the buildings." He pointed at various doorways. "The Courtyard library. You can borrow books there or buy them at Howling Good Reads if there is something you want to keep. Music and Movies both loans and sells. We have a grocery store, a butcher shop, an office for the *terra indigene* bodywalkers—what you would call doctors—a toother, a drugstore, general store, clothing . . ."

"Sparkles and Junk?" she asked, catching sight of a sign next to a shop door.

"Five of the Crows run that one. You can find fake diamonds, real diamonds, or a one-armed doll. The humans who are allowed to shop at the Market Square say the Crows' store is a cross between a stall market and a jewelry store. Mostly it's other Crows who find it appealing, but I'm told humans find good stuff if they know what they're looking for."

Sparkles and Junk sounded like an interesting place, and she caught sight of other simple signs that intrigued her, including a store that sold ice cream and chocolate. But Simon was already retracing his steps, so she hurried to catch up.

He stopped at the back of the Liaison's Office and pointed again. "Those are the back entrances for Howling Good Reads and A Little Bite. Tess is providing the midday meal as part of your pay, so you can go in through that door when you take your meal break."

Her head was spinning. So many images in such a short time. So many things to remember! But she recognized the back stairs they had come down a few minutes ago, and felt easier for it. Now if she could just figure out why he was annoyed with her. It wasn't like she had asked for a tour. *He* was the one who had kept them out in the cold, despite sniffing frequently as if he had a runny nose.

"The fourth key on the ring opens the back door," Simon said, sounding even less friendly than he had a moment ago.

Meg felt him bristling, taking up too much space and air as she fumbled to get the keys out of her coat pocket.

"Whatever you did to your hair, don't do it again," he growled.

His face was suddenly so close to hers, she dropped the keys. The area in front of the door had been shoveled, but she still had to use a glove to wipe off the keys after picking them up.

"What's wrong with my hair?" she said, hating that her voice sounded small and defensive.

"It stinks." Nothing small or defensive about *his* voice.

"I used the shampoo that was in the apartment. It's all I had." And even more than hating the way her voice sounded defensive, she hated the thought that she might have to act submissive to someone else who assumed he had the right to control her life.

"And it's all you *will* use. The *terra indigene* make those products and sell them at our stores because they don't stink up the air. But I wasn't talking about the soap or shampoo. Whatever you did to make your hair look like old blood and orange peels also makes it stink, and you're not going to do it again!"

Oh, gods. She'd been in a hurry to disguise herself in some way, so she must have done something wrong when she'd used that bottle of red dye on her hair. *I guess the change in color that I saw this morning wasn't bad lighting in the apartment's bathroom.*

"Get this into your head, Meg Corbyn. We don't let humans live in our part of the world because we like you. We let you live here because you can be useful, and you've invented things that we like having. If it wasn't for that, you'd all be nothing but meat. Which is something *you* should remember."

"Being mad about my hair isn't fair," she muttered, trying to hide that she was starting to shiver. She didn't think shivering would be a good idea right now.

"I don't have to be fair," he snapped. "You're in the Courtyard. Whatever rules humans have for employers aren't my rules unless I say they're my rules. So I can hire you even though you don't have any idea what you're doing, and *I can fire you for having stinky hair!*"

"Unless you want me to cut it all off, there's nothing I can do about the hair!" she snapped back. And then she felt terrified that he might want her to do exactly that.

Growl. Roar. Shout. She couldn't begin to describe the sound that came out of him.

She shook. She couldn't help it. He still looked human, but he also looked wild and savage.

"Is this a bad time for an introduction?" a voice rumbled.

Big man with a shaggy mane of medium-brown hair that tumbled to his shoulders. Jeans and a flannel shirt, with an open coat, as if the cold didn't bother him.

"You going to keep her shivering in the cold or show her where she works?" he asked, looking at Simon. "Or should I—"

Simon snarled.

The big man just waited.

Pulling a set of keys out of his pocket, Simon opened the door. Then he tipped his head toward her. "She's Meg Corbyn." He gave the man a narrow-eyed stare. "And that's Henry Beargard." Without another word, he shoved her inside and closed the door.

Even through the closed door, Meg heard Henry's booming laugh.

"Pegs on the wall are for coats," Simon said, sounding snappish. "The mats are for wet boots and shoes. Floor can be slippery when it's wet. Our bodywalkers don't know anything about mending actual humans, so if you slip and break a leg, we'll eat you same as we would a deer." He took off his boots and put on a pair of loafers that were on the mat. "Toilet and sink behind that door. Storage area is next to it. The bins that have clothes are for the *terra indigene*. Don't touch them. Under-the-counter fridge. A wave-cooker and an electric kettle to heat water. Cups, plates, and utensils are stored in the cupboards below. You're responsible for cleaning what you use." He gave her a slashing look. "Well? Are you just going to stand there?"

She took off her coat and boots, put on the shoes she'd brought with her, and remembered to take the keys when he growled at her.

He was not a nice man, and she was going to learn this job as fast as she could so she wouldn't have to deal with him too much.

He opened another wooden door that led into another big room.

"Sorting room," he said as he moved to a panel in the wall and flipped a switch. "This panel unlocks the delivery doors. They stay locked unless you're accepting an approved shipment or handing out mail."

"How will I know if it's appro—"

"The pigeonholes on this wall hold mail for the Market Square stores. The larger partitions hold packages and anything that needs to stay flat. Parcels can also be stored under the sorting table or in those cupboards." Simon gave her a hostile look as he opened another door and pointed to the sign screwed into the wood. "See that? It says PRIVATE. No one who isn't *terra indigene* comes into the sorting room except you. Is that clear?"

"It's clear but . . . why?" she asked.

"Because I said so. Because what goes on inside the Courtyard is no one's business except ours." Simon looked at the clock on the wall and growled. "I have other things to take care of, so you'll have to figure out the next steps on your own."

"But—"

"Deliveries are accepted from nine a.m. to noon. Afternoon deliveries usually arrive from two to four in the afternoon. *Terra indigene* delivery trucks come at other times, but those aren't your concern. There's a list of phone numbers in that drawer. If you have questions, you can call Howling Good Reads or A Little Bite. All those bags of mail and those packages have to be sorted for delivery. We did what we could while we were looking for a Liaison, but we all have our own work and don't have time to do yours."

"But—"

"The door opens at nine," he said as he headed out of the room.

Meg stared at the door leading to the back room, then jumped when the outer door slammed shut.

She held her breath until she was sure she was alone. Then she let it out with a muttered "Bad Wolf," and hoped she could figure out how to start her workday.

Simon wanted to bite someone, but the person leaning against the wall next to HGR's back door was Henry, and a lone Wolf didn't mess with a Grizzly, especially when that Bear acted as the Courtyard's spirit guide and was one of the few beings Simon could talk to without guarding his thoughts or words.

"You sure have your tail in a knot this morning," Henry said easily. "Might not want to scare off our new Liaison before she gets some of that mail sorted for us."

He rammed his key into the lock and turned it, but he didn't open the door. "She doesn't smell like prey. She's rested and fed and not cold. Why doesn't she smell like prey?"

"Not all humans do," Henry replied quietly.

Simon shook his head. "With some, we decide they're not edible because it's smart to have them around. But they still smell like prey, and *she doesn't.*"

"Not all humans do," Henry repeated. "There aren't many that give off that signal, but there have been some." He paused. "Maybe you're not picking up the prey scent because of the stinky hair?"

Simon stared at the Grizzly. "You could smell it from where you were standing?"

"No, the wind wasn't in the right direction for me to smell it, but I could hear you yelling about it. So could everyone else who's aflutter at this time of day."

He rested his forehead against the door. "The lack of prey scent confuses me."

"I can see that. But she's not *terra indigene*. Of that much I'm sure."

"So am I. She smells human. She just doesn't smell like prey."

"If she's causing this much trouble before most of us have even seen her, maybe you should force her out of the Courtyard."

Simon stepped back from the door and sighed. "I'll let the rest of the Business Association take a look at her before I decide. We need a Liaison. Might as well let her stay for a while."

Henry nodded. "Did you explain what she's supposed to do?"

He snarled, a frustrated sound.

"Then stay away from her for the rest of the morning and let someone else explain it."

"Who?"

"You know who."

Yes, he did know. He also knew that if he argued about it, Henry would swat him into the wall to knock some sense into him. For friendship's sake.

"All right. Let the Coyote deal with her for a couple of hours."

It wasn't until he was inside the bookstore and hanging up his coat that he realized he was still wearing the loafers and his feet were wet. He'd been so annoyed and confused and desperate to get away from Meg before he shifted and bit her just to prove she was prey that he'd forgotten to exchange the loafers for his boots.

Savagely angry now at all humans—and that stinky-haired one in particular—he stomped up to his second-floor office to deal with paperwork before checking out the new stock that had arrived yesterday. The store didn't open for another hour. If everyone was lucky, he'd have himself under control by then and wouldn't eat any of the customers.

The freaking Help Wanted sign was gone.

Asia stared at the glass door, not daring to get closer when the shoveled delivery area was a sign that the Others were up and about.

She wanted that damn job. *Really* wanted that job. She'd been in Lakeside for months now and hadn't gotten a look at *anything* in the Courtyard that everyone else hadn't seen. Her backers were getting restless, were starting to hint that they might need someone more professional for this assignment.

Her looks had gotten her out of Podunk and the nothing future she would have had in her hometown. Her looks had carried her all the way to Sparkletown and into a few auditions. But she'd done more acting on the casting couches than she'd done in front of a camera—until she uncovered a tidbit about a Sparkletown bigwig's wife that gave him the leverage he needed to divorce the wife without financial penalties.

Under the guise of developing her for a starring role in a to-be-determined television show, he helped Asia refine her natural intelligence-gathering skills and then sent her off to find some information about a competitor.

She still wasn't sure if that first assignment had been a test, but she was given another assignment and a fat envelope of cash when she returned with the information.

It was like being paid to research a role as an undercover cop or a corporate spy. Yes, that would be the perfect role for her: Asia Crane, Special Investigator. Sometimes she spent time in one of the bigger cities and had fancy clothes and baubles. Other times she spent a few weeks in a town that was a variation of Podunk, playing the role of shy young widow starting a new life, wearing twin sets and pumps while she ferreted out information about the selected target—or helped ruin his business career or political ambitions.

The work was exciting, it was fun, it paid well, and now that Bigwig had brought in a few other interested parties to finance her, she was being given extended assignments with more challenging targets. It wasn't the way most actresses built their careers, but she'd return to Sparkletown in another year or two with enough juice to get any part she wanted.

Infiltrating a Courtyard was her biggest and riskiest assignment to date. She had relocated to Lakeside because it was the only Courtyard in the whole of Thaisia that had any human employees beyond the Liaison. Even Toland on the East Coast and Sparkletown on the West—the financial and entertainment centers of the continent—didn't have Courtyards with as much tolerance for humans. Her task was to get in, observe, and report anything and everything that might help with dealing with the Others or, better yet, breaking their stranglehold on the human cities in Thaisia.

With minimal information to work with, despite having friends who had friends in Lakeside's government, Bigwig had suggested two potential targets as her ticket into the Courtyard: Elliot Wolfgard and Simon Wolfgard. With Elliot, she would have rubbed elbows with government officials and social climbers who might have provided other information of monetary value. But at the last minute, Bigwig discovered that, before relocating to Lakeside, Elliot had once told a society girl who was flirting with him that monkey fucking wasn't any different from barnyard banging, and neither was of interest to him. No one remembered what she said in reply, but a few days later, the society girl was found partially eaten in her own bedroom. So Asia crossed Elliot Wolfgard off the list.

That left Simon, who looked to be in his mid-thirties—young enough to like a frequent rub and old enough that he wouldn't be likely to lose control, leaving a human partner rutting with a Wolf. So she'd chosen a persona and a look that fit in with the other university and tech-college girls who hung around the store. She even signed up for a couple of classes at Lakeside University as a way to fill time. And what had she gotten for her efforts so far? Nothing. No job, no sex, no pillow talk, not even a few minutes in the stockroom for some tongue and tickle. She couldn't even wangle a membership to the fitness center.

She needed to show some progress soon. If she didn't, her backers might end the assignment and send in someone else. And if they did *that,* Bigwig wouldn't deliver on his promises, and she could end up back in Podunk instead of being the star of her own TV show.

Cawing announced the arrival of a handful of Crows who landed on the shoulder-high brick wall that ran along the left-hand side of the delivery area. One flew down to a flat-topped wooden sculpture positioned in front of one of the Liaison Office's windows. That one watched whatever was going on inside the office. The other four watched *her.*

Turning as if she had paused momentarily and had no interest in anything that concerned the Courtyard, Asia walked away.

She wasn't getting anywhere with Simon Wolfgard. Maybe she would have better luck with the new Liaison.

Meg opened the door marked PRIVATE, then closed her eyes and pictured the Liaison's Office as if it were drawn on paper. A rectangular building divided into three big rooms. The back room had the washroom, which contained the toilet and sink. It also served as break room and storage, and had a door that led outside and one that accessed the sorting room. The sorting room had a large outside delivery door, an *inside* delivery door that provided access to the front room, and the door with the PRIVATE sign that was directly behind the three-sided counter area. The front room, where she assumed most deliveries would be made since it had the counter, had the one glass door and two large windows.

She studied the sorting room again and wondered who had designed the Liaison's Office. For a room that was supposed to be private, private, *private,* the sorting room had an awful lot of doors, not to mention a window that would accommodate illicit access.

Not her problem. As long as she kept the delivery doors locked when they weren't needed, she could avoid being eaten. Maybe. Hopefully. Right now, she had to get ready for business.

Turning on the lights in the front part of the office was easy—the switches were on the wall next to the Private door. Getting to the outside door to open it was a problem because she couldn't figure out how the short left end of the counter opened to let someone into the main part of the room. So she got the stool from the sorting room and used it to climb over the counter. She turned the simple lock to the open position and then realized the simple lock was augmented by a heavy-duty dead bolt that required a key—which might or might not be on the key ring she'd left in the sorting room.

Caw caw

Three black birds were perched outside on a flat piece of wood, maneuvering to get a better look through one of the windows. She almost dismissed their presence, then wondered if they were *terra indigene* Crows that had come to take a look at the new Liaison.

Trying for a happy smile, Meg waggled her fingers and mouthed the words *Good morning.* Then she went back to the counter and tried to boost herself up enough to swing her legs over.

The Walking Names didn't tell the girls anything about themselves, but she had overheard some things. She was twenty-four years old. She was sixty-three inches tall. She had black hair, gray eyes, and fair skin. Her cheeks had a light rosy hue that would show scars to advantage, but her face was still unmarred by the razor. The girls in the compound were kept healthy and were walked daily, but they were not allowed to do things that would give them unnecessary stamina or make them physically strong.

Sometimes determination could make up for stamina and strength. But sometimes it couldn't.

The fourth time she landed back on the wrong side of the counter, a voice quietly said, "While this is highly entertaining, why don't you just use the go-through?"

Meg backed away from the counter as a lean man stepped through the Private doorway. He had light brown eyes and brown hair that was made up of a variety of shades, including gray.

"Sorry," he said. "Didn't mean to startle you. Name's Jester. Henry thought you could use a little help figuring out what to do, and since Simon's chewing his own tail this morning, and I look after the ponies, I was elected to help." He held up both hands. "No tricks. I promise." Then he gave her a smile that was both friendly and sly. "At least, not today."

"I have to get the door open before the deliveries start arriving," she said, wishing she didn't sound so anxious. "The keys I was given are on that ring in the sorting room, but I'm not even sure there's a key on it for this door."

"There isn't," Jester replied, disappearing into the sorting room. "You have a key to the back door," he continued when he walked into the front room and vaulted over the counter. "I'll show you where the office keys are kept."

He unlocked the dead bolt, studied the Crows for a moment, then grinned as he walked back to the counter. "You've been on the job for less than an hour and you're already the most entertaining Liaison we've had."

"Thanks," she said, trying not to sound sour. She could imagine what Simon Wolfgard would say if he heard about this. "You won't tell anyone about the counter, will you?"

"Me? No. Them?" Jester tipped his head toward the windows. There were Crows vying for a spot on the wooden sculpture, and a couple were standing in front of the door, looking in. "Most of the Courtyard will hear about this within an hour."

She sighed.

"Come on. I'll show you the trick with the go-through." He pointed to the slide bolt that connected the go-through with the long counter.

"I tried that," she said.

"That one keeps it closed during the day when you might be going in and out a lot." He reached under the wide top. A moment later, Meg heard a bolt drawing back, then another. "There are two bigger slide bolts that keep the go-through closed the rest of the time. Those are locked when you leave the office for a meal break or at the end of the day."

Jester pushed the go-through open, then stood aside to let her enter. He followed her in, closed the go-through, and used the visible slide bolt to secure it. After showing her where the other bolts were located, he pointed out the supplies and other items that were on the shelves under the counter.

A clipboard with a pad of paper. A round ceramic holder full of different color pens. Paperclips and rubber bands. A telephone at the other short end of the counter and its directory on the shelf underneath. And catalogs. Lots of merchandise catalogs from various stores, as well as menus from local eateries.

"We have a little bit of most everything in the Market Square, but not a lot of anything," Jester said. "There is a plaza a few blocks from here that serves the humans who live in this part of Lakeside. It has all sorts of stores and more variety in terms of merchandise. A Courtyard bus provides transportation twice a week for anyone who wants to shop there."

"Isn't that dangerous?" she asked, remembering training images of fighting, blood, and slashed bodies.

He gave her an odd look. "It's always dangerous when there are only a few of us among the humans." He waved a hand to indicate the Crows, then touched his fingers to his chest. "Remember this, Meg Corbyn. We're the ones you can see, but we're not the only ones who are here. Which is why we have so many catalogs," he continued in a lighter tone. "Our shops order things directly from manufacturers, just like human stores do. Some of it stays here; some is sent on to our kin who enjoy the things but want no contact with humans. But there are plenty of other bits of shiny that are ordered from a human store and delivered here, which is where you come in."

Meg nodded, not sure what to say. So many warnings layered in his words. So many things to think about.

"Ready to start?" Jester asked.

"Yes."

They went into the sorting room. Jester took the top bag from a pile of bags, opened it, and dumped the contents on the sorting table.

“The mail truck comes in the morning,” he said. “Give them back their bags as you empty them. You’ll get used to sorting the mail more specifically, but to start, sort by gard or location. Then . . .”

Caw caw

Jester smiled. “Sounds like your first delivery.”

Meg went out to the front room, closing the door partway. She put the clipboard and pad on the counter, tested a pen to make sure it worked, and carefully noted the date at the top of the page—and hoped the calendar under the counter had the days crossed out accurately.

The Crows scattered, most heading out while a few settled again on the brick wall and the sculpture sticking out of the snow.

As a man got out of the green van and opened its back door, Meg wrote down the time, the color of the truck, and the name Everywhere Delivery.

He was an older man whose face had been lined by weather and years, but his movements looked efficient as well as energetic. He elbowed the van door closed, glancing at the Crows as he pulled the office door open. Balancing four packages, he hesitated at the doorway.

“Good morning,” Meg said, hoping she sounded friendly but businesslike.

He relaxed and hurried to the counter. “Good morning. Got some packages for you.”

Suddenly remembering that every face could belong to an enemy, she fought to hold on to the businesslike demeanor. “It’s my first day. Do you mind if I write down some information?”

He gave her a smile wide enough for her to think his teeth weren’t the ones he’d been born with.

“That is a very good idea, Miz . . .”

“Meg.”

“Miz Meg. I’m Harry. That’s H-A-double-R-Y. I’m with Everywhere Delivery. Not a fancy name, but a true one. I’m usually here closer to nine on Moonsday and Thaisday, but the plows are still clearing the streets and the driving is slow this morning. Four packages today. Need to have you sign for them.”

She wrote down his name, the days and time he usually made deliveries, and the number of packages she signed for.

Harry looked at her clipboard and let out a happy sigh. “Warms the heart to see someone behind the counter doing the job proper. The last one they had here?" He shook his head. "I'm not surprised they gave him the boot. I'm surprised they kept him as long as they did. Couldn't be bothered to care about anything, and that's just not right. No, that's not right. Say, it can get pretty chilly out here with that door opening and closing all the time. You might want to get a pair of those fingerless gloves. The wife wears them around the house and swears they help her stay warm. You should look into getting a pair."

"I'll do that."

"You take care, Miz Meg."

"I will. See you on Moonsday, Harry."

He gave the Crows a friendly wave as he walked to his van.

Meg put the ceramic pen holder on the counter but put the clipboard on a shelf out of sight. Then she returned to the sorting room.

Jester grinned at her. "He's not peculiar, if that's what you were wondering. He's just relieved to be dealing with someone safe. So being concerned about you catching a chill is as much for his sake as yours." He eyed her. "Besides, he's got a point."

"Does he?" She didn't like the way he was eyeing her, especially when he grabbed her arm and gave it a squeeze, letting go before she had a chance to protest.

"You're not fat, but you don't have much muscle. You need to work on that. Run and Thump has treadmills and—"

"I don't like treadmills." She heard panic rising in her voice. *Don't think about the compound. Don't think about the Controller or the treadmills or anything else about that place.*

"Plenty of places here for you to walk." His voice was mild, but something sharp filled his eyes as he watched her. "But you couldn't get over the counter, so I'd say you could use some exercise to strengthen muscle. And the second floor of Run and Thump has classes for dancing or bending or some such thing."

"I'll think about it."

"Sort by gard, then by individuals," Jester said after an uncomfortable pause. "I'll be back with some of the ponies in a couple of hours."

"Ponies?"

"They act as couriers around the Courtyard when they feel like it."

He left her—and she wondered if she had already said too much.

Jester quietly closed the back door and looked around. The Crows were on the move, spreading out to watch and listen—and to hear what the regular crows had to tell them. The Hawks were soaring high above, also watching.

And inside the Human Liaison's Office?

Secrets. Fear.

He wanted to poke his nose into the reasons for both.

Couldn't talk to Simon. Not today. Henry had already warned him about that. But Tess? Yes, Tess might know how they had acquired their new Liaison. And she kept a supply of long-grass tea for him. A Little Bite wasn't open to human customers yet, so she might have time to gossip—if he phrased his comments and questions in the right way.

He was glad Henry had told him that Meg didn't have the prey scent that was typical of humans. He would have felt a lot more wary of their Liaison if the Grizzly hadn't already known there was something peculiar about her.

He wanted to know how and why Simon hired Meg Corbyn. And, most of all, he wanted to know what it was about her that made him feel she could be a danger to them all.

Monty paid the cab driver and got out at the corner of Whitetail Road and Chestnut Street. Taking a cab wasn't a luxury he could afford every morning, but he didn't want to be late on his first day. He'd have to check out bus routes and schedules until he had time to consider if he needed to purchase some kind of car.

He looked at his watch and hesitated. The Chestnut Street Police Station was in sight, and he had half an hour before his meeting with Captain Burke. Across the street from the station was a diner, the kind of place that served hearty meat-and-potatoes meals and coffee strong enough to help a man stay upright when he was too tired to stand on his own. In the middle of the block was a small Universal Temple.

Checking his watch once more, Monty crossed the street and walked to the temple. Whether it was true or not, it eased his heart to think there was something beyond the physical plane, something that felt benevolent toward humans, because the gods knew there wasn't much on the physical plane that felt benevolent toward them.

He opened the door to the entranceway, stomped the snow off his boots, then went into the temple itself.

Soft natural light filtered through snow-dusted windows. Vanilla candles delicately scented the air. The random tones of meditation bells drifted through the temple from the hidden sound system. The padded benches could be arranged in various patterns. Today they were scattered to provide seating at each of the alcoves that held representations of guardian spirits.

Mikhos, guardian of police, firefighters, and medical personnel, was in an alcove nearest the door, which made sense with the temple being so close to a police station.

Taking a match from the holder, he lit a candle in front of the alcove, then settled on the bench and practiced the controlled breathing that would clear his mind of busy thoughts in order to hear the quiet voice of wisdom.

It wasn't wisdom but memory that filled his mind.

You shot a human to protect a Wolf.

I shot a pedophile who had a girl imprisoned in his house. He had a knife and threatened to kill her.

You left a wounded human with one of the terra indigene.

I didn't feel a pulse. I didn't realize he was still alive when I went to check out the rest of the house.

He hadn't known the girl was a *terra indigene* Wolf. He hadn't known the bastard he shot was still technically alive when he called for help and a medical unit and then left the girl so he could quickly check the rest of the house. He hadn't known how much destruction a starving young Wolf could do to a human body in so short a time.

He shouldn't have gone in alone. He shouldn't have left the girl. There were a lot of things he shouldn't have done. Considering what it cost him afterward, he regretted doing the things he shouldn't have done. But shooting the pedophile? He didn't regret *that* choice, especially after he found the bodies of six other girls.

If the girl he saved had been human, he'd still be living in Toland with his lover Elayne Borden and their daughter, Lizzy. He'd still be reading a bedtime story to his little girl every night instead of living in a one-bedroom apartment a few hundred miles away.

But he had shot a human to protect a Wolf, and no one was going to forget that. The Toland police commissioner had given him a choice: transfer to Lakeside or resign from any kind of police work forever.

Elayne had been furious, appalled, humiliated that he had brought the scandal down on her by association, making her a social pariah, making Lizzy the victim of teasing and taunts and even pushing and slaps from schoolmates who had been friends the week before.

No legal contracts bound them together. Elayne hadn't wanted that much structure—at least until he proved his work could provide her with the social contacts she craved. But she'd been quick enough to call a lawyer and turn his promise of support money for Lizzy into a legal document after she flatly refused to consider coming with him and starting over. Live in Lakeside? Was he insane?

Lizzy. His little Lizzy. Would Elayne allow her to visit him? If he took the train back to Toland for a weekend trip, would Elayne even let him see his daughter?

I didn't see a Wolf, Lizzy. I saw a girl not much older than you, and for a moment, I saw you in the hands of such a man. I don't know if a policeman or a father pulled the trigger. I don't know if you'll ever understand. And I don't know what I'm going to do in this place without you.

Taking a last deep breath of scented air, he left the temple and went to the police station to find out if he had a future.

Captain Douglas Burke was a big man with neatly trimmed dark hair below a bald pate. His blue eyes held a fierce kind of friendliness that could reassure or frighten the person meeting those eyes across a desk.

In the moments before Burke gestured to the seat in front of the desk and opened a file folder, Monty figured his measure had been taken: a dark-skinned man of medium height who stayed trim with effort and tended to bulk up when he ate bread or potatoes for too many meals in a row, and whose curly black hair was already showing some gray despite his being on the short side of forty years old.

"Lieutenant Crispin James Montgomery." Giving Monty a fierce smile, Burke closed the file and folded his hands over it. "Toland is a big city. Only Sparkletown and two other cities on this entire continent match it in population and size. Which means people living there can go their whole lives without knowingly encountering the Others, and that makes it easy to pretend the *terra indigene* aren't out there watching everything humans do. But Lakeside was built on the shores of Lake Etu, one of the Great Lakes that are the largest source of freshwater in Thaisia—and those lakes belong to the *terra indigene*. We have a few farming communities and hamlets that are within thirty minutes of the city boundaries. There is a community of Simple Life folk who farm on Great Island. And there is the town of Talulah Falls up the road a piece. Beyond that, the nearest human towns or cities are two hours by train in any direction. All roads travel through the woods. Lakeside is a small city, which means we're not big enough to forget what's out there."

"Yes, sir," Monty said. That had been one of Elayne's objections to moving to Lakeside: there was no way to believe social connections meant anything when you couldn't forget you were nothing more than clever meat.

"This Chestnut Street station covers the district that includes the Lakeside Courtyard," Burke said. "You have the assignment of being the intermediary between the police and the Others."

"Sir . . ." Monty started to protest.

"You'll have three officers answering to you directly. Officer Kowalski will be your driver and partner; Officers MacDonald and Debany will take the second-shift patrol but will report any incidents to you day or night. Elliot Wolfgard is the consul who talks to the mayor and shakes hands with other government officials, but you'd be better off becoming acquainted with Simon Wolfgard. For one thing, he manages a *terra indigene* store that has human employees and tolerates human customers. For another, I believe he has a lot more influence in the Courtyard than our governing body thinks he does."

"Yes, sir." Deal directly with the Others? Maybe it wasn't too late to go back to Toland and find some other kind of work. Even if Elayne wouldn't take him back, he'd still be closer to Lizzy.

Burke stood and came around his desk, gesturing for Monty to remain seated. After a long look, he said, "Do you know about the Drowned City?"

Monty nodded. "It's an urban legend."

"No. It's not." Burke picked up a letter opener from his desk, turned it over and over, then set it back down. "My grandfather was in one of the rescue teams that went to find the survivors. He never spoke of it until the day I graduated from the police academy. Then he sat me down and told me what happened.

"From what was pieced together afterward, three young men, all full of loud talk, decided getting rid of the Others would put humans in control, would be the first step in our dominating this continent. So they dumped fifty-gallon drums of poison into the creek that supplied the water for that Courtyard.

"The Others caught the men on land that was under human control, so they called the police. The men were taken to the station, and their punishment should have been handled by human law and in human courts."

Burke's expression turned grimmer. "Turned out that one of those young men was the nephew of some bigwig. So it was argued that while those boys were standing next to the drums, no one saw them dump the poison into the creek. They were released, and the city government was foolish enough to let them publicly declare their 'actions without consequences' as a victory for humankind. And the *terra indigene* watched and listened.

"Late that night, it started to rain. The skies opened up and the water came down so hard and so fast, the underpasses were flooded and the creeks and streams had overflowed their banks before anyone realized there was trouble. Precise lightning strikes knocked out electric power all over the city. Phone lines went down about the same time. Middle of the night. No way to see in the dark, no way to call for help. And it kept raining.

"Sinkholes big enough to swallow tractor trailers cut off every road leading out of the city. Bridge supports that had held for a hundred years were torn out of the ground. Localized earthquakes shook buildings into pieces, while sinkholes swallowed others. And it kept raining.

"People drowned in their own cars trying to escape—or in their own homes when they couldn't even try to get away.

"The rain stopped falling at dawn. Truckers coming into the city for early-morning deliveries were the first ones to realize something had happened and called for help. They found cars packed with women and children floating in fields on either side of the road."

Burke cleared his throat. "Somehow cars that just had women and children got out. And most men who were around the same age as the ones who had poisoned the Others' water supply didn't die of drowning."

Monty watched Burke's face and said nothing. This was nothing like the version of the Drowned City he'd heard.

"As the water began to recede, rescue teams in boats went in to find survivors. They weren't many beyond the ones who had been washed out of the city. There wasn't a government building or a police station still standing. My grandfather's rescue team got close to the Courtyard and saw what watched them. That was their first—and only—look at the truth about the Courtyards and the *terra indigene*."

Burke took a breath and blew it out slowly as he returned to his chair behind the desk and sat down. "The Others, like the shape-shifters and bloodsuckers?

The ones who venture out to shop in human stores and interact with humans? They're the buffer, Lieutenant. As lethal as they are, they are the least of what lives in a Courtyard. What lives unseen . . . My grandfather said the term used in confidential reports was *Elementals*. He wouldn't explain what they were, but a lifetime after he saw them, his hands still shook when he said the word."

Monty shivered.

Burke linked his fingers and pressed his fisted hands on the desk. "I don't want Lakeside to become another Drowned City, and I expect you to help me make sure that doesn't happen. We've already got one black mark. We can't afford another. We clear on that, Lieutenant?"

"We're clear, sir," Monty replied. He wanted to ask about that black mark, but he had enough to think about today.

"Stop by your desk to pick up your cards and mobile phone. Officer Kowalski will be waiting for you there."

He stood up, since it was clear that Burke was done with him. With a nod to his captain, Monty turned to leave.

"Do you know the joke about what happened to the dinosaurs?" Burke asked as Monty opened the office door.

He turned back, offering the other man a hesitant smile. "No, sir. What happened to the dinosaurs?"

Burke didn't smile. "The Others is what happened to the dinosaurs."

Officer Karl Kowalski was a personable, good-looking man in his late twenties who knew how to handle a car on Lakeside's snowy streets.

"Hope the salt trucks and sanders make a pass pretty soon," Kowalski said as they watched the car in front of them slide through a traffic light. "Otherwise, we're going to spend the day dealing with fender benders and cars that spun out and are stuck."

"Is that what we're checking out?" Monty asked, opening the small notebook he carried everywhere.

"Hope so."

An odd answer, since their first call was to check out a car abandoned on Parkside Avenue.

Monty checked the notes he'd made. "A plow spotted the car late last night but it wasn't reported to us until this morning? Why the delay?"

"Car could have slid off the road and gotten stuck," Kowalski replied. "Owner could have called a friend and gotten a ride home, intending to deal with the car in the morning. Or he could have called a towing service and found shelter somewhere, since every towing business would have lists of calls in weather like this, and it could have taken the truck hours to get to the owner of this car."

"But the car is still there."

"Yes, sir. The car is still there, so now it's time for us to take a look." Kowalski pulled up behind the abandoned car and turned on the patrol car's flashing lights. He looked toward the bushes that provided a privacy screen behind a long stretch of fence. "Ah, sh— Sorry, Lieutenant."

Monty looked at what might have been a trail from the car to the fence. "What is it?"

"Nothing good," Kowalski replied grimly as he got out of the patrol car.

Monty got out, testing the ground beneath the snow to make sure he wasn't going to tumble into a ditch. Reassured, he plowed through the snow next to the indentation that might have been another person's footprints.

Caw caw

He glanced to his right at the handful of birds perched in the nearby trees.

The chest-high fence didn't have those decorative spikes to deter someone from scrambling over. The bushes wouldn't be much of a wall, especially if someone hopped the fence to look for help. Noticing the broken tops of two bushes, Monty reached over the fence and parted them.

Caw caw

"Oh, gods, there's a lot of blood," Monty said, catching sight of the trampled snow beyond the bushes. "Give me a boost. Someone's hurt and needs help."

"*Lieutenant.*" Kowalski grabbed Monty's arm and hauled him back a couple of steps before saying in a low voice, "That's the Courtyard. Believe me, there is no one wounded on the other side of that fence."

Hearing fear beneath the conviction in Kowalski's voice, Monty looked around. The handful of Crows had swelled to over a dozen, and more were flying toward them. A Hawk perched on top of the streetlight and another soared overhead. And all of them were watching him and Kowalski.

Then Monty heard the howling.

"We need to go back to the car now," Kowalski said.

Nodding, Monty led the way back to the car. As soon as they were inside,

Kowalski locked the doors and started the engine, turning the heater up all the way.

"I thought the barrier between humans and Others would be more . . . substantial," Monty said, shaken. "That's really the Courtyard?"

"That's it," Kowalski said, studying Monty. "You didn't work near the Courtyard in Toland?"

Monty shook his head. "Never got near it." He noticed that Kowalski's hands hadn't stopped shaking. "You sure there's nobody hurt on the other side of that fence?"

"I'm sure." Kowalski tipped his head to indicate the open land on the other side of the four-lane avenue. "Once the tow truck arrives, we can check the cairn to find out who went over the fence."

"I don't understand."

"Every Courtyard has its own policy when it comes to dealing with humans. The Wolfgard have been running this one for the past few years, and their rules are clear. Kids who hop the fence to look around on a dare get tossed back over the fence and sat on until we pick them up and arrest them for trespassing. Teenagers will get roughed up, maybe get a bad bite or a broken bone before they're tossed back over the fence. But any adult who goes in without an invitation doesn't come back out. And if any human—kid, teen, or adult—hops that fence and is carrying a weapon . . ." Kowalski shook his head. "The Others will leave wallets, keys, and other belongings at the cairn so we know that person isn't coming back. We fill out a DLU form. You know about those?"

Monty shook his head.

"DLU. Deceased, Location Unknown. A family needs one of those to get the death certificates when a body can't be produced."

Monty stared at the bushes and thought about the trampled snow and the blood.

Kowalski nodded. "Yeah. With a DLU, we all try hard not to think about what happened to the body, because thinking about it doesn't do anybody any good."

How many people in Toland who had been listed as missing were actually DLU? "What's so special about the cairn?"

Kowalski checked the trees and streetlight. Monty didn't think there had been any change in the number of Others watching them, but his partner would have a better sense of that.

"Two years ago, Daphne Wolfgard and her young son were out running. Right around here, in fact. She was shot and killed by one man. The other man shot at her son but missed. They drove away before the Wolves reached her or had a chance to go after the men. But the Wolves found the spot in the park where the men had waited to take a shot at whatever might get within range. They followed the men's scent, but lost the trail where a getaway vehicle must have been parked.

"That spring the Others planted all those junipers to limit the line of sight, and our mayor and Lakeside's governing body changed the parkland directly across from the Courtyard to a wildlife sanctuary that is off-limits to people, except for guided walks and restricted hunting. Anyone caught in the park at night is arrested and fined. Anyone caught with a weapon at any time goes to jail unless it's deer season and every person in that party has a permit for bow hunting.

"Captain Burke pushed hard to find the men who killed Daphne Wolfgard, but it looks like they left Lakeside right after that. Speculation was they weren't from Lakeside to begin with—just came in for a trophy kill and then disappeared. It's still an open case."

"Why keep it open?"

Kowalski's smile was grim. "Did you wonder about the water tax, Lieutenant?"

"Yes, I wondered." He'd been shocked when his landlady explained her strict rules about water usage. Other tenants in his building told him about using the water in the rain barrels for washing cars and watering the little kitchen garden. It had struck him as odd that no one wanted to tell him *why* there was a tax on water when they lived right next to the lake that supplied it.

"The Others control all the fresh water. Rates for water and the lease for the farmland that supplies most of the food for Lakeside are negotiated with this Courtyard. The year Daphne Wolfgard died, a water tax was added to the standard rates. Nothing was said then, and nothing has been said since, but the captain keeps the case open because what also isn't said is that if the men responsible for the murder are caught and punished, that tax will go away."

Monty drew in a breath. "Is that why you took this assignment? For the hazard pay?"

Kowalski nodded. "I'm getting married in six months. That extra check each month will help us pay the bills. You take a risk every time you encounter one of the Others, because you never know if they're going to look at you and see a meal. They're dangerous, and that's the truth of it, but a person can deal with them if he's careful."

"The fence is the boundary?" he asked.

"Nah, their land comes right up to the road. The fence is more a warning than a barricade. In between the road and fence is considered an access corridor for utilities and city workers."

"Who are watched," Monty said, looking at the Hawk who stared right back at him.

"Always. And they watch a lot more than the Courtyard and the park." Kowalski checked his mirror. "There's the tow truck and another patrol car. If that team can stay with the truck, we can leave."

As Kowalski opened his door to go talk to the other officers, Monty thought of what would happen after they checked the cairn. "When there's a DLU, who informs the families?" *Please don't let it be me.*

Kowalski paused with the door open. "There are a special team of investigators and a grief counselor who take care of that." He closed the door.

Monty blew out a sigh of relief.

We are the tenants, not the landlords, a temple priest once said at a weekly gathering. *We only borrow the air we breathe and the food we eat and the water we drink.*

That was easy enough to forget in Toland. He suspected the water tax helped everyone in Lakeside remember the truth of it.

Kowalski returned and drove up to the traffic light, then back around the wide median, pulling up almost directly across from where they had been parked a minute ago.

Even with all the snow that had fallen yesterday, the pile of stones and the discarded personal effects weren't hard to find.

Three wallets with ID and credit cards. Three sets of keys.

"There's some cash here," Kowalski said. "Probably not all the cash that was in the wallets to start with, but the Others never take all of it."

Not kids, Monty thought as he looked at the IDs. Young, sure, but old enough to have known better—which wasn't going to help their families face the loss. "I would have thought young men would carry more in their pockets."

"Probably did. The wallets and keys are usually all that's left here. Jewelry, weapons, trinkets, stuff like that will end up in one of the Others' stores here, in another Courtyard in the Northeast Region, or somewhere else on the continent. Even the weapons will get sold, although not back to any of us. The Others won't kill to steal, but once the meat is dead, they make use of everything they can."

A sick feeling churned in Monty. "Is that how you think of your own kind? As meat?"

"No, Lieutenant, I don't. But the *terra indigene* do, and I've seen the results when humans—police officers or otherwise—forget that."

Better not start wondering if you should have used one more bullet after you saw that young Wolf turn back into the girl you rescued. Better not start wondering. Not here. Not now.

"Let's get these items back to the station," Monty said. "Families may be starting to wonder why their boys didn't come home last night."

"Then what?" Kowalski asked.

"Then I think I should introduce myself to Simon Wolfgard."

Boxes and packages piled up on two handcarts as delivery trucks arrived in a flurry, their drivers nervously glancing at the Crows perched on the wall outside and visibly relaxing when they noticed the short human behind the counter. They were all quick to point out the name of their company as well as their own name, spelling out both for her as she wrote them down on her pad. Identification. Validation. Some of them had to make two trips to bring in all the deliveries, and Meg wondered whether they had avoided this stop for as many days as possible.

That first hour, the door opened and closed so often, she decided to look for those fingerless gloves Harry had mentioned and find some kind of insulated vest to wear over the turtleneck and sweater.

Wanting a little more warmth and to show some progress before Jester returned, she went into the sorting room to work on the mail.

Sorting mail turned out to be a challenge. Some was addressed to a person, some was addressed to a group, some had a street—maybe it was a street—and some had a designation she didn't understand at all. The only thing the mail and packages she'd signed for had in common was they all said Lakeside Courtyard.

"No wonder they have a hard time getting their mail," she muttered.

She managed to rough sort the first bag of mail and take two more deliveries before Jester returned.

"Not bad," he said as he began shifting a few pieces of mail from one stack to another. "Corvine goes with Crowgard. It's what they call the complex where most of them live. The Chambers goes with the Sanguinati. The numbers indicate a particular part of the Chambers. The Green Complex is the only residence that isn't species specific. It's located closest to the Market Square, and the members of the Business Association live there."

"Is there any kind of map or list that would tell me who goes with what?" Meg asked.

Jester's face went blank for a moment. Then he said, "I'll inquire. Now come meet your helpers." He walked over to the panel in the wall and unlocked the sorting room's outside door.

Meg thought about dashing into the back room to grab her coat. Then she saw her helpers and forgot about the coat.

"This is Thunder, Lightning, Tornado, Earthshaker, and Fog," Jester said. "They were the only ponies willing to make deliveries today."

They were tall enough to look her in the eyes. Meg wasn't sure if that meant they were typical pony size in terms of height, but what she saw were furry barrels with chubby legs and grumpy faces. Thunder was black, Lightning was white, Tornado and Earthshaker were brown, and Fog was a spotted gray.

"Hello," Meg said.

No change on the grumpy faces.

"Each of them has delivery baskets," Jester said, going back to the table for two handfuls of mail. "The baskets have the Courtyard sections written on them—see? So, for instance, the mail going to Corvine or anyone named Crowgard would go in Thunder's baskets." He put smaller mail in four compartments of one basket and then added the larger envelopes and catalogs to the basket on the other side. He looked at Thunder. "You go to the Crows today."

The pony bobbed his head and moved out of the way.

Lightning was given the mail for the Wolfgard complex, Tornado went to the Hawks, Earthshaker to the Owls and the Pony Barn, and Fog to the Sanguinati.

"What happens when they get to the complexes?" Meg asked.

"Oh, there is always someone about who will empty the baskets and distribute the mail to the individuals," Jester replied as he closed and locked the outer door. "Hmm. No one to take the mail to the Green Complex or the lake. Guess those will have to wait until tomorrow." He tipped his head and smiled at her. "Did Simon give you your pass?"

She shook her head.

The smile gained a sharp amusement. "Well, he's been a bit preoccupied today. Basically, once you step out the back door of this office, you need a pass to visit the Market Square or the Green Complex, which is the only residential area that isn't completely off-limits to human visitors. The pass is something you should always carry with you to avoid misunderstandings."

"Where do I get one?"

"From the consul's office, which is the other building that uses the same street entrance as this office. I'll pick that up for you and drop it off."

"What do I do with the handcarts in the front room that are full of packages?"

Jester opened the interior delivery door and pulled the handcarts into the sorting room. "That depends," he said as he secured the door. "If a package can fit in the basket, a pony can take it with the rest of the mail. Or you can deliver it in the BOW. We haven't encouraged our previous Liaisons to make deliveries in the Courtyard, but it is loosely within the parameters of your job if you choose to include it."

Was making deliveries really part of her job, or was Jester trying to get her into trouble for some reason? "Bow?" she asked.

"Box on Wheels. A small vehicle we use within the Courtyard. It runs on electricity, so remember to charge your BOW if you don't want to be stranded. The one for the Liaison is in the garage directly behind the office. Can't miss it."

"I have a car," Meg said, pleased.

"You have a Box on Wheels," Jester corrected. "Not a vehicle you want to take out on the city streets."

Leaving the Courtyard wasn't something she planned to do.

"Do you want to take a break?" he asked.

She looked at the clock on the wall and shook her head. "I'm supposed to be available for deliveries until noon, so I'll keep sorting the mail."

"Suit yourself. I'll get that pass for you." Jester went out the Private door and vaulted over the counter. He returned a few minutes later. He didn't have her pass, but he laid something else on the sorting-room table.

"This is a map of the Courtyard," Jester said quietly. "It shows the driving roads and where each gard lives."

My Controller would have paid a fortune for this, Meg thought as she studied the map. *He would have killed without a second thought to get this much information about the interior of a Courtyard.*

Wolfgard. Crowgard. Hawkgard. Owlgard. Sanguinati. Green Complex. Girls' Lake. Ash Grove. Utilities Complex. Lakes. Creek. Water reservoir.

"I suggest you tuck this in a drawer when you're not using it," Jester said. "The last two Liaisons weren't trusted with this at all and, like I said, we didn't encourage them to explore. You should be careful about who knows you have this, Meg Corbyn."

"Does Mr. Wolfgard know I have a map of the Courtyard?"

"Simon gave it to me to give to you."

A *test,* Meg thought. Simon Wolfgard was giving her a test to see if he could trust her. Which meant she shouldn't count on the map being accurate. If he thought she was some kind of spy trying to gain access to the Courtyard, providing an enemy with false information was almost as good as providing no information at all.

Then Jester grinned, an expression that was at odds with his sober tone of a moment ago. "I'll get you that pass now." And he was gone again.

When a half hour went by without a delivery or any sign of Jester, Meg checked out the music disc player. No discs, which was a disappointment, but as she fiddled with the buttons, she found the one that changed the player from discs to radio and connected her with Lakeside's radio stations. She spent a few minutes turning the dial as she tried to tune in a station that had approved music. Then it struck her. She didn't need anyone's permission or approval. She could try a different kind of music every day and decide for herself what she liked.

Excited, she tuned in a station and got back to work.

"Run and Thump?" Monty asked as he read the sign over one of the *terra indigene* storefronts.

"Fitness center," Kowalski replied. He turned into the parking lot that had a third less space for cars because the slots near the lot's back wall were taken up by mountains of snow on either side of a wooden door. "Treadmills for running, and the thumpy sound of weight machines. Not sure what they do on the second floor. Not sure why the Others would want such a place when they can run around in more than three hundred acres."

Maybe even they were bothered by the smell of wet fur and preferred to run indoors in inclement weather. “What about the storefront that doesn't have a sign?”

“Social center. This Courtyard does employ some humans and occasionally lets some of them live in the apartments above the seamstress/tailor's shop. But entertaining outsiders in an apartment that can access the Courtyard?” Kowalski shook his head. “You gather with friends at the social center. And you gather there if you want to socialize with an acquaintance who is *terra indigene*.”

“And if you want a more private kind of date?” Monty studied the younger man.

“The rooms above the social center can be used for that kind of date.”

“Is this street talk or personal knowledge?”

“Am I ever going to introduce you to my mother?”

Monty hid a smile, but it took effort. “Probably.”

Kowalski blew out a breath. “I really don't have *that* much personal knowledge. I've *heard* that if you use one of those rooms, you're responsible for putting fresh linen on the bed and tossing the used sheets in the laundry cart that's left at the end of the hall. There's a jar next to the laundry cart. Five dollars for the use of the sheets and the room.”

“And if the money in the jar doesn't match the number of sheets that were used?”

“The next time there aren't any clean sheets—and girls get pretty insulted if they're asked to cuddle on seconds because you were too cheap to put five dollars in the jar the last time.”

Now Monty didn't try to hide the smile. “You are a font of information, Officer Kowalski.”

Kowalski slanted a look at him.

Laughing, Monty got out of the car. Despite the wind, which was still cold enough to cut to the bone, he left his topcoat open so that his holstered gun showed. Then he pulled out his leather ID holder so it would be in his hand when he walked into Howling Good Reads.

“After the shooting two years ago, all the windows in these stores were refitted with bulletproof glass,” Kowalski said.

“A gunman could walk into the store and start shooting,” Monty countered.

“He could walk in, but he wouldn't get out alive.” Kowalski tipped his head slightly as he pulled the door open.

Monty looked in that direction as he walked into the store—and froze.

Amber eyes stared at him. Lips lifted off the teeth in a silent snarl as the creature lying in front of a bookcase rose to its feet. The damn thing was *big.* Its shoulder would be even with his hip if they were standing side by side, and he was sure it outweighed him.

The girl he'd rescued had looked like a rough version of the wolf puppies he'd seen in documentaries. But there was no mistaking *this* for the animal. There was something more primal about its body than the animals that lived in the world now. The first humans to set foot on this continent must have used the word *wolf* as a way to lessen their fear of what stared at them from the edge of the woods—or hunted them in the dark—and not because it was an accurate description.

Kowalski quietly cleared his throat.

Aware of how everyone was standing still—and trembling while they did it—he held up the leather holder that contained his ID and walked over to the counter.

At first glance, he thought the man behind the counter was human. The dark hair was a little mussed but professionally cut. The shirt and pullover sweater were workplace casual and equal in quality to things he'd seen in the better shops in Toland. And the wire-rimmed glasses gave the handsome face an academic quality.

Then the man looked at him with eyes that were the same amber color as the Wolf's.

How could anyone look into those eyes and not understand that a predator was looking back at you? Monty thought as he took the last steps to the counter. *How could you not know that there was nothing human behind those eyes?*

"Mr. Simon Wolfgard?" Monty asked, still holding up his ID.

"I'm Wolfgard," he replied in a baritone that was pleasing if you couldn't hear the growl under the words.

Pretending he didn't hear the growl, Monty continued. "I'm Lieutenant Crispin James Montgomery. My officers and I have been assigned as your police contacts, so I wanted to take this opportunity to introduce myself."

"Why do we need police contacts?" Simon asked. "We handle things on our own in the Courtyard."

The Wolf snarled behind him.

Several girls who had been hanging out at the front of the store squealed and headed farther back where they could hide behind the shelves and peek out to watch the drama.

"Yes, sir. I'm aware of that," Monty replied, lacing his voice with quiet but firm courtesy. "But if you know we will respond to any call for assistance, I'm hoping that you won't feel you always have to handle things on your own. Take shoplifting, for example."

Simon shrugged. "Steal from us, we eat a hand. But just one if it's a first offense."

Nervous titters from behind the nearest shelves.

"What if it's a second offense?" Kowalski asked, moving closer to the counter while keeping an eye on the Wolf that was in Wolf form.

The predatory look in Simon's eyes sharpened, just like the smile sharpened. "For a second offense, we don't bother with a hand."

Threat understood.

He could see the effort it was taking for Wolfgard to assume the mask and body language of human shopkeeper—which he assumed was the purpose of the glasses and clothing.

Not quite pulling it off today. Not quite able to hide the predator.

Or maybe this was as much as it was ever hidden.

"Why don't we go next door for a cup of coffee," Simon said, making the words less a question and more of a command. "Police officers like coffee. Don't they?"

"Yes, sir, we do," Monty replied.

Simon wagged a finger at a black-haired, black-eyed girl who hadn't bolted to the back of the store with the others—had, in fact, been eyeing them all with a bright intensity that made Monty want to buy her some popcorn to eat while she watched the show.

"Jenni," Simon said when she hopped onto the counter and then over it. "Can you watch the register for a few minutes?"

The smile she gave Simon had Monty reaching for his wallet to make sure it was still there.

"If someone wants to buy something, they will give you money and you will give them change," Simon said.

"But not the shiny," Jenni said, cocking her head. "We keep the shiny."

Simon looked like he wanted to bite someone, but all he said was, "Yeah, okay, you don't have to give anyone the shiny." Then he looked at the Wolf, who came over and sat in front of the register—a large, furry deterrent to anyone who wanted to check out before Wolfgard returned.

He led them to the adjoining store.

Not a lot of customers, Monty thought as he looked around. A couple of people were working on portable computers while sipping from large mugs, but that was all.

"Tess?" Simon called to the brown-haired woman behind the counter. "Three coffees here."

They sat at a table. Monty tucked his ID in his pocket when Tess set three mugs and a plate containing slices of some kind of cake on the table. When she returned with the pot of coffee, napkins, and a little pitcher of cream, Simon introduced Monty and then waited for Monty to introduce his partner.

Simon studied Kowalski. "Have I smelled you before?"

Kowalski turned bright red and almost dropped the mug. "No, I don't think so."

"You carrying another scent on you?"

A head shake. Then Kowalski paled and whispered, "My fiancée."

"She likes books?"

"Yes." Kowalski took a sip of coffee. His hands shook when he set the mug down. "We both do. We read a lot."

Simon continued to study the officer in a way that made Monty want to knock over the table or start shouting just to break that focus.

"Polite," Simon finally said. "Smells good. Doesn't screech when she talks. Asked about books she couldn't find in a human store. Should have that shipment tomorrow. She can pick up the ones that are available." A teeth-baring smile. "Or you can."

Kowalski looked Simon in the eyes. "I'm sure she would rather pick up her order personally to make sure the books are what she wanted."

"Books weren't the only thing your fiancée was interested in, but HGR doesn't sell music discs, and the music store isn't open to anyone but Courtyard residents." Simon smiled at Monty. "But we could arrange a tour of our Market Square for our new friends in the police department. You could each bring a guest, even do some shopping."

"As long as we don't expect the merchants to give us the shiny?" Monty asked, struggling to remain calm and polite—and hoping Kowalski would do the same.

Tess, who had been about to top off their mugs, jerked back. "Ah, Simon. You didn't let one of the Crows watch the register, did you?"

"It will be fine," he said tightly.

"Say that when you're trying to balance the cash drawer tonight." Shaking her head, she walked back to the counter.

Monty looked away before anyone noticed him staring. Her hair had been brown and straight when they walked in. Now it looked like she'd poured green food coloring over strands of it and used one of those curling irons. But she hadn't left the room. He *knew* she hadn't left the room.

"Since I'm closing up tonight, maybe I should take over the register now," a man said as he approached their table.

Black hair, dark eyes, black sweater and jeans. More olive-skinned than fair, and dangerously good-looking.

"This is Vladimir Sanguinati, the comanager of Howling Good Reads," Simon said.

Kowalski bobbled the mug and sloshed coffee on the table.

"Sorry," he muttered, grabbing the napkins Tess had put on the table.

"This is Lieutenant Crispin James Montgomery and Officer Karl Kowalski, our new police contacts," Simon said.

"How intriguing," Vladimir replied.

Monty didn't know why it was intriguing, or why Kowalski reacted to the name like that, but he did know there were things he wanted to think and say, and it wasn't safe to think or say them while he was in that store.

"I won't take up any more of your time, Mr. Wolfgard," Monty said quietly as he pushed his chair back and stood up. He pulled one of the new business cards out of his pocket and handed it to Simon. "My number at the station and my mobile phone number. If you need assistance—or just want it for any reason—please call me."

Rising, Simon slipped the card into his trouser pocket without looking at it.

"Since we're all friends now, you should come in for coffee again," Tess said.

"Thank you, ma'am. We'll do that," Monty said. He buttoned his coat as he and Kowalski walked to the outside door. "Wait until we're in the car," he added to his partner, feeling the Others' eyes watch them as they walked past the store windows to the parking lot.

When they got in the car, Kowalski blew out a breath and said, "Where to, Lieutenant?"

"Nowhere yet. Just start the car so we don't freeze out here." Monty stared straight ahead, letting thoughts solidify into words. But he wasn't quite ready to say what he suddenly understood, so he asked a question. "Sanguinati. You jumped like you were poked with a needle when you heard that name. Why?"

"Doesn't mean anything to you?" Kowalski waited a moment. "Are you familiar with the term *vampire*?"

Monty turned his head and stared at the other man. "That was one of the bloodsuckers?"

Kowalski nodded. "As in *drain their prey of blood*. In popular fiction they're called vampires, but that species of *terra indigene* call themselves Sanguinati. No one really knows much about them except that they drink blood, don't seem to have anything else in common with the fictional version, and they're just as dangerous as the shape-shifters. And there's been some . . . evidence . . . that they have another way of extracting blood besides biting you."

Glad he hadn't drunk much coffee, Monty swallowed to push down his churning stomach. "Do you think they're using those stores as easy places to hunt?"

Kowalski tipped his head back. Finally he said, "Can't say for certain about the Sanguinati, but the shifters aren't using the stores that way. Wolfgard wasn't kidding about them eating a shoplifter's hand, but we've never filled out a DLU because someone went into one of those stores." He turned his head and looked at Monty. "What's on your mind, Lieutenant?"

"I've been thinking that most of what you know about the *terra indigene* you learned because you've been brushing against them all your life. You probably grew up in a neighborhood that's close enough to the Courtyard that you know the rules for the social center."

"I'm not the only cop in Lakeside who's brushed up against the Others at a social occasion. The *terra indigene* control most of the world. It's foolish not to take an opportunity to figure out more about them. And, for the record, before I met Ruthie, I did some necking and petting with a girl who worked in the Courtyard, but we parted company after a few dates and I never used one of the rooms above the social center for a romp between the sheets."

A silence filled the car. Monty ended it before it became a wedge between him and the younger man. "*Terra indigene.* Earth native. At the academy, no one ever explains exactly what that means. Maybe command doesn't know exactly what it means or is afraid the truth would scare too many of us, and frightened men with guns would get us all killed."

"What's scarier than knowing you're always surrounded by creatures who think you're edible?"

"They really aren't human, Karl," Monty said. "Intellectually, I knew that. Now I know that with body as well as brain. The *terra indigene* aren't animals who turn into humans or humans who turn into animals. They really are something unknown that learned how to change into a human shape because it suited them. They gained something from the human form, whether it was standing upright or having the convenience of fingers and thumbs, just like they gained something from the animal forms they absorbed."

"You support the first-form theory?" Kowalski asked.

"That wasn't taught at the academy," Monty replied with a forced smile.

"Something Ruthie found in some moldy old history book a while back. There was a theory that the Others have had a lot of forms, changing their shapes as the world and the creatures around them changed so that they remained the dominant predators. But the first form, whatever it might be, is the evolutionary ancestor of all the *terra indigene* and is the reason they can change shapes. The theory also says they take on some of the traits of the forms they use—like that girl Crow attracted to something shiny."

"That's close enough to what I was thinking," Monty said. "They have learned a human shape, but there is no humanity in them, nothing that recognizes us as more than meat. More clever than deer or cattle, but still meat. And yet, when they couldn't find the men who killed one of their own, they understood how to punish everyone in the city by tacking on a tax to the water rates. Which means they do have feelings about their own kind."

"Okay. But what does that have to do with Wolfgard offering to let us see something that's usually off-limits or making sure I knew they recognized Ruthie? You were polite and got back threats."

"I don't think it was a threat. I think Simon Wolfgard was trying to be friendly. But the *terra indigene* line he comes from has absorbed the wolf for thousands of years and the human side for a few centuries at best, so he sounds threatening even when he isn't trying to be. He has his own motives for opening those stores to human customers and inviting us to see a market I'm guessing has been seen by very few visitors."

"So?"

"So we're going to take him up on his offer," Monty said. "We're going to tour the market. Ruthie too, if you're comfortable asking her to join us. We're going to stop in and have a cup of coffee on a regular basis. We're going to be faces the Others recognize. We're going to try to change the dynamic, Karl. They aren't human, will never be human. But we're going to try to get them to see at least some of us as more than useful or clever meat. Then maybe—*maybe*—the next time adult men act like fools and enter the Courtyard uninvited, we'll get a call instead of having to fill out a DLU form."

"I'm not sure anyone ever tried to change the dynamics between us and the Others," Kowalski said cautiously.

"Then maybe it's time someone did." Monty sighed. "All right. One more stop, then I'd like to drive around for a bit to get the feel of the area."

"Where to?"

"To introduce ourselves to the person who could be our best ally—the Human Liaison."

They pulled out of the parking lot and turned left at the intersection of Crowfield Avenue and Main Street. They passed one storefront before turning into the delivery area for the Liaison's Office and the consulate.

"That store is called Earth Native," Kowalski said. "*Terra indigene* sculpture, pottery, paintings, and weavings that are pricey but available for sale to humans. A sculptor who works in wood makes something called garden totems from the trunks of downed trees. Big things that can weigh a couple hundred pounds, or pieces small enough to be used as an accent table. Ruthie wants to buy a piece for our new apartment."

Monty filed all that information away as they pulled in and parked.

Kowalski pointed to their right. "That building is the consulate. Elliot Wolfgard has an office there, and the meeting rooms are usually as close as any city official gets to being inside the Courtyard."

"Stay here," Monty said. The moment he stepped out of the car, half the Crows perched on the shoulder-high wall took off and the other half began cawing at him. Someone on the other side of the wall had been working with some kind of hammer, and the rhythmic sound stopped.

Monty walked to the office door and pulled it open, pretending he didn't see the Crows—pretending there was nothing ominous in the silence coming from the other side of the wall.

As he walked up to the counter, the first thing he noticed was the woman's hair. It made him think of one of Lizzy's dolls whose hair was made of orange yarn. Then he noticed how her smile slipped when she looked past him and saw the police car.

"Good morning, ma'am," he said, pulling out his ID. "I'm Lieutenant Crispin James Montgomery."

"I'm Meg Corbyn," she replied. There were nerves—maybe even fear—in her gray eyes, and her hands trembled just enough to be noticed. "Is there something I can do for you?"

He'd seen the sign over the door. He knew what HLDNA meant. In his experience, women usually weren't afraid without a reason. "No, ma'am. I'm the police contact for the Courtyard, and I just wanted to introduce myself." He pulled out a business card and set it on the counter. When she didn't reach for it, he gentled his voice more than usual. "Ms. Corbyn, are you here by your own choice? I can't help noticing that you seem nervous."

She gave him a wobbly smile. "Oh. It's my first day. I want to do a good job, and there's quite a bit to learn."

Monty returned the smile. "I know what you mean. It's my first day on the job too."

Her smile firmed up and warmed, and she picked up the business card. Then her forehead puckered in a little frown. "But, Lieutenant, human law doesn't apply in the Courtyard."

"I know that, ma'am. Even so, if you need my help, you just call."

Meg hesitated, then said, "Do you know anything about ponies?"

Monty blinked. "Ponies? Not particularly. But I rode horses when I was young. Used to bring chunks of carrot or apple with me. The horses weren't much interested in being saddled, but they would come up to the fence for the carrots."

"Maybe that will help," Meg muttered.

"Well, then. I have been of service today."

She laughed as if she didn't quite know how, as if it wasn't a familiar sound. It bothered him that laughter was an unfamiliar sound.

That wasn't the only thing about her that bothered him.

He wished her luck on getting through the rest of her first day, and she wished him the same. Satisfied, he walked out of the office—and noticed Kowalski's tight face and unwavering attention. Looking toward the left corner of the building, he saw the big man dressed in jeans and a flannel shirt, holding a chisel and mallet. Must be the sculptor.

"Good morning," Monty said, continuing to the car.

The man didn't reply. Just watched him.

"Sir?" Kowalski said as soon as Monty got in the car.

"We've met enough residents of the Courtyard for one day," Monty replied. "Give me a tour of the district."

"Glad to."

"What qualities do you think a Liaison normally has?" he asked when they drove away from the Courtyard.

"Moxie. Savvy," Kowalski replied without hesitation.

"Innocence?"

Kowalski gave Monty a startled look before turning his attention back to the road. "That's not a label I would give to anyone who works for the Others."

"I got the impression Ms. Corbyn lacks the maturity of her physical age. If I hadn't seen her, I would have placed her at half her age."

Kowalski gave him another look. "The Simple Life folk sometimes give that impression because they live without most of the technology that the rest of us use. You think she left the community on Great Island and took the job here?"

He'd never met any of the Simple Life folk, so he couldn't offer an opinion, but he said, "It's worth checking out."

"Thing is, Lieutenant, the Others control everything on that island except the land they leased to the Simple Life community and a couple dozen families who live along the southern shore and make a living fishing, running the ferry, or working in the stores and shops that supply goods and services. A girl from that community would be used to seeing Others and might find it less scary to deal with them than be alone in the big city."

The explanation might be as simple as that, Monty thought. But he still wondered if being in the Courtyard was the reason Meg Corbyn was so nervous, or if she had another reason to be afraid.

Asia swore under her breath. The damn Crows were paying too much attention to the Liaison's Office, and if she kept driving past, one of them was going to realize they kept seeing the same car. Seeing the police car in the parking lot earlier had been reason enough to go on by. Her looks were memorable, and she didn't want cops taking any notice of her. But she did want to get a look at the new liaison Simon had hired instead of her. By the time she had done the slide and spin on some of the side streets—where were the freaking plows?—and gotten back to the street entrance, the damn cops were pulled up in front of the Liaison's Office!

She thought her luck had changed when she saw them drive away, but the earth native who sold sculptures and other artsy crap was going into the office, and there was something about him besides his size that made her uneasy.

Try again tomorrow, she thought.

As she flicked off the blinker, she realized the white van in front of her had done the same thing moments before.

"I guess I'm not the only one who is curious," she muttered to herself. She smiled as she followed the van long enough to memorize the license plate. Then she pulled in to the first cleared parking area and wrote down the numbers. This was something she could tell Bigwig. He kept saying information was a valuable commodity. Knowing that someone was interested in the new Liaison was the kind of information he and the other backers might find profitable.

CHAPTER 4

The experiment with the coffeemaker was an unqualified disaster, so Meg settled for a bowl of cereal and an apple—and promised herself a ten-minute break to run over to A Little Bite and get a large cup of coffee as soon as the shop opened.

Wearing the blue sweater and jeans again so the black outfit would still be clean, she made a second promise to stop at the clothing store in the Market Square and buy enough clothes to get her through the work days, or as many clothes as she could afford right now. How did the Others do laundry? Simon Wolfgard's clothes hadn't smelled, so the Others must have a way to wash clothes. She just had to find out where and how.

So many things to learn. So many things she knew only as images or snips of action. How was she going to find out what she needed to know without revealing how little she knew?

Those were thoughts for later. Now she had to finish getting ready for work.

Taking three carrots out of the refrigerator, she washed them, patted them dry, and set them on the cutting board. She pushed up the sleeves of her turtleneck and sweater, then pulled the large knife out of the cutting block.

Flesh and steel. Such an intimate dance.

Every cut brings you closer to the cut that kills you, Jean had said. *If you keep using the razor once you're free of this place, then you become your own killer.*

The knife clattered on the counter. Meg stepped back, staring at the shiny blade as she rubbed her left forearm to relieve the pins-and-needles feeling under her skin. She got that feeling sometimes just before it was time for the next cut. If the cut was delayed, the sensation got so bad it felt like buzzing or, even worse, like something trying to chew its way out of her skin.

Just a small cut, she thought as she pulled the folding razor out of the pocket of her jeans. *Just a small cut to see if the carrots will work, if the ponies will like me.*

She tried to convince herself that nothing terrible would happen if this gesture of friendship didn't work, and using up flesh for something insignificant was foolish. And how would the Others react to a fresh cut and the scent of blood? She hadn't considered that when she took the job.

But she was pulling a couple of paper towels off the roll and making a pad on the counter next to the sink. She opened the razor, lined up the back edge with the first knuckle of her left index finger, then turned the razor so the honed edge rested against skin. She took a slow breath and pressed the razor against her finger, making a cut deep enough to scar.

Pain flooded her, a remembered agony from the times she'd been punished for lies or defiance. She saw the ponies and . . .

The pain was washed away by an orgasmic euphoria. *This* was the ecstasy the girls craved, the ecstasy that only came from the razor kissing skin. *This . . .*

Meg blinked. Swayed. Stared at the blood on the paper towels.

Something about the ponies.

In order to remember what you see, you have to swallow the words along with the pain, Jean had said. *If you speak, what you saw will fade like a dream. You might remember wisps, but not enough to be useful to you.*

She must have spoken, must have described what she had seen. But there was no one to hear the words, so the prophecy and whatever she might have learned about the ponies was lost.

She looked at the razor and considered making another cut. Then she looked at the clock. She'd lost too much time already.

Hurrying into the bathroom, Meg washed the cut, then found a partially used box of bandages and tape in the medicine chest above the sink. After tending to the cut, she hurried back to the kitchen, cleaned the razor, and slipped it in her jeans pocket. Then she grabbed the kitchen knife and cut up the carrots. If anyone noticed the bandage or smelled the blood, she could explain it.

Accidents happened in kitchens all the time. A cut on her finger wouldn't be unusual, wouldn't give anyone a reason to wonder about her.

She put the carrot chunks in a bowl with a locking lid, tidied up the kitchen, then put on her outer gear and gathered the rest of her things. As she left the building and hurried down the back stairs, she was glad she didn't have to walk far to get to work.

It was still lung-biting cold, but far more peaceful than the previous morning. Or it was more peaceful until she reached the bottom of the stairs and spotted Simon Wolfgard coming out of A Little Bite with one of those big covered mugs she had seen yesterday when she stopped in the Market Square grocery store to buy apples and carrots.

He jerked to a stop when he saw her. Then he sniffed the air.

Hoping her hair still smelled enough to discourage him from coming closer, she said, "Good morning, Mr. Wolfgard."

"Ms. Corbyn."

When he said nothing more, she hurried to the Liaison's Office, aware of him watching her until she unlocked the back door and stepped inside. Hopefully now he would just go on about his own business and let her get on with hers.

She hung up her coat and swapped boots for shoes. After a debate with herself that consumed five minutes, she decided carrots at room temperature were probably better for pony tummies and left the container on the counter. Wishing she had something warm to drink, she checked the cupboards in the small kitchen area. The last person to work as the Liaison had been a slob, and she wasn't putting anything she wanted to eat on those shelves until she cleaned them. Which meant actually learning how to clean.

At least she had music this morning. She had stopped at Music and Movies yesterday and taken five music discs out on loan. She would get a notebook and keep track of the music she liked and didn't like, and the food she liked and didn't like and . . . everything else.

She put the first disc in the player, then set about opening the office. She put a fresh sheet of paper on the clipboard to take notes about the deliveries. Retrieving the keys from the drawer in the sorting room, she breathed a sigh of relief when she fiddled the slide locks open on the go-through and managed to unlock the front door.

The birds were back—three on the wall and one on the wood sculpture.

Since she wasn't sure if they were crows or Others, she stuck her head out the door and said, "Good morning."

A startled silence. As she pulled her head back inside, a couple of them cawed. It sounded more mellow than other caws, so she decided to take it as a return greeting.

She barely had time to take the map out of the drawer and drag one of the mailbags over to the table before the first delivery truck pulled in.

Don't need a bell on the door when there were Crows on watch, she thought as she dated the page and made her notes about the truck.

Same wariness as yesterday when the delivery people opened the door. Same relief when they saw her and realized they didn't have to deal with one of the Others. Same helpful information about who they were and what days they usually made deliveries.

She found it interesting that two or three trucks arrived at almost the same time, which made her wonder if the drivers had some agreement among themselves about delivering at a specific time so they wouldn't be in the Courtyard alone—especially since most of them greeted one another by name.

When the first flurry of deliveries was done, she opened the door into the sorting room and pushed one of the handcarts inside. She didn't like treadmills—too many memories of being exercised in the compound—but maybe she should go over to Run & Thump and see what she could do to gain some muscle. Not being able to lift packages or mailbags wasn't going to win her any gold stars from Simon Wolfgard.

She turned on the disc player and started sorting mail, her hips following the beat of the music.

"Courtyard Business Association," Meg muttered as she read the name on the envelope. "They have a business association? Where?" She put the envelope on the ask-Jester stack.

There were several envelopes for the Chambers that had a red FINAL NOTICE stamped on them. She had a feeling she would find earlier warnings in the mailbags at the bottom of the pile.

Was there some kind of rule that Others couldn't sort mail, or did they expect that everything would go on as it was until they got someone to do it? Or were they really all so busy doing Other things that they didn't have time to take care of mail and packages?

She was still pondering that when the front door opened. Meg set down the stack of envelopes and went to the counter, closing the Private door partway.

The woman approaching the counter had sleek, shoulder-length blond hair, brown eyes, and a carefully made-up face that Meg decided matched the "beautiful" training images. The woman's parka was unzipped, revealing a curvy body in snug jeans and sweater.

Having no yardstick for the outside world, Meg couldn't decide if a woman dressed like that in the daytime indicated a movie star or a prostitute.

"I'm looking for the new Liaison," the woman said.

"I'm the Liaison," Meg replied.

"Really?" Anger flashed in the woman's eyes at the same time she gave Meg a wide smile. "Why, you're almost a pocket pet."

Anger and a smile were conflicting images, but a conflict she had seen often enough on the faces of the Walking Names, especially when Jean had caused trouble and stirred up some of the other girls.

Unsure of how to respond, Meg took a step back. If she needed help, there was a phone in the sorting room as well as on the counter here, and the Private door had a lock.

The woman studied her, then said, "Oh, honey, you don't have to be scared. I'm annoyed with Simon for hiring someone else after he all but promised me this job, but I'm not upset with *you*."

"Excuse me?"

The woman waved a hand. "Water under the bridge, as they say." A friendly smile now. "I'm Asia Crane. I'm a student at Lakeside University. Howling Good Reads is sort of my home away from home, so I expect we'll see a lot of each other."

Not likely, since she didn't intend to spend much time at the bookstore—at least, not when Simon Wolfgard was around to glare at her or take offense at her hair. "I'm Meg Corbyn."

Asia clapped her hands. "Crane. Corbyn. Our names are so similar, we could be sisters!"

"Except we don't look anything alike," Meg pointed out. Was Asia's behavior typical of the way people responded to meeting a stranger?

"Oh, poo. Don't go spoiling things with details! And please don't be insulted about the pet remark. It's a phrase I must have picked up from the romance novels I've been reading for fun."

Meg couldn't picture Simon stocking romances. Maybe someone else had a say in ordering books for the store?

"It was nice to meet you, Asia, but I have to get back to work," Meg said.

"Doing what?" Asia leaned on the counter and wrinkled her nose as she looked around. "It doesn't look like there's much to do here to keep from dying of boredom. Maybe I'm glad I didn't get this job after all."

"There's more to do than watch the counter and sign for packages," Meg said defensively.

"Like what?"

She hesitated, but answering the question didn't seem like a terrible thing to do, especially since Simon had all but promised thc job to Asia.

But if he promised the job to her, why did he hire me? "I sort the mail for the Courtyard," she said, trying to ignore the prickling that suddenly filled her right arm.

Asia's eyes widened. "For the whole Courtyard? Not just the stores, but the *whole thing*? By yourself?"

Meg nodded.

"Oh, honey, if that's the case, I'm not sure that man can pay *anyone* enough to do that much tedious work."

"It's not tedious, and it's not that much work—or it won't be after I take care of the backlog." The prickling in her arm got worse, and she began to feel uneasy. She shouldn't have that sensation so soon after a cut. Was it a sign that there was something wrong with her? The Walking Names always told the girls they couldn't survive long outside the compound because they would be overwhelmed by the world. Jean said that was a lie, but it had been a long time since Jean had lived on the outside, so maybe she didn't remember things correctly anymore.

"Well, why don't you bring some of that mail out here so we can get acquainted? I could even give you a hand," Asia said.

Meg shook her head and shuffled her feet back another half step toward the Private door. "It's nice of you to offer, but the mail has to stay in the sorting room, and no one else is allowed in there without Mr. Wolfgard's permission."

"Well, *Simon* isn't going to mind me helping out." Asia braced her hands on the counter. A little jump and turn had her sitting on top and swinging her legs over.

That was when the Private door opened all the way and Simon lunged out of the sorting room, knocking Meg aside. As he made a grab for Asia, she squealed, swung her legs back over the counter, and scrambled out of reach.

"Simon *does* mind," he snarled. "And the next time you swing a leg over a counter and try to put it where it doesn't belong, you're going back over the counter *minus* a leg!"

Asia bolted out the door and ran until she reached the sidewalk. Then she turned and stared at them before hurrying down the street.

Meg pressed herself against the wall, wanting to get farther away but not daring to move. "M-Mr. Wolfgard, I told her she wasn't allowed, but it sounded like—"

"I heard what it sounded like," he snarled. "I don't pay you to yak with other monkeys when there's work to be done. And if you want this job, there's still plenty of work in there."

"I—I know."

"Why are you stuttering? Are you cold?"

Not daring to speak, she shook her head.

His next snarl sounded as full of frustration as anger. After one more menacing glance outside, he walked back into the sorting room.

Moments later, Meg heard the back door slam.

Shaking and still too scared to move, she began to cry.

Simon stormed through the back door of Howling Good Reads, stripped off his clothes, and shifted to Wolf, unable to stand being in that human shape a moment longer. Then he howled, letting all his fury ride in the sound.

He didn't know why he was so angry. He just knew that something about the tone of Meg's voice when she was trying to defend her territory—and being so *damned* inadequate about it!—had tripped something inside his brain.

John was the first to reach the stockroom, but one look at Simon had him backing away. Tess came next, her hair streaked green *and* red.

"Simon?" Tess said. "What's wrong?"

Before he could answer, the back door opened again, almost smacking his hindquarters. He whirled and snapped at Jenni, who had shifted from Crow and now was a naked, shivering human.

She ignored the cold and she ignored him, which was beyond insulting since he *was* the leader of this Courtyard. Instead, she focused on Tess.

"Simon was being mean. He made the Meg cry. I'm going over to the store to see if I can find a sparkly that will make her smile again. The Meg smiles a lot—when the Wolf isn't snarling at her."

Jenni stepped back outside, shifted into a Crow, and flew off to Sparkles and Junk.

<Didn't snarl at Meg,> Simon growled.

Swinging around him and following Jenni out of the door, Tess said over her shoulder, "I'll talk to Meg and see if I can repair the damage."

He wasn't sure she intended for him to hear the muttered, "Idiot."

He looked at John, who was now crouched to bring his head lower than Simon's.

<Bring clothes,> Simon ordered. Then he bounded up the stairs to the store's office.

John brought his clothes up, set them on the nearest chair, and hurried back downstairs.

Simon prowled the office, then howled again.

He *hadn't* snarled at Meg. Not exactly. But he doubted there was a female in the Courtyard who was going to see it his way today.

Shifting back to human, he got dressed. Then he went to the window facing Crowfield Avenue and stared out. The streets were in decent shape. Not down to pavement yet, but passable.

Turning away from the window, he looked at the stacks of paperwork waiting for him because he had encouraged more contact with humans as a way of keeping better track of them.

"It was easier when all we wanted to do was eat them and take their stuff," he grumbled.

And it had been easier when he hadn't cared if he made any of them cry.

Asia shook so hard she couldn't get the keys in the ignition to start her car.

Bigwig had told her dealing with the Others was a risky assignment, which was why he and the other backers had been willing to let her take her time infiltrating the Courtyard. In the months she'd been living in Lakeside and hanging around HGR, she hadn't seen more than posturing and snarls from the Wolves and not even that much menace from the rest of the Others. Now she realized Bigwig had paid her so much up front because *he* had known that *risky* could mean *deadly.*

Pulling the flask out of the glove box, she took a long swallow of whiskey to steady her nerves. Then she took another to dim the image of her legs being torn off by a Wolf.

"Freaking Wolf," she said after the third swallow. "Damn freaking Wolf should have been in his own store instead of sniffing around a no-looks female." And he hadn't just hired a female with no looks and no sense of fashion to represent the Courtyard; *he had hired a feeb!*

She had expected a man, had dressed to introduce herself to a man, had figured the reason Wolfgard hadn't chosen her was because Liaisons were usually men and a man had applied for the job. Instead, Wolfgard had hired a feebleminded, weird-haired girl who thought sorting mail was *interesting.*

Asia took another sip, then put the flask back in the glove box.

If Meg *wasn't* a feeb, what kind of person *would* want the Liaison's job for its own sake? Someone who had a reason to hide—that's who. From what? From whom? The driver of that white van was keeping tabs on something or someone in the Courtyard, and Meg Corbyn was the only new employee.

She had a name and description to give Bigwig when she reported in tonight. That might help him figure out who would be interested in someone like Meg. Until he got back to her with whatever information he could gather at his end, she was going to be Meg Corbyn's new best friend and use that friendship to learn whatever she could about the Courtyard. And that meant dealing with Simon Wolfgard.

Suicide by Wolf. She'd heard the phrase plenty of times. Now she understood what it meant. But if she didn't push Simon now, she'd never get another shot at Meg.

She debated for a moment, then decided whiskey breath would suit this little drama. After all, no human in the bookstore would expect someone to start a confrontation with a Wolf unless that person was a little drunk. And she thought Asia Crane, SI, would be the kind of investigator who would have a checkered past and the need to have a daytime drink once in a while.

She needed to write these ideas down for the day when she met with Bigwig to discuss her TV show.

She got out of her car and strode to Howling Good Reads. As soon as she walked into the store, she balled her hands into fists and shouted, "Simon Wolfgard! You get your butt over here! I have words to say to you!"

Several people dropped books. Then an awful silence filled the bookstore when Simon appeared. Asia hoped the lenses of his glasses were picking up some kind of light that made his eyes look glowing—and red.

Before he got too close, she launched her verbal attack. "Simon Wolfgard, you are meaner than a rabid skunk!"

"You were where you didn't belong!" he roared.

"Well, pardon me for trying to be friendly! I just dropped by to introduce myself and give your new employee a bit of a welcome. I didn't realize she was *forbidden* to have a simple conversation with *another human*. It's plain as plain that poor girl has some challenges." Asia tapped her temple. It didn't matter if Simon understood the gesture; all the humans in the store would recognize it and assume he had hired a feeb. "And then when someone takes an interest in her, all *you* do is make threats. It wouldn't surprise me one bit if she slips away some night and doesn't come back because of the way you treated her. Do you know what you are, Simon?"

"No," he growled. "What am I?"

"You're nothing but a bully with fangs! A human would have to be *desperate* to work for someone like you!"

"You were willing to work for me—and do more."

Her face heated, but she lifted her chin. "That was before I realized you Others mimic humans to get what you want, but you don't know anything about what's inside a human."

Simon bared his teeth. "We know what's inside a human. Tasty bits. Especially the heart and liver."

Her knees weakened and her heart pounded. Her voice quavered, but she shifted to quiet and dignified when she said, "I have nothing more to say to you."

She walked out of the store. When she reached the parking lot, she bolted to her car, braced a hand on the hood, and threw up.

Fear and whiskey aren't a good mix, she thought as she drove to her apartment. She would take a hot shower, put on some comfy clothes, and indulge herself by watching her favorite movies for the rest of the day.

In a couple of days, she'd go back to Howling Good Reads and see if she had a shot at spending time with the new Liaison.

At least she accomplished one thing. If Meg Corbyn disappeared one night, for whatever reason, everyone would figure she was running away from Simon Wolfgard and no one would make much effort to find her.

Meg sniffled and sorted mail. She didn't have enough money left to run again, so she had to hang on to this job long enough to get paid.

She glanced up when the door to the back room opened but didn't say anything until Tess stood on the other side of the table.

"Mr. Wolfgard left his coffee." She glanced at Tess, then focused on the mail. She remembered seeing green in Tess's hair yesterday, but not the red. Was changing hair color some kind of hobby? And if it was, why was Simon snapping about *her* hair?

Tess pursed her lips as she studied the insulated, covered mug. "Actually, he brought that for you."

Startled, Meg looked up.

Tess nodded. Then she said gently, "What happened, Meg? You've been crying, Simon's riled up, and the Crows just told me that Asia bolted out of here like the whole pack was on her heels."

"I was starting to sort the mail when she came in and introduced herself. She said Mr. Wolfgard had promised she could have this job, but he hired me instead. So she was curious about what I did besides sign for packages."

"Did you tell her?"

"I said I sorted the mail for the Courtyard."

"Did you tell her anything about who is in the Courtyard? Mention any names?"

Meg shook her head. "I guess it's natural for people to be curious about this place, but offering to help me sort the mail seemed too forward. But some people are like that," she added defensively. "Outgoing and chatty. Harry from Everywhere Delivery is chatty too, but Jester didn't say talking to Harry was wrong, and I *did* tell Asia I needed to get back to work. She shouldn't have sat on the counter or swung her legs over, but people do that when they want to chat. They sit on a piece of furniture and swing their legs."

Now that she wasn't as scared, Meg started to get mad. "Then Mr. Wolfgard showed up and threatened to bite Asia's leg. So she ran off, and she'll probably never come back."

"Do you want her to come back?" Tess asked.

"I have questions," Meg countered. "Things I can't ask *him*."

Tess raised her eyebrows. "He's a Mr. Wolfgard and a him?" She sighed. "What kind of questions?"

"I didn't see a place in the Market Square to wash clothes. Am I supposed to wash them in the bathroom sink or . . ." Going to a laundry beyond the Courtyard wasn't something she wanted to consider.

Looking thoughtful in a scary kind of way, Tess picked up the insulated mug and handed it to Meg. "It won't be hot, but it should still be warm. By the way, that mug isn't something you should put in the wave-cooker."

"Okay." Meg took the mug, removed the lid, and obediently took a sip of coffee.

"As for doing laundry, we send out some things to a laundry service—like bedspreads, curtains, and . . . other things we don't want to handle. There is also a coin-operated washing machine and dryer in the social center that employees are allowed to use. And each residential complex has a laundry room."

"Are there instructions for using the coin-operated machines?"

Training image. A commercial laundry, its walls spattered with blood, and two people dead on the floor.

Meg shivered.

"Tell you what," Tess said. "I'll come by around four thirty. That's long enough past the office's usual closing for any delivery trucks that are still slowed down by the snow. We'll go to the clothing store and pick up whatever you need to get you through a few more days. Then I'll take you over to the laundry room at the Green Complex. Did anyone give you your Market Square card?"

"Jester dropped it off with my pass, but he didn't explain what it did."

"Typical," Tess muttered. "Do just enough to stir things up. It goes like this. Everyone who works at any of our stores is paid in human currency and also receives credit that can be used at any store in the Courtyard. So while your pay may not seem like much in terms of the money you get, you're also getting double that amount credited on your card each week. At the end of each month, you can stop in at our bank and receive a slip telling you what you have left on the card."

Since she didn't have to pay for her apartment, the wages were more generous than she'd thought.

"I don't pretend to understand humans," Tess said. "Giving both sides a chance to understand each other is the reason the Business Association decided to open up some of the stores to human customers. So I'll talk to Simon about letting Asia Crane drop by to chat—as long as you and she understand that Simon will kill her if he catches her scent where it doesn't belong. But if you have questions about being in the Courtyard, you can ask me. All right?"

"Yes. Thank you."

Tess smiled and glanced at the clock on the wall. "Then I'll let you get back to work. The ponies will be coming soon. Don't forget to come by on your lunch break. A Little Bite is providing the midday meal."

"I'll remember."

She waited until Tess left, then put the Back in Five Minutes sign on the counter, locked the Private door, and went into the bathroom to wash her face. Nothing she could do about the puffy eyes, but dust could cause puffy eyes too, couldn't it? And that corner that held the older mailbags and packages *was* dusty.

She unlocked the Private door and tucked the sign under the counter just in time for another delivery truck to drive up.

It looked like she'd get to try out the dust excuse and see if anyone actually believed it.

"SIMON!"

Hearing Tess's voice, Simon vaulted over the checkout counter, an instinctive response to some knowledge embedded into the essence of his kind. When she strode from the back of the store, he knew why he wanted to give himself room to fight.

Her hair was completely red and coiling as she walked toward him.

Not black. Not the death color. But close enough.

Tess looked around. Her voice thundered through HGR. "Howling Good Reads is closed for the day. *Anyone* who is still in the store sixty seconds from now will never be seen again."

Others and humans ran for the nearest door, whether it was HGR's street door or the archway to A Little Bite.

"Tess?" Julia Hawkgard called from the archway. "Are we closing too?"

"Customers go. You and Merri Lee stay to close up."

When Simon turned toward the street door to lock it and flip the sign to CLOSED, Tess snarled, "Not you, Wolfgard."

He walked up to her. "I'm the leader of this Courtyard. You live here because of *my* invitation. Remember that."

Threads of black appeared in her red hair.

"If I have to make friends with a monkey in order to clean up your mess, you're going to make some concessions," she said.

"You don't have to make friends with anyone." He wasn't sure she *was* capable of making friends. And despite the efforts he and Henry had made over the years, they still didn't know what kind of *terra indigene* Tess was. But they knew she could kill. They did know that.

"Well, I have. For the sake of the Courtyard, I have made friends with our Human Liaison. Now it's your turn."

"What do you expect me to do? Asia Crane would have pushed where she didn't belong, and she'll keep pushing."

Tess tipped her head. "Even now?"

"Even now. And Meg isn't strong enough to hold her ground." But she had been strong enough to run from something—or someone—and had enough spine to ask him for a job.

"You've turned Asia into forbidden fruit," Tess said.

"What?"

"You've read enough human stories to know the lure of forbidden fruit."

Yes, he had. And if Meg smelled like prey the way she was supposed to, he wouldn't have responded in a way that was closer to protecting one of his own. Oh, he still would have forced Asia to back down, but he would have done it the same way he dealt with a customer in the store who wanted access to places that were private.

So it was Meg's fault that he hadn't behaved correctly.

"Simon?"

He heard the warning note in Tess's voice. "I won't forbid Asia from visiting with Meg, as long as she stays on her side of the counter."

"And I'll talk to my employees about helping me befriend the Liaison," Tess said.

"And keep a sharper eye on Asia?"

"That too."

Her hair was still red, but the black threads were gone and the coils were relaxing.

Since it wouldn't be viewed as a retreat now, Simon took a step back and looked around. "I don't feel like opening up again."

"No one will come in today anyway," Tess said. "But tomorrow the fear will have faded just enough." She smiled. "I heard John mention you received a shipment of terror books."

"Horror books." Now he smiled. "Including a couple of boxes of *terra indigene* authors I don't usually put out for human customers."

"Maybe you should make a display of them and put them on sale tomorrow. I expect we'll be busy."

"We could have tripled sales if we'd eaten one of the customers before they'd all gotten out."

Tess laughed. "Maybe we can do that next time."

Simon sighed. "I need a day out of this skin."

"And I need a few hours of solitude. See you tomorrow, Wolfgard."

"Tomorrow." He tipped his head toward A Little Bite. "What about your shop?"

"Julia and Merri Lee will clean up and close up. I'll tell them to take something over to Meg before they leave."

Choosing to be satisfied with that, Simon pulled out his keys and secured the dead bolt on HGR's street door. He checked the office, and stopped long enough to call Vlad and tell him the store was closed and also mention doing a display of horror books by *terra indigene* authors. Then he turned off lights as he went through the building, put on his winter coat when he reached the stockroom, and left, locking the back door.

He didn't want to be in this skin. He wanted to wear the body of a Wolf. But he had to stay in human form until he got Daphne's son, Sam, outside for a few minutes of fresh air—which was all the pup could tolerate since the night Daphne was shot. Once he got the youngster settled inside again, he could shift and run alone for a few hours.

So he set off for the Green Complex, hoping a walk on a cold day would frost some of his anger and frustration—and wishing again that he could find something that would break the fear that kept Sam locked in a single form.

Meg had her coat on and the bowl of carrot chunks on the sorting table with the mail when the ponies neighed. She opened the sorting room's outer door and smiled at their grumpy faces.

"Good morning," she said, hoping they couldn't recognize forced cheer. "I brought a treat for all of us, since we're all working hard to get the mail to everyone in the Courtyard. So let me get the baskets filled, and then I'll show you what I brought."

Maybe they aren't grumpy, Meg thought as she filled the slots in Thunder's baskets. *Maybe that's just what pony faces look like.*

When Thunder moved away, she wanted to remind him she had a treat for all of them, and felt disappointed that he was leaving without giving her a chance to make friends. But he simply circled around until he was behind Fog and would be first in line again.

She brought the bowl with her when she picked up the last stack of mail for the Green Complex—Fog's destination today.

Apparently, ponies *did* have more than one expression. When she offered two carrot chunks to Thunder, he took the first warily and the second eagerly. Bobbing his head, he trotted off while the others jostled one another to reach the bowl.

"Wait your turn," Meg said. "I brought plenty for all of us."

They settled down and waited for their treats, looking as interested in her as they were in the carrots. When Fog trotted off, Meg closed the door and felt that something had finally gone right that day. Setting the bowl on the table so that she could munch on the rest of the carrots while she worked, she went into the bathroom to wash carrot flecks and pony spit off her hands—and put a clean bandage on her finger.

As Kowalski drove down Crowfield Avenue, Monty noticed the Closed sign on Howling Good Reads' door and said, "Pull over." He studied the sign, then looked at the Closed sign at A Little Bite. "Is it usual for them to be closed when most other places are open?"

"No, it's not," Kowalski replied. "The Others can be whimsical about business hours, and sometimes the stores are closed to humans so that the *terra indigene* can shop without being around us. But when that happens, there is usually a Residents Only sign tacked on the door, the lights will be on, and you'll see people in the stores."

"So whatever caused this can't be good."

"No, sir, it can't be good."

Monty opened his door. "I see some movement in A Little Bite. Wait here."

Getting out of the car, he went up to the door and knocked loudly enough to ensure that the two women in the shop wouldn't ignore him.

The dark-haired one hurried to the door and pointed to the sign. He responded by holding up his ID.

She flipped the lock, pulled the door open, and said, "We're closed."

"Is there something I can do to help?" Monty asked, his voice quiet and courteous.

She shook her head and started to close the door when the other woman called out, "Let him in, Merri Lee. He can take some of this coffee and food. He is police. Tess said we should be polite to him."

Merri Lee pulled the door open enough for him to slip inside, then locked it again.

"Sorry," she said, keeping her voice low. "There was an . . . upset . . . earlier, and it's better for humans not to be around here today."

"What about you?" he asked.

"Julia is a Hawkgard, so I'm okay." She raised her voice to a normal volume and addressed the woman pouring coffee into two large travel mugs. "I'm supposed to bring some of the food to Meg."

"Already have everything set aside for her," Julia replied. "For you too. And me. You have a carry sack?"

It took Monty a moment to realize the question was aimed at him. "No, ma'am, I don't."

"We usually sell them, but you are the police, so I'll give you one," Julia said.

The heavy fabric sack had two sleeves with stiff bottoms that were sized for the insulated travel mugs, plus a zippered compartment that could hold sandwiches or containers of food. There was even a section to hold cutlery.

He watched her fill up the sack with sandwiches and pastries. It looked like they were cleaning out anything that was intended for sale that day and wouldn't be held over for tomorrow.

"What happened here?" he asked.

"Jenni said Simon upset the Meg and made her cry," Julia replied. "Then that Asia came into Howling Good Reads and yelled at Simon, and then Tess and Simon yelled at each other over what happened with the Meg. That's when they closed the stores. It's not safe when Simon and Tess yell at each other."

"Is Ms. Corbyn all right?"

Merri Lee nodded. "Just upset." She watched Julia zip up the sack and added, "You should go now."

Concern mixed with a warning. Whatever had happened today had happened before. The humans—and the Others—knew how to ride it out.

And hoped they lived through it?

Nothing he could do, so he accepted the carry sack and food with warm thanks, and slipped one of his cards to Merri Lee when she let him out of the shop.

"Lieutenant?" Kowalski asked when Monty got in the car.

"Pull into their parking lot. I'd like a few minutes to think while we have something to eat."

Once Kowalski parked the car, Monty handed out coffee and food.

Merri Lee, being human, might not say anything about him being in the shop, but Julia Hawkgard would report his presence to somebody. So he couldn't stop by and talk to Meg Corbyn and reassure himself that she was just upset, but there were other ways of checking on things that weren't officially his concern.

Telling himself to be satisfied with that, he enjoyed the unexpected meal.

Someone knocked loudly on the office's back door, then knocked again before Meg could reach it.

"Hi," the woman said when Meg opened the door. "I'm Merri Lee. Can I come in far enough so you don't lose all the heat?"

Still feeling raw about Simon's reaction to Asia—and feeling a touch defiant because *this* woman was holding up a pass that said she was allowed to be in this part of the Courtyard—Meg stepped aside.

"I brought your midday meal," Merri Lee said as she came in. "Things are churned up today, so . . . Wow." Her eyes widened as she looked around. "Is the other room any cleaner?"

"A little. Not much." Meg looked around too. "It is pretty dirty, isn't it?" She thought it was, but she hadn't been sure other humans would see it that way.

"Here." Merri Lee handed her the carry sack. "Look. No one but the Liaison and the *terra indigene* are supposed to be in this office, but I wouldn't want to work here until it's clean."

"There's a lot of mail that needs to be sorted," Meg said.

"And you have to do that," Merri Lee agreed. "But A Little Bite is closed today, so I could put in my work hours by helping you clean this room at least."

"If you're not allowed to be here, you'll get in trouble." There was a natural warmth to Merri Lee's friendliness, so Meg didn't want her to get hurt.

"Not if I get permission from a member of the Business Association." Merri Lee looked nervous. "Can't ask Simon or Tess, and I'd rather not ask Vlad or Nyx." Her face cleared. "But if Henry is working in his studio, I can ask him. Are there any cleaning supplies here?"

"Not that I found."

"Not even for the toilet?"

Meg shook her head.

"Oh, gods. Well, I'll pick up some supplies after I talk to Henry." She glanced at Meg's hands. "What did you do to your finger?"

"I was cutting up carrots for the ponies," Meg replied. "Got a little careless. It's not a deep slice."

Merri Lee nodded. "I'll get some cleaning gloves to protect your hands. The cleansers will sting if they get in that cut." She held out another carry sack. "That's my food. Could you stash it someplace until I get back?" Giving Meg a smile and wave, she darted out.

Meg put the carry sacks on the sorting table. It felt uncomfortable to lie to someone who was being kind. She hadn't known a lie could have a physical weight. But she wasn't going to tell anyone the truth about the cutting and the prophecies until she had no other choice.

Having decided that much, she unzipped the compartment that held her food. Before she could remove a sandwich, something small and brown ran across the floor and darted into the pile of packages that still needed sorting.

When Merri Lee returned a few minutes later with Henry Beargard and two females, Meg was kneeling on top of the sorting table, staring at that corner of the room.

Merri Lee stopped in the doorway and looked ready to run. Henry and the females stepped into the sorting room.

Meg pointed a shaking finger. "Something is hiding in that corner."

Henry moved silently to that corner and sniffed. "Mouse."

"Oh, gods," Merri Lee said.

"They're easier to catch if you leave food in the middle of the floor," the brown-haired woman said.

"Why would you do that?" Meg asked.

"Fresh snack," the black-haired woman replied brightly.

Merri Lee said, "Oh, gods" again before clamping a hand over her mouth. Meg just stared.

Henry studied Merri Lee, then Meg. "Humans don't like mice?"

"Not in the building!" Meg said.

"And not around food," Merri Lee added.

The three *terra indigene* looked baffled.

"But it's fresh meat," the brown-haired woman finally said.

"Humans don't eat mice," Merri Lee said. "Or rats. We just don't."

Silence.

Finally, Henry sighed—a big, gusty sound. "We will put aside other work today and make this place human-clean for the Liaison." He pointed at Merri Lee. "You will show us how this is done."

"I'll go to the Market Square and pick up the supplies we'll need to put some shine on these rooms," Merri Lee said.

The black-haired woman cawed. "You can make things shiny?"

"In a way."

So the Crow went with Merri Lee while Henry began excavating the mailbags and boxes piled in the corner of the sorting room.

The brown-haired woman was an Owl named Allison. She was quite pleased to catch two mice—and less pleased when Henry made her go outside to eat them.

When five people cleaned three rooms—and one of them was a man as strong as a bear—the work went quickly, even with Allison taking two more breaks to devour mouse snacks. Some of the packages in that corner had been nibbled; others were smashed. Meg noticed how many of them were addressed to people living in the Chambers, which made her wonder who the Sanguinati were that the previous Liaisons wouldn't deliver packages to them.

On the other hand, Jester had said the previous Liaisons hadn't been encouraged to make deliveries to anyone in the Courtyard. But *something* should have been done to get the packages to the people waiting for them.

She had made excuses for not eating while they were working—especially when there was still the possibility of finding another mouse. Since Merri Lee was also making excuses, despite a growling stomach, the Others accepted the strange behavior.

Finally, all the old packages were neatly stacked on one of the hand carts; the counters, tables, cupboards, and floors were washed; the wave-cooker and fridge were clean; and the bathroom didn't make her shudder when she used the toilet. Allison went back to the Owlgard Complex to report this peculiar aversion humans had to mice. Crystal Crowgard ran off to Sparkles and Junk with rags and the spray bottle of cleaner that would make all their display counters shiny.

Henry pointed at Meg. "The rooms are clean. Now you will eat." He pointed at Merri Lee. "You may sit with her in the back room and visit."

Meg looked at the clock on the sorting-room wall. "It's almost two o'clock. I need to take deliveries."

"You will eat," Henry said. "I will watch the counter until you are done."

Meg went to the back room and frowned at the small round table and two chairs. "Those weren't here this morning."

"No, they weren't," Merri Lee replied, pulling food out of the fridge. "But I mentioned to Henry that it would nicer if you had a place to eat when you didn't want to go out during your break, and he got these from somewhere." She looked around the room and nodded. "This is much better."

"Definitely better," Meg agreed. "Thank you."

They didn't talk much. Maybe they were both too hungry to focus on anything but food. Maybe they had learned enough about each other for the moment. Whatever the reason, Merri Lee left as soon as she had enough to eat.

Meg stored the rest of the food, then went out to the front room in time to greet the two deliverymen who had taken one look at Henry and were backing away.

When the men gave her the packages and drove off, Henry nodded as if he was pleased about something.

"I don't answer the telephone when I'm working with the wood," he said. "But if you need me, you tell the Crows and I'll come."

"Thank you for all the help today," Meg said.

He left, saying nothing more.

Meg went back to sorting mail for the remaining time in her workday, but she kept glancing at those old packages. She would do something about them tomorrow.

She was about to close up for the day when a patrol car pulled into the delivery area.

He found me, she thought, her heart jumping. *The Controller has found me. That's why the police are here.*

She hadn't seen these men before, but they seemed to know something about the Others because they both got out, removed their hats, and looked straight at the Crows before entering the office.

"Ma'am," one of them said when they reached the counter. "I'm Officer Michael Debany. This is my partner, Lawrence MacDonald. We work with Lieutenant Montgomery and just wanted to introduce ourselves and let you know we're available if you need any assistance."

As they chatted and Officer Debany mentioned again that they would provide help if it was needed, Meg realized the men were fishing for information about what happened this morning to close Howling Good Reads and A Little Bite, but mostly they were trying to find out if she had been hurt but was afraid to leave.

She wouldn't have gone with them even if she did need help, but it made her feel better that help was available for the other humans who worked for the *terra indigene.*

When the police officers left, she locked up the front room and continued sorting mail until Tess arrived to help her with clothes shopping and laundry. That turned out to be a more pleasant experience than she'd expected.

The only thing that marred the evening was when she looked out her apartment window before going to bed and spotted a man standing across the street, watching her.

CHAPTER 5

Eight ponies showed up the following day, looking for mail and carrots. Meg filled their baskets, handed out treats, and breathed a sigh of relief that she had just enough carrot chunks to go around. She wasn't sure they could count and would know if the last pony only got one chunk instead of two, but it wasn't a chance she wanted to take.

She waved when they trotted away, then closed the door, washed her hands, and got back to sorting. Apparently, Watersday was a light day for deliveries from human businesses, but the number of trucks with the earth native symbol on the cab more than made up for it. They didn't stop at her office, though; they continued up the access way between the Liaison's Office and the consulate to the delivery area for the Market Square.

According to Merri Lee, the Lakeside Courtyard served as a way station for *terra indigene* who wanted to enjoy human goods without having to deal directly with humans. Meat, dairy, and produce came in to the Courtyard from the farms run by the Others; clothes, books, movies, and incidental products that appealed to them went out.

Meg looked at some of the old packages. The labels said IN CARE OF THE LAKESIDE COURTYARD. Should those be going out to *terra indigene* settlements with the other merchandise? She didn't want to bother Henry, who usually didn't answer the telephone anyway. And she certainly didn't want to call the big, bad Wolf. But she had to ask someone, so she called the bookstore and listened to the phone ring.

"Maybe he got run over by a tree," she muttered as she imagined a log rolling down a hill and flattening a certain Wolf. It happened in some of the videos she had watched, so it *could* happen. Couldn't it? The thought cheered her up, so she pictured it again, changing the log to a rolling pin that rolled out the Wolf like a furry piecrust.

"Howling Good Reads," said a male voice that wasn't *his*.

It took her a moment to realign her thoughts. "This is Meg Corbyn."

"Do you want to talk to Simon?"

"No."

"Oh."

She tried to think of a question that anyone at the store could answer so she could hang up before someone told *him* that she had called. Then she looked at the packages.

Rememory. A woman locked in a box—a surprise to be delivered as a special gift. Except no one had known what was in the box, and no one had recognized the urgency of finding it when the box hadn't been delivered as promised.

The girls might not remember a prophecy at the time they spoke the words, but the images weren't lost. They were absorbed like the training images, connecting something remembered with something present. Jean called those images rememories because they were more than training images but less than personal memories.

There wasn't a woman in any of the packages that had been left in the sorting room, and a life wasn't lost in any of those small boxes. But each of those packages was stained by disappointment.

"Could someone tell me if any of the packages I have at the office should be going out on the earth native trucks with the other deliveries?"

A pause. "Someone who isn't Simon?" the voice asked cautiously.

"Yes."

Voices were muffled by a hand over the receiver, but Meg could still hear the emotion in those voices and wondered how much of a problem she was causing for whoever was working at HGR today.

The silence that followed was so full she thought she'd been disconnected. Then the voice came back and said, "Vlad will come over and look."

"Thank you."

She hung up and went back to sorting. She wasn't sure Vlad would be any better than *him*, but at least Vlad hadn't yelled at her. Yet.

Vlad leaned against the office doorway and gave Simon a smile that made the Wolf's canines lengthen and his fingernails change into hard claws.

"I'm going to the Liaison's Office," Vlad said pleasantly.

"Why?" Simon snarled.

"Because it seems Meg is good at holding a grudge and doesn't want to talk to *you*. And you must feel she has a reason for that grudge. You wouldn't have spent all morning doing paperwork you don't like if you didn't have to make up for something."

"I don't have to make up for anything!"

"You stirred things up plenty yesterday."

"*She* stirred things up."

"You can tell the story any way you like," Vlad said, pushing off from the doorway. "That's not going to change what is."

"Bite me."

"You're too sour today. I'd rather . . ."

Simon shot to his feet.

Vlad stared at Simon, then held up his hands. "I'm going over there at her request to answer her questions—nothing more. You have my word on that, Wolfgard."

It was foolish to fight with a friend when he knew Vlad was pulling his tail because of his behavior yesterday, and it was worse than foolish to fight with one of the Sanguinati. But it took more effort than it should have to accept Vlad's word.

Forcing himself to shift all the way back to human, Simon sat down and picked up a pen as if everything was settled. "If you have to sample someone, do us all a favor and bite Asia Crane."

Vlad laughed. "Now you're just being mean."

Based on the pictures she had studied as part of her identification training, Vlad would have been labeled the tall, dark stranger, the dangerous thrill.

He scared her. His movements were more sinuous than the other earth natives she'd seen. *They* practically shouted they were predators. With Vlad, she didn't think humans realized the danger until it was too late.

And yet he was courteous and didn't crowd her while he checked the labels on the boxes she had set aside, and agreed that they should go on the trucks delivering supplies to other *terra indigene*.

He called Jester and asked for a pony and sled to transport the packages, explaining while they waited that the drivers would know better which packages should go in which truck.

Jester arrived with a pony named Twister, and he and Vlad loaded the packages into the small sled. Then Twister pulled the sled to the area where the trucks were parked.

"If there is nothing else, I must get back to the store," Vlad said with a smile. "Simon is doing paperwork today, so it's better for the customers if someone else deals with them." As he walked away, he added, "But I expect the Wolfgard will be ready for a break and some fresh air around lunchtime."

Which meant the Wolf might poke his nose around the office and find something else she had done wrong—at least according to the whims of Simon Wolfgard.

"What are you going to do with these packages?" Jester asked, looking at the ones still on the handcart. "Do you want me to send Twister back for them?"

"No," Meg said quickly. "I thought I would take out the BOW and deliver these in person. You did say I could do that as part of my duties."

"Yes, I did." The laughter in his eyes told her plainly enough he knew why she didn't want to be around during the lunch break. "Have you unhooked the BOW from its energy cord yet?"

She shook her head. That was just one of the things she hadn't tried to do yet.

"Then I'll do that and bring it around for you this time."

"Would it be all right if I take the map with me until I learn my way around?"

No laughter now. "It's not something you want to misplace."

Or give to anyone else. "I'll be careful with it."

A different kind of laughter filled his eyes now. Sharp, almost predatory. "Why don't I get another copy for you at the Three Ps? It's just across the way. Lorne is a human, but he's dependable despite that." Jester's smile told Meg plainly enough that not all humans who had worked for the Others had been dependable. "Three Ps stands for Postage, Printing, and Paper. Lorne sells different kinds of stationery, as well as the stamps needed to mail things outside the Courtyard. And he prints the Courtyard's weekly newsletter."

"You have a newsletter?" Surprise made her blurt out the words.

"Of course we have a newsletter. How else would we know which movies are being shown at the social room in each residential complex? How else would everyone know about the new books that arrived and are available in our library?" Jester pressed one hand to his chest. "How else would we learn from Ms. Know-It-All's column, 'Others Etiquette'?"

"An advice column?" Meg stared at him. "You're kidding."

"We don't kid about Ms. Know-It-All," he replied. Then he snatched up the map and left.

Meg stood where she was, trying to sort out the words and the change in Jester's attitude when she asked if she could take the map. He'd brought her the map in the first place and warned her to be careful. Now he was telling her where to make copies and that she could buy stamps to mail letters to people outside the Courtyard. Was he *trying* to get her into trouble?

A *test,* she thought. Maybe lots of other people had seen the map. Maybe it wasn't as big a secret as she had been led to believe. Maybe this was a way for the Others to decide if they could trust a human. *And maybe any human who fails this test is never seen again. I'm going to die in this Courtyard. I know that. Is it because of the map or because I fail some other kind of test?*

A couple minutes later, she heard the *beep beep* of the BOW's horn. Pushing aside all thoughts of tests, she put her coat on, opened the sorting room's delivery door, and began loading the back of the vehicle.

The BOW really was a box on wheels. It had two seats in the front. The rest of it—what there was of it—was a cargo area.

Plenty of room for a Wolf in the back, Jester told her after he dropped the copy of the map on the passenger's seat and returned the original to the sorting room. Like she wanted a Wolf breathing down her neck while she was driving—or doing anything else.

Did they all think if they kept mentioning Simon she would forget how *scary* he had been yesterday? Maybe fear wasn't something the Others retained, but humans certainly did.

Even humans like her.

It was a little before noon when she locked up the office and got in the BOW, making sure she had her pass in the side pocket of her new purse, where it would be easy to reach.

When Jester tapped on the window, she rolled it down.

"You all set?" he asked.

"All set." She hoped she sounded confident. She really wanted him to go away before she put the BOW in gear.

"I'll tell Tess you'll be by later for your meal."

She wondered what else he was going to tell Tess, but she smiled and said, "Thanks."

The laughter was back in his eyes when she made no move to shift the gear to drive. Then he walked away.

Recalling training images of car interiors, she found the lights and the windshield wipers. She found the dial that controlled the heater. Shakily confident that she would be fine—as long as she didn't have to do anything but go forward—she headed out to make her first deliveries.

After a couple of minutes of white-knuckle driving on a road that had been plowed, more or less, Meg began wondering if the pony and sled wouldn't have been a better idea. The pony wouldn't be inclined to slide off the road. Not that the BOW wasn't a game little vehicle. It growled its way up an incline, struggling to find the traction it needed to get to the next piece of level ground.

From what she could tell from the map, she was on the main road that circled the entire Courtyard, so it should be sufficiently cleared all the way around. As long as she didn't stray off it, she should be fine. Besides, the thought of going back and running into Simon was reason enough to keep going forward. That and not knowing how to drive backward.

It wasn't her fault she'd never driven in snow—or in anything else. A sterile, restricted life meant the girls had no other stimulation except the images, sounds, and other visuals in the lessons, and what was used as reference for the prophecies could be verified because it was assumed all of the girls saw and heard the same thing. And it had been proven by the Walking Names that that kind of life made the girls more accepting of any kind of actual stimulation because they were starved for sensation.

Would the cutting be as compelling if there were other ways to feel pleasure, other sensations?

But that sterile life was her past. Now she was gaining the experience of driving in snow, and as long as she didn't run into another vehicle or end up in a ditch, the Wolf had no reason to criticize.

The road forked. The left fork curved toward the Owlgard Complex and the

Pony Barn. The right fork was the main road and had a sign that read, TRESPASSERS WILL BE EATEN.

Meg swallowed hard and continued on the main road, passing the Green Complex. Then she passed the Ash Grove and the Utilities Complex. Finally she reached the ornate black fences that marked the Chambers, the part of the Courtyard claimed by the Sanguinati.

She tried to pull up some memory about that name, was sure she knew something about them even though the girls had been taught very little about the Others. But Jester's warning when she was packing up the BOW was clear enough.

The fences around the Chambers aren't decorative, Meg. They're boundaries. You never push open a gate and step onto the Sanguinati's land for any reason. Anyone who enters without their consent doesn't leave—and I've never known them to give their consent.

What unnerved her about the words was the certainty that they applied to the rest of the *terra indigene* as well as humans.

But she didn't have to break the rules to deliver the packages. When she pulled up to the first white marble building positioned in the center of its fenced-in land, she saw nine metal boxes outside the fence, painted black and secured to a stone foundation. They didn't have individual numbers, so they must be used by everyone who lived in the . . . Was that a mausoleum? It seemed small if the handful of names with this particular address actually lived inside.

She opened the door of the first box. Roomy enough for magazines and other mail of similar size. Another box was wider and the packages she had fit well enough. She put packages in three more boxes, then got back into the BOW and went on to the next building.

Four packages for the residents of this part of the Chambers. This time, as she closed the door of the last box, she noticed the soot around the mausoleum. Or was that smoke? Was something on fire inside?

She leaned into the BOW and fumbled for the mobile phone Tess had arranged for her to have. She had dutifully put in the contact numbers for Simon, Tess, and the consulate. But whom should she call to report a fire? How did the Courtyard handle emergencies?

Then the smoke drifted away from the structure with a deliberate change of direction—toward her.

She stopped fumbling for the phone, got into the BOW, and headed for the next fenced area.

This mausoleum didn't look any different from the other two, except there was a smaller one built close to the fence separating the two structures. The walkway from the gate to the elaborately carved wooden door was clear of snow, as was the marble stoop.

Smoke drifted close to the fences.

Jester didn't say she wouldn't be harmed if she was on this side of the fence. He just said being harmed was a certainty if she went inside the fenced area.

Maybe they would appreciate someone finally delivering their packages?

Tucking her pass inside the coat pocket, she got out of the BOW, raised the back door, pulled out the packages, and filled several of the boxes.

Then she pulled out a package for Mr. Erebus Sanguinati. It was one of the packages shoved farthest back in that corner of the sorting room, so it had been there for weeks, maybe even months.

It wasn't a heavy package, but it was square rather than a rectangle, making it too high to fit into the metal boxes. She chewed on her lower lip, wondering what she should do.

"Something wrong?"

She stumbled back a step. She hadn't seen anyone approach, hadn't heard anyone, but a beautiful woman with dark eyes and black hair that flowed to the waist of her black velvet gown now stood near the fence that separated the two mausoleums.

"I have a package for Mr. Erebus Sanguinati, but it won't fit into the boxes."

"You're the new Liaison?"

"Yes. I'm Meg Corbyn."

The woman didn't offer her name. Instead, she looked toward the larger mausoleum—whose door was now open just enough for someone to peek out.

"You could leave a form saying there is a package being held at the Liaison's Office," the woman said.

"It's been at the office for a while," Meg replied. "That's why I thought I should deliver it in person."

The woman's smile was more lethal than encouraging. "You could leave it in the snow. The previous Liaisons would have—if they had been brave enough to come at all."

Meg shook her head. "Whatever is inside might get damaged if it got wet."

A sound like dry leaves skittering over a sidewalk came from the larger mausoleum.

The woman looked startled, then studied Meg with unnerving interest. "Grandfather Erebus says you may enter the Chambers and set the package before the door. Stay on the walkway, and you will come to no harm."

"I was told I wasn't allowed to enter the Chambers," Meg said.

The woman's smile sharpened. "Even the Wolfgard accommodates the Grandfather."

Which meant Mr. Erebus was a very important person in the Courtyard.

Smoke flowed swiftly over the snow, gathering to one side of the gate. Part of it condensed, becoming an arm and a hand that pulled open the gate before changing back to smoke that moved away.

Something about smoke and the name Sanguinati that she needed to remember.

Pushing open the gate a little more, Meg walked up to the mausoleum. A hand curled around the edge of the door—an old hand with knobby joints, big veins, and yellowed, horny fingernails. A dark eye in a lined face peered out at her.

Not quite looking him in the eye, in case that was offensive to him, Meg carefully set the package down on the dry marble stoop.

"I'm sorry it took so long for you to receive your package, Mr. Erebus. I'll watch for them from now on and get them to you as soon as I can."

"Sweet child," he whispered in that dry-leaves voice. "So considerate of an old man."

"I hope nothing spoiled," Meg said, stepping back. "Good day, sir." She turned and walked back to the BOW, aware of all the smoke gathering just inside the fences. The gate closed behind her. The woman continued to watch her as she got into the BOW and drove off.

She had another set of packages for another address in the Chambers, but she was feeling shaky and wanted to get away from that part of the Courtyard. She continued driving until she passed the last of those ornate black fences and was heading for the Hawkgard Complex.

Then she remembered. Smoke. Sanguinati.

She hit the brakes and almost slid into a snowbank. She managed to put the BOW in park and crank up the heater before she started shaking.

Vampire. In one of their hurried, forbidden conversations, Jean had told her *vampire* was the street name for the Sanguinati. Smoke was another form they could take when they were hunting.

And when they are killing?

Now she understood why it was so dangerous to set foot on their land—and why no one who did left the Sanguinati's piece of the Courtyard.

But an old, powerful vampire had given permission for her to enter the Chambers and deliver a package.

"Oh, I feel woozy." She leaned back and closed her eyes. A moment later, she opened them, too uneasy about not being able to see what might be approaching.

How many of them had been out there, watching her?

That didn't make her feel any less woozy, so she put the BOW in gear and trundled the rest of the way to the Hawkgard Complex, which consisted of three U-shape buildings, two stories tall, that were separated by driveways that led to garages and a parking area.

Every apartment had a patio or balcony with its own entrance. What she didn't see were mailboxes or the nest of large boxes for packages. Which meant there had to be a room somewhere for those things.

Pulling up in front of the middle building, Meg got out of the BOW.

"What do you want?"

She squeaked and grabbed for the door handle before she regained control enough to look over her shoulder. The brown-haired, brown-eyed man who stared at her didn't look the least bit friendly.

"Hello," she said, trying out a smile. "I'm Meg, the new Liaison. I have some packages for the Hawkgard Complex, but I don't know where I should leave them. Can you help me?"

He didn't answer for so long, she didn't know what to do. Finally, he pointed to the center room on the ground floor. "There."

"Does each building have a mail room?" she asked, wondering how she could figure out what package went to which building.

He huffed. She could have sworn his hair rose like feathers being fluffed in annoyance.

"*There.*" He went to the back of the BOW and opened the door. He sniffed, then began rummaging happily through her ordered stacks.

"What are you doing?" she asked.

"Mouse," he replied, picking up each package and sniffing it.

"There aren't any mice in the packages." At least, she hoped there weren't. "But there were mice around where the packages were stored."

He stopped rummaging, apparently losing all interest. But he did help her carry the packages to the mail room. Judging by the cubbyholes built into one wall and the large table at a right angle to them, this was where all the mail for the Hawkgard Complex was delivered. The cubbyholes had numbers but no names, and most of the packages were addressed as Hawkgard with a number.

Come to think of it, a lot of the mail she had sorted for all the complexes was the same way. The gard and maybe an initial was the most identification shown. Hard to know how many of each race was living in a Courtyard if only a few, like Erebus Sanguinati and Simon Wolfgard, provided a full name.

Were they that uncaring about such things or that cautious about how much humans knew about them?

What did that say about Erebus that he used his full name? Was it a way of indicating his lack of concern about who knew he was residing at the Lakeside Courtyard or was it a warning?

She thanked the Hawk for his help, and had the impression he had to dig into his knowledge of humans for the "You are welcome" reply.

When she reached the bridge that spanned Courtyard Creek, she pulled over and studied the map. If she kept going straight, she would be at the Wolfgard area of the Courtyard, and she didn't want to go there and take the chance of running into *him*. Besides, she needed to head back to the office. But she had time to look at one place that made her curious. So she drove over the bridge and turned left on the road that ran along the small lake.

When she spotted the girl skating on the lake, she stopped the BOW and got out. The air was so clean and cold it hurt to breathe it in, and yet the girl, wearing a white, calf-length dress with short sleeves, didn't seem to notice.

Meg made her way to the edge of the ice and waited. The girl looked at her, circled away, then skated over to where she stood.

A girl in shape, but not human. The face, especially the eyes, passed for human only from a distance.

"I'm Meg," she said quietly, not sure why she thought this girl was more of a threat than the Sanguinati.

"You stopped," the girl said. "Why?"

"I wanted to introduce myself." She hesitated. "Are you alone here? Where are your parents?"

The girl laughed. "The Mother is everywhere. The Father doesn't spurt his seed in this season." She laughed again. "You don't like the spurting? Never mind. My sisters and cousins are with me, and that is enough. Our homes are over there." She pointed to a cluster of small buildings that were made of stone and wood.

"I'm glad you're not alone."

An odd look. "That matters to you?"

"I know how it feels to be alone." She shook her head, determined to shake off the memories of being isolated in a cell—or watching a movie clip in a room full of girls and feeling even more alone. "Anyway, I'm planning to make regular deliveries from now on, so I wondered if there was anything you wanted from the Market Square. It's a long walk for you and your sisters. I could give one or two of you a ride up to the shops."

"Kindness. How unexpected," the girl murmured. "There is a Courtyard bus that comes through twice a day that any *terra indigene* can take up to the shops, and the ponies are always willing to give me a ride. But . . ."

"But . . . ?"

The girl shrugged. "I put in a request for some books from our library. They weren't dropped off."

"Wait a moment." Meg went back to the BOW, retrieved the notepad and pen from her purse, and retraced her steps back to the lake. She held them out. "If you write down the titles, I'll go to the library after work and see if any of them are available."

The girl took the pad and pen, wrote several titles, then handed the pad and pen back to Meg.

"If your sisters are out when I return, whom should I ask for?"

Another odd look that was frightening because there was amusement in it.

"My sisters mostly sleep in this season, so only my cousins might be around," the girl replied. Then she added, "I am Winter."

"It's a pleasure to meet you, Winter," Meg said. Her teeth began to chatter.

Winter laughed. "Yes. But you've had enough pleasure, I think."

"I guess so. I'll look for those books." She hurried back to the BOW, but once inside with the heater doing its best to thaw her out, she waved to the girl.

The girl waved back, then turned to stare at the Crows and Hawks gathered in trees on the other side of the lake. They all took off in a flurry of wings, as if they were nervous about drawing the girl's attention.

But Meg noticed at least some of them followed her all the way back to the office.

She and the BOW crawled into the garage, one turn of the wheels at a time. The opening was almost twice as wide as the vehicle, but Meg's nerves still danced until she got the BOW inside and turned off.

Her nerves did more than dance when she got out of the BOW and saw the man standing there. Dressed in a mechanic's blue jumpsuit, his only concession to the biting cold was a thin turtleneck sweater under the jumpsuit. He had brown hair, the amber eyes of a Wolf, and an annoyed expression that said plainly enough she had already messed with his day and he didn't like it.

"I'm Meg, the new Liaison," she said.

"The Wolfgard says I'm to take care of charging up the BOW for you this time."

"Oh." She looked at the cord and buttons on the garage's back wall. "I suppose I should learn how to do that."

"The Wolfgard said I'm to take care of it. You're supposed to get food and open the office before the deliveries start arriving. The fools won't get out of their trucks if they see a Wolf instead of you, and I'm waiting for parts." He ran a possessive hand over the BOW's hood. "Wouldn't have been up this close to the monkeys if I wasn't waiting for parts that are supposed to come today."

"Then I'd better get my lunch and open up the office," Meg said brightly as she edged away from him. This one seemed wilder than Simon in a way she couldn't explain, and she wasn't sure "think before you bite" was a concept he understood. "Thank you for taking care of the BOW."

"Just because *he* slams your tail in the door, the rest of us have to be polite," he grumbled. Then he sniffed the air, sniffed again as his head turned in her direction. "What did you roll in to make your fur smell that stinky?"

Irritation wiped out caution. Were they *all* obsessed with smell? "I didn't roll in anything. And my hair stinks less than it did."

"So does a skunk."

Since that seemed to be his final opinion, she marched over to the back door of A Little Bite.

Tess took one look at her face and grinned. "I see you've met Blair."

"Maybe," Meg muttered. "Does he like any humans?"

"Sure," Tess replied cheerfully. "Although he's pretty opinionated about the lack of lean meat on most of them."

"I don't think I want lunch."

"Yes, you do. Vegetable soup and a turkey sandwich. I'll pack it up for you."

Meg followed Tess back to the counter. "So, who is he?"

"Third Wolf, after Simon and Elliot. Those two deal with humans and the world outside the Courtyard. Blair takes care of the inside of the Courtyard. He keeps track of the game on our land, leads the hunt when the butcher puts in a request for venison, and is the primary enforcer. He's also the one here at Lakeside who is most intrigued by mechanical things and energy sources, so he oversees the *terra indigene* who care for the windmills and solar panels we use to power most of the buildings outside the business district." Tess smiled as she handed Meg the carry sack. "Keeps him busy and limits his contact with humans—which is the way he and Simon like it."

"He's waiting for a package. If it arrives, whom should I call?" Meg asked. Tess looked at her until she sighed. "I should call Simon."

The BOW's garage door was closed by the time she reached the back door of the office, and she didn't spot a Wolf lurking nearby. But when she unlocked the front door, she did see three trucks idling while the drivers waited for her—and she saw the black sedan stuck behind them, unable to enter until at least one truck departed.

It looked like the kind of car she imagined a consul would drive—or would he have a driver?—so she signed for packages as quickly as possible, making hasty notes so that she wouldn't be the one causing a delay. It seemed the delivery people shared that feeling. Within a couple of minutes, they were gone and the sedan pulled up in front of the consulate door.

The man who got out had a slim build and receding hair. He stared in her direction, then went inside.

"If that's Elliot Wolfgard, I guess I won't be getting any gold stars from *him*," she muttered.

She could live without gold stars. Today she would be happy if she got through the rest of the day without being eaten.

She put the turkey sandwich and soup in the fridge, too unsettled to consider food. After a peaceful hour of sorting mail and packages, she called Howling Good Reads and left the message that there were a couple of items for B. Wolfgard, as well as other packages simply addressed to the Utility Complex, and was informed that Blair would pick up all of them after the office closed.

Maybe there was an advantage to having stinky hair if it encouraged the Wolves to keep their distance.

Cheered by that thought, she warmed up the turkey sandwich and enjoyed a late lunch.

Looking out the back window of HGR's office, Simon watched Blair come out of the Liaison's Office with a package and load it into the BOW assigned to the Utility Complex. The Wolf had waited only long enough to be sure Meg had left for the day before going in to retrieve the bits and pieces for whatever he was currently tinkering with.

She had headed for the Market Square, which meant she would be coming back this way when she went to her apartment. Better for both of them if they didn't see each other. Better for him, anyway. Henry would smack him if an encounter with him upset Meg today—and getting smacked by a Grizzly wasn't fun, even for a Wolf.

He put on his coat and stopped at the counter long enough to tell Heather, one of his human employees, that she was supposed to inform Vlad if Asia Crane entered the store. Then he went out the back door and walked over to the Liaison's Office.

"You got your parts?" Simon asked when Blair came out with another package that he tucked in the BOW.

Blair nodded as he closed the vehicle's back door. Then he locked the door of the Liaison's Office. "You need a ride?"

He didn't *need* a ride, but maybe he could coax Sam to spend a little more time outside if he got home while it was still light. And if Blair was unhappy with Meg for some reason, it was better to know before blood was spilled. "Thanks."

Neither spoke until they were headed for the Green Complex. Then Blair said casually, "The Liaison. Think we could wash her in the same solution we use for youngsters who get skunked?"

Simon barked out a laugh. Then he considered the appeal of doing just that—and the consequences—and reluctantly shook his head.

Blair sighed. "Didn't think so." A pause. "Elliot might want to have words with you. The delivery trucks backed up for a couple of minutes while the drivers waited for her to return, and his shiny black car couldn't get around them."

"He doesn't care about the shiny black car."

"No, but he does care about maintaining status in a way the monkeys understand, and I don't think having to wait for your human to open the door for afternoon deliveries is going to encourage him to tolerate her."

"She's doing her job."

"And causing trouble."

Simon growled—and noticed the way the other Wolf's lips twitched in amusement.

Blair didn't say another thing until he pulled up at the Green Complex. Then he looked straight ahead. "It's still deer season, so there will be some bow hunters in the park for a couple more weeks."

"So?" Simon opened the passenger's door and got out.

"If she doesn't wear a hat, the Liaison won't need the orange vest hunters use to keep from shooting each other."

Simon closed the BOW's door a little harder than necessary, but he still heard Blair laughing as the Wolf drove away.

Fishing out his keys, Simon walked to his apartment. The Green Complex apartments were a mix of sizes that shared common walls and accommodated the different species of *terra indigene* who chose to live there. Some were more like two-story town houses, while smaller apartments were contained on a single floor. Like the other residential complexes, the Green was U-shaped, with the connecting section containing the mail room, laundry area, and a social room on the second floor where movies were played on the big-screen television and a couple of tables provided an area to play board games the Others had converted from the human versions of those games.

The moment his key slid into the front door lock, he heard the squeaky-door sound that was Sam's howl.

His big living room had a carpet and a sofa, a couple of lamps, a television and movie disc player, a low table with storage baskets, and the cage where Sam lived.

Sam was all wagging tail and happy-puppy greeting—until Simon opened the cage door. Then the youngster huddled in the back of the cage, whimpering.

Simon held out his hand. "Come on, Sam. It's still light outside. We'll be safe. Come outside for a pee and a poop."

When the pup continued to shake and whimper, Simon reached in and hauled him out, ignoring Sam's attempts to bite him and escape. They did this several times a day—had been doing it since Daphne was killed and Simon became Sam's guardian. Sam was terrified of outside because outside was where his mother had died right in front of him.

Sam had stopped growing that night, hadn't continued his development the way pups should. They had no way of knowing what had happened to his human form because he hadn't shifted in two years.

Simon couldn't imagine being stuck in one skin his whole life, unable to shift. And he didn't want to imagine what it felt like to be so afraid that he could no longer make that choice.

He took the struggling pup outside and firmly closed the apartment door.

"A pee and a poop," he said, walking over to a potted tree that was part of a central garden area. He put Sam down and placed himself between the pup and the apartment. They weren't going in until Sam obeyed, but it broke his heart a little more every time they did this, and the fangs of his hatred for the men responsible grew a little longer.

Someday, he promised himself as Sam took care of business.

Sam was trembling and on the verge of panic from being outside for so long when the shiny black sedan pulled up in front of the complex. The back door opened and Elliot Wolfgard stepped out. Like Daphne and Sam, Elliot had gray eyes instead of amber, but it was a cold gray that suited the stern expression that was usually worn on the human face.

Now the stern expression shifted into a warm smile as Elliot came forward with open arms. "Hello, Sam." He crouched in the snow to rub the pup's ears and ruffle his fur. "How's our boy?" He looked up at Simon when he asked the question.

Simon shrugged to say *same as always.*

Elliot's smile dimmed as he rose. "You should tell the Liaison to wear a watch if she can't get back to work on time without one."

"Actually, she was making deliveries in the Courtyard, not dawdling for her own amusement," Simon replied with just enough tooth to remind Elliot who was dominant.

"I stand corrected," Elliot said after a moment. "I should have known that she was attending to her duties. The Crows are such gossips and find her entertaining, if the number of them gathering to watch the office is any indication.

I prefer not to deal with them, but my staff would have heard if we had cause to complain about her."

"She doesn't like mice for snacks. That makes her peculiar—at least according to the Owls."

"All right, Simon, you made your point," Elliot said. "If we finally have a Liaison who will do the work we pay for, I'll try to show more tolerance."

"Appreciate it."

"Has Blair met her yet?"

Simon nodded. "And didn't bite her."

"That's something. I'll be out tonight for a dinner—a guest of the mayor. I'll have my mobile phone if you need me."

"Enjoy your evening."

"That will depend on the menu. If it's beef, it will be a tolerable meal. If it's chicken . . ." Elliot shuddered. "What is the point of *chicken*?"

"Eggs?"

Elliot waved a hand dismissively. "I'll see you tomorrow."

As soon as Elliot drove away, Sam began pawing at Simon's leg, trying to jump into his arms.

"You need to work your legs," Simon told the pup, making him walk back to the apartment. But he picked up Sam before opening the door, grabbed a towel from the basket in the entryway, and dried off feet and fur.

As soon as he was free, Sam raced to the safety of his cage.

Determined not to let his disappointment show, Simon went into the kitchen, hung up the towel on a peg near the back door, and made dinner for himself and Sam. Then he turned on one of the movies Sam used to love watching, settled in the living room with food and a book, and gave his nephew as much comfort and company as the pup would accept.

Meg opened the journal she had found at the General Store. She labeled the first page *Books*, skipped a page, then labeled the next one *Music*. She skipped another page, put the date at the top of the page, and stopped.

What was she supposed to write? *Dear Diary, I didn't get eaten today.* That was true, but it didn't really say much. Or maybe it said everything that needed to be said.

She still wasn't sure if humans didn't stay long in jobs at the Courtyard because they quit or because they didn't survive dealing with the Others. Except for Lorne, who ran the Three Ps, and Elizabeth Bennefeld, the therapist who was available at the Good Hands Massage Parlor a couple afternoons each week, Merri Lee was the longest-employed human in the Courtyard, and she had been working at A Little Bite for just over a year. Sure, employees were considered not edible, but that didn't mean anything if the person did something the Others considered a betrayal.

What would the Others consider a betrayal? Certainly a physical act against them would count, but what about a lie that didn't have anything to do with them? Would that be seen as betrayal?

In the end, afraid that privacy was still an illusion, she avoided mentioning names or what parts of the Courtyard she had visited while making deliveries, but she did mention attending the Quiet Mind exercise class, which was held on the second floor of Run & Thump, and visiting the Courtyard library.

She had found three of the books Winter had requested and two for herself before running into Merri Lee, who had talked her into trying the Quiet Mind class, then went with her to a couple of stores to select an exercise mat and workout clothes.

She was making friends, developing a routine that could become a satisfying life for however long it lasted. If she just remembered to stop at the grocery store to pick up food for the evening meals, she would be all set. As it was, she scrounged what was left of the food Tess had brought, too tired to go back out once she staggered up to her apartment.

Now, muscles loosened from a hot shower and adequately fed, she tucked herself into bed with one of the books, content to read while cars rolled by and people's voices carried in the still air as they headed home.

She heard Wolves howling, but she wasn't sure how close they were to this part of the Courtyard. How far did the sound travel? The library had computers that could access information through the telephone lines. Maybe she could find information about the animal wolf that would help her understand the *terra indigene* Wolf.

She tensed when she heard a heavy footfall near her door, but she let out a sigh of relief when that was followed by the rattle of keys in the door across from hers. She had passed Henry in the Market Square that afternoon, and he had mentioned that he would be staying in one of the other efficiency apartments tonight because he wanted to remain close to his studio.

Picking up her journal, she made a note to herself to look up sculpture and totems when she had a chance to use the computer at the library.

Henry's door opened and closed. Cars crunched by. Meg got up to make a cup of chamomile tea, then went back to bed and kept reading, slightly scandalized by the story—and more scandalized by the fact that no one had stopped her from taking out the book.

Then there were no sounds of cars, no people heading home.

Meg looked at the clock and reluctantly closed the book. She got up long enough to put her mug in the sink and go to the bathroom. Tomorrow was a rest day, and the Liaison's Office and most of the Courtyard stores were closed. Hopefully that didn't include the grocery store. Apples for the ponies on Moonsday? She would need to cut them just before the ponies arrived. Otherwise the chunks would turn brown from the air. She knew that from training images. The girls had spent an entire week one year looking at captioned pictures of different kinds of fruit, from fresh to rotted. In a prophecy, seeing fruit that had been rotting for a specific number of days could indicate the time a person had been missing . . . or dead.

Meg let out a gusty sigh. Maybe her kind always saw the world as images that could be recalled to create a whole picture for someone else. Or maybe it was the way she had been trained to think and learn. Jean hadn't used the standard images all the time, but she had been unusual, difficult. Different.

You'll have a chance to escape this life, Meg. You'll have a chance to be someone for yourself. When the chance comes, take it and run—and don't come back. Don't ever let them bring you back here.

What about you?

The Walking Names made sure I can't run, but I'll be free someday. I saw that too.

The prickling under Meg's skin started in her feet and ran up both legs. She stifled a cry, not wanting Henry to hear her and come pounding on the door, demanding an explanation.

She walked toward the bathroom, hoping to find something in the medicine chest that would ease the feeling.

She knew what would make the prickling go away, but it was too soon to cut again. Besides, she also knew how much it hurt to hold in a prophecy, and speaking without a listener would relieve the pressure but it wouldn't do her any good otherwise.

As she tried to talk herself out of making another cut, the prickling faded on its own.

Meg splashed some water on her face, then returned to the living area of her apartment, determined to focus on the present and not the past because, most likely, her present could be measured in days or weeks.

The Moonsday treat. How many apples for how many ponies? She'd better bring extra in case more ponies showed up. How many lived in the Courtyard anyway? She'd have to ask Jester, since he was the one who looked after them.

Her mind on ponies and apples and what she might do on her day off, Meg pulled aside the drape and looked down at the street—and forgot all about sleeping.

The man was there again. She couldn't make out his features, but he was wearing the same dark coat and watch cap as the man she'd seen the other night. She was sure of it.

As she watched, he crossed Crowfield Avenue, heading straight for the glass door that provided street access to the apartments. But that door was locked. She was still safe because that door was locked.

Training image. Hands manipulating slim metal instruments to open a lock.

A locked door wouldn't keep her safe. Panic held her frozen at the window. Then the prickling returned in her legs as she heard a sound she couldn't identify. Her hands and arms began to tingle as she remembered the last time she and Jean had spoken.

Don't ever let them bring you back here.

Meg bolted across the room, certain now that the man had been sent by the Controller.

Couldn't get out. Locked in, just like before when she lived in the compound! No, not like before. Now *she* had the keys. The dead bolt just needed a key.

She scrambled for the keys in her purse, panting as her shaking hands tried to fit the key in the lock.

Was the man coming up the stairs? Creeping down the hallway? If she opened the door, would he be right there, waiting to grab her?

The tingling in her hands became a buzz that was so painful she dropped the keys. Unable to escape, she pounded on the door and screamed, "Henry! Henry!" Could he hear her? *Please, gods, let him hear me!*

She felt as well as heard the roar that filled the hallway, followed by a startled cry and the clatter of boots.

Racing to the window, Meg saw the man running across the street, angling for the corner and disappearing from sight. Retracing her steps, she picked up the keys with shaking hands and finally managed to open the door.

Henry stood at the end of the hallway, looking down the stairs. She couldn't see his expression—the lights from his apartment and hers didn't reach that far, and he hadn't turned on the hallway light—but she had the impression he was very angry.

"Henry?" she said hesitantly. "Should I call someone?"

"Who would you call?" he asked, sounding more curious than angry.

"I don't know. The police? Or someone in the Courtyard?"

He walked back to her door and studied her. Then he shook his head. "No need to call anyone. I'll take a look around now and talk to Simon in the morning. Keep your door locked, Meg, and you'll be all right."

No, she wouldn't be all right. She couldn't explain that to Henry, so she closed the door and turned the key in the lock. Then she pressed her ear against the door, listening as she counted slowly.

She reached one hundred before Henry walked back down the hallway to the stairs. As soon as she was sure he wouldn't hear her, she moved with controlled desperation, changing into jeans and a sweater, packing up a small bag of toiletries, tucking her book, a jar candle, and box of matches into one of the zippered carry bags. She rolled her pillow into the spare blanket from the chest at the end of her bed. Then she put her coat and boots on and held her breath while she turned the key, listening as hard as she could for Henry's footsteps.

She slipped out of her apartment and locked up, then fled to the back entrance and down the stairs. She hurried to the Liaison's Office, fumbled to get the door open, and let out a sob of relief when she was inside.

Just as exposed here as in her apartment. Just as alone, since the shops and the consulate wouldn't be open tomorrow. But no one knew she was here. The low light in the front part of the office was always on and wouldn't attract attention. Light from the candle would be visible only from the window in the sorting room, and that window looked out on the yard and sculpture garden behind Henry's studio.

She would be safe here tonight—or as safe as she could be.

Unwilling to turn on the overhead lights, she slipped off her boots, then padded her way to the sorting room, dropping the pillow and blanket on the table before going to the counter that ran under the window. Retrieving the candle and matches from her carry bag, she lit the candle. She didn't need to cut her skin to figure out the Controller had found her. It was just a matter of time before his man found a way to reclaim her.

Just a matter of time.

Spreading the blanket out on the sorting table, Meg climbed up and got as comfortable as she could on her hard, makeshift bed.

In the western part of the continent, where the *terra indigene* Grizzlies ruled as many Courtyards as the Wolves, some humans called his first form spirit bear.

Spirit bear moved through the world unseen, but some could sense his passing. Some would know he was there before he took on the tangible shape that had teeth and claws.

Now Henry followed the stranger's trail until it ended farther up the street where the man's vehicle had been parked.

Turning back to the Courtyard, he went to the glass door and studied the broken lock as he considered what it meant.

So much fear behind Meg's door, so much desperation when she screamed his name.

If he hadn't wanted to be close to the wood tonight, would she have disappeared, leaving them to think she was just another human who had used them for a few days' shelter? Or would the broken lock on the door and the scent of a stranger stir up Simon and the rest of the *terra indigene* who lived here?

Turning away from the door, Henry walked up to the corner and turned left, following the boundary of the Courtyard, not sure what he was looking for but letting instinct guide him.

He prowled the delivery area, taking in the scents around the front of the Liaison's Office and the consulate. The stranger's scent wasn't there, but moving closer to the sorting-room delivery doors, he picked up another scent that was fresher than it should be.

Moving around the office to the yard behind his studio, he saw the flicker of light in the sorting room. Taking up the full Grizzly form, Henry braced a paw on the wall and looked in the window.

Meg, sleeping on the sorting table.

Meg, who wasn't in the apartment where someone would expect to find her at this time of night.

Moving away from the window, Henry called, <Owls!>

Five of them answered his call, landing on the wall that separated his studio from the delivery area.

<Why do you want us?> Allison asked.

<Intruder,> he said. <Keep watch here. Meg is inside the office.>

Two of the owls flew off, taking up position on the roof of the consulate. Another flew up to the roof of his studio. Allison and a juvenile male remained on the wall.

Satisfied that he would have plenty of warning if the stranger returned, Henry ambled back to the efficiency apartment, changed to human form, and retrieved his clothes where he had left them in the stairwell. He made himself a cup of strong black tea generously laced with honey, then settled into the rocking chair near the window that gave him a view of the Liaison's Office. As he drank his tea, he wondered about the female who had suddenly come into their lives.

Throughout the rest of the night, he wondered a lot.

And he wondered what Simon was going to say in the morning.

CHAPTER 6

Simon got out of the shower and rubbed the towel briskly over his skin. He didn't like conforming to the way humans chopped up days into little boxes. The sun and moon and change of seasons should be enough for anyone. But if he *had* to conform in order to run a human-type business, he shouldn't have to think about it on the one day each week when he could live as Wolf from one sunrise to the next.

Earthday was the day of rest, the day the Courtyard was closed to humans so that the *terra indigene* could run and play and be what they were: earth natives. It was the one day he didn't have to shift into the skin that was useful but never felt like *home.*

Because he dealt with humans so much, he *needed* a day with the Wolfgard, *needed* his own kind. That was the trap for Others who had excessive contact with humans—if you adapted too much in order to deal with them, you ran the risk of forgetting who you were and you could end up being neither and nothing. That was why even Sam's distress at seeing him as a Wolf wasn't enough for him to give up what he needed for himself.

But *Henry's* message on the answering machine this morning had him breaking his own rule, since the Beargard had made it clear that it was the Wolfgard in human form that was needed at the studio.

He got dressed, then stopped in the living room to make sure Sam had food and water—and hadn't messed in the cage. Since he was in this form anyway, he'd take the pup out before shifting to fur and meeting Blair and some others for a run.

After considering the benefits of walking from the Green Complex to the studio in order to give the human form exercise, he went around to the garage and got one of the BOWs. He made sure this form got plenty of exercise. Today, the sooner he could shed this skin, the happier he would be.

A couple more inches of snow had fallen overnight. Combined with what was still on the Courtyard roads, it added a little sliding excitement to an ordinary drive—and reminded him to talk to the *terra indigene* who worked at the Utilities Complex and also handled clearing the Courtyard's roads. If Meg was going to be out making deliveries tomorrow, he'd have Jester explain about sticking to the main roads to avoid getting stuck. The BOWs could handle the snow just fine—as long as the driver wasn't stupid.

When he reached the Courtyard's business district, he parked the BOW in the employee parking lot, which put him in between the Market Square and the other shops, including Henry's studio. Getting out of the BOW, he stopped and listened to the rhythmic sound of someone using a snow shovel.

Leaving the parking lot, Simon walked around the garages, then stopped when he saw the footprints outside the Liaison's Office. There were no deliveries on Earthday, so there shouldn't be fresh footprints coming *out* of the office this morning.

He walked up to Henry, who was shoveling the area between the back doors of the shops and the Liaison's Office. Removing the snow. Eliminating the footprints.

"Hard not to leave a trail when there's fresh snow," Henry said. The look in the Grizzly's eyes made Simon wary, especially after Henry added, "We had a visitor last night."

Simon looked at the office's back door. "An intruder?"

"Not there," Henry said, tipping his head toward the office. Then he wagged his thumb toward the stairs leading up to the efficiency apartments.

For a moment, Simon just stared at Henry. Then he absorbed the meaning of the words and snarled as his canines lengthened, his nails changed, and fur sprang out on his chest and back.

"I told Meg we had rules about visitors. I *told* her . . ." He choked on the fury rising inside him—fury that wanted to rip and tear and destroy this strange and awful feeling of betrayal and the person who had caused it.

"Simon."

He'd thought she was different from the other damn monkeys. He'd thought there was finally one of them the *terra indigene* might be able to work with, despite the way she made him half crazy with the *not prey* confusion. He'd consented to let her have a map of the Courtyard because she seemed to want to do her job. If he'd wanted a liar as their Liaison, he would have hired that Asia Crane!

"Simon."

Hearing the warning in Henry's voice, he made an effort to stuff himself back into the human skin.

"If you want to sneak a visitor past us, you don't have him break the lock on the street door. And you don't call attention to someone's presence by yelling loud enough to be heard by the Grizzly staying in the apartment across the hall."

"She didn't know you'd be there," Simon said, choking on the effort to get his teeth back to human size.

"Yes, she did. I saw her in the Market Square yesterday and told her I would be there so she wouldn't be frightened if she heard me."

Frightened. The word cleared away his fury and let him think again.

Meg was hiding from something or someone. He'd realized that when he hired her, but he'd been chasing his tail so much because of her—or dodging to avoid having it stomped on by someone else—he'd forgotten she had run away from something or someone.

He looked at the footprints coming out of the office.

"After the intruder ran off, she slipped out and spent the night on the sorting table," Henry said.

Too afraid to stay in her own den? Unacceptable!

It took effort to shape words. "Did you see the intruder?"

"Not well enough. But I got the scent of him, and I'll recognize it again if he comes around."

If this stranger was hunting Meg, he would come around again. "Can't get that lock fixed until tomorrow." A Wolf and a Hawk were learning how to change and fix locks. They might be able to replace that broken one, but the Courtyard had an understanding with a lock company, and being willing to teach Others this skill was the reason Simon did business with Chris at Fallacaro Lock & Key.

"The Owls who kept watch last night will keep watch again," Henry said. "I've already talked to a couple of Hawks and some of the Crows about keeping watch on this part of the Courtyard today. And I'll be staying at the efficiency apartment again tonight."

"What about today? With the stores closed, she'll be alone up there during the day." Not likely that someone would come in daylight, but imagining Meg by herself all day felt too much like watching a deer that was the perfect prey because it was separated from the rest of the herd.

And that reminded him too much of Daphne and Sam running alone that terrible night, thinking they were safe.

"Should we call the police?" Henry asked.

"And tell them what? That someone broke a lock? Nothing was taken. We aren't sure the intruder was after Meg. We've had people try to sneak in and use the apartments. Could have been someone who just wanted to get out of the cold for a night and thought they could slip away before we noticed."

"That's called trespassing," Henry pointed out. "Humans have a law against it too."

"We'll deal with it our own way," Simon said. "I'll get another shovel and help you clear the snow." And erase the footprints that might tell a different kind of predator where to find his prey.

"What about Meg?"

She hadn't asked for his help. It bothered him that she hadn't asked for his help. He was the Courtyard's leader, after all. "We'll keep watch today. Tomorrow we'll consider what else might be needed."

Like getting some answers about who she was running from—and why someone would want her back.

Meg heard the howling as soon as she turned off the shower. Sounded like a whole pack of them was right under her windows. Drying off as quickly as she could, she wrapped the towel around her head, pulled on a bathrobe, and went to the windows to look out.

No sign of them, but judging by the way a car skidded as it came abreast of the Courtyard's parking lot and the driver tried to accelerate to get away from whatever he saw, they weren't far away.

There had been no sign of Henry when she hurried back to her apartment.

Did he work in his studio on Earthday, or was she alone in this part of the Courtyard? Merri Lee had told her none of the shops were officially open on Earthday, but the library was never locked, and in the morning a couple of the Others served leftovers at the Market Square's restaurant, Meat-n-Greens. So she could walk over to the restaurant for a meal and then spend some time browsing through the library's books.

Another howl, easily heard despite the closed windows.

We are here.

Above her, somewhere on the roof, she heard several Crows cawing.

We are here.

Something that had been wound tight inside Meg since last night began to relax. There weren't any humans around this part of the Courtyard today, but she wasn't alone. She could spend the afternoon reading or napping, maybe even do some chores now that she'd learned how to clean. Not all human stores were closed on Earthday, so there were cars going by—including, she noted before stepping away from the window, a police car. She would be safe enough while there was daylight.

She could decide later about where she would hide after dark.

That afternoon, Asia Crane slowly drove past the entrance to the Liaison's Office and the consulate. As usual on Earthday, a chain stretched across the street entrance, a metal Closed sign hanging from the center. It was a simple but efficient way to keep people from using the delivery area as a parking lot for the restaurants and other businesses across the street from the Courtyard.

Bigwig hadn't been able to give her any information about the white van or the driver who seemed to be casing the Courtyard. Probably nothing more than a disgruntled husband or boyfriend looking for an opportunity to haul his dumb-ass woman back home. Although why anyone would go to that much trouble for no-looks Meg was a mystery.

She didn't care about the who, how, or why as long as Meg no longer filled the Liaison's job, leaving it open for her to have another shot at access to the Courtyard.

Damn it! There wasn't anything that looked like the Help Wanted sign taped to the office door. That meant White Van Man hadn't taken care of business yet. Well, she might be able to help with that.

Tomorrow she would make a two-prong attack. She would test her welcome at Howling Good Reads, and she would make an effort to befriend Meg.

Her next step would depend on her reception, but one way or another, Simon Wolfgard was going to pay for her backers becoming impatient with her lack of progress.

Simon flipped the lock on Howling Good Reads' front door, flipped the sign to Open, put on the wire-rimmed glasses, and started the rest of the routine for opening the store.

A minute after he opened HGR, Asia Crane strutted through the door. She was a determined bitch, so he wasn't surprised that even a bad scare hadn't kept her away for long. If he'd liked her at all, he might have admired her determination to lure him into having sex.

And if he ever found out she was sniffing around the Courtyard—and him—for something more than a walk on the wild side, he would kill her.

Asia gave him a slashing look as she opened her parka and walked toward the display of new books, every bump of her hips a sharp movement in the skin-tight jeans.

He watched the shallow way her chest rose and fell under the short, tight sweater, watched the way her encased hips kept moving even though she was picking up books and looking at the back copy—almost like she didn't dare stop moving because there was a good chance she wouldn't be able to start up again. When he saw her little, self-satisfied smile, he realized she was watching him watch her. Why would she be satisfied? Considering the way she struggled to expand her chest, she didn't even look bitable this morning.

Or maybe he was still full from the deer they'd brought down yesterday and wasn't interested in another weak animal.

"Mr. Wolfgard?"

He focused his amber eyes and most of his attention on Heather, one of his human employees.

"If you're going to man the register, do you want me to stock the shelves?" She gave him a hesitant smile and suddenly smelled nervous.

"You are a sensible female," he said, raising his voice so Asia would stay at the new books display and not feel the need to slink over to hear what he was saying.

"Thanks," Heather said. "Um . . . why? I haven't done anything yet."

He waved a hand at her. "Your clothes don't lock up your body. You can take a full breath. If you were being chased, you wouldn't fall down after a few steps from lack of air." He was thinking of her escaping a human pursuer. A Wolf would run her down in seconds whether she could breathe or not.

Heather stared at him.

He continued to study her, understanding by the fear scent that he had taken a misstep somewhere in the past minute. He'd been indicating approval, because it was now clear to him that Asia did those exaggerated hip movements to hide the fact that she couldn't walk quickly without being out of breath. He didn't know what he'd said that had frightened Heather, but the look in her eyes made him think of a bunny just before it tries to run.

Even when he wasn't hungry, he liked chasing bunnies.

"I'll go stock some of the shelves," Heather said, backing away from him.

"All right." He tried to sound agreeable so that she wouldn't quit. Vlad hated doing the paperwork as much as he did when a human employee quit, which was why they'd both made a promise not to eat quitters just to avoid the paperwork. As Tess had pointed out, eating the staff was bad for morale and made it so much harder to find new employees.

When Heather came out of the back room with a cart of books—instead of running out the back door after leaving the words *I quit* on a note taped to the wall, like a couple of previous employees had done—he turned his attention to Asia.

She must have been waiting for that moment. Her cheeks were a blaze of color and she looked ready to spit stone. She slammed a book back down on the display and raised her chin.

"I guess there isn't anything of interest here this morning," she said coldly.

"Then you should go," he replied. "Although . . ." He vaulted over the counter, went to the other side of the display, picked up a book, and held it out. "You might find this one interesting."

It was one of the horror books written by a *terra indigene*. The cover was black with the open mouth of a Wolf just before it took a bite out of its enemy. Or maybe it was the second bite, since there was a little blood on the teeth.

Asia forgot everything she knew about Wolves and bolted out the door.

He watched her run toward the parking lot and decided two things: one, she couldn't run worth a damn in those clothes, and two, on her, he found the fear scent agreeable.

Monty adjusted the collar of his overcoat with one hand while he knocked on his captain's doorway.

"Come in, Lieutenant," Captain Burke said, waving him in while most of his attention remained on the sheet of paper he was studying. "Are you getting settled in all right?"

"Yes, sir. Thank you for asking."

Yesterday he'd gone to the temple near his apartment building and had found some peace and fellowship there. Then he called Elayne in the hope of talking to Lizzy, and got stonewalled. Lizzy had never been allowed to go over to a friend's house before the midday meal on the day of rest and meditation. He didn't think Elayne would change that rule, but if she had, it was only to deny him some time to talk to his little girl. Until that phone call he'd still thought of himself as Elayne's lover, despite the current estrangement, but she made it clear she was looking for someone whose social standing would erase the "stain" he'd put on all their lives.

And that told him plainly enough that his chances of talking to Lizzy, let alone having her come to visit during her summer vacation, had gone from slim to none.

"A couple of calls about Wolf sightings yesterday," Burke said. "You can hear them howling for miles, so people are used to that, but having Wolves gather in the Courtyard parking lot during the day is unusual."

"I'll check it out," Monty said.

Burke nodded, then turned the paper he'd been studying so Monty could see it. "Your priority is the Courtyard, but keep your eyes open for this individual while you're on patrol. Somebody wants this thief caught and the stolen items returned in a hurry, and has the clout to pull strings with the Northeast Region governor. And the governor pulled our mayor's strings, and you know how it tumbles down from there."

Monty stared at the Most Wanted poster and felt the blood drain from his head.

May all the gods above and below have mercy on us.

"I'm going to get copies of this made and distributed, and—"

"You can't."

Burke folded his hands and gave Monty a smile that was full of friendly menace. "You're telling your captain what he can or can't do?"

Monty pointed to the face on the poster, noting the way his hand trembled. He was sure Burke noticed that too. "That's the new Liaison at the Lakeside Courtyard. I met her the other day." Being wanted for the theft of something that would have somebody leaning on the governor for its return could explain why Meg Corbyn had been so nervous when he'd met her. She hadn't been worried about working with the Wolves; she'd been worried about being recognized by *him*.

"Are you sure, Lieutenant?" Burke asked quietly.

Monty nodded. "The hair looks darker here . . ." A bad dye job would explain the weird orange color. "But that's her."

"You've met Simon Wolfgard. Do you think he'd hand her over to you?"

Human law didn't apply in the Courtyards—or anywhere beyond the land the humans had been allowed to lease from the *terra indigene* in order to have farms and cities—and it *never* applied to the Others. But Simon Wolfgard ran a business and had no tolerance for thieves. Would that make a difference?

"I can stall putting out copies of this poster," Burke said, "but I'm sure every police station received it and every other captain is going to be handing out copies to his men. So if I'm going to be the only captain defying a direct order from the mayor to apprehend this woman, you'd better give me a reason I can take to His Honor."

"I'd like to make a copy of this and take it to Mr. Wolfgard," Monty said. "I'll show it to him and let him decide."

"Just remember, that woman is the only one who knows where the stolen property is hidden. We need a live person, not a DLU. Make sure he understands that."

"Yes, sir."

"Get your copy made and keep me informed."

Monty took the poster, made his copy, and returned the original to Burke. When he finished, he found Kowalski leaning a hip against his desk.

"We're going to the bookstore," Monty said.

"Going to ask about the Wolf sightings?" Kowalski asked.

Monty carefully folded the Most Wanted poster into quarters and tucked it in the pocket of his sports jacket. "Something like that."

As they drove to Howling Good Reads, Monty considered various ways to approach Simon Wolfgard with this information. He didn't know if there was a way to get the result the mayor and governor wanted, but he did know one thing: if the Others chose not to cooperate, that Most Wanted poster could be as dangerous to the humans in Lakeside as barrels of poison were to another city a couple generations ago.

Simon pulled all the slips of paper out of the envelope and arranged them on the counter according to gard. Most were book orders from the *terra indigene* settlements that were serviced by the Lakeside Courtyard. A few were orders that he'd pass along to other stores in the Market Square.

Like telephones, electronic mail through the computers was a useful way to communicate when information had to travel from one Courtyard to another quickly or when dealing with humans. But *terra indigene* who didn't have to deal with the monkeys had only a passing interest in electrical things, so a territory that covered three times the area of the city of Lakeside might have a dozen buildings that had phone lines and the electricity for computers. Except in emergencies, most Others still used paper when sending an order or request to a Courtyard.

A Little Bite always did a brisk business on Moonsday mornings, but HGR was usually quiet until lunchtime, which was why he set aside this time for filling orders. Retrieving a cart from the back room—and taking a moment to make sure Heather was actually working and not curled up somewhere in an effort to hide from him—Simon returned to the front of the store. After a quick scan of titles, he rolled the cart to the new-books display and filled the top shelf with a handful of each book. Then he rolled the cart back to the counter, picked up the first slip of paper, and began filling the order.

"Rubber bands," he muttered. Rubber bands were small, useful items and were a perk that came with placing an order. Even if only one book was ordered, he sent it out with a rubber band around it.

Before he could vault back over the counter to get the bag of rubber bands, the door opened and Lieutenant Montgomery walked in.

The lieutenant and his men had been very much in sight since that first meeting last Thaisday. Not a dominance challenge or anything foolish like that. More like a quiet version of a Wolf howl—a way to say *we are here*. Kowalski had come in and bought a couple of the horror books the day after the arguments had closed HGR and A Little Bite.

Simon wasn't sure Kowalski or his female was interested in those kinds of books or if it had been an excuse to look around. He had a feeling the police officer had been as relieved not to see any fresh bloodstains as the other customers were disappointed by that lack of excitement.

The lieutenant approached the counter. "Mr. Wolfgard."

"Lieutenant Montgomery." Simon absorbed the look on the face, the expression in the dark eyes, and the smell of nerves that wasn't quite fear. "You aren't here to buy a book."

"No, sir, I'm not." Montgomery pulled a piece of paper out of his sports coat pocket, unfolded it, and set it on the counter between them. "I came to show you this."

His mind took in the words *most wanted* and *grand theft*, but what he saw was the picture of Meg.

He didn't realize he was snarling until Montgomery eased away from him, a hand brushing the overcoat and sports jacket out of the way in order to reach the gun. Knowing what he would do if the hand touched the gun, he stared hard into Montgomery's eyes. The man instinctively froze, not even daring to breathe.

Satisfied that Montgomery wouldn't do anything foolish—at least not right now—Simon looked at the poster again.

"It's not a fuzzy picture," he said after a moment. "So why is there no name?"

Montgomery shook his head. "I don't understand."

"I watch your news shows sometimes. When you catch a picture of someone stealing in a store or bank and don't know them, the picture is fuzzy. When you have a picture like that"—he pointed at the poster—"the police always know the name of their prey."

He'd known she was running from someone. He'd known Meg Corbyn wasn't her name. He should have let her freeze in the snow instead of taking her in. But now that she *was* in, what happened to her was *his* decision.

"Why is there no name?" Simon asked again.

He watched Montgomery study the poster and smelled the man's uneasiness.

"Looks like an ID photo, doesn't it?" Montgomery said softly. "Like a driver's license photo or . . ." He reached into a pocket, pulled out the leather holder, and flipped it open to show his own ID. Then he put the holder back in his pocket. "If someone could supply that kind of photo, why wouldn't they be able to supply the name?"

Simon was going to get an answer to that question. He'd decide later if that answer was something he would share with humans.

Taking the poster, he refolded it and slipped it into his trouser pocket. "I'll talk to the members of our Business Association. If we have any information about this person, we'll let you know."

"I must emphasize that we're looking to apprehend and *question* this person about the theft."

Simon smiled, deliberately showing his teeth—especially the canines that he hadn't been able to get all the way back to human size. "I understand. Thank you for bringing this to our attention, Lieutenant Montgomery. We'll be in touch."

Dismay. Worry. But Montgomery had sense enough to walk out of the store without further argument. There was *nothing* the police could do about whatever happened in the Courtyard.

He waited a few moments, then called Vlad.

"Simon," Vlad said. "Nyx and I need to talk to you."

"Later," Simon replied, trying not to snap. "The Business Association has something to discuss. I need you to call them. I want everyone who's available in the meeting room in an hour. And call Blair and Jester. I want them there too. And a representative from the Owlgard, Hawkgard, and Crowgard."

"Anyone else?" Vlad asked quietly.

He knew why Vlad asked the question, just like he knew which group of *terra indigene* was being left out of this discussion. But *they* were never interested in such things.

"No, that should be sufficient," Simon said.

"In an hour, then. But, Simon, we still need to talk. It's important."

Simon hung up. Then he shouted for Heather, passing her on his way to the stockroom. "Man the register and work on filling the orders. Call John. Tell him to come in."

He put on his coat and boots for the walk to the Liaison's Office. That was acting civilized and controlled. If he didn't stay in control . . .

She *lied* to him.

. . . he was going to shift to Wolf, and they would never be able to clean up the blood well enough to hire someone else after he tore *her* throat out so she couldn't lie to him anymore.

The office's back door wasn't locked, so he slipped inside, removed his boots, and padded across the back room in his socks. He could hear low music even through the closed door that connected to the sorting room. As he entered the room, he saw Meg take a CD out of the player and say, "I don't like that music."

"Then why listen to it?" he asked.

She whirled around, wobbling to keep her balance. She put the CD back in its case and made a notation on a notebook sitting next to the player before answering him. "I'm listening to a variety of music to discover what I like."

Why don't you know what you like?

"Is there something I can do for you, Mr. Wolfgard? Today's mailbag hasn't arrived yet, but there are a few pieces of old mail. I put them in HGR's spot." She indicated the cubbyholes in the sorting room's back wall. "Also, I'm still not clear if the ponies deliver mail to the Market Square businesses or if someone from the businesses is supposed to stop in for that mail."

Right now he didn't care about the mail or packages or any other damn monkey thing.

He took the poster out of his pocket, opened it, and set it on the table. "No more lies," he said, his voice a growl of restrained menace. "What happens next will depend on whether you answer two questions honestly."

She stared at the poster. Her face paled. She swayed, and he told himself to let the bitch fall if she fainted.

"He found me," she whispered. "I wondered after the other night, but I thought . . . hoped . . ." She swallowed, then looked at him. "What do you want to know?"

The bleakness in her eyes made him just as angry as her lies.

"What was your name, and what did you steal?" Couldn't have been a small thing. They wouldn't be hunting for her like this if it was a small thing.

"My name is Meg Corbyn."

"That's the name you took when you came here," he snapped. "What was it before?"

Her expression was an odd blend of anger and pride. It made him wary because it reminded him that she was inexplicably *not prey.*

"My designation was *cs759,*" she said.

"That's not a name!"

"No, it isn't. But it's all they gave me. All they gave any of us. A designation. People give names to their pets, but *property* isn't deserving of a name. If you give them designations instead of names, then you don't have to think about what you're doing to them, don't have to consider if *property* has feelings when you . . ."

Her eyes stayed locked on his, despite her sudden effort to breathe.

Simon stayed perfectly still. If he moved, fangs and fury would break loose. *What did they do to you, Meg?*

"As for what I stole, I took this." She pulled something out of her pocket and set it on the wanted poster.

He picked it up. Silver. One side was decorated with pretty leaves and flowers. The other side had *cs759* engraved into it in plain lettering. He found the spot that accommodated a fingernail and opened the thing to reveal the shining blade of a thin razor.

He had seen one of these twenty years ago. Seeing another one now made him shiver.

"It's pretty, but it can't be worth all that much." His voice sounded rough, uncertain. He felt as if he'd been chasing a rabbit that suddenly turned into a Grizzly. Something wasn't right about this. So many things weren't right about this.

"By itself, it probably isn't worth much," Meg replied. "The second thing I stole is this." She pulled off her sweater and tossed it aside. She pushed up the left sleeve of the turtleneck until it was above her elbow. Then she held out her arm.

He stared at the evenly spaced scars.

An old woman, her bare arms browned by the sun so the thin scars showed white, sitting behind a little table where she set out cards and told fortunes to earn the money that paid for her room and board. A little community of humans who eked out a living at the edge of an earth-native settlement that amused itself by taking tourists into the wilds for pictures and stories and sometimes even movies that would be shown in theaters. Some taught the Others basic skills like weaving or carpentry. Some assisted with the tours. And there were always a few who were looking for an excuse to die and were just biding their time, knowing the Wolves and Grizzlies would oblige them eventually.

She sat there in the baking sun, her head covered by a straw hat, smiling at the youngsters, human and Other, who laughed at her as they went by in their various groups.

But he hadn't laughed, hadn't walked by. The scars intrigued him, bothered him. The look in her eyes unnerved him. And then . . .

"Not much good skin left, but this was meant for you . . ."

The silver razor flashed in the sun as she took it from the pocket of her dress. A precise cut on her cheek, its distance from an existing scar the width of the blade.

What he saw that day, what she said that day, had shaped his life.

"Blood prophet," Simon whispered as he continued to stare at Meg. "You're a *cassandra sangue*."

"Yes," she replied, lowering her arm and pushing down her sleeve.

"But . . . why did you run? Your kind live in special places. You're pampered, given the best of . . ."

"Whether you're beaten or pampered, fed the best foods or starved, kept in filth or kept clean, a cage is still a cage," Meg said with fierce passion. "We are taught what the Walking Names want us to know because what good is a prophet if she can't describe what she sees? We sit in classrooms, day after day, looking at pictures that describe things that exist in the world, but we're never allowed to know one another, never allowed to have friends, never allowed to speak unless it's part of an exercise. We are told when to eat, when to sleep, when to walk on the treadmill for exercise. They even schedule when we take a shit! We are alive, but we're never allowed to live. How long would *you* last if you were kept like that?"

She was shaking. He couldn't tell if she was cold or upset, even when she retrieved the sweater and put it on.

"Why don't more of you run away?" he asked.

"I guess living in a cage and not having a name doesn't bother most of them. Besides, where would they go?" She wouldn't meet his eyes. "Will you let me stay until dark? I might be able to slip past whoever the Controller sent after me if I can stay here until dark."

Simon tipped his head, struggling to understand her. "You're going to run again?"

Now she looked at him. "I would rather die than go back there."

A quiet statement. The honesty scared him because there was a little too much Wolf in her voice when she said those words. She wasn't *terra indigene,* but she also wasn't human like other humans. She was a confusion, and until he understood more, all he had to work with was instinct.

A few days ago, she came looking for a job because she wanted to live. If that wasn't true, she would have gone to sleep in a snowbank somewhere. Now she was willing to die?

He didn't like that. He didn't like that at all.

He pocketed the silver razor and the wanted poster.

"The razor is mine," she protested.

"Then you'll have to stay until I give it back."

"Mr. Wolfgard . . ."

"You're staying, Meg," he snarled. "Until I say different, you're staying." He heard a truck pull in, then another. "You've got work."

As he passed through the back room, he grabbed his boots but didn't stop to put them on. Instead, he ran back to HGR.

Cs759. The meaning of the letters was clear enough. He didn't want to think about the significance of the number.

That Controller was trying to set the police on her trail. Were other kinds of hunters searching for Meg? Was it a hired predator who had tried to break in the other night?

After telling John and Heather he was back, he went up to his office and put on dry socks. While he waited for the members of the Business Association to arrive for the meeting, he stared out the window that gave him a view of the Liaison's Office.

Power. When the *terra indigene* dealt with humans, it always came down to power and potential conflict.

He was the leader of the Lakeside Courtyard and what he wanted would carry weight, but this choice was too big for him to make alone.

Meg turned off the CD player. There was no point in playing music to learn what she liked. Instead, she pulled mail out of the last old sack and tried to keep her mind on sorting it, on finishing *something* before she herself was finished.

A white room and one of those awful beds. And Simon Wolfgard. She had seen those things in the prophecy that had revealed her own future.

Was he going to hand her over to the Controller, maybe even barter for some prophecies? Or now that he knew what she was, would he do the same thing the Controller had done? Would he know how? Was that why she'd seen the bed that was used when the girls were bound for the most intimate kinds of cuts?

She focused so hard on not thinking about what Simon would decide, she jolted when she heard the neighing outside the sorting room's outside door.

"Oh, gods," she muttered, glancing at the clock. She'd meant to run over to the grocery store for carrots or apples. No time to do that now. "Just a minute," she yelled when the neighing became a chorus. She could imagine what Elliot Wolfgard would say about the noise if the workers at the consulate were disturbed.

Rushing into the back room for her coat, she looked around for *something* that would serve as a treat. She didn't want to think about the reaction the ponies would have if she *didn't* have something for them.

The only things in the kitchen area besides a jar of instant coffee and bags of herbal tea were a box of sugar lumps, a box of crackers, and a storage tin that held an open package of chocolate cookies.

She shrugged into her coat, grabbed the box of sugar lumps, then rushed to open the door, because the next chorus of neighs was now accompanied by the cawing of the Crows.

"I'm here, I'm here," she panted as she got the door open, set the box on the sorting table, grabbed the first stack of mail, and began filling the baskets.

The ponies shifted, jostled, nipped at her coat in a way that made her think of a child tugging on an adult's sleeve in a bid for attention.

She didn't have enough mail sorted to fill the baskets for the eight ponies who had shown up, but she made sure they all had something to carry. Then she opened the box of sugar lumps.

"A special Moonsday treat," she said, holding out two lumps to Thunder. He took them happily. They all did. So happily, in fact, they all tried to get in line again for another serving.

When she closed the box and waved bye-bye, they all stared at her—and the box—for a long moment before trotting off to deliver the mail.

Sighing and shivering, Meg closed the door, returned the sugar to the cupboard in the back room, and continued with her work.

The Business Association's meeting room had a ring of wooden chairs set around a low, round sectional table. It also had a secretary desk and filing cabinets, as well as a computer on another desk that could be used for e-mail or placing orders with human companies.

Since the Business Association's office filled the other half of HGR's second floor, Simon was the first to arrive. He chose a seat and waited through the usual shuffling for position that took place because the bird gards wouldn't willingly sit next to one another and *none* of them wanted to sit next to the Sanguinati.

Vlad and Nyx arrived a minute after he did. Everyone else came in a moment later, leaving their outer garments on the coatrack in the small waiting room and delaying their entrance long enough for the Sanguinati to choose their seats.

Vlad sat next to him and Nyx sat on Vlad's right. From there, the chairs around the table filled in—Jester, Blair, Jenni Crowgard, Tess, Julia Hawkgard, and Henry. Allison Owlgard took the last chair.

Jenni was part of the Business Association, but Julia and Allison weren't. Which meant the leaders of their gards had probably chosen them as representatives because they did work around or in the businesses that had contact with humans.

"We're all here, Simon," Henry said in a quiet rumble.

"Lieutenant Montgomery came to see me this morning," Simon said.

"We stayed on our own land yesterday," Blair growled. "Or on the sidewalks that butt up against it, which are considered public property. The humans have no cause for complaint about that."

"I heard some youngsters had fun digging in the compost pile," Jester said. "Could someone have reported that?"

Blair shook his head. "That's technically our land, but we let the Lakeside parks and utilities people use it too. Both sides add to the compost piles and can make use of the material. The park and utility workers don't mind us digging. Saves them some work turning the piles. Besides, the youngsters didn't have that much fun with it. The stuff is frozen just like everything else right now."

"He wasn't here about our being seen or about the compost," Simon said.

Shifting his hip, he pulled out the paper and razor from a pocket. He opened the paper and set it in the center of the round table.

"Oh," Jenni said, sounding pleased. "The Meg looks more like a Crow in that picture."

Jester sat back, as if he wanted distance from the poster. Vlad shifted uneasily, and Nyx was unnervingly still. Tess's hair turned green and began curling wildly.

Blair's eyes were filled with hot anger, but his voice was quiet when he asked, "What did she steal?"

"This." Simon set the silver razor, designation side up, on the poster.

"Shiny!"

Jenni made a grab for the razor, then jerked her hand back when Blair turned his head and snapped at her. She made a show of holding her hand protectively against her chest and leaning toward Tess.

Henry leaned forward. "What is *cs759*?"

"Her designation." Simon hesitated. "Meg is a *cassandra sangue*."

"A blood prophet?" Jester said. "Our Liaison is a *blood prophet*?"

Simon nodded. "She ran away from the place where she was kept. That's how she ended up here."

"It's rare for them to be out in the world," Henry said thoughtfully. "We know little about her kind of human because so few of them are out in the world. I wonder if Meg doesn't smell like prey because she is a different kind of human."

"I don't think the Owlgard knows much about them except for a few rumors, and those always make them sound special and pampered," Allison said.

"Caged. She said they were caged," Simon said. After a moment he added, "She said she would rather die than go back there."

An awkward silence. Caging a *terra indigene* was considered an act of war—which was why keeping Sam in a cage for the pup's own safety was killing Simon a little more every day.

"Did you see any scars?" Nyx asked.

He nodded. "On her left arm, above and below the elbow. Evenly spaced."

Jester blew out a breath. "Meg is the first decent Liaison we've ever had in this Courtyard—at least since I've been living here. But if the police have this poster and are showing it to you, they know she's here. Do we want to get into a fight with them over another human? We don't even know enough about blood prophets to know if it's worth the fight."

Tess suddenly shifted in her chair—a jerky, angry movement. Her hair was now bloodred with green streaks and black threads.

Jenni looked at Tess, let out a caw, and scooted her chair as close to Blair's as she could.

"Don't ask me how I know these things," Tess said in a rough voice. "Just know that they are true."

"Tell us," Simon said, struggling not to make any changes that would look aggressive.

"Cassandra sangue," Tess said. "Blood prophet. A Thousand Cuts. Apparently, someone determined that was how many could be gotten out of one of these girls. The distance between cuts is precise. Too close and the prophecies . . . smudge. Too much space and skin is wasted. A precise cut with a very sharp blade to produce the euphoria and the prophecies. The girls become addicted to the euphoria, crave it beyond anything else. Which is what kills them in the end. Unsupervised, they might cut too deep or nick a vein and bleed out while their minds are within the euphoria and prophecies. Or they cut too close and the mixed prophecies drive them insane. However it happens, most of them die before they're thirty-five years old."

"Then the caging is done as a kindness?" Henry asked, sounding reluctant.

"You'd have to ask someone who has lived in that kind of cage," Tess said. "While she has any skin that can be cut, Meg is a valuable asset to someone—a source of potential wealth to someone. Like every other kind of creature, the *cassandra sangue* have different levels of ability. A cut on a thick-skinned, thick-headed clunker is still worth a couple hundred dollars. A sensitive skin, combined with intelligence that has been educated? Depending on what part of the body is being cut for the prophecy, you're talking about anywhere from a thousand dollars a cut to ten thousand or more."

Blair whistled. "That raises the stakes."

Simon looked at the people around the table. Yes, that raised the stakes. Meg could be worth thousands of dollars to the human who had controlled her.

What is she worth to us?

"I gather the reason you called us here was because of the potential fight if we allow Meg to stay," Vlad said.

Simon nodded.

"Then Nyx and I would like to add some information that the rest of you need before you make a decision." Vlad looked at Nyx, who nodded. "Meg met Grandfather Erebus."

Everyone jerked in their chairs.

"She came by delivering packages," Nyx said, "and she fretted over one that wouldn't fit in the boxes. It had been in the office for a while, so she didn't want to take it back, and she wouldn't leave it in the snow the way other humans would have done. So Grandfather gave her permission to enter the Chambers and place the box in front of his door. It turned out to be the box of old movies he'd been waiting for these past few months."

"He has decreed that the sweet blood may enter the Chambers to deliver packages, that the Sanguinati will do nothing to harm or frighten the sweet blood within the Chambers or anywhere else in the Courtyard," Vlad said.

"Sweet blood?" Simon said. "Does he know she's a *cassandra sangue?*"

Vlad shrugged. "Does it matter? There is a sweetness about her that appeals to him, and he's made it clear what he expects from his own as far as Meg is concerned."

Simon didn't comment. Meg had an annoying appeal, but *he* wouldn't call her sweet. Puppylike in some ways, which would interest Wolves, but definitely not sweet.

Now Julia and Jenni shifted in their chairs.

"She met the girl at the lake," Julia said.

Jester whined.

"Which one?" Blair asked.

"Which one would be out there skating, wearing nothing but a short-sleeved white dress and shoes?" Julia replied.

"Winter," Simon breathed. "Meg talked to Winter?"

"The Hawks and Crows were warned off. Apparently, the Elemental didn't want to share the conversation. We don't know what was said, but she and the Meg chatted for a while, and then the Meg left."

So at least one of the Elementals also had an interest in Meg. And Winter, if provoked, could be a terrifying bitch even for other *terra indigene.*

They looked at one another. Then they all turned to him and nodded.

"Meg stays," Simon said in confirmation. "And we'll make sure Meg—and the police—know we consider her one of us now."

"How are you going to do that?" Tess asked as the black threads faded from her hair.

Simon picked up the razor and the wanted poster. "With a slight change of address."

Meg didn't need to see the deliveryman suddenly tense to know Simon was standing in the Private doorway. When the man left, she continued to stare out toward the street rather than look at the Wolf.

"Should I close up the office?" she asked.

"The office is closed from noon until two p.m., and it's almost noon," Simon said. "So, yes, you should close up until you reopen for afternoon hours."

Now she turned to look at him. "I can stay?"

"With some changes."

"What kind of changes?"

"Close up, Meg. Then we'll talk."

She closed up the office, put on her coat and boots, then followed him out the back door, which he locked before she could pull out her keys.

He led her to a BOW parked near the door and stuffed her into the passenger's seat. By the time she got herself sorted out, he was behind the wheel and headed into the Courtyard.

She started to ask again what changes she had to make, but he was frowning more and more. Then he hit the brakes, and the BOW slid sideways before it stopped.

Those amber eyes stared at her. The frown deepened. "How were you taught things in that place where you were kept?"

She noticed he didn't say where she had lived. At least he understood that distinction. "We were shown pictures. Sometimes drawings, sometimes photographs. We watched documentaries and training films. Sometimes scenes from movies. After we were taught to read, we were given reading assignments, or an instructor would read aloud. Or we read aloud in order to learn how to speak properly and pronounce words." And there were things that had been done to them "for the experience," or things they had been made to watch being done to a girl who was used-up or too deficient to earn her keep through the cutting.

Simon's frown deepened a little more. "You took the BOW out the other day. How did you learn to drive?"

"It's not that hard," she muttered. Then she added defensively, "At least I didn't slide like you just did."

He straightened the BOW and continued down the road. "You weren't taught to drive. Were you taught to do anything except speak prophecies?"

"You aren't dependent on your keepers if you can do for yourself," she replied quietly.

The sounds he was making were terrible and frightening. When he glanced at her, he stopped the sounds, but in the moment when his eyes met hers, she saw a queer red flicker in the amber.

"Where are we going?" she asked. It looked like they were headed for the Green Complex. A minute later, he pulled into a parking space across the road from the complex.

"This is guest parking or temporary parking," Simon said as he got out of the BOW. When she joined him, he pointed to a lane that ran alongside the U-shaped building. "That leads to the garages and resident parking. The morning bus wouldn't get you to work on time, so you need to use the Liaison's BOW—once you learn to drive."

"I can drive," she protested. "At least, going forward."

He stared at her. "You can't back up?"

She didn't answer.

"Right. We'll drive to work together for a few days."

"But . . ."

"You can't stay in that efficiency apartment over the shops, Meg. You're too vulnerable there. So if you're going to stay and be our Liaison, you're going to live here."

"Here? But this is inside the Courtyard. Humans don't live here."

"You do."

There was a finality to the way he said the words, the way he took her arm and led her across the road. She'd seen some of the Green Complex when Tess brought her here to wash her clothes.

Out of sight. Out of reach. Safe.

"Second floor," he said, leading her to a stairway. The porch had latticework on both sides and along half the front. She guessed it would provide shade, shelter, and some privacy in the summertime. And some shelter from the snow now.

He pulled a set of keys out of his coat pocket, opened the door, and stepped aside.

She stepped on a welcome mat, toed off her boots, and placed them on a cracked boot mat. Then she looked around.

Big living room. Natural wood and earth tones. Some furniture that didn't fill the space, but was as much as she had in the efficiency. She glanced back at Simon. He stayed near the door, an unreadable look on his face. Hesitantly, she explored.

Two bedrooms. One was empty; the other had a double bed that had been stripped and a dresser. The bathroom looked modestly clean, and the kitchen had a pleasant, airy feel and included a dining area. It also had a door that led to an interior landing and a back staircase that went down to an outer door—both of which were shared with the apartment next to hers.

"Acceptable?" he asked when she returned to the living room.

"Yes. Thank you."

He turned his head toward the door, listening for a moment before nodding. "Some females will help you make your den human clean. I'll drive you back to the office in time for the afternoon deliveries."

When he opened the door, she heard Merri Lee and Jenni Crowgard talking as they came up the stairs.

"Mr. Wolfgard?" she said before he stepped out the door. "I noticed the kitchen door shares a landing. Who lives in the other apartment?"

He gave her a long look. "I do."

Then he was gone, and Merri Lee, Jenni, Allison Owlgard, and a young woman who introduced herself as Heather Houghton were piling in with food and cleaning supplies. By the time they all piled out again to go back to their usual jobs, the only thing left for her to do was bring over her clothes and the bits and pieces she had acquired.

Simon was waiting at the bottom of the steps. As the women passed him, Jenni said, "The Meg didn't want to ask you, but there's no television or movie player here. Could she bring the one from the little apartment?"

Simon stared at them, then at Meg. "Anything else?"

"Meg likes books," Merri Lee replied cheerfully. "If there's a spare bookcase at the efficiency apartment, you could bring that too."

"I didn't say . . . I wasn't asking . . ." Meg stammered.

He took her arm and led her to the BOW. The other women piled into the one parked beside his, Merri Lee in the driver's seat, Heather beside her, and Jenni and Allison curled in the back. They took off while Simon watched them.

Shaking his head, he opened the passenger's door and, once again, stuffed Meg inside. Getting in the driver's side, he said, "Merri Lee doesn't drive any better than you do."

"I drive just fine," Meg snapped.

"Considering you don't know how." He pulled out of the parking space and sent the BOW flying down the road at a speed she wouldn't have considered.

Folding her arms, she stared out the side window and muttered, "Bad Wolf."

His only response was to burst out laughing.

Monty followed the man named John up the stairs and down a hallway to the door that had OFFICE painted in black letters on frosted glass. John knocked, swung open the door, and retreated.

"Come in, Lieutenant," Simon said, rising from the chair behind an executive's desk made of a dark wood.

The quick glance he allowed himself before giving the Wolf his complete attention gave him the impression of a typical office—desk with phone, computer, trays for paperwork; a large calendar that also served as a blotter and a protection for the wood. There were filing cabinets along one wall, and a lack of anything personal—no photographs or even framed prints—but some men preferred an austere work environment, so that wasn't altogether out of the ordinary. The only thing in the room that wasn't typical of a human businessman's office was the pile of pillows and blankets in one corner.

"I appreciate you responding so promptly," Simon said.

"Frankly, Mr. Wolfgard, I'm surprised you asked for me at all," Monty replied. Something about those amber eyes. They were more feral now than they had been this morning, if that was possible.

"I talked to the members of the Business Association, and we all agree that while the woman in the wanted poster bears a strong resemblance to our Liaison, they are not the same person."

Monty opened his mouth to disagree, then realized there was no point. Wolfgard knew perfectly well Meg Corbyn was the woman on the wanted poster.

"Furthermore," Simon continued, "it seems the police are not the only ones who have made that mistake. Late Watersday night, someone tried to break in to the efficiency apartments we keep over the seamstress/tailor's shop. He only got as far as breaking the lock on the outside door and climbing the stairs before being scared off by Henry Beargard."

"You're sure it was one man?" Monty asked.

"There might have been another waiting in the vehicle, but Henry smelled only one intruder."

While Wolfgard's form didn't change, he wasn't making any pretense now at passing for human.

"You didn't report the attempted break-in," Monty said, shoving his hands in his overcoat pockets to hide the trembling.

"I'm reporting it now. A broken lock wasn't sufficient reason to trouble our friends in the police, but if it was an attempt to take our Liaison against her will, then it deserves everyone's attention. We have, of course, taken precautions. Meg Corbyn is now residing in the Green Complex, where safe access is only possible by prior arrangement. I live there. So does Vladimir Sanguinati and Henry Beargard."

Message understood. No one who tried to reach Meg Corbyn when she was asleep or otherwise vulnerable would survive.

"I'm sure Ms. Corbyn appreciates your interest in her well-being," Monty said.

Simon barked out a laugh. "Not enough to notice." Then his face took on that feral look that was terrible to see on an otherwise human face. "Human law doesn't apply in the Courtyard, Lieutenant. No matter what anyone else thinks, Meg Corbyn is ours now—and we protect our own. You make sure you send that message back to whoever made the poster."

"Do you know why someone is making so much effort to find her?"

"It doesn't matter anymore."

One other angle to try. "If the items that were stolen were returned, I don't think Ms. Corbyn would be of interest to—"

Flickers of red in Wolfgard's amber eyes. When he spoke, Monty didn't think Simon was even aware of the way his voice snarled, "Meg is *ours*."

Another message there—and a sudden suspicion that he might be dealing with something far more delicate and dangerous than he'd realized.

"Thank you for your time, Mr. Wolfgard." It was hard to do, but he turned his back on the Wolf and walked out of the office, closing the door behind him.

He didn't get all the way down the stairs when the howl came from the floor above him.

He nodded to the pale young woman behind the counter and walked out of Howling Good Reads—and noticed how many people who had been browsing in the front of the store looked up and then headed for the checkout counter.

Kowalski was waiting for him when he slid into the passenger's side of the patrol car. On the other side of the snow-shrunk parking lot was a van with FALLACARO LOCK & KEY painted on the sides.

"Anything?" he asked as he adjusted his seat belt.

Kowalski tipped his head toward the three men crowded around a glass door. "Break-in the other night. Broken lock. Intruder didn't get far enough to enter any of the apartments and take anything. Chris Fallacaro runs this side of the business. His father is semiretired, which I took to mean has some prejudice against the Others and doesn't take these particular service calls."

"Does Mr. Fallacaro do any of the residential locks in the Courtyard?"

Kowalski shook his head. "He's teaching a couple of the Others about replacing locks, and they've got their own key-cutting machine set up in their Utilities Complex. I had a chance to talk to him for a minute before the Others showed up. He says they don't quibble about a bill, pay in cash, and outside of crowding him to watch what he's doing and sniffing him—which can be unnerving because they can tell if he's been with his girlfriend or what his mother served for dinner the previous night—there's nothing hard about working with them."

"If a key ever found its way into the wrong hands, that boy wouldn't survive a day," Monty said.

"Oh, he knows that, Lieutenant. That's why he's very careful about handing over all the keys, and goes to their complex to help them make extra sets."

"All right. Let's go back to the station. Looks like I'm going to spoil Captain Burke's afternoon."

Monty watched his captain's expression turn stonier as he gave his report.

"You really think they'll fight about this?" Burke asked.

Monty nodded. "They'll fight."

Burke leaned back in his chair. "You have any thoughts about why this woman is so important to them—or what she stole?"

"Why do any of us bring a stray kitten into our home and feed it?" Monty replied. "It may have been no more complicated than that in the beginning, but now that someone has invaded their land to get to Ms. Corbyn, the Others are a lot more invested in keeping her." He paused, not sure how much to reveal about his own suspicions. "Something Simon Wolfgard said has been bothering me. If the victim of the theft knew who had taken the items and could give us what amounts to a photo ID for the wanted poster, why couldn't he supply a name? If this is some kind of corporate theft and Meg Corbyn was an employee, why weren't we told her name?"

"You're edging toward a point. What is it?"

"What if she didn't have a name? Or what if anonymity is for her own protection?"

"Everyone has a—" Burke slowly sat forward.

"From what I understand, those compounds are as well guarded as any Courtyard, and no one, including the clients who go to those places, really knows what goes on inside."

Burke sighed. "We are standing on thin ice, Lieutenant, and if any part of what you've just implied is true, there are going to be some powerful people dropping boulders off a bridge, trying to hit the ice beneath your feet—and mine. Gods above and below, if our city government is seen to be on the wrong side of this argument, and our mayor, along with our jackass governor, has already put us on the wrong side by giving the order to circulate that wanted poster . . ."

He didn't finish the thought. He didn't need to. Finally, he pushed himself up. "I'd better talk to the chief and see what he can do about getting those posters off the streets before someone tries to make an arrest. What are you going to do?"

"Talk to MacDonald and Debany when they come on shift and make sure they're aware of the potential conflict brewing. And I'm going to see if I can confirm or deny my suspicions about why Ms. Corbyn is so interesting to so many people."

Monty hung up his overcoat and made himself a cup of green tea. Then he sat at his computer and spent the next couple of hours hunting for what little the police actually knew about the race of humans known as *cassandra sangue.*

CHAPTER 8

Timing her approach, Asia drove her car into the Liaison's Office delivery area and parked in a way that guaranteed her vehicle would clog up the most space. Then she plucked the takeout cup out of the cup holder and hurried into the office. Seeing Meg hesitate in the doorway of the room marked PRIVATE, she widened her smile and strode up to the counter.

"I'm working an earlier shift and only have a minute," Asia said, sounding a little breathless. "We got off on the wrong foot the other day, and it was totally my fault. I get too enthusiastic sometimes, and I really did want to get acquainted because I don't have many friends and I think you're someone I could talk to, you know? Anyway, here's a little peace offering." She set the takeout cup on the counter in front of Meg. "I wasn't sure how you take your coffee or even if you drink it, so I brought you a cup of hot chocolate. Can't go wrong with chocolate, I always say."

She shifted position, her body language signaling awkward but sincere. "Anyway, I hope I didn't cause you any trouble."

"You didn't cause trouble," Meg said. "I appreciate the hot chocolate, and I'd like to chat with you sometime, but . . ."

"But right now you've got work and I've got work." Asia looked over her shoulder when a horn beeped and the Crows perched on the stone wall responded. She rolled her eyes as she turned back to Meg. "And I am in the way of those delivery trucks and creating a roadblock on the highway of commerce."

Meg smiled. "More like the cart path to the petty cash box."

Waving, Asia hurried out to her car, flashed a smile at the deliveryman that wiped the sour look off his face, and drove out of the Courtyard. As she glanced in her rearview mirror before pulling out into traffic, she noticed two Crows taking off.

Score, Asia thought. Let those black-feathered gossips tell everyone she'd stopped by the office. Meg Corbyn had no social skills and couldn't lie worth a damn with body or words. The feeb had bought the new version of Asia Crane, and that's all Asia had been aiming for today.

A cup of coffee here, a slice of pizza there, and she would become the friend Meg couldn't say no to. And then she would be able to get on with her assignment and make her backers happy.

A shiver went through Monty when he walked into the station's assembly room and saw Captain Burke passing out the wanted posters of Meg Corbyn.

"Lieutenant?" Kowalski whispered behind him. "Maybe we should take a seat."

Burke understands the danger. Why would he . . . ?

Monty looked at the faces of the other men as they glanced at the poster and then studied their captain, and their reaction to this particular assembly began to sink in.

When everyone was seated, Burke gave them all that fierce smile.

"Most wanted," Burke said. "Grand theft. You will notice there is no mention of what was stolen or the identity of this person, despite an indication that she is, in fact, known to the person or persons who reported the theft. I've been told that all cities in the eastern half of Thaisia have been asked to be on the lookout for this person, and we will do our duty to our government and our city by keeping our eyes open.

"But, gentlemen, there are a couple of things I want to emphasize. First, nothing leads me to believe this person is armed or dangerous or in any way a direct threat to us or the citizens of Lakeside. So if you believe you have sighted this woman, force is not required for initial contact. Be clear about that.

"Second, it's been said that every person has a doppelganger—someone who looks so much like you as to be mistaken for you. That can make for interesting stories of mistaken identity—unless that doppelganger happens to live in a Courtyard."

Sudden shifting in the chairs. Nervous twitches. Nervous coughs.

"It has come to my attention that someone living in the Lakeside Courtyard bears a strong resemblance to this woman on the poster. I trust you can all appreciate the consequences to this city if we try to apprehend the wrong person. Lieutenant Montgomery and his team are assigned to handle any incidents that deal with the Others, whether the *terra indigene* are in the Courtyard or out amongst us in the city. If you see someone with the Others who looks like the woman in the poster, you call Lieutenant Montgomery. If he or any of his team asks for backup or assistance, the rest of you will provide it.

"The governor wants this alleged criminal apprehended and the stolen property returned to its rightful owner. He's given his orders to the mayors of all the cities and towns in the Northeast Region. Those mayors have given their orders to the police commissioners of their cities, who have passed those orders down to the chiefs of police, who have passed them down to the captains, who are, like me, passing them down to the rest of you."

Burke paused and looked at all of them. He was still smiling, but his blue eyes were bright with anger. "So now you know what His Honor wants you to do. I hope you all understand what *I* want you to do."

Monty walked out of the assembly, saying nothing. He stopped at his desk long enough to grab his coat, then left the station. Kowalski caught up to him at the patrol car.

"Where to, Lieutenant?" Kowalski asked as he started the car.

Monty released his breath in a sigh. Burke had walked a verbal tightrope to warn the men of a potential conflict with the Others. He hoped his own careful talk would be as successful. "Howling Good Reads."

Kowalski drove away from the station. "I don't think HGR is open this early, but A Little Bite should be open by now."

Monty glanced at the other man before staring out the passenger's window. "Karl, coffee on the house is one thing, but we can't accept breakfast sandwiches and pastries every morning. And MacDonald and Debany shouldn't be going in for free soup every afternoon."

A quick smile, there and gone. "I don't think Officer Debany is stopping by for the soup."

"Oh?" He thought of the human woman who worked for Tess and understood Debany's interest. "Nevertheless, this constant largesse could be misunderstood, and we might be creating a tab we don't want to pay."

"The last time I offered to pay for the food, the owner seemed insulted, and, frankly, Lieutenant, I'm a lot more scared of her than I am of you."

Tess. Definitely not someone he wanted to insult. "All right. But . . . restraint." Monty sighed again. "Besides, if I keep eating like this, I'll have to find a gym."

Kowalski was suddenly paying the roads an excessive amount of attention. "Ruthie has been making noises about joining a gym or fitness center—specifically, joining Run and Thump, since it's the closest place to the apartment we're moving into. All the residents and employees of the Courtyard can use R and T, but there are also a few memberships open for humans who don't work for them."

"This might not be the best time for such a membership," Monty said. "If anything goes wrong . . ."

"I know, but Ruthie thinks giving the Others positive exposure to humans might help us in the long run. She goes into HGR all the time and says she never feels threatened. If she's polite, the Others are polite."

"Help who? The police?"

"Help all of us. Isn't mutual exposure the whole reason Simon Wolfgard opened a few stores to humans?"

Maybe, Monty thought. After a few days of contact with the Others, he didn't think Wolfgard wanted to be friends with humans any more than the Wolf wanted to be friends with deer, but having a better understanding of one's prey was useful for all kinds of reasons.

"Just be careful, both of you," Monty said.

"Count on it."

When they reached the Courtyard, HGR still had a Closed sign on the door, but A Little Bite was open. Kowalski pulled into the parking lot.

"Wait here." Monty reached for the door handle, then stopped. Something about the way Burke had worded things when talking about the Courtyard. Something about the way the men suddenly got twitchy.

He sat back. "Karl? Has a shield ever shown up at that cairn in the park?"

"There wasn't a specific place to look for identification on a DLU until Daphne Wolfgard was murdered two years ago." Kowalski stared straight ahead. "It hasn't happened since Captain Burke took over as patrol captain at the Chestnut Street station, but there have been times in the past when an officer was reported missing and the abandoned patrol car and a blood-smeared badge were the only things that were found. There's some speculation that the chief and the captain have an . . . understanding . . . because if Captain Burke wants *anyone* transferred out of the Chestnut Street station, that person is gone the next day, no arguments made or questions asked." A hesitation. "There's a saying among the officers: it's better to get transferred than be a DLU."

"Is the hazard pay for being on this team worth the risk?" Monty asked.

"Lieutenant, if things go really wrong between us and the Others, no amount of pay will be worth the risk. But there also won't be any place in Lakeside that *is* safe, so maybe taking those risks is what will make the difference for everyone."

Since Kowalski didn't seem inclined to add anything else, Monty got out of the car and went into A Little Bite.

Tess was behind the counter. The smile she gave him made him feel as if someone had sliced his back open, leaving him weak and trembling.

"Lieutenant. Coffee is fresh; the pastries are from yesterday. Everyone seems to be getting a slow start this morning."

"Coffee would be appreciated," Monty replied. "But I stopped by to see if I could have a word with Mr. Wolfgard. I noticed Howling Good Reads isn't open yet, so I wondered if you had a way of getting in touch with him."

"Regarding?"

"A discussion we had yesterday."

Black threads suddenly appeared in Tess's brown hair as it began to coil.

"This way." Her voice hadn't been warm before. Now it was brutally chilling.

He followed her to the lattice door that separated the two shops. She opened the door, went into HGR, and said, "Vladimir. Lieutenant Montgomery wants a word." Turning to Monty, she added, "The members of the Business Association know all about your discussion. Simon isn't available right now, so you can talk to Vlad."

She walked back into her shop and closed the lattice door, leaving him with one of the Sanguinati.

Vladimir's smile was as brutally chilling as Tess's voice had been a moment before. It took all the courage Monty could gather to approach the book display the vampire was rearranging.

He did not want to tell the Others anything about Meg Corbyn they didn't already know, but not telling them enough could lead to a slaughter. And maybe—*maybe*—there was one bit of information that might persuade the *terra indigene* to let humans deal with humans.

"I wanted Mr. Wolfgard to be aware that the poster I showed him yesterday has been distributed to all the police stations in Lakeside—to all police stations throughout the eastern part of Thaisia, in fact."

"Is that significant?"

Vlad sounded like he was making an effort to show polite interest, but Monty wondered how long it would take for that tidbit to reach the farthest Courtyard on the eastern seaboard—and what it would mean to the police in those other cities. "I also wanted to make him aware of some details I came across while checking the information on the poster." He paused to consider his words. "There is a small segment of the human population that is considered at risk. Their deaths are mostly caused by self-inflicted wounds, so a provision was made in human law to allow another person to have a 'benevolent ownership' of such an individual."

"Wouldn't this benevolence be called slavery if it was forced on any other kind of human?" Vlad asked, now sounding a little puzzled. Before Monty could respond, the vampire continued. "What about the segment of your population that chooses suicide by Wolf? As a defender of your people, you know it happens. Does your law insist on this benevolent ownership for them if they're stopped before they throw themselves in front of a pack?"

Suicide by Wolf. The phrase chilled Monty—and the vampire noticed.

"No," Monty said. "Our law has no provision for that." He didn't think explaining about the mental wards in city hospitals was a good idea, since he wasn't sure Vlad would understand—or care—about the difference between being held in such a ward and benevolent ownership.

Vlad looked more and more coldly delighted. "There are always the stronger and the weaker, the leaders and the followers. Don't you force the weaker among you to accept the scraps that are left when the stronger have eaten their fill? Don't they wear the worn-out rags instead of warm clothes? Stronger and weaker exist in any group, but you've clearly decided some *kinds* of humans are more important than others. Some kinds of humans are human and other kinds are . . . property? Is that how it works? I didn't realize you monkeys had such savagery in you. Next you'll be eating your weak in order to keep the strong healthy."

"*No.*"

Monty knew the look Vlad gave him would haunt his dreams for years to come.

"How long will that attitude last if there is no other food?" Vlad asked softly.

For a moment, Monty couldn't breathe. Was this a real threat to cut off food as an experiment in cannibalism or just the peculiar intellectual workings of a *terra indigene* mind?

"Was there anything else you wanted Simon to know?" Vlad asked.

This, at least, was a piece of what he was here to say. "Yes. There is concern that with so many police officers looking for the individual on that wanted poster, mistakes in identification could be made."

"You're referring to that person who looks similar to our Liaison?"

Monty nodded. "I would appreciate being informed whenever Ms. Corbyn leaves the Courtyard. My men and I won't interfere with her, but I would feel more comfortable being present. To avoid any misunderstandings."

"That's an excellent suggestion, Lieutenant Montgomery." Vlad smiled. "Misunderstandings have been so costly in the past."

Thinking of the Drowned City, Monty shivered. "Yes, Mr. Sanguinati, they have." When silence was the only response, Monty took a step back. "I'll leave you to your work. I appreciate you taking the time to talk to me."

Vlad took a step forward and held out his hand. "Anytime, Lieutenant."

Not daring to give offense, Monty took the vampire's hand—and instantly felt a prickling that was gone a moment later. And in that same moment, he felt the odd sensation of Vlad's strong grip being less substantial.

"You can go out through A Little Bite," Vlad said, releasing Monty's hand and turning back to the display of books.

Glad to leave, Monty went to the lattice door. As he reached out to open it, he noticed the pinpricks of blood on his palm.

He swayed as understanding replaced puzzlement. He didn't dare turn around and look at the vampire.

How much blood had Vlad taken from him in the few seconds their hands had touched? Was that a feeding, a warning, or a threat?

He hurried into the coffee shop and turned toward the door, wanting to escape. But Tess's voice saying, "Don't forget your coffee," made him turn back.

The threads of black were gone, but the hair was still unnaturally curly.

She handed him some paper napkins first—and smiled.

It took effort not to run, but he walked out of A Little Bite and joined Kowalski, who was leaning against the patrol car, watching the roofs of the buildings.

"They sure are keeping close watch," Kowalski said as Monty handed him one of the coffees. "A dozen Crows and a couple of Hawks have come and gone while you were inside. You all right, Lieutenant?"

"Let's get in the car," Monty replied.

When they were inside and partially sheltered from feathered observers, Monty pulled the napkins away from his hand.

"Gods above and below," Kowalski said, whistling softly. "What happened?"

"I shook hands with Vladimir Sanguinati."

"Why?"

"Didn't have a good alternative, and considering the conversation prior to it, it didn't seem smart to insult him."

Kowalski paled. "They can take blood just by touching you?"

"Apparently. You had mentioned there was some evidence that they could take blood without biting a person. Looks like we've just been given a demonstration of what that other method is."

Monty raised the cup to his lips, then lowered it without drinking. "Let's get out of here, Karl. I need something to eat, and I need to get away from the Courtyard for a while."

Kowalski secured his cup in a holder and drove out of the parking lot.

Warning signs everywhere, Monty thought. The mayor wanted the dangerous criminal caught and the stolen property returned to its rightful owner. Except the property wasn't a thing; it was a person. Meg Corbyn had stolen her own body, had run away from someone's "benevolent ownership."

Considering what the *cassandra sangues* could do, how much of that benevolence was about profit?

Monty closed his eyes, letting Kowalski choose the place for a light meal.

Now that Vladimir Sanguinati had put the thought on the table, Monty wasn't sure that, in this case, *benevolence* wasn't another word for "slavery." He also wasn't sure if leaving a blood prophet on her own wasn't a passive form of murder.

But he *was* sure that any intervention with regard to Meg Corbyn and her addiction to cutting would have to come from Simon Wolfgard now and not him.

The phone rang as Meg was pulling on her coat. "Hello?"

"Meg? It's Jester. Listen, old Hurricane is coming up with the other ponies. He's retired now—that's why he's living at Lakeside—but it would be good for him to feel useful. Could you give him the mail for the Owlgard or the Pony Barn?"

"Sure. How will I know which one he is?"

"White mane and tail, and a gray coat with a hint of blue. Can't mistake him for any of the others."

"Have to go," Meg said when she heard the chorus of neighs.

She opened the delivery door and then stared.

There were twelve ponies waiting for her. Meg didn't recognize four of them, but she figured out which one was Hurricane based on the description Jester gave her. Instead of forming their usual line, the ponies were all jostling for first position at the door, pushing and crowding until Thunder stamped a foot.

The *boom* shook the building and had Meg grabbing for the doorway to keep her balance.

She looked at the pony. *Oh, he couldn't have . . .*

Suddenly a voice yelled, "Blessed Thaisia! What is going on?"

She'd never heard that voice before, but she was willing to bet it was Elliot Wolfgard yelling out a window in the consulate.

In the absolute silence that followed, she heard a window slam shut.

"You're going to get me in trouble," she told Thunder in a loud whisper.

The pony wouldn't look at her, which confirmed he had been responsible for that roll of thunder.

"Now," she said firmly. "Lakeside mail carriers are good-mannered ponies. Anyone who can't behave will have to go home."

She couldn't actually make them go back to the Pony Barn if they weren't good mannered, but she just stood in the doorway of the sorting room. The ponies stared at her as if trying to decide if she was bluffing. Then they sorted themselves out in a neat line, with Thunder in his usual first position.

"Thank you." Giddily triumphant, Meg went to the table and picked up the stacks of mail for Thunder's baskets. As each pony shifted in the line, she filled baskets for Lightning, Tornado, Earthshaker, and Fog. Going back to the table for the last three batches of mail, she wondered about the ponies' names. If Thunder could make so much sound by stamping his foot, what could Tornado and Earthshaker do if they pitched a fit?

Couldn't think about that. Just like she *wouldn't* think about having Wolves and vampires living in the same apartment complex that she did—or why she felt safer being around them than the humans she had lived with in the compound.

Just like she wouldn't admit to being curious about seeing a Wolf in Wolf form. She didn't have a training image of a *terra indigene* Wolf, just images of the animal. Even her Controller, with all the money he acquired from the use of his property, hadn't been able to buy a photograph of a Wolf to use as reference.

Shaking off those thoughts, Meg fetched the treat bowl and held out two carrot chunks for Thunder.

He looked at her, looked at the carrots, and shook his head.

"Carrots," Meg said. "You liked carrots last week."

Another head shake. Thunder lifted a hoof, looked toward the consulate, and put the hoof down carefully.

Meg studied the ponies and felt her stomach flutter. *Oh no.*

Retreating—and becoming aware of just how cold the room was because she'd already had the door open too long—she hustled into the front room, grabbed the calendar and a marker, then hustled back to the ponies.

"Look." She made a big S on Moonsday, then turned the calendar around for the ponies to see. Not that she thought they could read, but they seemed to understand words. "We had sugar lumps on Moonsday as a special treat. We don't get sugar lumps again as a treat until *next* Moonsday, which is here." She made another S on the calendar. "*Today* we have carrots as our treat."

She put the calendar and marker down, picked up the treat bowl, and returned to the doorway. "Carrots today." She held out two carrot chunks.

Managing to convey disappointment and resignation, Thunder ate his carrot chunks and headed out to deliver his mail.

All the ponies ate their carrots, including the ones who must have shown up today because they expected sugar.

Meg closed the outside door, checked the front room to make sure no delivery trucks were pulling in, then went into the back room to make herself a cup of peppermint tea. If they were going to have a treat discussion every day, she was going to put on her boots and stand outside from now on. At least that way she could warm up afterward.

Simon hung up the office phone and sat back in his chair. That was the third West Coast Courtyard leader to call him this morning, asking if there had been any peculiar attacks in the Lakeside Courtyard's territory.

Something new had found its way among the humans. Something that was absorbed by the *terra indigene* when they ate the meat. Humans were turning savagely aggressive, and not just among their own kind. They were *attacking* some of the Others. Mostly Crows were being attacked, were being ripped apart in both forms, by packs of humans that were so aggressive, they had no survival instincts. The top predators in those Courtyards had taken down the monkeys, then began to fight among themselves soon after consuming the meat.

Just as disturbing were the Wolves and Grizzlies and Cats that were suddenly so passive, they couldn't defend themselves against an attack by a gang of humans.

The bodywalkers, the healers among the *terra indigene*, could find no evidence of poison or drugs, but *something* was making humans behave strangely and was also affecting the Others.

More humans in the bigger cities took drugs that not only damaged their lives but also spoiled them as meat. But none of the incidents being reported were in the big cities. This new danger was happening in small farming hamlets or industrial centers that had a few hundred citizens. The kinds of places where the Others had minimal contact with humans and wouldn't know there could be reasons not to eat a kill.

The kinds of places that, if the Others felt threatened and decided to eliminate those humans, the number that were killed would be howled at as tragic on the television or in the newspapers, but in truth would be no more than an inconvenience. Another group of humans would be selected to work the farms or run the machines, would scrub off the blood and move into the houses—if the Others didn't get there first and simply reclaim the land and property for themselves.

Didn't humans understand how expendable they were? The *terra indigene* were as old as the world, as old as the land and the seas. They learned from the top predators and became *more* than those predators. Always adapting, always changing as Namid changed. *They* would be forever.

The *terra indigene* in Thaisia didn't need humans anymore in order to have the material things they wanted. If the monkeys became a real threat, they no longer had enough to offer to make their presence endurable. If that day came, humans would follow the same path as other creatures before them and become an extinct meat.

Meg wasn't surprised when Jester showed up an hour after the ponies trotted off. She put down the stack of mail she'd been sorting and held out the treat bowl. "Have a carrot."

Jester leaned over the bowl, sniffed, then leaned back. "I prefer meat."

"Set a good example," Meg growled. "Eat a carrot."

Jester took a step back and eyed her. "You're sounding rather Wolfish. Was there a problem with the ponies this morning?"

Meg set the bowl on the table. "Only that they didn't get sugar lumps today, but sugar is a special treat and isn't something they should have every day, so today the treat was carrots, and Thunder . . . thundered . . . which upset Elliot Wolfgard, who sent some stuffy Owl to remind me that the consulate dealt with human government and shouldn't be embarrassed by the Courtyard help's shenanigans!"

She hadn't realized how much the reprimand had upset her. After all, she hadn't done anything to deserve it.

No. She wasn't upset. She was *mad.*

It felt good to be mad. It felt invigorating to be able to feel emotions without fearing punishment. It felt *alive.*

She stared at Jester.

"You gave sugar to the ponies?" he asked.

"So what? An occasional lump of sugar won't hurt them."

"No. Of course it won't." He took another step away from the table. "I'd tuck my tail between my legs, but it's very uncomfortable growing one while wearing trousers, and I think we'd both prefer that I remain dressed."

She picked up the bowl and held it out. "Eat a carrot instead. It won't hurt you either."

Sighing, he took a carrot chunk and nibbled on it. "Will there be sugar again?"

The calendar was now sitting next to the music player. She held it up and tapped the big black S. "Moonsday is sugar day."

"Right. I'll explain it to them."

Her anger fizzled out. "I'm not upset with you, Jester. It's just that I want to do a good job. I really do. But I haven't been here a week yet, and I keep getting into trouble."

Smiling, Jester held thumb and forefinger close together. "A little bit of trouble, which is amply compensated for by the entertainment you've been providing."

"Thanks a lot." She hesitated. She didn't know much about anything, but she didn't have to know much to figure out she was going to have time on her hands. "Jester? When they were caught up with their work, what did the other Liaisons do while they waited for deliveries?"

He looked around the room. "You cleared out all the old mail and packages?"

"Yes."

He looked a little bewildered. "I don't know, Meg. I don't remember seeing this room so clean. Maybe . . . read books?"

"Is there something else I could do to be helpful?"

"What do you want to do?"

Good question. One that deserved some thought.

"Your suggestion about reading is a good one. I'll start with that." She could study anything she wanted, could read about a subject from beginning to end if she wanted. She could learn how to do things instead of having a head full of disconnected images.

"Good," Jester said. "Fine. I'll talk to the ponies. From now on, they'll be happy with whatever treats you give them."

Then he was gone, slipping out the door so fast she almost wondered if he'd been there at all.

Meg shook her head. She wasn't sure humans could—or should—understand how the Others thought. But Jester's suggestion was a good one, so during her lunch break she would pick up a book to study and a book to read for fun, and ponder what else she could do to earn her keep.

Then it occurred to her that if the Others had no suggestions about what she should do with her time, she could adjust her job to include whatever *she* wanted. Hadn't she already done that by making deliveries?

Putting a music disc into the player, Meg filled the room with a lively tune and went back to sorting.

Hearing the crunch of tires behind him, Simon shifted over to the side of the road. But the shiny black sedan slowed to keep pace with him, and the rear window rolled down.

"Want a ride home?" Elliot asked.

Simon shook his head. "Need to walk."

"Stop the car," Elliot said to his driver.

Simon waited for Elliot to exchange the expensive leather shoes for practical boots and get out of the car. The sedan drove off, leaving the two Wolves walking toward the Green Complex.

"What's wrong?" Elliot asked. "Has your Liaison caused another problem? Isn't one a day sufficient?"

"Could have been worse," Simon replied, a low growl under the words. "At least it was Thunder expressing an opinion. And if he hadn't been showing off or trying to scare her or whatever it was he was trying to do, his stamping a hoof wouldn't have done that."

"And if it had been Twister or Earthshaker expressing an opinion around so many buildings?"

"It wasn't." If it had been, he would have had an unpleasant conversation with the girl at the lake, since the ponies were the Elementals' steeds. Instead he'd had a baffling talk with Jester. The Coyote was delighted that Meg was able to pull Elliot's tail with so little effort, but Jester was also wary of their weird-haired Liaison. She didn't behave like other humans, so none of the Others were quite sure how to deal with her—which made her the most interesting and frustrating thing to cross their paths in quite some time.

"There's trouble in the western Courtyards," Simon said. As they walked, he told Elliot about the phone calls, the attacks, and the deaths. "Select Courtyard leaders might be meeting in the Midwest Region to discuss this new threat."

Elliot frowned. "This . . . disease. It's contagious?"

Simon shook his head. "It's not a disease. It wears off like a drug in a few hours. There are *two* pieces of foulness trickling into small human settlements, and our bodywalkers can't find the source of either of them."

"You're going to represent the Northeast Region?"

"If the meeting is called, I'll be the one to go for the Courtyards in this part of Thaisia."

A brief, uncomfortable silence. Then Elliot said, "What about Sam? I'll take care of him. You know that. But I will not have him in a cage."

"The cage is for his protection." An old argument. In his terror and grief after seeing his mother killed, Sam had gone on a binge of self-destructive behavior no amount of pack discipline could stop. After the second time the pup had come too close to killing himself, Simon had gotten the cage, intending to get rid of it as soon as the pup settled down. But by the time he could trust Sam to be alone, the pup had decided the cage was the *only* safe place, and getting him to come out for even a few minutes at a time had become a daily battle.

As much as Elliot loved Sam and still mourned the loss of Daphne, it was a battle the older Wolf refused to endure. And the sight of Sam in a cage upset everyone in the Wolfgard complex, especially the other pups.

"Henry will look after him. Or Vlad."

"How long will you be gone?"

"A few days. Maybe a week." He didn't want to consider what could happen in a week—or who might not be in the Courtyard when he returned. "Try to get along with Meg, all right? She's the first Liaison we've had in a long time who actually does the work, and that includes making deliveries to the Chambers."

Elliot looked uncomfortable at the reminder that Erebus Sanguinati approved of their new Liaison. "Well, I will say this for her. She's the first monkey who bothered to walk the few steps between buildings and deliver the consulate's mail personally so that I receive correspondence in a timely manner."

Having that much settled, they finished the walk to the Green Complex in easy silence. The black sedan was waiting in a visitor's parking space.

Elliot opened the door, then paused. "By the way, the mayor called me to whine about a dangerous thief and about a rumor that she may be hiding in the Courtyard, even posing as our Liaison, and it was vitally important that the property that was taken be returned to its owner."

Simon twitched. Should he tell Elliot about Meg? The decision the Business Association had made not to tell anyone that Meg was a blood prophet was sound—and it had taken a threat from Tess to get Jenni Crowgard's promise not to share that information with anyone, including the other Crows. But maybe knowing would help Elliot deal with the monkeys who chattered in his ear?

"What did you tell him?" Simon asked, knowing his hesitation had given Elliot a clue that he had reasons for wanting to hold on to their new Liaison besides her ability to sort mail and deliver packages.

Elliot bared his teeth in a smile. "I told him our Liaison didn't have the backbone to be dangerous or the intelligence to be a successful thief."

"That will do." Not a compliment to Meg, but the kind of answer that the human government could find useful. Then something occurred to him. "How did the mayor know that Meg looked like the woman on the wanted poster? Only a handful of police have seen her, and the deliverymen would have no reason to know about the poster."

"The mayor said he received an anonymous tip," Elliot said.

"Male or female?"

"He didn't say."

How would Asia Crane have seen one of those posters? She wasn't above causing mischief for the person who had the job she claimed she wanted. Or was it someone else? Someone who might be able to charm information out of a policeman. Or someone who worked for the Others and had earned some degree of trust.

Something else he would discuss with Henry, Vlad, and Tess, especially if he had to leave for that meeting.

Simon watched Elliot drive off to the Wolfgard Complex before crossing the road and going to his apartment. Sam's greeting ended as soon as Simon opened the cage door and reached for the pup.

Ignoring the whimpers, he hauled Sam out of the cage and took him outside. As usual, as soon as Sam's feet touched the ground, he tried to bolt for the apartment.

Growling, Simon turned to give chase. Having to use the damned cage scraped at him as much as it did Elliot, but what were they supposed to do—let the pup die?

What will you do if he starts growing again, if he ever matures into a full-grown Wolf and still needs a cage?

He'd taken a couple of steps after the pup when Sam slid to a stop and headed away from their door, sniffing the ground with an interest he hadn't shown in much too long.

Intrigued, Simon joined the pup and bent low to see if he could pick up whatever scent Sam found so interesting.

Meg.

As he straightened up, he saw her coming through the archway that led to the garages and parking area behind the complex. She had carry bags in both hands and was puffing a bit.

One way or another, he was going to make sure she got more exercise—even if he had to chase her like a bunny.

"Meg," he said, nodding.

"Mr. Wolfgard."

Calling him Mr. Wolfgard was becoming an effective door she kept slamming in his face, and he didn't like it. If she kept doing it, thinking of her as a two-legged bunny was going to have more and more appeal.

Then she looked down, smiled, and said, "Hello. Who are you?"

That's when he remembered the pup, who was halfway hiding between his legs.

Sam gave her his squeaky-door howl of greeting.

When young, *terra indigene* Wolves didn't look much different from wolves. As they matured, the differences in size and shape became apparent.

"This is Sam," Simon said. He didn't offer an explanation of who Sam was. Meg didn't seem to notice.

"Hello, Sam."

The pup grumbled and howled in conversational tones. Still safe between Simon's legs, he edged forward to sniff at Meg, then jumped back to hide. And all the while, Sam's body quivered and his tail thumped against Simon's leg.

Not one of us, but she doesn't smell like prey either, Simon thought. *Doesn't smell like the kind of humans who had destroyed Sam's world.* Meg was something new, and her scent made the pup forget he was afraid of being outside.

Wasn't that interesting?

"You need any help getting those up the stairs?" Simon asked.

"No, thank you. The stairs are clear of snow, so I'll be fine. Besides, this is my second trip. Good evening, Mr. Wolfgard. Bye, Sam."

He watched her go up the stairs before he took the pup over to the area Sam was using as a dumping spot. The rest of the residents were tolerant because it was Sam and because it was so cold and because the Hawks and Owls didn't object to the rats and mice that were drawn to the feces. But sooner or later he was going to have to clean up all the poop.

As soon as the pup had done his business, Sam made a dash for the stairs leading up to Meg's apartment. Simon caught him halfway up and took him inside their own place.

"No," he said firmly. "I don't think she wants to play tonight."

He could picture, too clearly, the two of them romping with Meg in the snow.

"Come on. I'll give you a good brushing. Girls like a well-groomed Wolf."

Meg doing the brushing, her fingers deep in his fur.

It was better not to think of *that* picture either.

Sam got a good brushing and remained fairly calm about having to stay out of the cage while Simon gave it a thorough cleaning—calm enough to venture to the front door by himself and sniff around the entrance.

It was easy enough to figure out what scent the pup was looking for.

And wasn't that interesting?

CHAPTER 9

Meg bobbled the jar of sweet pickles when something thumped on her kitchen door. Her hands shook as she put the jar on the table, and her heart bounced in her throat. Someone had found her, but she couldn't seem to move, wasn't able to run for the front door and escape.

Then the thump was repeated, followed by a growled "Open up, Meg!"

Relief made her dizzy. No one had found her except the annoyed Wolf whose apartment also accessed the common hallway and back staircase.

"Just a minute!" Keys. She needed . . .

A key turned in the lock, but the door was still held shut by the sliding bolt. That resistance was followed by a snarl that made her shiver as she hurried to the door and slid the bolt to an open position.

Simon burst into her kitchen, grabbed her before she could scramble out of reach, and hauled her out to the landing and then through the open doorway into his apartment.

She struggled—an instinctive need to escape from an angry man—until he snapped at her, his teeth so close to the tip of her nose, she wondered if he'd stripped off a layer of skin.

"I don't have time to play." His growl rumbled under the words as he pulled her through an empty room, down a hallway, down the stairs, and into his kitchen. "I have to go away for a few days, and I need you to take care of Sam."

That pins-and-needles feeling filled her arms and hands as soon as he said the words, but she didn't dare rub her skin and call attention to herself.

"Why are you going away? Where are you going?" It wasn't just curiosity or concern that made her ask. Simon still had her razor. She'd gritted her teeth for an hour yesterday evening while a craving seemed to eat its way through her chest and belly. Not sure how far blood scent could travel and being sensibly afraid of exciting the predatory nature of her neighbors—especially the vampire, Grizzly, and Wolf—she'd managed to resist using a kitchen knife for a cut. But she wasn't going to be able to resist much longer.

"It doesn't concern you," Simon said. "Just do your work until I get back, and you'll be fine." He opened a bottom cupboard, hauled out a bag of dry dog food, and scooped some into a bowl. "This is Sam's food. I give him a scoop in the morning and another around dinnertime. And he gets fresh water at the same time."

Staggered by the responsibility he'd just dumped on her, Meg said, "But I don't know anything about taking care of a puppy!"

"Just give him food and water twice a day." Simon repeated as he shoved a set of keys into her hand. "Keys for this apartment. If you have any questions, ask Vlad or Henry."

Meg hurried after him as he strode to the front door and picked up the carryall beside it. "Mr. Wolfgard!"

He turned and looked at her. The prickling under her skin turned into a harsh buzz that filled her legs as well as her arms.

Something bad has happened. Something very bad.

"What about taking Sam outside?" she asked, forcing her voice and body to imitate calm, a skill she had learned out of necessity. No matter what the Walking Names had said about professional manners and being clinical while handling female bodies, when girls struggled against being strapped down for a cut, it provoked some of them into doing . . . things . . . after the cut and prophecy in order to relieve their own response to the girls' distress. And as long as no usable skin was damaged, the Controller chose not to see what his people were doing. After all, some experiences provided richer details to the visions—especially the darker visions.

To her surprise—and relief—Simon responded to her calm manner by calming down.

He shook his head. "If Sam got away from you, he could get hurt before you could catch up to him. He'll have to do his business in the cage. I'll clean it up when I get back."

The whole apartment would stink of poop if the cage wasn't cleaned for a few days.

A horn beeped.

Simon reached for the carryall.

"Mr. Wolfgard." When he looked at her again, she lifted her chin. "You have something that belongs to me."

He didn't do anything except straighten up and face her, but she felt the underlying menace. Anyone seeing him now would know he wasn't human. Because of that, she felt certain this was one time she couldn't afford to back down. If she did, something in him would force her to remain submissive.

"You don't need it," he said.

"That's not for you to decide. But you're right—I don't need it. A kitchen knife will do just as well, but mistakes happen more often when the blade doesn't have a familiar weight and the sharpest edge."

It wasn't a bluff. Most girls who used some other kind of sharp edge when they couldn't get their hands on the proper razor ended up ruined in one way or another if they didn't end up dead.

He stared at her, red flickers in his eyes. Then he bared his teeth, and she watched in disbelief as his canines lengthened and then returned to almost human size.

The Wolf was definitely too close to the surface this morning.

Saying nothing, he reached into the pocket of his jeans, pulled out the silver razor, and handed it to her.

Someone outside laid on the horn.

Simon grabbed his carryall and went out the front door, not bothering to close it behind him.

Meg rushed out after him and watched him get into a small passenger van. She couldn't see who was driving, but it looked like there were a couple more people in the back seats.

When the van drove off, she remembered she was outside and it was cold. But when she turned to go back inside, a fierce need to cut washed over her. Remembering the euphoria produced a flutter through her pelvis, that delicious pull of arousal.

One cut for a good cause. Something bad had happened. Something that was taking Simon away from the Courtyard. One cut might tell him so much.

Meg went inside, closed the door, and then leaned against it as she opened the razor.

One cut to help Simon and get rid of that awful buzzing under her skin. But with no idea of why he left, what should she focus on? Prophesies became too general if the *cassandra sangue* wasn't focused on someone or something specific. Even a photograph wasn't usually enough because the prophecy could be about the person who *took* the photo, not the subject *in* the photo. That was why the Controller's clients had to be in the same room as the prophet in order for her visions to be about the right person.

As she raised her left arm and studied the skin on her forearm and hand, she heard a whimper. She walked into the living room and studied the pup in the cage. He was huddled in the back corner, looking scared.

A prophet needed someone to listen to the prophecy, needed to speak the words in order to feel euphoria from a cut. Swallowing the words and enduring the pain was how she had remembered the visions that had shown her how to escape.

Was she brave enough to suffer like that again?

Simon was gone, but there was still someone who could listen. Except the pup wouldn't be able to tell her what was said, and she wouldn't remember enough for the cut to be useful for anything but some physical relief.

Caw caw caw

Meg jolted at the sound of the Crows leaving. Gods above and below, she was going to be late for work!

Flustered, she closed the razor and tucked it into her pocket. She fetched the bowl of puppy food that Simon had left in the kitchen and put it in the cage. Then she locked the front door and bolted up the stairs to the back hallway and her own kitchen, locking doors as she went. The beef slices and jar of sweet pickles were shoved into the refrigerator. She'd return during her lunch break to check on Sam and put everything away properly.

A last look around to make sure everything was turned on or off as it should be. Then she grabbed her coat and the bag of apples for the ponies, stuffed her feet into her boots, and locked her door. Rushing down the stairs, she ran to the garage that held her BOW.

It wasn't until she was driving toward the Liaison's Office that she realized Simon hadn't told her what to do if the Wolf pup shifted into a boy.

Simon waited until they reached the Utilities Complex before he turned his head and looked at Nathan Wolfgard and Marie Hawkgard, who were sitting in the back of the van. "You going somewhere?"

"They're going with you," Blair growled, slowing at the Utilities gate.

The Wolf manning the gate pulled it open just enough to allow the van to exit. He nodded at Simon, who nodded in return.

Blair pulled out into traffic, still growling. "The train isn't going to wait for you, and we don't have time to spare with all these monkeys on the road. Why are they on the road?"

"They're going to work," Simon replied. Glancing at Nathan and Marie, he added, "I don't need company."

"They aren't company," Blair snapped. "They're guards. You're the leader of the Lakeside Courtyard. You don't travel alone. Especially not now. Humans see a Wolf on his own in a train compartment, they might get stupid and kill you. You remember what happened the last time a *terra indigene* was mobbed on a train?"

It was like a line had been drawn between the east and west of Thaisia. For three months any train traveling across the continent was hit by a tornado at the line that served as the designation for where the Hawk had been killed by humans.

Three months of bodies and freight torn up and thrown along the tracks. Then the Elementals, having made their point, went back to their usual way of interacting with the world.

"I remember," Simon said.

Blair nodded. "That's why enforcers from the Wolfgard and Hawkgard are going with you. That's also why I called the train station to tell them you would be on the westbound train this morning, and why I asked Henry to call that policeman so that some of his people would be at the station."

"This is supposed to be a quiet gathering of leaders to talk about what happened in Jerzy yesterday."

"Once you get off the train at the Midwest station, you'll disappear into *terra indigene* land. Until then . . ." Blair glanced at him. "Simon, there's nothing obvious, but you can't pass for human today. The police and the train workers need to keep their kind under control because humans can't afford to cause another problem."

The humans in this part of Thaisia might not have heard the news yet, but once they did, they would be full of shock and anger and panic. Not a good time for *terra indigene* to be among them for anything but a massive hunt. But the Others were also full of anger. A wrong move by humans right now, and a lot of their hamlets, towns, or even cities could disappear.

"What about Sam?" Blair asked.

"Meg will take care of him."

"Meg?" Blair took his eyes off the road to stare at Simon a moment too long and almost rammed the car slowing down in front of him. "Why?"

"Because she's the first thing in two years that made him curious enough to forget he's afraid of being outside."

A soft whine from Nathan.

"What did Elliot say?" Blair asked.

"I didn't tell him."

Blair looked thoughtful. Then he nodded. "When he finds out, I'll deal with it."

"I want the Crows watching the office," Simon said. "Tell Vlad and Henry to keep an eye on Meg. She hasn't had much contact with other *terra indigene,* and her *not prey* scent might cause confusion." *In someone besides me,* he added silently. Although knowing her scent was caused by her being *cassandra sangue* had eased that confusion inside him. She was still a puzzle, but that just made her something interesting to explore.

"Jester has had the most contact with her," Blair said. "He finds her entertaining, but he's also wary of her."

<If anyone picks up the faintest scent of blood on Meg, I want Vlad or Henry to know about it,> Simon told Blair. If he couldn't stop her from cutting, he was damn well going to know every time she did it.

Blair nodded.

They drove the rest of the way to the train station in silence. Simon's thoughts were full of Sam and Meg. He regretted not being there to watch them, but maybe that was better. They would have to figure out how to deal with each other on their own.

When they pulled into the train-station parking lot, Simon noticed the police car as he got out of the van, letting Nathan retrieve his carryall from the back. Lieutenant Montgomery stepped out of the car.

"Have to go, or we'll miss the train," Nathan said.

Simon nodded to Montgomery, then strode into the station, followed by Nathan and Marie.

When he boarded the train, he and his guards had the back half of a passenger car all to themselves. A sweating conductor blocked the aisle after they took their seats, directing the humans who hadn't found a seat elsewhere to the front half of the car.

Nervous glances. A buzz of whispers once the train started moving. And a railroad security guard taking the place of the conductor to ensure there wouldn't be any trouble.

Nathan was a couple of seats in front of Simon. Marie was a couple of seats behind him on the opposite side of the aisle. They, along with the human guard, would keep watch; he didn't need to.

Nothing he could do for the moment. The new drug or disease that was touching humans and Others alike had become more than a worry. What had happened in Jerzy could start a war. *Terra indigene* leaders needed to meet, needed to talk, needed to decide what should be done. Humans had weapons that could challenge claws and fangs. They had guns and bombs that could kill the shapeshifters and even the Sanguinati when they were in human form—if they died before they could shift to smoke. But nothing could stop the Elementals, which was something humans tended to forget until it was too late. And that was one of the reasons the *terra indigene* rationed the metals and fuels and other materials humans needed to create their weapons. The outcome of a war wouldn't change, so why should shifters have to die before the monkeys were extinguished? Besides, killing the humans all at once was a waste of meat.

Simon closed his eyes. Nothing he could do for the moment. Blair would look after the Courtyard—and keep an eye on Sam and Meg. As for the humans, he would have to trust Lieutenant Montgomery to keep the peace until he got back.

"Oh, that's not good," Meg muttered when she spotted the black sedan idling along the side of the Liaison's Office, unable to move forward because of all the delivery trucks that were in the way.

Parking her BOW willy-nilly and hoping no one needed to get another vehicle out of the garages, she bolted into the office. She had to get some of those deliveries taken care of before Elliot Wolfgard coughed up a hairball.

Did Wolves have hairballs? How could she find out such things?

Shaking her head, she removed her boots, hurried into the sorting room . . . and stopped. The Private door was wide-open, so she could see part of the front counter. The Hawk she had met the other day was standing behind the counter, his arms folded, his stance aggressive. He glared at someone she couldn't see and said, "Just write the words the Meg will want and leave the boxes."

One of the Crows, standing on the counter, cawed at the visitor, then walked over to the container filled with pens, lifted one out and, holding it in his beak, walked back. He tapped one end of the pen on the counter, then held it up as if offering it to someone—who obviously didn't take it because the pen was tapped on the counter again.

Hurrying to the doorway, Meg poked her head into the front room and got a look at the deliveryman.

"Hi, Dan. Sorry I'm late. Slept through the alarm. Just give me a second to get my coat off and I'll be with you."

She hadn't realized how nervous he'd been about being alone with the Others until she saw the relief on his face. She hadn't thought the Hawks and Crows were that dangerous, but maybe he knew more about them than she did.

"Oh, that's all right, Ms. Meg. Happens to all of us."

The Crow tapped the pen on the counter and held it up again.

Meg beamed a smile at the Hawk in human form and the Crow. "And you two opened up the office? That's great. Thank you. Be right with you, Dan."

"I know what you need."

And he didn't wait for her.

As she ducked back into the sorting room, she saw him gingerly take the pen from the Crow. By the time she hung up her coat and pulled on her shoes, Dan was outside, talking to a couple more deliverymen, and Harry was pulling open the door, juggling his delivery on one arm.

"Good morning, Harry," Meg said. Had she remembered to brush her hair? Simon's grab and hustle this morning had wiped her routine right out of her mind. She touched one side of her head.

"Morning, Miz Meg." Harry looked at her hand and smiled. "I see you've got a couple of helpers today. You take your time getting settled. We'll do fine."

The Crow grabbed the pen lying on the counter and held it up.

Taking Harry at his word, Meg retreated to the washroom and looked in the mirror. Her hair wasn't sticking up every which way, but it had been flattened by her hat. She ran a comb through it, decided that was as good as things would get, and went back to the counter.

The last deliveryman was writing down his information under the Crow's watchful eye. He looked at Meg and smiled. "Figures the day you're late to arrive is the day we've all got the Courtyard down as our first stop."

"Well, you all took care of it, and I thank you for that," Meg replied as she watched the black sedan pull out on Main Street.

"The Beargard said to help the Meg today," the Hawk said.

"Oh." The Crow was entertaining himself by pulling pens out of the container and arranging them on the counter, but what was she supposed to do with the Hawk? And how long did they expect to "help" today?

Since he was in human form, there was one thing the Hawk could do.

"I didn't have time for breakfast this morning," Meg said. "Would you go over to A Little Bite and ask Tess for some coffee? Tell her it's for me, and she'll know how to fix it. And ask her if Howling Good Reads has any copies of the Lakeside newspaper."

The Hawk stared at her. "The Lorne makes the newspaper. He's over there." He pointed in the direction of the Three Ps.

"Not the Courtyard's newsletter. I'd like a copy of the newspaper the humans read."

"Why would you want that?"

The Crow looked up from his pen arrangement to stare at her too.

Clearly being *too* interested in human activity was suspicious behavior here, even if the person was human. But something bad had happened, something that had caused Simon to leave in a hurry. Maybe she could find out what it was without cutting.

"As Liaison, I should be aware of what is happening in the human part of the city," Meg said, choosing her words with care. "And I can check store ads and make a list of things that might interest the *terra indigene*."

After a moment, the Hawk nodded and left. Meg smiled at the Crow and brought the handcart of packages into the sorting room.

Some were small enough to go with the mail. Others she would pack in the BOW for deliveries, along with her personal delivery.

The Hawk returned with a large coffee, a newspaper, and a small bag. He set them all on one end of the sorting table.

"HGR gets newspapers," he said. "Tess will tell Vlad that you are to get one now. There is food. There is no mouse in it, but the Merri Lee said you would like this meat better."

Thank the gods for Merri Lee. "Thank you." When he stared at her, she added, "I don't need any more help right now."

He turned and went into the back room. Meg was reaching for the coffee when he walked back out, naked. He went right by her, vaulted over the counter, then held out an arm for the Crow, who hesitated but hopped on his arm. The two of them left the office. The Crow joined its friends on the wall that separated the delivery area from Henry's yard. The Hawk stood in full view of anyone driving by long enough to make Meg wonder how to explain the cause of all the car accidents when the police came calling. Then he shifted and flew off.

Putting all the pens back in the holder, Meg went into the sorting room. There was nothing to do until the mail truck arrived, so she ate her breakfast and skimmed through the *Lakeside News* from first page to last. She found a few things she thought might be of interest to the Others, but she'd ask Tess or Vlad before doing anything.

What she didn't find was any kind of news that would explain why Simon had left in such a rush that morning.

Monty hesitated in the doorway of Captain Burke's office. Something about the way the man sat behind the desk gave the strong impression that intruding for anything but an emergency wouldn't be tolerated.

But when Monty took a step back, Burke said, "Come in, Lieutenant, and shut the door."

He shut the door and approached the desk.

"Something on your mind?" Burke asked. He sounded subdued.

"Simon Wolfgard and two other *terra indigene* caught a westbound train this morning," Monty said. "Henry Beargard called me with this information and suggested that a patrol car be at the station to ensure good behavior on the part of the humans. Officer Kowalski tells me this is unusual because the Others travel by train all the time and police presence isn't requested." He studied Burke. "It means something, doesn't it?"

"It means Simon Wolfgard knows more about what's happening out west than we do," Burke replied. He sighed and sat back. "Most likely, the newspapers and television news will receive a watered-down version to avoid things escalating out west or spreading to other parts of Thaisia."

Monty shivered. "Sir?"

"In hamlets that have less than a thousand people, the Others don't have a Courtyard. They don't need one because there is no way in or out of those places except on roads running through *terra indigene* land. But the Others usually have a house at the edge of the village, a place for mail and packages to be delivered and the place where they have electricity and telephones and where they enjoy the technology we've developed. The gards take turns using the house and looking after it, as well as dealing with the mail and deliveries.

"Last night in Jerzy, a farming hamlet that provides about a quarter of the food for one of the bigger cities on the West Coast . . ." Burke stopped and just stared straight ahead for a long moment. "Well, we don't really know what happened, except some young fools hopped up on some damn thing figured out the Crows had gathered for a movie night, broke into the house, and attacked the Others. One of the Crows managed to reach the phone and call for help, and a couple of them got away and alerted the rest of the *terra indigene*. The police officers who responded to the call were shot by the intruders, along with several Crows. That much is clear. After that . . . The Others caught some of the attackers and killed them, right out on the street. And then they went crazy. Some of the people in the village, instead of staying in their houses, grabbed whatever they could for weapons and went out and escalated the fight."

Burke clasped his hands and pressed them on the desk. "By the time police reinforcements from other hamlets arrived, the fight was over and the Others had disappeared into their own land. We don't know how many *terra indigene* died in that fight, but one-third of the people in Jerzy are dead. We know the humans started it, so the survivors are damn lucky the Others left anyone alive."

Burke's voice had risen to something close to an angry roar.

Out of the corner of his eye, Monty saw men jerk to a stop and stare before hurrying away.

"How did you find out about this, sir?" Monty asked.

Burke sagged, his face an unhealthy gray. "One of the officers who responded to the call is the son of a friend of mine. The Others found Roger and took him to the clinic. Saved his life. The other three police officers didn't make it. So Roger was the only one who knew for sure what happened up to his being shot. My friend called me this morning, both to tell me about Roger and to warn me about something Roger had heard before he passed out." He pushed back from his desk and stood up. "I will be talking—quietly—to the chief, to other captains, and to all the team leaders in this station. The chief will decide who else needs to know."

"About the attack?"

Burke shook his head. "About something that pumps up aggressive behavior. One of the attackers was boasting about having 'gone over wolf' and how they would become the enemy in order to defeat the enemy."

"Gods above and below," Monty whispered.

"So if you hear any whispers about humans having 'gone over wolf' or about something on the street that pumps up aggression, I want to know. Is that understood?"

"Yes, sir." He hesitated, not sure he wanted to know. "What about the rest of the people in that hamlet? What will happen to them?"

"The Others let an ambulance come in and take Roger to a city hospital. They did that because he had responded when the Crows called for help. Then they barricaded the roads. Now the only ways out of Jerzy don't lead to anyplace human, and right now it's unclear if people would survive if they tried to leave. But one thing has already happened in the city that is supplied by Jerzy."

"Rations," Monty said. He remembered a winter as a child when his mother was making more soups and got so angry when he or his siblings tried to take a second piece of bread. That spring, he and his father and brothers had turned a piece of their backyard into a vegetable garden, and his mother learned how to can fruit for the hard times, and never went to the butcher shop or the grocery store without her ration book.

"Rations," Burke agreed. "And you can bet *that* will be news in every city throughout Thaisia, even if the reason isn't. That will be all, Lieutenant, unless you have something to add."

"No, sir. Nothing."

As Monty walked back to his desk to check his messages, he remembered Vladimir Sanguinati's words.

Next you'll be eating your weak in order to keep the strong healthy.

He sank into his chair, his legs trembling. Was someone *trying* to provoke a war between humans and Others? Did anyone think humans could win?

And if humans started a war and lost, what would happen to the survivors? Would there *be* any survivors?

Monty took out his wallet and opened it to the picture of Lizzy. He stared at that picture for a long time.

I will do my best to keep you safe, Lizzy girl. Even if I never see you again, I will do my best to keep you safe.

Putting his wallet back in his pocket, he went out to find Kowalski.

"Yes?"

"By the gods! Did you hear about Jerzy? All those people dead!"

"There was some mention of a hamlet by that name, but the news reports were very vague."

"What are you going to do about it?"

"What happened has nothing to do with me. As for what you should do, this seems like the time to adjust the price for your crops. The prophecy did say an incident would create an opportunity for great profit."

"But the prophecy didn't say anything about slaughter!"

"Why should it? You wanted to know if you could make more profit on your farms without further investment. Prices always rise when there is a shortage. Since you own most of the farmland in another hamlet that supplies the same city, you'll have great influence in setting the prices for a variety of crops."

"But you didn't say the shortage would be caused by people being killed!"

"And you didn't ask about anything but profit when the girl was cut."

An uneasy silence. "I should have phrased my request more carefully. I didn't mean to imply I had been given an inferior girl."

Quiet menace. "You paid for a cut on one of my best girls, and that is what you received."

"Yes, of course. You run the finest institution, and all of your girls are of exceptional quality. But for my next appointment, could I reserve cs759?"

"Cs759 is not, at present, on the roster."

"That's a shame. She has the finest skin. It's like she begins to attune to a prophecy even before the cut. When will you put her back in the roster?"

"Soon. I anticipate that she will be available again very soon."

CHAPTER 10

Meg sat back on her heels and stared at the Wolf pup, who stared back at her. Sam seemed shy, which made sense since she was a stranger, but he also seemed interested in getting to know her. At least, he seemed that way while she refilled his food and water bowls. But when she reached into the cage with a couple of paper towels to pick up the poop in the back corner, he snapped at her—and kept snapping every time she tried to reach in farther than the bowls, which were in the front of the cage.

"Come on, Sam. You don't want to smell poop all day, do you?"

The pup talked back at her. Since she didn't speak Wolf, she had no idea what he said, but she had the impression he was embarrassed, and her noticing the poop only made things worse, but she didn't know what to do about that. The *terra indigene* weren't human, didn't think like humans even when they were in a human skin. She'd learned that much in the week she'd been working for them. But they did have feelings. She'd learned that too.

She glanced at the wall clock and sighed. If she didn't get moving, she'd be late for work again.

She secured the cage door. "All right. You win, because I have to go to work. But this discussion isn't over."

He talked back, then lowered his head.

She'd bet a week's pay—if she had a paycheck yet—that Simon didn't take that kind of lip from a puppy. Of course, she didn't think Simon Wolfgard took that kind of lip from anyone.

She got to her feet and studied the pup. Why was he in a cage? If she asked, would anyone tell her?

He wasn't always in the cage. Sam had been outside the other night. Simon would rip her to pieces if she let Sam go outside and something happened to the pup. But there had to be *something* she could do that would keep them both safe so she could take him outside.

"I'll see you when I get back from work." No response to the words, but as she locked Simon's front door, she heard Sam's squeaky-door howl.

Telling herself she shouldn't feel guilty about leaving Sam by himself—after all, Simon did it all the time—she hurried to the garage, unhooked the BOW from its power supply, and headed for work. She still tended to stomp on the power pedal when backing up. Remembering all those training images from movies—clips of cars speeding up a ramp backward and sailing over another vehicle—kept interfering with the reality of a flat exit. But she was feeling more confident about forward driving, especially now that the main roads in the Courtyard were down to pavement.

She turned the sign on the office door to OPEN one minute after nine o'clock. As she poked her head out the door to say good morning to the four Crows on the wall and the Hawk who had claimed the top of the wooden sculpture—and the best view inside the office—she noticed Elliot Wolfgard coming out of the consulate.

Good clothes. Power attitude. Most of the men who had come to the compound and looked at her skin with a greed that was almost sexual had good clothes and that attitude.

Giving him a brisk nod, she withdrew and went back to the sorting room, closing the Private door partway. Then she braced her hands on the table and closed her eyes.

It had been a week since her last cut. Fear of making a bad cut with an unfamiliar blade had sufficiently dulled the craving for the euphoria. Fear and remembering things Jean had told her.

"They cut us so often for the money. I remember my ma saying that the more you cut, the more you want to cut. But Namid gave us the good feelings as a reward for cutting when folks

need help." Jean paused. "Of course, when cutting is the only thing that makes you feel good, most girls won't fight when they're put in the chair."

Was this what withdrawal felt like? The Walking Names always said the girls *needed* the cutting. Truth or lie? Did she really need a cut or did she just want the euphoria? Since she could make her own choices about her body, did it matter?

Top side of the arms would be the safest place without a watcher. Or the legs, as long as she stayed away from the inner thighs.

Slipping her hand in her jeans' pocket, Meg caressed the razor, her thumb running over the *cs759* engraved in the handle. A designation, not a name. And that *did* matter.

She heard the thump of boxes being set on the counter. Pulling her empty, trembling hand out of her pocket, she went out to take the first delivery.

Asia bought two takeout cups of hot chocolate at A Little Bite, then walked over to the Liaison's Office.

She'd spent an evening at Lakeside University, hanging around the girls who liked taking a walk on the wild side. She had hoped to glean some ideas for getting that kind of interest from the Others, but after an hour, she realized there were boys out there claiming to be what they weren't, and the girls who thought they had romped with a Wolf or a vampire had never seen a real one.

That gave her an idea for a way to get in by a side door, so to speak, but it still meant becoming pals with Meg. She was bound to learn something of interest by hanging around the Liaison's Office, and she'd also be able to scope out any possibilities working at the consulate.

And there had been that interesting phone call from her backers, who had heard from their contact in the mayor's office. Apparently, Meg had been a naughty girl, and White Van was looking for a thief, not a runaway spouse. So keeping tabs on Meg could be profitable all by itself.

A deliveryman held the door for her. Asia flashed him a smile, but she didn't bother to flirt because Meg was at the counter, looking baffled, and that made her curious.

"Problem?" she asked, setting the cups of hot chocolate on the counter.

"This store sent me eight catalogs," Meg said. "Why would a store send me eight of the same thing?"

"So you could distribute them?"

"For what?"

Just where did you come from that you don't know about ordering from catalogs?

"Haven't you noticed the ads in the *Lakeside News*? There are only so many newspapers that can be printed each day, and they're allowed to have only so many pages. When a store is running a special or a sale, they list the page number of the catalog where you can find the description. Even when there isn't a sale, lots of people check catalogs before going to a store and using up gasoline for the trip."

Meg's face went from baffled to excited. "This is good! Or it could be if the Others understand how to use catalogs. I can send one to each complex and can keep one for reference."

"There you go." Asia nudged the hot chocolate closer to Meg.

"What happens to the old catalogs?"

"They get collected and returned to the stores. A store's paper allowance is based on the amount of paper it's returning for recycling. The fewer catalogs the store returns, the fewer new catalogs it's allowed to print. When the spring catalog comes out, it will be an even trade—you'll get as many new catalogs as you hand in."

"I'll make a note of that so I can get the old ones back. Thanks, Asia."

"Glad to help." Asia hesitated, then decided the timing was good. "Say, Meg. Have you seen Simon around lately? Taking even a couple of classes at the university is expensive, and I'm still looking for some other work to help pay the bills. I wanted to see if he could use someone for one or two evenings a week at HGR. Preferably evenings when he's not on duty. He makes me nervous, so I act like a dummy around him, but I am a good worker. I really am."

Meg hesitated. "I don't think Simon will be in the store for a few days, but you could talk to Vlad. He's polite."

Asia didn't have to fake a shudder. "No, thank you. I like my neck just the way it is." Seeing Meg's blank look, she added, "You do know what he is, don't you?"

"Oh. Yes. I haven't had a lot of contact with him, but he's been courteous. He's certainly not as grumpy as the Wolves I've met."

Good to know, Asia thought. Maybe that meant the vampires considered the Liaison off-limits for dinner. She would be willing to have sex with a *terra indigene,* but she wanted some assurance that she would survive the experience. Maybe her mistake had been to target Simon. Maybe Vlad would have been a better choice for a lover. Donating a *little* blood for some useful pillow talk would be a fair exchange.

She gave Meg the "woman down on her luck but still has some pride" look she'd practiced in the mirror last night. And she didn't look at the hot chocolate she shouldn't have bought if she was broke—especially when places charged extra for disposable takeout cups.

Meg fiddled with the pens on the counter. Finally she said, "I can ask Vlad if they hire extra help on occasion."

"Appreciate it." Asia took a deep breath and put just the right note of false cheer in her voice. "Time for me to get going."

"Thanks for the hot chocolate."

With a careless wave, Asia left the office and hurried back to her car. It sounded like a little thing, but Simon being away from the Courtyard so soon after that incident out west was a solid nugget of information—especially when the newspapers and television news still didn't know what happened in Jerzy. Simon's absence was a good indication that the Others were somehow involved, and informing her backers was money in the bank for her.

And Simon being away gave her time to find out more about Meg and the man in the white van.

Days and months and years of training images and sounds. Snips and clips and photographs of the beautiful and the terrifying. Movies and documentaries and carefully edited bits from the news. During all those lessons, the Walking Names never told the girls which images were make-believe and which ones were real. *Real* was a word with little meaning beyond the cells and the physical things done to girls who were no longer useful enough to be "pampered"—things that gave the rest of them "the full experience" for the visions required by particular clients.

And there were the other images, the ones that swam under the surface of memory and rose without warning or context. The ones that came from prophecies. They looked different, felt different. Sometimes felt too alive, were experienced too much. But they were veiled by the euphoria, and the Walking Names didn't know the girls never forgot anything that was seen or heard during the visions. No, nothing was really forgotten, but those rememories, as Jean called them, couldn't be deliberately recalled like the training images.

Meg shook her head, pushed those thoughts away, and went back to sorting mail. Thinking about the compound wouldn't do anything but give her bad dreams tonight. She needed to remember something that would help her deal with Sam. *Had* she seen anything in all those binders filled with images that would be helpful now?

"Meg?"

She heard the voice a moment before Merri Lee poked her head in from the back room.

"Would you like to split a pizza with Heather and me?" Merri Lee asked. "Hot Crust is in the plaza a few blocks from here, and today is one of the days a Courtyard bus takes *terra indigene* for a shopping trip. Henry said he would pick up the pizza for us as long as I ordered a couple of party-size pizzas for the Green Complex."

Meg frowned. "Doesn't Hot Crust make deliveries?"

"They used to, but there was an . . . incident . . . and they won't come to the Courtyard anymore." Merri Lee brightened. "But maybe they'll start delivering again now that you're the Liaison."

Meg searched her memory for images of different kinds of pizza. Images of people eating pizza. She had been given a piece once in order to know taste, texture, and smell.

"I don't like the little salty fish," she said. She wasn't sure that was true, but she hadn't liked the look of them.

"Neither do we," Merri Lee said. "We usually get half with pepperoni and mushrooms and half with sweet peppers. Is that good for you?"

"That's fine. But I don't have any money."

"This one is on us—a welcome to the Courtyard. The last Liaison made Heather and me uneasy, so we are really glad you're here. And speaking of money." Merri Lee handed an envelope to Meg. "Your first pay envelope. It covers the three days you worked last week."

Meg opened the envelope and stared at the bills in various denominations.

"I know," Merri Lee said. "Most companies write paychecks. In the Courtyard, you get cash, and it's up to you to set enough aside to pay your income taxes, because they don't bother with anything like that either. You can open an account at the Market Square bank so you could write checks for expenses outside the Courtyard. Or there's a bank in the plaza that the Business Association uses when they write checks for outside vendors."

"I don't think this is the right amount," Meg said, riffling through the bills. "It's too much for the hours I worked last week."

"That's the other thing about working for the Others. You will never get less than what they agreed to pay you, but sometimes they give you more without explanation. We figure it's their way of saying 'Good job—don't quit' without actually having to say it. They don't do it every week, but Lorne says if you don't get a bumped-up pay at least once in a month, you should take it as a warning that you're doing something the Business Association doesn't like." Merri Lee headed for the back door, saying over her shoulder, "They're predicting more snow tonight. I hope it misses the city. If it piles up any more, we'll have to climb snowbanks and go into our houses through second-story windows."

Training image. Snow and barren, vertical rock. Men clinging to the rock, tied together with ropes.

Ropes. Safety lines. Buddies.

Meg hurried to the back room, catching Merri Lee on the doorstep. "When does the bus leave for the plaza?" she asked, feeling her skin almost buzz in response to her excitement.

"Eleven thirty. It returns from the plaza at one thirty."

"Thanks."

As soon as Merri Lee left, Meg went back to the sorting room and pulled out the Lakeside phone book. Ropes wouldn't work, but . . . Yes! The plaza had a pet store. She should be able to find something there that would be comfortable for Sam and keep them together.

Her hand hovered over the telephone while she went through the list of Others she knew. Vlad and Tess would be working in their own stores. So would Jenni. And Henry would be on the bus. Julia or Allison? Maybe. Blair? Remembering what he said about deliverymen and Wolves, definitely not. Which left . . .

The phone was answered on the second ring. "Pony Barn. Jester speaking."

"This is Meg."

A pause. "Is there a problem, Meg?"

Did her name automatically mean trouble? "No, but I wanted to ask you for a favor."

"Ask."

"There's something I want to get at the plaza, and the bus leaves at eleven thirty. I need someone to watch the office in case a delivery comes in before we close for the afternoon break."

"I'll come up with the ponies and stay until you get back."

"Thanks, Jester."

After hanging up, she stared at the phone and thought about what she was about to do. It was safe in the Courtyard. No one could touch her in the Courtyard. But in a human plaza where human law *did* apply?

Risky.

She turned her right hand palm up and studied the scars on the back of each finger. Didn't usually get much from a finger cut. A few disjointed images at the most.

Get on a bus full of *terra indigene* with a fresh cut on her hand? Did she really want to take the chance of setting off an attack? Besides, she was pretty sure Henry knew she was a *cassandra sangue*, so how would she explain the cut if he noticed it?

"You don't need to cut to go to the store," she told herself. "Jester is the only one who knows for sure that you're leaving the Courtyard. You'll be fine. Just buy the things for Sam, then go back to the bus and wait for the rest of them."

She briskly rubbed both arms and tried to ignore the pins and needles under her skin by focusing on the mail she had to get ready for the ponies.

It's a good thing Captain Burke expects each of his lieutenants to report at least once per shift, Monty thought as he stepped into Burke's office. Otherwise, the other men would start wondering if he was screwing up big-time.

"Something to report, Lieutenant?" Burke asked.

"Someone named Jester called to tell me Meg Corbyn was on the Courtyard's shopping bus, along with about fifteen Others, including Henry Beargard and Vladimir Sanguinati."

Burke stared at him, and Monty couldn't read anything in those blue eyes that gave him a clue as to what the man was thinking.

"Give me a minute, and then I'll buy you lunch," Burke finally said. "We'll take my car, so tell Officer Kowalski to meet you at the plaza. Maybe he'd like to pick up some lunch or stretch his legs."

Leaving Burke, Monty waited at his own desk for Kowalski. No messages.

No reports. And thank the gods, no DLUs to fill out. He hoped that would still be true after the *terra indigenes'* shopping trip.

When Kowalski joined him, he told Karl about the call and that he and Captain Burke would be at the plaza.

"But he wants a patrol car parked nearby," Kowalski said, nodding. "I probably won't be the only one. The Courtyard bus brings Others to that plaza every Sunsday and Firesday at the same time. Patrol cars tend to drive through the parking lot or park for a while to pick up lunch. Helps to keep everyone honest."

"I'll see you there," Monty said as Burke walked out of his office, adjusting the collar of his winter coat.

He wasn't sure if Burke expected small talk from his officers or wanted silence in order to concentrate on driving. A thin layer of snow covered the streets, and after seeing a couple of cars fishtail while trying to stop at a light, he decided not to pull Burke's attention from the road.

Asia followed the Courtyard bus to the plaza, parking where she could see the dark green vehicle but wouldn't be noticed by the Others. Scanning the lot, she noticed a white van pull in from the other direction.

Not a good place for a snatch unless Meg walked so close to the van that the driver could grab her and be gone before the *terra indigene* realized there was trouble.

Then a patrol car pulled into the lot and parked a few spaces down from the bus, and another one pulled in from the opposite direction and also parked a few spaces away.

"Damn," Asia whispered. Wasn't unusual to see cop cars in the plaza on the Others' shopping days, but they weren't even trying to be subtle this time. Which meant they were more worried than usual and were going to shut down trouble before it started.

Were they antsy because of what happened in Jerzy, or was there a more immediate concern?

Asia figured she had an answer of sorts when Meg Corbyn stepped off the bus.

Burke parked a couple of spots from the small, dark green bus with LAKESIDE COURTYARD painted on the side.

"I wouldn't think they would want to advertise which vehicle was theirs,"

Monty said. He looked around at the rapidly filling parking lot. "Especially since they've parked the bus to take up four spaces."

"It's advertised so that the relatives of anyone who starts trouble can't claim the meat didn't know they were messing with the Courtyard's vehicle. Besides, the plaza blocks off those four spaces to give the *terra indigene* plenty of room. Safer for everyone that way."

Absorbing the significance of the word *meat,* Monty felt his stomach twitch and suddenly wasn't sure he wanted lunch.

Burke got out of the car and moved toward the bus. Hurrying after him, Monty saw the reason. Meg looked at both of them as she stepped off the bus, her face turning pale. Moving to one side to let the rest of the *terra indigene* exit, she stayed close to the bus. A big man whom Monty recognized as the sculptor and assumed was Henry Beargard stepped down, looked at them, and growled—and the rest of the Others, who had been heading toward the stores, all turned back to stare at him and Burke.

Beargard took a step to the right. Vladimir Sanguinati stepped down and, somehow, slid between Meg and the bus to stand on her left.

Feeling the tension, Monty wasn't sure what to do. They had called him, so why this hostility?

Because she's afraid, he realized as he looked at Meg. *She's afraid, and the Others are waiting to see what we do where human law could apply.*

"Ms. Corbyn," Monty said, forcing his lips into a smile. "May I introduce my captain, Douglas Burke?"

"It's a pleasure to meet you, Ms. Corbyn," Burke said, extending his hand.

She hesitated, and Monty didn't dare breathe until she shook Burke's hand.

"Thank you, Captain Burke," she said. "If you'll excuse me?" The rest of the *terra indigene* except Vlad and Henry scattered to take care of their own concerns while Meg hurried to the stores on the other side of the parking lot.

"When we called Lieutenant Montgomery, we weren't expecting to see an officer of such high rank," Vlad said, looking at Burke.

Burke's smile might have passed for genial if you didn't know the man. "I'm taking the lieutenant to the Saucy Plate for lunch to introduce him to some of the best red sauce in the city."

"An excellent choice for dining. I, too, enjoy a good red sauce," Vlad said.

Burke's smile froze.

"Captain?" Monty said. "We should get a seat before the lunch crowd arrives."

With a nod at Vlad and Henry, Burke turned and led the way to the Saucy Plate. Monty said nothing until they were seated and the waitress handed out menus and took their orders for coffee.

"Captain, I don't think he meant it to sound . . ." Monty trailed off, unwilling to lie to the man.

"To sound threatening?" Burke asked. "Oh, I'm sure he did. They floated that phone call to see what we would do, but they don't trust us—not in general and, specifically, not where Meg Corbyn is concerned." He smiled at the waitress when she brought the coffee and took their orders. "You've met Vladimir Sanguinati before. Any reason why you didn't introduce me?"

Monty shivered and rubbed the palm of his right hand. "I didn't want to put you in the position of having to shake his hand."

Burke gave Monty's hand a long look, then turned the conversation to small talk and stories about Lakeside.

When Meg reached the Pet Palace on the other side of the plaza, she glanced around. The Others who had been on the bus with her weren't in sight, but there were birds on most of the parking-lot lights. She couldn't tell if they were crows or Crows. Not that it mattered. If this worked, everyone in the Green Complex would know about her purchases.

Hopefully the Others would realize she was just trying to help Sam and not eat her for doing it.

"Can I help you?" the clerk asked as soon as she walked in the door.

Meg gave the man a bright smile. "I'm looking for a dog harness and a long leash."

He led her to an aisle that had a bewildering assortment of leashes, harnesses, and collars.

"What size dog?" he asked.

She chewed on her lower lip. "Well, he's still a puppy, but he's a big puppy. At least, I think he would be considered a big puppy."

"Your first dog?" The clerk sounded delighted. "What breed is it?"

"He's a Wolf."

She thought the movie clips of someone's skin turning a sickly green had been make-believe. Apparently not.

"You want to put a harness *on a Wolf*?"

There was something in the clerk's voice—shock? fear?—that made her wonder how much trouble she was going to be in until she could think of some other way of getting Sam safely outside. "He's young, and I don't want him to get hurt if I take him for a walk."

She didn't see anyone else in the store, but he leaned closer. "How did you get your hands on a Wolf pup?"

"I'm the Courtyard Liaison. He lives in the apartment next to mine. Are you going to help me or not?"

She wasn't sure he would, but he finally reached for a harness. His hands shook and his voice cracked, but based on what information she could give him, he found a red harness that he thought would fit and a long red leash that would give Sam room to roam.

"Will there be anything else?" the clerk asked.

Meg thought about it. "What kind of toys would a puppy like?"

She ended up with a ball and a length of knotted rope. Then she spotted dog cookies and picked up boxes of beef flavor and chicken flavor.

The clerk looked so relieved when she handed over her big zippered shopping bag, she wondered if the store would be closed from now on when the Others usually came to the plaza.

"Do you have a catalog?" she asked.

He slipped two into the bag. "Orders are usually next-day delivery."

She paid for her purchases and sighed with relief when she was on the sidewalk. She hadn't done anything wrong, but she wasn't sure how the Others felt about pet stores. She started to walk between two parked cars, then stopped, unable to take another step.

Rememory. A car door suddenly opening as a young woman walked past. Strong hands reaching, grabbing. Dark hood. Hard to breathe. Impossible to see. And those hands touching and . . .

"Are you all right?"

Meg jerked back and almost slipped, then almost slipped again trying to avoid the hand reaching for her.

Crows cawed, sounding a warning.

She focused on the man, who now stood very still. Police officer. Not one of the two who had introduced themselves, but not unfamiliar.

"Officer Kowalski, ma'am. I work with Lieutenant Montgomery."

She let her breath out slowly. She'd seen him in the car the day the lieutenant stopped in.

"My thoughts wandered," she said. "I wasn't watching where I was going." That wouldn't explain whatever he'd seen in her face when he reached for her, but the way he looked at her told her plainly enough her explanation, while true in its way, wasn't quite good enough to be believed.

"Let me give you a hand back to the bus. The parking lot is a little slick today."

Feeling unsteady and understanding that making an excuse to refuse his help would cause trouble, she accepted his arm—and noticed, even across the parking lot, the way Vlad stiffened as he watched them. She also noticed the way two more police officers got out of a patrol car and began looking around.

"Was anyone abducted from this plaza recently?" Meg asked, only noticing the prickling in her legs when the sensation began to fade.

"Ma'am?" Kowalski gave her a sharp look.

Rememories and images didn't use to flood her mind like this when she wasn't focused on a particular question, wasn't strapped in for a cutting and prophecy. When other people talked about recalling memories and information, was this what they experienced—this immediate association of one thing to another?

Did that mean she was starting to process the information around her like other people did, or was this the first stage of madness in a *cassandra sangue*? The Walking Names told the girls they would go mad if they tried to live outside the compound. Only Jean insisted that they wouldn't, but she really was half mad.

"It's nothing," Meg lied. "Overactive imagination. I have to stop reading scary stories before bedtime."

He nodded. "My fiancée says the same thing. Doesn't stop her from reading them."

Releasing his arm when they reached the bus—and Vlad—Meg smiled at Kowalski. "Thank you for the escort."

"My pleasure, ma'am." Nodding to Vlad, he returned to his patrol car.

"Problem?" Vlad asked.

She shook her head.

"You want to do any more shopping?"

She shook her head again. She wanted to get out of sight, wanted to hide. The need to do that was almost painful, and she didn't know what was making her feel that way. But she did remember how Simon had calmed down in response to her acting calm, so it wasn't hard to guess that predators didn't react well around fear.

"I'd like to put this in the bus and then make some notes about what stores are here," she said.

"I'll take that." Vlad's hand closed around the top of her carry bag.

She couldn't think of a way to refuse his help without making him curious about her purchases, so she surrendered the bag, then pulled a notebook out of her purse. As the Others trickled back to the bus with sacks bulging with merchandise, Meg made a list of the stores—and tried to ignore the feeling that more than the police and the *terra indigene* were watching her.

Asia slumped in her seat, peering over the dashboard as the Courtyard bus pulled out of the parking lot.

"Gods," she muttered when White Van pulled out moments later. "Can you be more obvious?" The fool had been walking toward Meg and was barely a handful of cars away when that police officer approached her. Cops and Crows and a freaking vampire all watching the parking lot. Watching *Meg*. Did that idiot really think he could have gotten away if he'd even made a grab for her? At best, he'd be having a long chat with the cops. At worst, pieces of him would be all over the damn parking lot.

Satisfied there was no one left who would notice her, she started her car.

Time to call Bigwig to see if he had any other information about Meg Corbyn. Someone who was supposed to be a thief shouldn't be getting police protection. Could be a cover story. A woman on the run being smoked out of hiding by a false accusation of theft. She's taken into custody, and one cop believes her story and helps her escape. Then the two of them are on the run, racing against time to uncover a deadly conspiracy.

That kind of movie could be a hit. She'd have to write up the idea and talk to Bigwig about it. Instead of a movie, maybe it could be a two-part special story in the Asia Crane, SI, TV show that would introduce the cop who might be an information source and/or lover.

While she was discussing that story idea with Bigwig, maybe he would be able to find out why so many people were paying attention to the Courtyard's Liaison.

Meg knelt in front of Sam's cage. She had hoped that everyone else would still be working, but apparently even the businesses available to human customers sometimes closed on a whim.

Or maybe the pizzas Henry took up to the social room were the reason the residents of the Green Complex were home early.

If she waited until dark to try this, they had less chance of being seen, but it might be scarier for Sam. So they would do this now.

"Sam," she said. "I think we should try the buddy system so we can go outside together."

He whined and shivered.

"When humans climb mountains, they tie a rope around themselves that connects them to their buddy. That way, if one of them gets stuck in a snowdrift, the other can pull him out."

She was mashing images together in a way that might not make a realistic whole, but she figured Sam wouldn't know that. Besides, there weren't any mountains in the Courtyard, but there were significant drifts that could bury either one of them.

"So I bought these." She held up the leash. "See? It's a safety line. I loop this around my waist, like this." She slipped one end of the leash through the wrist loop, then stepped into the bigger loop and pulled it up to her waist. "This end clips to a harness that you wear, since that's better than squashing you around the middle." She clipped the leash to the harness and held it up for him to see. "Want to try the buddy system? We wouldn't go far. Just a walk around the inside of the complex. What do you think?"

She opened the cage door. She was pretty sure Sam couldn't get out of the apartment, but she remembered movie clips of what a house looked like after a dog, chased by a human, ran through it.

If that happened, Simon would take one look at his home when he returned and eat her.

Sam crept to the door of the cage and stretched his neck to sniff the harness. He looked at the harness, then looked at her . . . and stepped out of the cage, making anxious little sounds.

"All right," she said brightly. "Let's go walk in the snow!"

She shimmied out of her end of the leash and put the harness on him, double-checking to make sure nothing was too tight. Then she put on her coat and shimmied the leash back up to her waist. Sam hesitated and looked ready to bolt back into his cage, but he followed her to the front door and pressed himself against her legs, which made putting on her boots a balancing act.

Zipping Simon's keys into her jacket pocket, she opened the front door, and she and Sam stepped outside.

Closing the door, she took a deep breath, grabbed her end of the leash before the loosened loop slipped down, and moved away from the building. After a moment, Sam followed her.

"There's Henry and Vlad," she said, spotting the vampire and Grizzly on the other side of the complex. "Let's go over and say hello." She started walking but stopped as soon as she felt a tug around her middle. She looked back at Sam, who hadn't moved but was now studying the red leash stretched between them.

Meg smiled. "See? Safety line."

His tail began to wag. He trotted up to her, and the two of them followed the walkway until they reached Vlad and Henry.

She couldn't identify the expressions on their faces. Since they weren't yelling at her—or threatening to eat her—she gave them a bright smile and said, "Sam and I are mighty adventurers, just like in the movies."

"I can see that," Henry replied after a moment. He looked at Sam. "You can follow a scent better than she can, so you make sure our Liaison doesn't get lost."

Sam replied in Wolf, and she and the pup continued their circuit around the complex.

Watching the woman and Wolf pup, Vlad felt relieved that Simon wasn't going to be within easy reach of a telephone. When he'd promised to keep an eye on those two, he hadn't anticipated Meg doing anything like *this.*

"That's Sam," he said, struggling to keep his voice neutral and not provoke the Grizzly.

"It is," Henry agreed.

"That's Sam *on a leash.*" Because their second form couldn't be contained by such things, the Sanguinati didn't have the hatred of chains and cages that filled the shifters, but even he felt anger at seeing a *terra indigene* being treated like a . . .

a . . . dog. He could imagine what Blair or, even worse, Elliot would say if they found out.

Hearing the Crows, he amended that thought to *when* they found out.

"And that's Meg with a leash around her waist," Henry said as Sam ran around her in circles and pulled her legs out from under her, dumping them both in a snowbank. "Hard to get away from what's on the other end, but a good way to haul someone back if there's trouble."

A good way to capture two instead of just one. But Vlad didn't say that. He just watched while girl and pup got untangled and climbed out of the snow.

"Something frightened her at the plaza," Henry said. "For a moment, the air carried the scent of the man who tried to break in to the efficiency apartments. But with all the police around, it was not a good time to hunt."

Vlad watched as Meg and Sam started the second circuit around the complex, heading back toward him and Henry. Sam was ahead of Meg now, sniffing at everything. Then he bounced back to Meg for a moment before bounding into the lead again.

This was the Sam he remembered before Daphne was killed—an exuberant pup. How could a piece of leather that should have offended make so much difference? *Why* did it make so much difference?

Sam was digging at something in the snow, and Meg was watching Sam. So neither of them saw Blair standing at the entrance to the complex, his mouth hanging open as he stared at the leash and harness.

"Henry," Vlad said.

"I see him."

Before Meg and Sam noticed him, Blair stepped out of sight. Not gone, no, but watching as Sam took a running leap and disappeared in a drift.

He howled that squeaky-door sound that couldn't be mistaken for any other Wolf. Meg laughed and took a step back. "Climb, Sam. Climb! We are adventure buddies scaling the mighty snow!" She pulled, and Sam climbed until he got out of the drift. He shook himself off and looked at Meg, tail wagging, tongue hanging out in a grin.

"Time for dinner?" she asked the pup.

His answer was to set off at a brisk pace, pulling her along behind him.

When Meg and Sam were inside Simon's apartment, Vlad watched Blair reappear at the entrance, looking wary. That harness and leash would infuriate all the Wolves in the Courtyard. Without Simon's presence, Blair, as the Courtyard's main enforcer, would either defend Meg or let the other Wolves have her for this offense. Which would bring the Wolves into conflict with the Sanguinati, because Grandfather Erebus was entertained by the Liaison and her courtesies, and he had made it clear that Meg was under his protection until he said otherwise.

Blair looked at them, nodded, and walked away.

"What do you think?" Vlad asked.

"See what you can find in the books or the computer about adventurers and ropes. See if you can find out why Meg did this."

"I can look. Or I can just ask her."

"Or you can just ask her." A thoughtful pause. "She does not think like other humans, and she does not think like us. She is something new, something little known and not understood. But she found a way to quiet Sam's fear, and that should not be forgotten."

No, that shouldn't be forgotten, which was something he would point out to Blair.

Henry blew out a breath. "Come. There is pizza and a movie. What was chosen for the entertainment?"

Vlad smiled, revealing the Sanguinati fangs. "*Night of the Wolf.*"

CHAPTER 11

Her coat dangling from one arm, Meg rushed back into Simon's living room and shrieked, "Sam! What are you doing? Stop that! Stop!"

The pup continued chewing at the cage and pushing his little paws against the wires so hard that it looked like his toes had elongated into furry fingers that were trying to reach the latch.

She banged the cage with the flat of her hand, startling him enough to take a step back.

"Stop that!" she scolded. "You're going to break a tooth or cut your paws. What's wrong with you?"

He talked at her. She threw her hands up in exasperation.

"You have food. You have water. You already ate the cookies, and we had a quick walk. I have to go to work now. If I'm late again, Elliot Wolfgard will *bite* me, and I bet he bites *hard*."

Sam lifted his muzzle and wailed.

Meg stared at him and wondered what happened to the sweet puppy she had brushed yesterday evening, the puppy who had snuggled on the couch with her while she watched a television program. He'd been fine about going into the cage when she said it was time for bed. He hadn't made a fuss about her going back to her own apartment. And he'd been fine when she came over this morning—until she tried to leave.

"You can't go to work with me," Meg said. "You'd be bored, and I can't be playing with you. You stay home all the time when Simon goes to work."

Sam howled.

"I can come back during my lunch break for a walk."

Sam *howled*.

If she left, would he stop howling? If she left, would he *still* be howling when she got back? How much longer before Vlad or Henry or Tess started pounding on the door to find out what was wrong? Or was this something Sam did every morning and the residents were used to it?

Maybe they were, but she wasn't.

"All right!" she yelled. She opened the cage door. "Out! Out out out. Wait for me by the door."

Sam rushed out of the cage and busied himself trying to tug harness and leash off the coat peg by the front door.

Meg grabbed his food and water bowls and hurried to the kitchen. Finding a clean, empty coffee can with a lid in one of the bottom cupboards, she filled it with kibble and threw a few cookies on top, poured the water down the sink and dried the bowl, then grabbed one of the big carry sacks hanging from a peg and filled it with Sam's things. A moment's thought about snow and puppies had her running upstairs to snag a bath towel from the linen closet.

"I'm late, I'm late, I'm late," she muttered as she ran down the stairs. She stuffed Sam into the harness, ignoring his complaints because she didn't smooth all of his fur in the right direction. "I'll fix it after we get to the office."

Pup, purse, her carry sack, Sam's carry sack. The towel over one arm, the leash looped around her wrist. Juggling everything, she opened the door, fumbling for the keys in her pocket. Just as she pulled them out, Sam jerked on the leash, yanking her off balance.

She dropped the keys—and an olive-skinned hand caught them before they hit the ground.

"Need a hand?" Vlad said, smiling at her.

"Or a mallet."

He looked baffled—and very amused. "I don't understand."

She shook her head.

He locked Simon's front door and handed her the keys.

"Thank you," she said, dumping the keys in her purse and digging for the BOW's key. "I'm having a difficult morning. Sam! Stop tugging at me!"

"Is it that time of the month?" Vlad asked.

Some feeling blew through her. It might have been embarrassment, but she suspected it was closer to rage. "*What?*"

He studied her. "Is that not an appropriate question to ask?"

"No!"

"Odd. In many novels I've read, human males often ask that question when a female is acting . . ." Puzzlement as he continued to study her face. "Although, now that I consider it, they usually don't make that observation to the female herself."

"I have to go to work now," Meg said, enunciating each word.

"Ah." He looked at Sam, then at the carry sacks and the towel. "Where is Sam going?"

"He's coming with me."

Something in Vlad's eyes. Surprise? Panic? She would be okay with panic. It would mean she wasn't the only one who felt out of control today.

Although a vampire feeling out of control might not be healthy for the people around him.

"I'll help you with those," Vlad said.

She didn't argue, especially since she hadn't found the BOW's key yet. Vlad flung the towel over his shoulder and held the handles of the carry sacks in one hand as if the sacks weighed nothing, then led the way to the garages, leaving her to deal with Sam. She shortened the leash to keep the pup from running around her in circles. The way things were going, she would end up face-first in the snow. Again.

The way things were going, if she didn't put her foot down, she would end up puppy-sitting a little tyrant.

She was still trying to find her key—and wondering if she'd left it on her kitchen table—when Vlad dipped a hand in his pocket, pulled out a key, and opened the back of her BOW.

"What?" she stammered. "How?"

"Any BOW key works for all the BOWs in this Courtyard," Vlad said. "Makes it easier, since very few of them are designated for a particular individual."

While she stared at him, he picked up Sam, wiped the pup's feet, then placed pup and towel where Sam could look out between the front seats. He tucked the sacks in the back. "Are you riding in the back?" He wagged a finger at the leash still looped over her wrist.

She stripped off the leash and tossed it in the back. Vlad closed the door and walked over to the driver's side. He was courteous, and except for that crack about PMS, he was polite. But she had the distinct impression he was laughing at her.

"It's my BOW, so I'm driving," she said.

"Found your key yet?" He didn't wait for her answer. "Since I do have a key, I'm driving—and neither of us will be too late for work."

She made a growling sound that had his eyebrows shooting up in surprise, but she was beaten for the moment, so she went around to the passenger's side and got in.

The BOWs were built to tootle around an enclosed community like a Courtyard, but knowing Elliot had been grumbling over the Liaison's tardiness, Vlad nudged the vehicle to its top speed, aware that Meg was trying to watch him without appearing to watch him. From what the members of the Business Association had been able to piece together by observing her, Meg absorbed what she saw and heard with unnerving clarity, and those remembered images became her reference to the world. What she saw she could repeat and do—up to a point. There were gaps, omissions of information, that they suspected were deliberate, so that blood prophets could do very few things independently. From what Tess had gleaned from questioning Merri Lee, Meg could identify a lot of objects, but she knew what very few of them did.

Which made her escape from the compound where she had lived to her arrival at their Courtyard all the more remarkable. Somehow, she had figured out enough to run away—and stay alive while she did it.

Thinking about what Henry and Tess—and Simon—would say if Meg ended up in a ditch because of watching how *he* drove, Vlad slowed to a moderate speed and took care not to do anything that would be considered bad driving. That was something they had agreed on—be precise when showing the Liaison how to do something so that she learned what she needed to know.

Of course, Simon had ignored that completely when he rushed off and dumped a Wolf pup in her lap.

Something new, Henry had said about her. Something little known and not understood. She was all of that. And she was a potential threat, because someone with Meg's ability to remember images and accurately describe them could tell an enemy too much about their Courtyard and about the *terra indigene.*

He pushed those thoughts aside when a Hawk, an Owl, and four Crows all came winging toward them from the direction of the Liaison's Office.

<Monkeys are waiting for the Meg,> the Hawk told Vlad.

<We're almost there,> he replied to all of them. <The humans will wait for her.>

<We will tell Nyx,> the Crows said as they circled around, and went winging back.

He wasn't far behind them, so a minute later he pulled up at the Liaison's Office, parking close to the back door. "You go in and get settled. I'll bring Sam and the bags."

"Thanks," Meg replied, jumping out of the BOW.

Sam tried to scramble into the front seat and follow her, but Vlad grabbed him as Meg closed the door. The pup struggled for a moment, then stared out the window, making anxious sounds.

<Listen to me, Sam. Listen,> Vlad said. <This building is a place where we deal with humans. There will be many of them coming and going. Meg will be talking to them. You're afraid of them, but if you're going to stay here with Meg, you have to be brave. Do you understand?>

No answer except that shallow, anxious breathing, accompanied by a whine.

Vlad sighed. How had Simon endured this silence from a pup he loved?

He got out of the BOW, carrying Sam so he wouldn't have to dry off the pup. After setting him on the floor in the back room—and watching while Sam rushed into the sorting room to find Meg—he took the sacks and towel out of the BOW and carried them inside.

Moving silently, he entered the sorting room. Sam was sniffing one corner of the room, now oblivious to everything except the scent he'd found. Opening the Private door all the way, he looked at the tableau and thought, *A Crow, a prophet, and a vampire walk into an office . . .*

Then he huffed out a breath. It sounded like the beginning of one of those stupid jokes the *terra indigene* never understood.

Three deliverymen, all holding boxes and all standing back from the counter. Dropping the pen it was holding, the Crow cawed at them, walked to one end of the counter, selected another pen, then returned and tapped the pen on the paper clamped to the clipboard.

The men hesitated to approach, as if that small distance would make any difference. If Nyx wanted to feed, there wasn't anything her prey could do to stop her. If she had been wearing jeans and a sweater, the men wouldn't have known she was one of the Sanguinati. But Nyx preferred wearing a long, black velvet gown that had a modest train and those draping sleeves—the kind of garment female vampires often wore in the old movies Grandfather loved so much. Wearing it amused her because she said it was a way to tell her prey what she was, even before she began to feed.

Still in her winter coat, Meg took the pen from the Crow. Smiling and talking to the men, she quickly filled out the information while they set the packages on the handcart and kept glancing at Nyx.

Realizing none of the men were leaving, Vlad said, <Nyx.>

<I have done nothing. It is their own fear that holds them,> she replied, her dark eyes watching the men while she remained perfectly still. <Meg will do her work, and I will remain where I am.>

<Why stay?> he asked, although he made no move to withdraw.

<To teach the humans that they're not prey when they are in this office. They will learn we do not harm those who deal with Meg, even if she is delayed. They will value her because of that and be a different kind of guard.>

<Have you heard something to indicate there is a reason for another kind of guard?>

<She pleases Grandfather. That is reason enough to keep her safe,> Nyx replied.

Meg smiled at the deliverymen as they walked out the door together and got into their trucks or vans. She continued to smile until they drove away. Then she blew out a breath and turned to Nyx and the Crow.

"Thank you for opening the office. I don't mean to be late every morning. Things have gotten complicated the past couple of days."

Looking over his shoulder at Sam, who was still busily sniffing his way around the sorting room, Vlad said, "That's understandable."

"It was entertaining," Nyx said. "And Jake knew what to do."

The Crow who was pulling pens out of the holder and arranging them on the counter looked at them and cawed.

"I think there is a package for Mr. Erebus from the movie place," Meg said. "Do you want to take it with you?"

Nyx laughed. "And deprive him of a visit from you? No. But I will tell him a package has arrived." She changed to smoke, from feet to chest, and floated over the counter. Returning to solid form, she held out her arm to the Crow, who hopped on to be taken outside.

Meg stared as the Crow flew off and Nyx changed completely to smoke that flowed toward the access way leading to the Market Square. Then she stared at the counter, and finally at Vlad. "Am I the *only* one who needs to use the go-through?"

Feeling Sam come up beside him, Vlad grinned at her. "No, you're not the only one. At least for now. I'll park the BOW in the garage for you. If you don't find your key, let me know and I'll drive you home."

He didn't wait for her answer. He needed to open HGR, and he wanted to let Henry know Sam was with Meg—assuming Jake hadn't already told the Courtyard's spirit guide.

And he still needed to find a subtle way of warning everyone in the Courtyard that, until Simon returned, he and Henry Beargard would be looking after Meg and Sam.

Meg put out kibble and water for Sam, smoothed the fur under the harness, and let him roam the sorting room without the leash. After she barely missed stepping on his tail or toes a couple of times, he settled down where he was out of the way but could watch her sort the mail and packages. The package for Mr. Erebus from the movie place was small enough to go with the mail, but remembering what Nyx said, Meg put it with the afternoon deliveries—including a special delivery for Winter that she hadn't yet had a chance to make.

The morning passed quickly. When she heard the ponies, she snapped the leash to Sam's harness and slipped the other end over her wrist before opening the outer door, just in case the pup decided to bolt outside. But Sam, while intrigued, was happy to stay with her as she walked back and forth from table to ponies. For their part, the ponies seemed curious but unconcerned about the pup.

Congratulating herself on getting through another week without getting eaten or fired, she tapped the stack of papers that held her notes about the week's deliveries. Her little finger slid along the papers' edge.

A shiver of pain came before blood welled from the slice along the joint. She stared at her left hand, trying to remember something from her lessons that would explain the cut, unwilling to believe that paper could slice skin. Then the *pain* came, smothering her chest and twisting her belly.

Sam howled in terror.

She looked at the pup to reassure him, hoping to shape ordinary words before the prophecy began flowing through her.

Except Sam wasn't howling. He stood next to her, watching her anxiously as her own body told him something was wrong.

Sam wasn't howling. But she could hear him. Even now, knowing he wasn't making a sound, she could still hear him.

The vision had started. She didn't know what was coming, what images she would see. But if Sam was part of it . . . If she spoke to experience the euphoria, she wouldn't remember enough, if she remembered anything at all, and no one would know why Sam was afraid. But if she didn't speak, if she swallowed the words so that *she* could see the prophecy . . . For Sam's sake, could she endure the pain?

"Stay here," she said through gritted teeth. She hurried to the bathroom and shut the door before Sam could follow her.

Her throat felt clogged with terrible things. Leaning over the sink, she struggled to breathe as pain crawled through her and the vision filled her mind as if she were watching a stuttering movie clip.

Men. Dressed all in black. Even their faces, their heads, were black. Some had guns; others carried rifles . . . *skip* . . .One man was grabbing at something, but she couldn't see . . . *skip* . . . A sound like a car mated to a hornet . . . *skip* . . . Snow falling so fast and fierce and thick, she couldn't get a sense of place, couldn't tell if she was seeing the Courtyard or the city or somewhere else that had a snowstorm . . . *skip* . . . But Sam was there, howling in terror.

Meg came back to herself when the muscles in her hands cramped from holding on to the sink so hard.

Focus on breathing, she told herself. *The pain will fade. You know it will fade.*

She washed her hands, taking care to thoroughly clean the little finger.

Such a small slice along the edge of that joint. If she sliced it again to lengthen it, maybe she could see more. And maybe she would see another prophecy, but it would be mashed with the images she'd already seen in this small cut. The

Walking Names called the result of cutting over a previous cut a double vision, that nightmarish occurrence when one prophecy imposed itself over another and the images collided in ways that usually had terrible, mind-breaking consequences for the girl who saw them.

Sometimes the colliding images weren't terrible. Sometimes, if the girl could accept what she was seeing, the images could change a life. They had changed hers when the Controller had cut across old scars as a punishment. The colliding prophecies had shown her the first steps of her escape.

Just because she had survived double visions before didn't mean her mind wouldn't break if she tried it again.

She dried off her hands, got antiseptic and a bandage from the first-aid kit, and took care of the slice. Moving slowly, she returned to the sorting room and Sam. Opening her personal notebook to a clean page, she wrote down what she had seen while the details were fresh.

She had to tell someone, but who would listen?

Wishing she could talk to Simon, Meg reached for the phone and made a call. The phone at the other end rang and rang. Then the answering machine picked up.

"Henry? This is Meg. I need to talk to you."

Henry arrived a minute after she locked up for her lunch break. Leaving Sam in the sorting room with a couple of cookies, she found herself unable to look at the big man, let alone say anything.

"You're hurt," he finally said.

She shook her head.

"You smell of pain, of weakness."

Not weakness. No, she wasn't weak. But the pain, while fading, was still a fearsome thing.

Henry's voice was a quiet rumble. "What did you do to your hand, Meg?"

"I didn't know paper could cut." Even to her own ears, she sounded whiny. "I thought that was a make-believe image."

"Make-believe?"

"Not real."

He looked puzzled. "Let me see your hand."

"My hand is fine. That's not why—"

He took her left hand and unwrapped the bandage on her little finger. His hands were big and rough, but he touched her with surprising gentleness.

"You have scars," Meg said, looking at his fingers.

"I work with wood. Sometimes I am clumsy with my tools." He studied the slice on her finger, then bent his head and sniffed it. Shaking his head, he re-wrapped the bandage. "Such a small cut shouldn't cause so much pain."

He wanted an explanation, but her pain had no significance in what she had seen, so right now it wasn't important. "Henry, I saw something."

Releasing her hand, he straightened to his full height, towering over her. "You saw . . . ?"

Easing around him, she picked up her notebook from the table in the back room and handed it to him.

She watched him read the words, the frown line between his dark eyes getting deeper as he read them again.

"Some prophecies look like a series of images or sounds," she said. "Some, like this one, look like a movie clip, or a series of clips with sounds and action. The same image might appear in a hundred prophecies, so it's up to the person who wanted the vision to understand the meaning."

Henry studied her. "You heard a Wolf howling. Are you sure it was Sam?"

"Does any other Wolf howl sound like Sam's?"

"No." Henry thought for a moment. "Why would you have a vision about Sam? He could not have asked you to see anything."

"No, but he was the only person with me when I got the paper cut." Meg shivered. "Who are those men? Why do they want Sam?"

With Henry standing in the middle of the room, she didn't have room to pace.

"I'm so useless!" she cried. "I see this, but I can't tell you where it will happen or when or why!"

Henry held up her notebook. "I need to talk to some of the others. May I take this? I will return it."

"Okay. Yes. What about Sam?"

"Vlad will take Sam home. He has been here long enough for one day."

"But . . ."

The back door opened and Vlad walked in, giving Henry a questioning look. Then he glanced at her hands and stiffened.

Something passed between Grizzly and vampire that neither shared with her. Vlad slipped into the sorting room while Henry fetched her coat from the peg on the wall.

"Come with me," Henry said.

"My purse is in the sorting room, and my keys are in it."

Before she had both boots on, Vlad opened the door enough to hand her purse to Henry, and used one of his feet to block Sam's attempts to join her.

"Where are we going?" she asked when she and Henry stepped outside.

"Not far."

He led her to the yard behind his shop. A narrow path ran down the center of it to his studio door, which wasn't locked. Big windows filled the back wall on either side of the door, providing light. The sides of the studio were the building's brick walls. The floor was wood chips—or was covered in a layer of wood chips so thick she wasn't sure what the floor was supposed to be. The room felt warmer than outside, but not warm enough that she wanted to give up her coat, and Henry didn't indicate she should remove her boots.

He pointed to a bench. She sat down, wondering why she was there. Besides several pieces of wood and a cart filled with tools, there was a storage cabinet with a granite top and a round carved table that held a music player.

Henry stripped off his own coat and hung it on a peg before plugging in an electric kettle that sat on the cabinet. While the water heated, he placed her notebook on one of the cabinet's shelves, then selected a music disc and put it in the player. A few minutes later, he handed her a mug, turned on the music, and began working on the piece of wood in the center of the room.

The scent of peppermint rose from the mug. Not sure what he wanted from her, she cupped her hands around the mug for warmth and watched him as he coaxed a shape from the wood. The music, a blend of drums and rattles and something like a flute, flowed in the air, and the sound of Henry working seemed to blend with the rest.

"I like the music," Meg said. "What is it?"

He looked at her and smiled. "Earth-native music. When humans invented the music players and the discs that held sounds so that songs and stories could be shared by many, we saw the value of those things and arranged to record the music of our people."

"Do you like human music?"

"Some." Henry caressed the wood. "But not here. Not when I touch the wood and listen to what it wants to become."

Meg studied the rough shape that seemed to be leaping out of the block of wood. "It's a fish."

He nodded. "A salmon."

When she said nothing more, he picked up his tools and began working again. She watched the salmon emerge from the wood, its body a graceful curve. Not finished, to be sure, but not unformed.

She hoped she would still be there to see it when it was done.

The music ended. Her mug was empty. Taking it from her, Henry said, "The pain is quieter now. Eat some food. Rest a little more before you return to your work."

She stood. "Thank you for letting me sit here. I'm sorry I couldn't be more helpful."

"You gave us warning. That is help. As for the rest, you are welcome to come here and let your spirit touch the wood."

Now that the pain had dulled, she was hungry for more than the usual soup and sandwich she could get at A Little Bite, so she walked over to Meat-n-Greens, the restaurant in the Market Square. Training images told her this wasn't a high-end restaurant—the tablecloths were the kind that could be wiped down instead of cloth that needed to be laundered—but the menu listed everything from appetizers to full dinners. She ordered a small steak with mashed potatoes and peas, savoring the experience of making a choice.

When she got back to the office, she found a container of soup and a wrapped sandwich in the little fridge, and her lidded mug filled with fresh coffee.

"Don't have to wonder about dinner," she said as she picked up the copies of the *Lakeside News* and the Courtyard's newsletter that someone had left on the back table. She took them and her coffee into the sorting room, then opened the office for the afternoon deliveries.

Henry, Vlad, Blair, and Tess gathered in the Business Association's meeting room.

Henry set the notebook on the table. "This is Meg's. I think whatever else is written here is private, but she offered these words for all of us to see."

None of them spoke as they read Meg's record of the vision, but Blair began growling.

"If this was a book, the vision would have included a newspaper that would indicate the date something would happen," Vlad said.

"But it is not a book," Henry replied. "She gave us much for such a small cut. An accident," he added when Blair stared at him.

Blair nodded and went back to studying the words.

Henry looked at Tess. "You said there was pleasure in the cutting. All I smelled in her was pain. Why?"

"I don't know," Tess replied. "Maybe it's the difference between an accidental cut and one made deliberately. Maybe it was because there was something she wasn't able to do alone, so she experienced pain instead of euphoria. I told you all I know about blood prophets."

"I used the computer to check for books or any writings about them," Vlad said. "There are stories that have *cassandra sangue* as characters, but they were listed under horror or suspense novels, so I doubt there is any useful information. I added a couple of them to the next book order coming to HGR. I'll keep looking."

"Someone knows about them," Tess said.

"Meg knows," Henry said quietly. "In time, she will tell us." He looked at the Wolf. "Blair?"

Blair let out a breath slowly. "Could be this year, could be five years from now. There's still plenty of time for a storm like that before the cold girl yields to her sister. That sound. Smaller than a car, but not a BOW. Has to move well over snow."

"I can help Vlad search the computers for such a vehicle," Tess said. She hesitated. "Should we tell that policeman who talks to Simon?"

"Are such visions ever wrong?" Blair asked. "Can we know that those men coming in with weapons and hidden faces aren't police?"

"Why would the police want Sam?" Vlad asked.

"Why would anyone?" Henry countered.

Flickers of red danced in Blair's amber eyes. "Daphne is dead, so Sam is the Wolfgard's child. Would anyone be foolish enough to touch him and start a war?"

"Someone *will* be foolish enough," Henry said. "Meg has seen it."

Silence.

Finally Blair said, "Clear skies today. Unless someone angers the girl at the lake, we shouldn't have another storm for a few days."

Tess leaned forward and brushed a finger over the page that held Meg's notes about the vision. "Even if a blood prophet is never wrong, what she sees is open to interpretation. Meg has shown us the beginning of a fight, but there is nothing here that shows how it will end."

She looked at the three men. Despite his strength as a Grizzly, Henry felt a shiver down his spine when he saw the way her hair began to coil.

Tess left the room, apparently deciding there was nothing more to say.

"Sam's not going to accept being left behind all the time," Vlad said. "And being around Meg is good for him." He gave Blair a pointed look. "You don't like the harness and leash, and I understand that, but a couple of days with Meg has pulled Sam away from the bad place he's been in since Daphne died. That should count for something."

"I can't speak for other Wolves, but it counts with me," Blair said. "We'll keep Sam safe. And Meg too."

Vlad shifted in his chair. "She hasn't seen a Wolf yet. Except Sam."

"There's always a Wolf on duty at HGR," Blair said.

"Yes, but she hasn't been in the store since she became the Liaison, so she hasn't seen one of you."

"I'll assign a couple of Wolves to keep watch around the office. In human form."

"Keep in mind that they'll see Meg and Sam," Henry said.

Blair growled. "*That* is for Simon to deal with when he gets back."

"Agreed."

Satisfied they had done what they could for the moment, Henry stood. "I am close by during the day, and the Hawks and Crows keep watch when Meg is working. They will alert the Wolves if there is a threat."

The three went back to their own work.

As Henry walked the narrow path to his studio door, he looked at the Crows gathered on the wall. <Anything to tell me?>

<Humans and boxes,> Jake replied. <The Meg does not need help with the writing.> He sounded disappointed.

Back inside, Henry hung up his coat and walked around the pieces of wood waiting to be given a new kind of life—and thought about the female who, despite being human, he was beginning to see as a friend.

In between deliveries, Meg scanned the *Lakeside News*, but didn't see anything she thought should be reported to Henry or Tess—and wondered if she was out of place to even be looking. Surely Tess or Vlad did that anyway. But they didn't have all the images she did and might not recognize something that could have an impact on the Others.

She noticed the sale ads, which were set up as Asia said, but she didn't know if any of the residents would be interested in such items.

She read the comics and didn't understand most of them. But there was a comic strip about the Others that disturbed her. It seemed to be part of an ongoing story, so the words had little meaning, but the slavering Wolf, standing upright and looking like a furry man with a wolf's head, made her uncomfortable. Maybe it was a way to diminish something that was feared, but it felt dangerous. She couldn't say if it was dangerous to the Others or to the humans, but she absorbed the image, then looked at the date at the top of the newspaper. Another image.

Folding the paper, she reached for the Courtyard's newsletter, then stopped. Too much information, too much to absorb already today. Besides, distributing that new catalog to the residential complexes had produced a flurry of orders that had arrived that afternoon, so she still had to separate a cartload of packages and contact the complexes to come and pick up their orders.

She locked up promptly at four o'clock, filled the back of the BOW with small packages for the Chambers and the Green Complex, made sure she had her package for Winter, and headed out to make her deliveries.

It still made her nervous to get out of the BOW at any of the mausoleums that housed the Sanguinati—except Mr. Erebus's home—but she was getting used to the smoke that flowed out of the buildings whenever she stopped the BOW. The Sanguinati in smoke form didn't flow beyond their fences when she was around, and the ones who remained in human form didn't speak to her or approach. She always bid them a good afternoon as she tucked packages into the delivery boxes—and always breathed a sigh of relief that none of them wanted to make a meal out of her.

Mr. Erebus, on the other hand, came down the walkway to meet her as she got out of the BOW.

"Your movies arrived," Meg said, holding up the package. She noticed his fingernails didn't look as yellow or horny as they had the first time she'd seen him, but maybe that was because she'd been nervous and the doorway had been dark.

"I do enjoy my movies," he said. "Such a sweet girl to bring them to me."

Then he pointed at the black delivery boxes to indicate she should put his package inside. Even when he came out to meet her, he wouldn't take a package directly from her hand.

"I'm pleased to do it," Meg said.

Erebus studied her as she put the rest of the packages inside the delivery boxes. "Vladimir is kind to you?"

The question surprised her. What surprised her more was the feeling that Vlad's well-being depended on her answer. "Yes, he is. He and Nyx were very helpful this morning."

"That is good." He stepped back. "Go finish your work, then enjoy the night."

"I will."

As she drove toward the lake, she wondered if that was a warning that she should stay within the Green area of the Courtyard after dark.

Winter was skating on the lake, wearing the same white dress. Meg parked in the same place as the first time she'd visited, pulled a scarf out of the shopping bag, then walked down to the edge of the lake.

The girl gradually joined her.

"It is the Liaison," Winter said. "Do you skate, Meg?"

"I never learned."

"Humans wear metal on their feet to glide over ice. I have no need of such things." Winter tipped her head. "Did you come to collect the library books? We have not finished reading them."

"No, I'm not here for the books. I brought you this." Meg held out the scarf.

The girl stiffened, and the eyes that fixed on Meg were filled with an inhuman anger.

"You brought me the color of Summer?"

Staggered by the depth of the anger, Meg looked at the green scarf. "Summer? No. I didn't think of it as a summer green."

Winter seemed taller than she'd been a moment ago—and less human. And the air, which had been tolerable that afternoon, suddenly had a bite.

She had insulted the girl. That much she understood. It sounded like Winter and Summer didn't get along, despite being sisters. *Were* they sisters?

"When I saw this, I thought of you," Meg said, hoping to explain.

"Me." The word was a furious whisper. Snow suddenly whipped around the other side of the lake, a curtain moving toward them.

"Because of this." Meg unfolded the scarf, revealing the snowflakes that became the white ends and fringe. She struggled to find the right words. "Winter isn't an absence of color; it has all these shades of white. And then there are the evergreens with their branches tipped with snow, their color an accent for the white. When I saw the scarf at a shop in the Market Square, I thought of you because your dress has shades of white, and the green would be an accent for the dress like the evergreens are for the land."

The snow on the other side of the lake quieted. Winter studied the land and the trees, then looked at the scarf. "It *is* the color of the evergreens." She reached out and rubbed the scarf between her hands. "Soft."

Meg hardly dared to breathe.

"Kindness," Winter murmured, taking the scarf and wrapping it around her neck. "So unexpected."

The eyes that would never be mistaken for human stared at her. "Thank you, Meg."

"You're welcome, Winter." She walked back to the BOW and waved before she got in. The girl didn't wave back, but as Meg drove away, a second girl glided over the ice and linked hands with Winter.

During the drive back to the Green Complex, Meg noticed how the snow beside the road swirled in the air like skaters twirling over the ice on a lake.

CHAPTER 12

After a long, hot shower and a late breakfast, Meg filled Earthday with chores, Sam, and her first social outing. While her clothes washed, she and Sam walked around the complex. While the clothes dried, she and Sam walked around the complex. By the time she got home and put her clothes away, Sam was sprawled on her bedroom floor, unwilling to move. She had to lug him back to his cage in Simon's living room.

Then it was time to meet the females who were gathering in the Green's social room to watch a chick movie. Jenni Crowgard and her sisters were there, along with Julia Hawkgard, Allison Owlgard, and Tess.

They rearranged the chairs and the sectional couch to their liking—and for ease at reaching the popcorn, nuts, and chocolate chip cookies Tess had brought. Then Jenni started the movie.

There were mothers crying about daughters, and daughters yelling at mothers. There were fathers arguing with sons. There were friends offering unwanted advice to everyone. But in the end, they were all smiling and hugging.

Meg couldn't decide if this was supposed to be a story about a real family or if it was make-believe and wouldn't actually happen in a human community. The Others didn't understand the story either, but they all agreed on one thing: there wasn't a single chick in the whole movie.

By the time she got back, Sam was awake and ready to play. So they ate and played and watched another movie that definitely had chicks and other animals in it.

"If you let me get some sleep tonight, you can come with me in the morning," Meg said when she latched the cage. "But if you start howling and keep everyone up, you'll have to stay home by yourself."

Sam whined, making Meg feel like a meanie. But he settled down, and she went back to her apartment and barely had time to go through her nightly routine before she fell into bed and was sound asleep.

The next morning, there wasn't a sound from Simon's apartment. Not a yip or a howl. Having slept through her alarm, Meg wasn't sure she would have heard Sam before she stumbled out of bed, no matter how much noise he'd made. However, by the time she got out of the shower, the silence had taken on an ominous feel.

What if she hadn't latched the cage correctly last night? What if Sam had gotten out and, feeling upset with her for leaving him, had done one of the things that had worried Simon enough to buy the cage in the first place?

Rubbing her wet hair, Meg stuffed the towel on the rack, put on her robe and slippers, and hurried over to Simon's apartment. She shivered as she worked the lock in the back hallway—a reminder that even indoors, this wasn't a good time of year for wet hair and minimal clothing.

She would fix both of those things as soon as she checked on Sam.

What if he wasn't making any noise because he was injured and couldn't howl for help? What if he was sick? What if . . .

She rushed down the stairs and into the living room.

. . . he was licking the last bits of kibble out of his bowl and waiting for her quietly so she would take him with her?

Sam wagged his tail and let out a soft *arrooooo* of greeting.

"Good morning, Sam," Meg said. "I just wanted to let you know that I'll come and get you in a few minutes. Okay?"

Taking the sound he made as agreement, she dashed back to her apartment to dry her hair and get dressed. She hurried through the rest of her morning routine, almost choking on her hasty breakfast of peanut butter and bread.

By the time she got her place locked up and returned to Simon's apartment, Sam was dancing in place. As soon as she unlocked the cage, he was out and dancing at the front door. She got him into his harness and packed up his bowls and towel. When she stepped outside, Vlad was waiting for her.

He took the two carry sacks and looked thoughtful. "What are you bringing every day?"

"Sam's food bowls," Meg replied, double checking that she had properly locked Simon's door, because she remembered images and clips of thieves breaking into houses. Then there was the recent vision of those men dressed in black and Sam being afraid. She didn't think anyone would sneak into the Courtyard and try to steal from the Others. On the other hand, people did foolish things all the time.

"Meg, if Sam is going to the office with you most days, get another set of bowls so you don't have to cart these back and forth," Vlad said.

"I'm going to look through the Pet Palace catalog this morning to see how much they cost," she said as the three of them set off for the garages, stopping every few steps for Sam to pee. She didn't want to be stingy, but the shopping trip on Firesday had shown her how quickly money was used up, and she didn't want to run out before the next pay envelope. And that thought reminded her to stop at the Market Square bank and find out how much store credit she could anticipate having each month. She was beginning to understand why so many of the Controller's clients had wanted prophecies about money.

"Buy what you want for Sam and charge it to the Business Association," Vlad said. "I'll authorize the purchases."

"Thank you."

They packed the carry sacks and Sam into the BOW. Then, despite her having her key that morning, Vlad drove the three of them to the Liaison's Office.

When she opened the front door, Harry from Everywhere Delivery was just pulling in.

Not late this morning, she thought as she waved at Harry—and caught a glimpse of someone watching from the second floor of the consulate. *But just barely on time.*

Since Harry always chatted with her for a few minutes, Meg took her time setting up her clipboard and filling out the information on the packages he brought. Unlike Asia Crane, he wasn't blatantly curious about the Courtyard. Harry chatted about his own life, a version of the human world that was as alien to her as the *terra indigenes'* way of life. But Meg absorbed the words, and whenever she had a few minutes of quiet time, she tried to match the things Harry talked about to the images and clips that had been part of her training.

"Pull up so we're not in the way of deliveries," Monty said as Kowalski drove into the Courtyard. "This won't take more than a couple of minutes."

There had been no further news from the West Coast, no confirmation of how many people in Jerzy had been killed last week, no information about why a pack of young men had attacked the Others and started the fight that escalated into a slaughter. And despite having a patrol car waiting at the train station whenever an eastbound train pulled in, there had been no sign of Simon Wolfgard.

Preferring to avoid more dealings with Vladimir Sanguinati, Monty had decided to approach the Liaison. He didn't think Meg Corbyn could—or would—tell him anything, but he wanted to remind her that he was there to help.

As he opened the office door, one of the Crows fluttered over the stone wall, while another went winging off, no doubt to tell someone that he was there.

There was that flash of fear in Meg Corbyn's gray eyes when she saw him, quickly followed by an effort to hide that fear. He wondered if she would ever look at him and not be afraid that he was going to take her back to whatever she had run away from. But why would she still be afraid? Didn't she know that the Others wouldn't tolerate her being apprehended?

"Good morning, Lieutenant Montgomery. Is there something I can do for you?"

Reaching the counter, Monty smiled and shook his head. "No, ma'am. I just dropped by to see if there was anything we can do for you."

"Oh." She looked at the catalog on the counter, as if searching for the correct response among the merchandise.

Since she wasn't looking at him, he focused on the room beyond the Private door, which she had left open. A back wall with slots and shelves. A box of sugar lumps sitting on a big table in the middle of the room. And a gray puppy standing in the doorway, its lips peeled back to reveal a mouth full of healthy teeth.

Not a dog puppy, Monty thought when the animal snarled at him. *A Wolf pup.*

Meg jerked at the sound. After staring at the Wolf, she looked at Monty and said, "This is Sam. He's helping me for a few days." Then she looked at the youngster. "Sam, this is Lieutenant Montgomery. He's a police officer." Back to him. "He's young. I'm not sure he knows what a police officer is."

When did the Others start shifting into human form? Was that pup also a boy? *Whose* boy?

He didn't need three guesses to figure *that* out, but it made him wonder what other duties Simon Wolfgard might require from his Liaison.

"Maybe the bookstore has one of those 'this is' books," Monty said. "I don't recall the actual name, but the gist of the books is to help children identify things. Like, 'This is a cat. This is a car. This is a mouse. This is a moose.'"

There was a queer look in her eyes, and her fair skin paled. "I remember those kinds of books," she whispered. "I didn't know other children were taught that way."

He'd been thinking of all the evenings he sat with Lizzy, reading those books to her, and how excited she had been when they went to the children's zoo and she could identify the goat, chicken, and bunny. But looking at Meg, he doubted she had the same kind of warm memories about those books.

"Thank you. That's a good suggestion," she said. "If HGR doesn't carry children's books, maybe the Courtyard library does."

Time to leave. He glanced at the catalog, which was open to a selection of dog beds, and noticed she had circled one. He took a moment to gauge the pup, then tipped his head to look at her choice.

"I'd go with the medium-sized bed, not the small," he said.

"But he is small," Meg protested. She paused. "At least, I think he's small. I haven't seen a full-grown Wolf yet."

He smiled, but he wondered *why* she hadn't seen a Wolf yet. "Take my word for it. Sam is already bigger than what people consider a small dog."

"Oh. Well, that's good to know."

"You have a good day, Ms. Corbyn."

"You too."

When he stepped out of the office, he caught sight of Kowalski's expression. Looking to the right, he saw the Grizzly who was standing on the other side of the wall, watching him. In those first moments, his lungs refused to breathe and his bowels turned to water.

"Good day, Mr. Beargard," he said quietly. Then he walked over to the patrol car and got in.

"We okay to leave?" Kowalski asked, still keeping an eye on the Grizzly.

"Yes. Let's go," Monty replied.

Henry Beargard watched them until they pulled into traffic.

"A guy from the consulate came out as soon as you went into the Liaison's Office," Kowalski said. "Mainly wanted to know what we were doing there. Told him it was a courtesy call."

"Which it was."

"The guy was in my line of sight, so when I first saw the Grizzly, I thought it was one of those carvings, until the bear turned his head and watched you talking to the Liaison." Kowalski braked carefully as they came up to a red traffic light. "Never saw one of the Bears before. Can't say I'm anxious to see another one." A pause when the light changed and they started moving again. "Do you think he could have gotten over that wall?"

Could have gotten over it or gone through it. Not finding any comfort in that certainty, Monty didn't answer the question.

Meg called the Pet Palace and placed her order with the shop's manager since the salesperson who answered the phone didn't want the responsibility of charging anything to the Courtyard. Receiving a promise that the bowls and bed would be delivered the following morning, she considered her next call.

Something was wrong with Sam—or had been wrong. She'd understood that from the cage in Simon's living room and the kibble, which she doubted was a typical food for any of the Wolves.

Something had changed in the past few days. Sam seemed more responsive, more like a curious puppy now. If he was behaving more like a typical Wolf pup, maybe that explained his increasing lack of interest in the kibble.

Although it didn't explain his interest in the cookies she had bought for him.

Since she couldn't ask Simon for advice—and she sure didn't want to ask Blair—she called the Market Square butcher shop to see if she could get an answer.

And as she listened to the phone ring, a thought niggled at her. She'd been in the Courtyard almost two weeks now and heard them every night, so why *hadn't* she seen any of the Wolves in Wolf form? Were they under orders to avoid her when in that form? Were they really that scary?

"We got meat and fish today," a male voice said. "Whaddaya looking for?"

"This is Meg, the Liaison. Do you have any special meat?"

Silence, followed by sputtering. "Special meat? *You* want some of the *special meat?*"

Obviously there was a special meat. Just as obviously, not everyone was allowed to have it.

"It's for Sam," Meg said. "He's not enthusiastic about the kibble, so I wondered if there was a special meat for puppies. Well, maybe something like rabbit or deer isn't really special, since Wolves eat it all the time. Don't they?" When he didn't say anything, she plowed on. "Little Wolves Sam's age do eat meat, don't they?"

A gusty sigh. Then that voice, sounding relieved, said, "Sure they eat meat. Sure they do. Got some nice bits of beef in today. That would be more of a treat than deer or rabbit—unless you want a whole haunch of rabbit. Got a haunch left from the one I caught this morning."

Suddenly feeling queasy, Meg said, "A small piece of beef would be fine. I don't want to give him too much if he hasn't had it for a while."

"I'll bring it over." He hung up.

Meg stared at the phone. "Why was he so upset about me asking for special meat?"

Not everyone was allowed to have it. Or was it just the *humans* who weren't supposed to want it because . . .

Before she lost her nerve, she called A Little Bite and silently thanked all the gods when Merri Lee answered.

"Are humans considered special meat?" Meg asked.

"This isn't a good thing to talk about over the phone," Merri Lee finally said.

For a moment, Meg couldn't think, could barely breathe as a drawing of a cow with arrows pointing to the various cuts of meat popped into her head. Then she imagined a drawing of a human with the same kinds of arrows. Could there be a sign like that in the butcher shop?

"Merri? Does the butcher shop in the Courtyard sell people parts?"

Silence.

"Oh, gods."

After another silence, Merri Lee said, "I'm pretty sure the special meat isn't sold in the butcher shop anymore, if it ever was," she said, her voice barely above a whisper. "And I'm pretty sure when the Others kill a human, that person is usually consumed on the spot and there aren't any leftovers." She swallowed hard enough that Meg could hear it over the phone. "But when special meat *is* available, you'll see a sign on the shop door. It's not obvious what it's for, but we've all been able to guess why it goes up. Like I said, I'm pretty sure they don't sell the meat there, but the sign tells all the Others that it's available."

"But we're supposed to shop there!"

"Have you been inside yet?"

"No. I don't know how to cook, so I haven't bought any meat there yet." And might never buy any.

"When you do, be sure to ask what meat you're getting. Or tell them what you're looking for. If you ask for a steak and don't specify the animal, you could get beef or horse or deer or moose or even bison. That can be interesting, but you don't always want interesting."

Feeling wobbly, Meg braced a hand on the counter and wished she'd never thought of getting a treat for Sam. "Okay." She blew out a breath. "Okay. Thanks, Merri."

She hung up and went back into the sorting room in time to hear a loud knock on the back door. Sam followed her, still wearing the harness and leash because he wouldn't let her unclip the safety line.

She opened the door. The man had the brown hair and eyes of the Hawks she'd met, and he was wearing a blood-smeared apron around his waist. He held out two packages wrapped in brown paper.

"Chopped up a few pieces of stew beef," he said. "Let it get body warm before you give it to Sam. The other package has pieces of dried stag stick. The pups like chewing on those."

"What's a stag stick?" Meg asked, taking the packages.

He stared at her for a moment. Then he put a fist below his belt and popped out a thumb.

"Oh," Meg said. "*Oh.*"

He spun around and ran back to the Market Square.

She closed the door, looked at the packages in her hands, and said, "Eeewwww."

But Sam was bouncing all around her, dancing on his hind legs to sniff at the packages.

The first package she opened had the beef. Figuring she could warm it in the wave-cooker, she put that package in the little fridge. The next package held three pieces of . . . stag. Using thumb and forefinger, she picked up a piece and gave it to Sam. Then she hurriedly wrapped up the rest and ran to the bathroom to wash her hands. Twice.

Of course, he wouldn't stay in the back room with his chewy, so she began sorting the mail while she studiously ignored what Sam was holding between his paws and gnawing with such pleasure.

Vlad looked up from the invoices he was sorting and studied the Wolf in the doorway. "Something wrong?"

Blair came in and took a seat on the other side of the desk. "Boone says he's not going to store special meat in the shop anymore because he doesn't want to get into trouble with Henry now and with Simon when the Wolfgard returns."

"Why is Boone worried about getting into trouble?"

"Because Meg asked if he had any special meat."

Vlad's mouth fell open. "*Meg?*"

"Boone says he'll get in trouble if he doesn't sell it to her when she asks for it, but he'll get into more trouble if she buys some and *then* finds out what it is. He can't sell what he doesn't have, so he's not going to have it."

"*Meg?*" Vlad said again. He couldn't decide if he was intrigued or disturbed by this information.

"Turns out she was looking for a treat for Sam." Blair's lips twitched in a hint of a smile. "From the sounds he was making when he called me, I'm guessing the Hawk is going to stress molt a few feathers before the day is done."

Vlad laughed out loud.

Blair pushed out of the chair. "Course, he also brought pieces of a stag stick for Sam."

"Stop," Vlad pleaded, laughing so hard he couldn't breathe. "No, wait. Did Meg know what it was?"

"She does now. I did tell Boone he should continue delivering a little meat for Sam." A pause. "Simon called. He'll be back on Windsday."

Still trying to catch his breath, Vlad waved a hand to acknowledge he'd heard.

"Doesn't sound like he got any answers," Blair said.

Sobering, Vlad nodded. "We'll all talk when he gets back." Once Blair left the office and he was sure the Wolf was out of hearing, he added, "About a lot of things."

Meg stared at the back door of Howling Good Reads. Bringing a Wolf into the store wasn't a problem; she'd heard that one or two Others were usually in animal form to provide store security. No, the problem was how they would react to Sam's harness and leash—and whether she would be breaking some unspoken rule by bringing a young *terra indigene* into a store frequented by humans.

Leaving Sam in the office had not been an option after she considered how much trouble he could get into on his own. So here she was, dithering at the door.

The wooden gate at the back of Henry's yard opened. The Beargard studied both of them for a long moment before he looked at HGR's back door. Stepping up to her, he took the leash.

"Come on, Sam. You play with me for a while. The sooner Meg takes care of her chores, the sooner you can both eat."

This was Henry, and Sam would be safe with the Grizzly, but Meg didn't feel easy about other people holding the leash and having control over Sam, and she especially didn't like the pup accepting that other people *could* hold the leash.

Her uneasiness must have shown on her face, because Henry said, "We'll be fine, Meg. Do your chores."

She looked at Sam. "It would be better if you stayed with Henry. Okay?"

She didn't wait for an answer. She went into HGR and hurried through the stockroom. But she didn't make it into the public part of the store before she heard that squeaky-door howl—Sam's protest at being left behind.

Already feeling guilty about leaving him, she let out her own squeak when Sam's howl was answered by a deeper howl somewhere in the store. She hesitated. Then curiosity pushed her into the store proper.

Maybe she would see her first grown Wolf.

Apparently, she wasn't the only one engaged in Wolf spotting after hearing that howl. All the customers she passed were looking for something that wasn't on the shelves, but she reached the front of the store without seeing one of the *terra indigene* in Wolf form. She did find John Wolfgard, who took her to the children's section. He seemed too cheerful to be a Wolf, and she wondered if customers who dealt with him were relieved or disappointed by that.

Called away by another customer, he left her browsing the picture books and "this is" books. She chose a couple of the "this is" books and a book of children's stories. Not sure how long she'd been browsing, and wanting a chance to look for a book for herself, she hurried out of the children's section and headed for the front of the store where she'd seen a display of books, and almost ran into the man blocking the way.

He was about Simon's age, with a lean face and body, but his hair was a blend of gray and black, and his gray eyes held the least illusion of humanity of any shifter she'd seen in the Courtyard so far. He wore jeans, a white sweater, and a scarred, black leather jacket. There was no doubt in her mind that he was the Wolf who had answered Sam's howl.

He didn't move out of the way so much as shift position enough for her to squeeze past him. When she did, he leaned in and sniffed her with no subtlety whatsoever. Then he sneezed.

Meg didn't bother to sigh about another Wolf who was going to complain about her stinky hair—which didn't smell anymore, thank you very much.

Even John's smile faltered when he noticed how the other Wolf followed her to the front of the store, but he rang up her purchases—including a novel that she grabbed from the display table to prove she could buy a book for herself—and put them in the carry bag she'd brought with her.

Thanking John, she headed toward the back of the store, more and more nervous about the Wolf who seemed intent on following her. She breathed a sigh of relief when he hesitated, then turned and went into A Little Bite. Wanting to get back to the office before he began following her again, she flung open the back door of HGR and hurried to the open door of Henry's yard.

A snowball hit her shoulder, surprising a squeak out of her. But it was the Wolf charging at her that made her scream so loud the Crows and Hawks that were all around Henry's yard and the Liaison's Office took off in a flurry of wings. Meg dropped to her hands and knees, then curled up, covering her head and neck with her arms.

The Wolf landed on her back, snarling fiercely as he slid off her in his attempt to grab at her arms.

Then a small head shoved its way under her arm, and a tongue gave her face a couple of quick licks. Sam talked at her for a moment before he pulled his head out of the space and happily jumped on her again.

Henry's laugh boomed out. "You caught her good and proper, Sam. Now let her up."

Meg counted to ten. When no one jumped on her, she slowly uncurled. A moment later, a big hand grabbed the back of her coat, hauled her upright, and began whacking the snow off her.

"You make a fine squeaky toy, Meg," Henry said, his voice suffused with laughter. "Sam, it's time for you to go."

"That's enough," she gasped, brushing the snow off the front of her coat.

Henry picked up her purse and the carry bag, brushing the snow off both of them. "It was nice of you to play at being prey."

She hadn't been playing at anything. The red harness or the size of the animal hadn't registered in her brain. All she'd seen was a Wolf heading toward her at a full run. Sam had looked a lot bigger in that moment, and dropping to the ground had been instinctive.

"I probably should have run," she murmured, taking the purse and carry bag from Henry. Sam returned, mouthing one end of the leash as he dragged it behind him.

"No," Henry said quietly, his attention on something behind her. "Running would have been the wrong thing to do."

Taking the leash from Sam, she clipped it to his harness and slipped the other end over her wrist before turning to look at whatever Henry was watching.

The Wolf who had followed her in HGR was standing nearby, holding one of the insulated lunch boxes Tess used to deliver food or coffee to people working in the Market Square. He stared at her with a fury that bordered on crazed hatred.

"What do you want, Ferus?" Henry asked.

It was Sam, standing between her feet and snarling at the other Wolf, that finally pulled Ferus's attention away from her. But not for long. He couldn't seem to tear his focus away from the harness and leash that attached Sam to a human.

"Ferus." Henry's voice was both command and warning.

"Tess asked me to carry this for the *Liaison*," Ferus said, the words almost lost in the growling voice.

"You should go now," Henry said to Meg, resting a hand on her shoulder. "You'll need to open up for afternoon deliveries soon." He gave her a little push toward the office.

"Come on, Sam," Meg said, too scared now to do more than whisper.

All the way back to the office, Sam ran to the end of the leash, then stopped and kept watch until she caught up to him. And all the way back, Ferus trailed behind them, a silent threat.

Memory. A movie clip showing a pack of ordinary wolves pulling down a deer. Beginning to feed before the deer was dead. Ripping. Tearing. Gorging on fresh meat.

They had watched that same clip for an entire afternoon because one of the girls had fought against being cut, and the resulting prophecy had been of inferior quality. And while the girls watched the clip, the Walking Names had whispered over and over, "That could be you. If we ever stop taking care of you, that is what the wolves will do to you."

They took care of property, not people. Willing to risk her life in order to have a life, she had run and had ended up in a Courtyard, hiding among beings who were even more dangerous than the man who saw her as nothing but a living tool. Despite Simon snarling at her about one thing or another and always threatening to eat her because she had done something he didn't like, and despite the conditioned fear of the Others the Walking Names had tried to instill in her, she hadn't thought of herself as prey. Until now.

She didn't need to cut skin to know that was exactly how Ferus saw her. To him, human equaled prey, equaled meat. She didn't need the razor to know it wasn't a question of *if* he would pull her down and rip her open like the deer she had seen in that movie clip; it was a question of *when.*

She had been so busy building a life here, she had forgotten the other part of her personal vision. She was going to die in this Courtyard.

But she'd also seen herself in that narrow bed, and Simon pacing in that white room. How could she be there if the Wolves tore her apart?

Sam yipped, and she realized they had reached the office's back door. Her hands shook as she struggled to get the key in the lock.

Once she had the door open and Sam had darted inside, she dared to look at the other Wolf. "Thank you for carrying the lunch."

He just stared at her. Then he held out the lunch box.

Taking it, she backed inside the office and closed the door—and almost wet herself when the furious howl sounded from the other side of the door.

Panting in her effort to breathe, she set all the bags on the small table and ignored the snow she was tracking on the floor. Slipping the leash off her wrist and stripping off her coat, she went into the bathroom, shutting the door before Sam could follow her.

She needed to pee but now she couldn't relax her muscles enough to go. Finally able to take care of business, she left the bathroom in time to see Sam climb up on a chair and try to snatch the lunch box.

Grabbing the pup, she dried off his feet, removed her boots, and cleaned up the floor. Then, with him dancing around her, she opened the lunch box. A container of beef and vegetable soup for her, and a smaller container of soup for Sam. Dumping out the untouched kibble, she poured the soup in his bowl, dipping her finger into it to make sure it wasn't too hot. He began lapping up soup as soon as she got out of his way, so she opened her own container. That soup was hot, and she realized Tess must have deliberately let Sam's serving cool off. A cheese sandwich was included with her lunch. Tearing off a piece, she gave it to Sam, then forced herself to eat a bite of the sandwich and a couple of spoonfuls of soup. Her stomach was still flipping with fear, so even that little bit of food made her queasy.

Giving up, she heated water while she wrapped up the food—and wondered if she was going to have to puppy-proof the fridge and lower cupboards.

After making a cup of peppermint tea, she grabbed the carry bag of books and headed for the front room, intending to open up early and take a better look at the books in between deliveries.

The box of sugar lumps she'd left on the sorting table was knocked over and the top of the box was torn. Drawers where she kept her office supplies were pulled open.

And there was someone making furtive noises in the front room.

Quietly turning the knob, Meg yanked the Private door open, then stared at the Crow who, flustered at being caught, almost fell off the counter.

"Jake?"

Jenni had told her that Jake liked playing the pen game with the humans who brought packages, and he intended to help the Meg whenever he was assigned to watch that part of the Courtyard.

Help was not the word that came to mind as Meg unlocked the front door. And how had Jake gotten in? As far as she knew, only a few members of the Business Association had keys to the Liaison's Office. Well, he could have slipped in with one of the deliverymen and hidden so he could rummage through the drawers while she was out of the office.

She picked up two empty boxes from the floor, then looked at all the pencils that were scattered on the counter, along with most of the pens she usually kept in the holder. She wasn't sure what the Crow was building, but he'd certainly gone through the drawers to find what he wanted.

"Jake, you can't have the pencils and pens," Meg said. She reached for one of the pens. He pecked her. "Hey!" She had had her fill of wildlife today and didn't need a pesky Crow stealing her things.

Caw!

"I need those pens!"

Caw!

"Jake!" Her eyes filled with tears, which was stupid. It was all stupid, but she had been scared twice in the space of a few minutes, and she didn't need this—whatever it was.

Jake tipped his head this way and that. Then he fluttered around his creation, pulled out a blue pen, and offered it to her. When she took it, he selected a red pen and offered it. Finally he gave back a black pen and began rebuilding whatever he was building on her counter.

"Mine," she said, sniffling as she put the three pens under the counter with her clipboard.

She was about to ask about the sugar when Asia dashed into the office.

"Gods above and below, Meg. What's going on? Is someone hurt?"

"Hurt?"

"That *scream*. Didn't you hear it? I was looking at the display of pottery in the window of Earth Native and I heard that *awful* scream. And all the birds suddenly flying around, going crazy and making a racket." Asia threw her hands up, causing Jake to flutter his wings and caw in protest.

Meg wanted to slink into the sorting room and lock all the doors and never come out. She would stay there until she dried up into human jerky.

Then she considered what the Wolves would happily do with that kind of jerky.

"You heard that?"

"Of course I heard that!" Asia edged away from the Crow and lowered her voice. "Do you know who it was?"

"Me," Meg mumbled, her face burning with embarrassment. "It was me."

"You?"

"I was startled. And even little Wolves look pretty big when they're running right at you."

Of course, that was the moment Sam chose to stand in the doorway, wagging his tail and licking his chops.

"Oh," Asia gushed, leaning on the counter but careful not to have any part of herself *beyond* the counter. "Isn't he the sweetest thing!" Her eyes flicked up to the doorway. "Speaking of sweetest things, you must have a mighty big sweet tooth, Meg."

Meg glanced back. "Oh, the sugar is for the ponies. They get a special treat on Moonsday." She looked at Jake. "Do you know how the box got knocked over and the top torn open?"

The Crow lifted his wings in a way that perfectly mimicked a shrug.

Meg leaned closer to Jake. "If someone hid a lump of sugar in order to attract bugs to eat, that someone isn't going to be allowed to play with the pencils anymore."

He stared at her. Then he fluttered down to the floor, pecked around the edge of the counter for a moment, flew back up, and dropped the sugar lump on the counter.

Sighing, Meg took the sugar lump—and heard something fall over in the back room.

"Asia, this isn't a good day for a visit."

"I can see that," Asia replied. "You take care. Maybe we can grab some lunch in one of those places across the street tomorrow."

"I'm not sure. I'm looking after Sam, and he's a handful."

A thump, followed by Sam loudly talking back at something.

"I have to go," Meg said, hurrying into the back room.

For a moment all she could do was stare. Sam had somehow dragged a chair across the room and was climbing up to reach the box of puppy cookies she'd left on the counter. The fridge door was open, and scraps of her cheese sandwich were scattered on the floor, along with the wrapping, which had been ripped into pieces. Either he wasn't interested or he hadn't been able to grab her container of soup. She didn't want to think of how much of a mess *that* would have made.

Deciding she would drink her now-cold peppermint tea before dealing with Sam's helping himself to her lunch, she grabbed the pup and went into the sorting room, firmly closing the door to the back room.

That's when she saw the box of sugar on the table and realized she no longer had the sugar lump she'd taken from Jake and had no clue where she'd dropped it.

Slipping into the front room to retrieve her tea, she saw Ferus standing outside the consulate, talking with Elliot Wolfgard and gesturing toward the office. Easy to guess what they were talking about: Sam on a leash. Vlad and Henry didn't seem concerned about it when she and Sam walked around the complex, but she had a feeling the Wolves weren't going to be as understanding about buddies and safety lines.

"Crow in the front room, puppy in the middle room, crazy Wolf outside," she muttered. "Could today get any better?"

Apparently, it could. Fortunately, she noticed the bug Jake must have dropped in her tea as a peace offering *before* she took a sip.

Entering the Stag and Hare, a restaurant directly across from the Courtyard's delivery entrance, Asia settled at a table by the windows. The cold came off the plates of glass in waves, and most of the customers were huddled at the tables closest to the fireplace in the center of the main room.

Keeping her coat on, Asia placed her order and stared out the window, turning over the things she had seen as she considered what she could use to her advantage.

Meg had screamed, and all the *terra indigene* in that part of the Courtyard had responded, even those who worked in the consulate. According to Darrell Adams, a human who worked for Elliot Wolfgard, everyone at the consulate thought of the Liaison's Office like a poor relation—something that had to be tolerated but was ignored as much as possible.

Poor relation or not, even they had paid some attention when Meg screamed. So there was a way to redirect the Others' attention, if only for a minute or two. Plenty of things could be accomplished in a minute or two.

And there was that Wolf pup *wearing a harness.* Could he shift into a boy, or did the harness constrict his ability to change into human form? If one of the Others *could* be contained and controlled, her backers probably knew a few collectors who would risk the wrath of the *terra indigene* to have a Wolf for a pet, if only for a little while. They might even consider using a tamed Wolf in a few horror movies—at least until he became old enough to be dangerous.

Asia smiled at the waiter when he brought her a bowl of soup. As the simple meal warmed her, she looked at the Courtyard and smiled again.

Meg was looking after a pup while Simon Wolfgard was away. Didn't need to be a genius to add up two and two and get *money.*

After all, holding someone for ransom was often a lucrative, if risky, business.

On Sunsday morning, the new set of bowls and the dog bed for the office were delivered as promised, and Sam was delighted to have his own comfortable spot where he could watch Meg as she sorted mail and packages. Boone brought over a small container of chopped meat, claiming it was now a regular order. Meg didn't ask what kind of meat it was or who had placed the order. She just warmed up the meat and stirred it into the kibble.

That morning, there was no sign of Jake Crowgard. There was also no sign of any of the pencils or pens he'd been playing with—including the three that were supposed to be hers. Between deliveries, she called toy stores, found what she was looking for, and got a promise from the store that she would have the merchandise by that afternoon.

Sometimes Sam hid from the deliverymen; sometimes he watched them from the sorting-room doorway—and Meg watched the way a couple of them studied the red harness just a little too long for her liking.

And too often throughout the day, when she thought about the vision of the men in black and Sam howling in terror, she found herself rubbing her arms to relieve the prickling under her skin while she struggled with the craving to make another cut.

By Windsday, Meg and Sam had a workable morning routine, and for the first time since beginning her puppy-sitting stint seven days ago, they got to the office without rushing.

As she opened the front door, Meg stuck her head out and smiled at the Crows who had taken up their usual position on the wall. "Tell Jake I have a package for him."

After setting up for business, she unclipped the leash and removed Sam's harness. She made that decision after waking up twice, scared by dreams she couldn't remember. She would keep the harness and leash handy, but she didn't want him wearing it when it wasn't necessary.

Besides, Merri Lee told her that Ferus had been reassigned to work with Blair at the Utilities Complex. And yesterday Henry suddenly came into the office several times to check on a delivery or look through a catalog he claimed he didn't have. It hadn't escaped her notice that the Grizzly showed up every time Elliot Wolfgard left the consulate. Realizing Blair and Henry had done those things because some of the Wolves were upset about the harness was another reason for Sam not to wear it.

"We don't need the safety line when we're inside the office," she told him when he tried to leap up and grab the harness off the counter. "All you have to remember is not to run out when we fill the mail baskets for the ponies."

He talked back, but she gave him cookies and another piece of the stag stick, which he took back to his bed to gnaw on, ending the discussion.

Jake Crowgard wasn't as easy to distract.

Meg didn't know how he was getting in, but he was on the counter, studying the empty pen holder when she came back to the front room. Setting her peppermint tea on the sorting table, where it would be out of reach of any gifts he might want to drop into it, she pulled out a box from under the counter, opened it, and showed him the wooden wheels, colored sticks, and various connectors.

"Give back all my pencils and pens—and promise to leave them alone from now on—and you can have this," she said.

Negotiations would have been simpler if Jake had shifted to his human form so that he could actually talk to her. She was sure that was the reason he didn't shift. He tried to pretend he didn't understand what she was saying, so she smiled at him, closed the box, took it into the sorting room, and shut the Private door.

She ignored Jake's cawing while she sorted the mail. She ignored Sam's howling when she unlocked the sorting-room's outside door, then went into the back room to fetch her coat and the bowl of carrot chunks that was the ponies' treat that day.

Sam stood in front of the outside door, mouthing his end of the leash and wagging his tail. Clearly, having a door open to the outside required the safety line. Wondering if she had emphasized the buddy system a little too much, Meg slipped the leash's loop over her wrist and picked up the first two bundles of mail just as a chorus of neighs announced the arrival of the ponies. Pleased with himself, Sam stayed beside her as she walked back and forth between the table and the ponies, loading their baskets with mail, catalogs from nearby stores, and flat packages.

Once the ponies were on their way and Sam had ducked out just long enough to yellow up some snow, Meg locked the doors. Then she checked the front room. Jake wasn't in sight, but there were three pencils on the counter.

She took the pencils and put two colored sticks and a wheel in their place.

When she closed for lunch, she snuck the toy box out of the office and locked it in her BOW. Then she dropped Sam off at Henry's yard for an hour of playtime while she went to A Little Bite for a leisurely meal.

Returning to the office, she found three more pencils and four pens on the counter—and a black feather in the sorting room. Apparently, Jake had tried to get around trading by searching for the box. She felt oddly proud that she'd been sneakier than a Crow.

She never saw him during the afternoon delivery hours, but every time she checked the front room, a few more pens or pencils would be on the counter. When the pen holder and the pencil boxes were full, Meg set all the remaining toy pieces on the counter and locked up for the day. She had deliveries to make, and she needed to get Sam settled at home before heading out.

As she and Sam went out the back door, Starr Crowgard ran up to them.

"Jake wants to know if you found the last pencils," Starr said.

"Yes, I did." Meg paused, her key in the lock.

"He wondered if he could have the rest of the sticks."

He wondered? Meg thought as she opened the door. "Sure."

They went to the front room. Meg put the remaining pieces back in the box and gave it all to Starr, who shifted from foot to foot.

It was a mistake to think the Others were exactly like the birds or animals they mimicked, but after living in those forms for so many generations, they had absorbed some of the behaviors of those animals. Putting together what she knew about crows with the way Starr was looking at her, Meg tried not to sigh. "How many boxes would you like for the Corvine social room?"

Starr held up five fingers.

"I'll order them tomorrow."

Smiling, Starr followed her out, then hurried toward the Market Square, where her sisters—and, no doubt, Jake—were waiting at Sparkles and Junk to finish building whatever they were building.

Once she and Sam were settled in the BOW, Meg let out a gusty sigh. It wasn't easy dealing with the Others, but at least she had shown the Crows that she wasn't a pushover.

The Crows might have learned she wasn't a pushover, but that particular lesson had been lost on the puppy. When she parked at the Green Complex, Sam wouldn't get out of the BOW.

"Sam," Meg said sternly. "I have deliveries to make before we can play. You have to wait for me at home."

He talked back, and she didn't need to speak Wolf to know he wanted to come with her and wasn't agreeing with anything she said about him staying home by himself.

Until a few days ago, he'd been home by himself all the time. Apparently, he didn't like it anymore.

Meg stared at the defiant pup and considered the problem. She could pick him up, but he was fast enough to bounce all over the inside of the BOW, and there was the possibility of him smashing a package that held something breakable. She could try to grab the harness, but he might forget they were friends and bite her. Or she could grab the leash and haul him out of the vehicle. But she had spent a lifetime of being controlled and held by one kind of a leash or another, and she didn't want Sam thinking that he should let someone control him without fighting that person all the way.

A human someone, anyway, since Simon Wolfgard controlled pretty much everything and everyone in the Courtyard. Which didn't help her now, as he was still out of town.

Leaning into the BOW, she shook her finger at Sam, bopping him on the nose a couple of times.

"All right," she said. "You can come with me. But, Sam, you have to mind me, or we'll both get in trouble. Do you understand?"

He licked her finger and wagged his tail. Once she was sure feet, tail, and leash were safely inside, she closed the door and went around to her side.

After starting the BOW, she considered her delivery route. She wasn't going near the Wolfgard Complex while Sam was with her. That would be asking for trouble. She had a box for Jester. The Pony Barn was safe enough. The Utilities Complex? Trickier if Blair and Ferus were there, but she had sent a note along with the mail telling Blair she would deliver his boxes when she made her afternoon rounds, and she didn't think it was a good idea to break a promise to the Courtyard's enforcer.

"I'm going to get bitten one way or the other," she muttered as she headed for the Pony Barn. When she pulled up in front, she counted four Owls perched on a decorative piece of wooden fence. Three Hawks claimed a similar bit of fence on the other side of the barn. And the trees around the barn held a dozen Crows. Apparently, she was still entertaining enough for the Others to watch her activities.

Jester walked over to the BOW, glanced in the passenger's window, and grinned. Coming around to Meg's side, he waited until she rolled down her window and blocked Sam's attempt to climb in her lap and poke his head out.

"Got a helper today?" Jester asked.

"I've got something," she replied. Then, "Sam! Stop it! You promised to behave."

"If you had a better sense of smell, you'd want to sniff around too," Jester said. He looked at her face and let out his yipping laugh. "I'll get my own box out of the back."

"Thank you." She grabbed Sam before he climbed in the back with the packages, but she couldn't stop him from howling to let the whole Courtyard know he was there. And the whole Courtyard *would* know, because the Crows cawed, the Hawks screamed, the Owls hooted, and the ponies neighed. And the damn Coyote raised his voice along with the rest of them, despite being in human form.

"Drive carefully," Jester said. "Got some snow coming." He closed the BOW's back door and headed for the barn.

As she drove off, several ponies, including Thunder, Lightning, and old Hurricane, left the barn and trotted along behind her, turning off on one of the unmarked tracks while she continued to the Utilities Complex.

Blair was there, waiting for his delivery. So was Ferus. When she pulled up, both of them were focused on her passenger.

"You have to stay inside," Meg said quietly. "Big Wolves don't like the safety line." She got out of the BOW and had the back door open before the two Wolves approached.

There were flickers of red in Ferus's eyes. He snarled at her. Blair immediately turned and snarled at him until Ferus lowered his eyes and took a step back. And Sam, poking his head between the seats to watch the Wolves, vocalized opinions to everyone.

Blair studied the pup. Then he studied Meg. Finally, he said, "You have any packages for the Wolfgard Complex?"

"Yes."

"You leave those here. I'll take them with me when I go home."

Relieved, she hauled out boxes and packages, which Blair handed to Ferus to take into the Utilities building.

"Simon will be home tonight," Blair said as he took the last box.

"Oh. That's good." It was good. It also meant she needed to have Sam tucked at home before Simon arrived.

Having sufficiently expressed his opinion, Sam was curled up in the passenger's seat, napping, when she got back into the BOW and headed for the Chambers.

Her hands shook a little as the BOW chugged up the road and snow swiftly covered the pavement. She wanted to finish her deliveries and get home before the snowfall surpassed her driving skills—and it wouldn't take much snow on the roads to do that.

Sam didn't stir when she stopped at the first set of delivery boxes for the Chambers, but he woke up when she rummaged through the BOW to find the snow brush and clean off the windows before she could drive to the next group of mausoleums the Sanguinati called home.

By the time she pulled up in front of Erebus's home, Sam was almost bouncing with excitement, pawing at the passenger's window and then at the door handle.

"Come out this way," Meg said, holding her own door open.

He leaped out of the BOW and dodged across the road to explore as far as the leash allowed.

"Over here, Sam." Meg breathed a sigh of relief when he immediately obeyed. Crouching, she put a hand on his head. "We must never run across a road without looking in both directions. There could be other vehicles on the road, and the drivers might not see us in time to stop. That would be very bad, especially if anyone got hurt. So you don't run across the road like that. All right?"

He licked her chin, which she took as agreement.

When they went to the back of the BOW and she began gathering the packages, she noticed the way the pup stared at the wrought-iron fence, and thought of what Jester had told her about the Chambers.

Getting Sam's attention again, she said, "This is also a very important rule that we all have to follow. *No one* is allowed to go inside the fence unless Mr. Erebus gives his permission. Even Simon doesn't enter the Chambers without permission. So we stay on this side of the fence and don't even poke our noses between the bars."

Sam sighed.

"I know," she said as she opened a couple of the delivery boxes and began filling them. "There are a lot of rules to remember when you go beyond the Green Complex—and even more rules when traveling outside the Courtyard. If you had let me take you home, you could have been in a warm house, watching a movie, instead of being out here in the snow."

"Do you like movies, little Wolf?"

Meg jumped and let out a squeak. Sam responded by making puppy growls and snarls—which would have sounded more impressive if he hadn't leaped behind her and then poked his head between her knees to voice those opinions.

She looked at the old man standing at the gate, smiling gently at her. "Mr. Erebus."

"I didn't mean to startle you."

"I know. I just didn't see you." She glanced at his mausoleum. The door was open, but there were no footprints marring the fresh snow on the walk. She had gotten so used to seeing smoke drifting over the snow, she hadn't even noticed it this time.

Erebus didn't comment. He just stood there, smiling gently.

"Sam does like movies," Meg said to fill the silence. She closed the full delivery boxes, then went back to the BOW for another group of packages. "But I don't think he watches the same kind of movies that you do."

"I like many kinds of movies," Erebus replied, looking at Sam. "Have you seen the movies called cartoons? I especially enjoy the ones where the animals or people do the most foolish things and still survive."

Sam stayed close to her while she filled the boxes, but when she went back to the BOW for the final packages—the ones addressed to Erebus—Sam eased up to the gate to study the vampire patriarch.

Erebus opened the gate, crouched down, and extended one hand beyond the Chambers boundary. Sam sniffed the hand, licked a finger, and wagged his tail.

Erebus laughed softly as he petted the pup. "You're a delightful boy. I'm glad you're looking after our Meg."

"Looks like you have another movie," Meg said. When Erebus rose, she expected him to tell her to put it in the delivery box. Even when she had gone up the walk and delivered his packages at the door and he was watching, she had set them on the stoop per his instructions. But he had petted Sam, and she had a feeling that meant something. So she held out the package.

He hesitated. Erebus actually hesitated before he took the package from her hand.

"Namid is full of many things, some wondrous and some terrible," he said softly. "And some of her creations are both. Thank you for bringing my movies, Meg. I do like my old movies."

She opened the passenger's door, made sure the towel was on the seat, and let Sam jump in. Once he was settled, she got in, waved at Erebus, and drove off.

Why had he always hesitated to take a package from her until now? Was there some taboo about Sanguinati touching *cassandra sangue*? Did he even know what she was? And why had he looked at *her* when he said some of the world's creations were both terrible and wondrous? Yes, prophecies could be either and sometimes both, but she didn't think Erebus had been talking about prophecies.

Which made her wonder what he knew about her kind that she didn't.

The snow was falling faster. Meg stopped the BOW and took out the copy of the Courtyard map that she tucked into her purse each time she went out to make deliveries. She wasn't ignoring the danger of taking a map out of the Liaison's Office, but she was careful to keep it out of sight. And while it did show where each gard lived within the Courtyard, the map didn't show any roads except the paved ones that were suitable for vehicles. It wasn't anywhere near as detailed as the map of Lakeside that she had found in the Courtyard's library.

The Controller would have paid a lot of money for even this much information about the interior of a Courtyard.

After studying the map for a minute, she tucked it back in her purse, put the

BOW in gear, and turned onto an interior road. She'd make the other deliveries tomorrow if the roads in the Courtyard were passable. Right now, she wanted to get back to the Green Complex while she could.

By the time the BOW slid across Ripple Bridge, Meg was gripping the steering wheel and hardly daring to breathe. Even with the wipers going and the heater switched to blow on the front window, it was getting harder and harder to see.

The white horse standing at the edge of the road blended in with the swirling snow, and she wouldn't have seen him on his own, but the black horse and his rider stood in the road, waiting for her.

She stopped the BOW and put it in park, afraid that if she shut it off, she would never clear the snow off the windows enough to drive home. Rolling down her window, she peered at the riders who came up alongside the vehicle. Not girls. Closer to adult women, but still looking a bit too young to be considered mature.

Their faces—eerie, seductive, and compelling—looked even less human than their child faces, but the green scarf confirmed the identity of the black horse's rider.

"Winter?"

Winter laughed, and the snow swirled around them. "Yes, it's me. Thunder and Lightning wanted to stretch their legs, so Air and I are out riding." Her smile was chilling.

Meg stared at the horses—beautiful, otherworldly creatures with flowing manes and tails, who, except for their color, didn't look anything like the chubby ponies who delivered the mail.

Then Thunder lightly stamped a foot, and sound rolled softly through the Courtyard.

"Be patient," Winter scolded mildly. "This is our Meg."

Thunder tossed his head as if agreeing. Then the horse poked his nose in the window at the same moment Sam clambered into Meg's lap. The two breathed in each other's scent and seemed satisfied.

"More snow is coming," Winter said once Thunder pulled his head back. "You should go home."

"I have the library books you requested." Nudging Sam back into the passenger's seat, she started to twist around to find the carry bag.

"Leave it with Jester," Winter said. "We'll fetch it on the way back." She studied the BOW, then exchanged a look with Air. "And we can give you a little help getting home."

"You don't have to do that." Meg wasn't sure what they were offering, but she didn't want to face Thunder and Lightning anytime soon if they ended up hitched to the front of the BOW to pull her back to the Green Complex.

"No, we don't. But it will be amusing," Winter replied.

"Do you think the storm will hold off long enough for Simon to get home?" Meg asked. It was more thinking out loud than an actual question.

Another look between Winter and Air. "The Wolfgard will be able to get home tonight. Follow us."

Turning, they cantered down the road.

Rolling up her window, Meg put the BOW in gear and followed.

Snow blew off the road in front of her, leaving the pavement clear so the BOW could keep up with the horses, and filling back in moments after Meg drove past. It was like driving through a snow-shaped tunnel that was lit up by flickers of lightning and trembled with the thunder that followed. It should have been frightening, but she felt oddly safe in the cocoon of weather the Elementals were shaping around her. A few flakes drifted down and were cleared by the wipers, but she could see the road and the horses up ahead, and that's all she really needed.

As they neared the Pony Barn, she spotted another rider heading out on a brown horse—and noticed the funnel of snow that followed Tornado.

They stopped at the Pony Barn long enough for Jester to run out and fetch the bag of library books. After that, Winter and Air escorted Meg and Sam all the way back to the Green Complex's garage.

"Thank you," Meg said, grabbing her own carry bag and Sam's towel as the pup jumped out of the BOW.

With a nod of their heads, Winter and Air turned the horses and rode off.

Meg paused long enough to check that she'd shut off the lights. She couldn't remember what the power gauge read, but she shook her head and closed the garage door. There should be enough power for her to get to the office, and she could charge the BOW in the garage there. Besides, the snow was coming down harder now, and it was lung-biting cold outside.

Sam didn't have any trouble running in snow, but after Meg skidded a couple of times and almost landed on her butt, he slowed down to accommodate human legs. Pausing at the bottom of her stairs to catch her breath, she noticed the black sedan idling at the side of the road.

"What does he want?" she muttered uneasily as she looked around. No lights on in Henry's apartment. Most likely he was still working in his studio. She paused a moment longer, then climbed the stairs to her apartment.

"Come on, Sam. You can stay up here with me until Simon gets home." She'd spent so much time in Simon's apartment these past few days, she hadn't had a chance to settle into her own place.

"Meg!"

Meg opened her door, tossed the towel on the floor near the boot mat, and told Sam to stay on the towel. Then she greeted Tess as the other woman bounded up the stairs.

"Here," Tess said, holding out a bakery tin. "Chocolate chip cookies, still warm from the oven. I booted everyone out and closed A Little Bite early, but after I got home, I felt restless and decided to bake."

Meg took the tin. "Thanks, Tess. Do you want to come in?"

"No. I've got a casserole in the oven now. You're shivering. You should get inside."

Tess wasn't shivering—yet—but she wasn't dressed for being outside for long.

Meg stepped inside.

Tess's hair began to streak with green. She shook her head, but the hair continued to change to green and started to curl. "It's this storm," she explained. "Everyone will be edgy if the Wolfgard gets stranded tonight."

"Winter said the storm will hold off and Simon will be able to get home," Meg said.

Tess gave her an odd look. "Did she? Well, she would know."

Bounding down the stairs, Tess ran back to her own apartment. Meg closed her door and set down the tin with the rest of her things as she took off her boots and hung up her coat.

Sam immediately began sniffing at the bakery tin. When he couldn't nose it open, he sat and grabbed it between his front paws, trying to hook his claws under the lid to pull it open.

"No," Meg said, taking it from him. Going into the kitchen with him bouncing beside her, she set the tin in the middle of her table, opened it, and recalled everything she could about cookies and animals.

The chocolate chip cookies smelled delicious, and she wanted to bite into one. But she looked at Sam, balanced on his hind legs with his front paws resting on the table's edge, and closed the tin.

"I'm sorry, Sam, but I don't know if Wolves can eat these cookies. I remember that chocolate is bad for dogs—" She held up a hand to stop him when he began vocalizing. "Yes, I know you're not a dog, and maybe since you can change shape you'd be fine eating chocolate even when you're furry, but I can't take the chance of you getting sick, especially tonight, when it would be hard to get help. So no people cookies. And I won't have any either." *At least, not until you go home.*

Sam howled.

Someone pounded on her front door.

Meg hesitated, rememories of bad things happening when someone answered a door flashing through her mind. Then, reminding herself that she was safe in the Green Complex, she hurried to the door. It was probably Vlad checking to make sure she and Sam had gotten home all right. Or maybe Henry had come home in the past few minutes and wanted to let her know he was close by.

But when she opened the door, Elliot Wolfgard stepped inside far enough to prevent her from closing the door. The hatred in his eyes froze her—more so when Sam bounded in from the kitchen, trailing the leash because she hadn't had time to remove the harness.

"Sam," he said, still looking at Meg. "Come with me."

Sam whined and looked at her.

"*Sam,*" Elliot snarled.

"It's all right," Meg told the pup. "Simon will be home soon."

Elliot scooped up Sam. "Once I get him settled, I'll be back. I have some things to say to you."

As soon as Elliot went down the stairs, Meg closed the door and hurried to the phone.

"Tess?" she said as soon as the other woman answered the phone.

"Meg? Is something wrong?"

"Elliot Wolfgard was just here. He took Sam back to Simon's place. Was it all right to let Sam go with him?"

A pause. "In human terms, Elliot is Sam's grandfather, so there's no reason why the pup can't go with him."

Then why didn't Simon ask Elliot to watch Sam? "All right. Thanks. Have to go. Someone is at the door."

"Call me when your visitor leaves."

She hung up without promising to call and hurried back to the door.

Elliot stepped inside, leaving her to shiver because, once again, he wasn't far enough inside for her to close the door.

"The enforcer may be willing to protect you, but the rest of the Wolves will never forgive what you've done," he snarled. "As far as I'm concerned, you're barely useful meat, and I am going to do everything I can to have you running before the pack as prey for what you did to Sam."

"I haven't done anything to Sam!"

He slapped her face.

"Enjoy your evening, meat. You won't live to see many more of them."

He went down the stairs, leaving her shaking. A few moments later, she heard Simon's front door slam.

She was going to die in the Courtyard. She'd known that since the first time she'd set eyes on Simon Wolfgard.

She swallowed convulsively, but her mouth kept filling with saliva. She barely made it to the toilet before she threw up.

Vlad flowed over the snow toward the Green Complex, ready to spend a quiet evening at home. Blair was on his way to pick up Simon and the two guards who had gone with him, Nathan Wolfgard and Marie Hawkgard. If the weather forecast was right about Lakeside getting another foot of snow this evening, the drive home would be slow going.

After hearing that report, he had sent Heather home, closed Howling Good Reads, and locked up the social center. Tess had already closed A Little Bite, and Run & Thump, along with the rest of the Courtyard businesses, had closed an hour after that. But a bar across the street from the Courtyard was still doing a brisk business. He had fed sufficiently on two delightful girls who claimed they had missed their bus and were in the bar drinking while they waited for the next one. He was suspicious about their reason for being in the bar, but he had no doubt they'd been drinking, because he was a little drunk from the alcohol in their blood.

If the weather had been milder, he would have let the girls find their own way to the bus stop, since it was within sight of the bar. By itself, the amount of blood he'd taken from each of them wouldn't do more than make them tired. But the police officer, Lieutenant Montgomery, paid attention to the Courtyard now, and Vlad didn't think Simon would appreciate questions about two girls falling into a drunken sleep and dying in a snowdrift so close to where the Sanguinati lived—especially when there was no reason for the girls to die. So he flagged down a cab and paid the driver to take the girls back to their residence at the nearby tech college.

He wasn't sure he liked thinking of humans as something other than useful prey or concerning himself with their welfare once he was done with them, but with humans stirred up about whatever had happened in the western part of Thaisia, being considerate of the prey here was just healthy self-interest.

As he flowed into the Green Complex and headed for his apartment, he became aware of sounds coming from Simon's apartment. Sam was howling, an unhappy sound. Probably meant that Meg wanted some time to herself or wasn't interested in taking any kind of walk with the temperature dropping and the snow falling so heavily.

Passing his own door, Vlad shifted into human form and walked over to the stairs leading to Meg's apartment. Since the cold and snow didn't bother him, he would offer to take the pup for a walk. That would at least give them all a bit of quiet.

Her front door stood open.

Shifting back to smoke, he flowed up the stairs and into her apartment. No sign of intruders. No sign of struggle. He flowed into the kitchen and found nothing. Nothing in her bedroom.

Shifting back to human form, he hesitated outside the bathroom door.

"Meg?" he called softly. "Meg? Are you in there?"

"I— Yes, I'm here."

Ignoring how many ways he might upset a human female by entering a bathroom uninvited, he pushed open the door, then rushed over to her. The room smelled of vomit, which he found repulsive, but not of blood. No injuries then, just illness.

"You're sick?" Should he call Heather to find out what medicine humans used for stomach sickness? Or maybe Elizabeth Bennefeld. Wouldn't she need to know about the human body for her massage work?

"No," Meg replied. "I'm . . ." Tears spilled down her face. She shook her head.

"Sam?"

"Home."

He knew that much. "You done here?"

She nodded. She flushed the toilet once more and closed the lid. When he helped her up, he saw the other side of her face.

"What's *that*?"

She shook her head. When he continued to block her way out of the bathroom, she whispered, "Please. Don't make this harder."

Make what harder? Vlad thought.

"I'd really like to be alone now," Meg said.

Not knowing what else to do, he left her apartment, closing the front door behind him. He hesitated at the top of the stairs, then went down and knocked on Simon's door.

He heard a crash, followed by Elliot's angry shout. He knocked again, harder. Elliot finally opened the door enough to look out, his body blocking the space.

Vlad smelled blood. "Problem?"

"A family matter," Elliot replied darkly.

He leaned closer to Elliot. "If Meg ends up with another unexplained bruise or is frightened into sickness again, that, too, will be a family matter. But the family involved won't be the Wolfgard's."

Threat delivered, Vlad went to his own apartment. He would inform Grandfather Erebus tomorrow. That would give Simon time to settle things in his own way.

Flanked by Nathan and Marie, Simon stepped off the train, walked through the station, and out the door that opened onto the parking lot. There had been bands of snow all along the way, but once the train reached Lake Etu, the snow had turned into serious weather. By the time they reached the train station at Lakeside, Simon figured the snow was going to make all but the main roads impassable.

He breathed out a sigh of relief when he saw Blair brushing off the van's windows—and he felt his muscles tense when he spotted the police car idling in the parking lot.

After handing his carryall to Nathan, who climbed into the back with Marie, Simon took the passenger's seat in the front of the van. Blair got in on the driver's side a moment later, turned on the wipers, and put the van in gear.

Simon tipped his head toward the police car. "Is there some trouble I should know about?"

Blair shook his head. "I think that lieutenant who comes sniffing around wanted to know when you returned."

The tire tracks from the cars that had arrived to pick up passengers were already filling in with fresh snow. Blair pulled out of the parking space and slowly drove toward the lot's exit.

"You think we'll get home tonight?" Nathan asked, leaning forward.

For a moment, Blair didn't answer. Looking at the other Wolf's face, Simon had the strong impression the Courtyard's enforcer wasn't easy about something. Maybe more than one something.

"Tess called while I was waiting for the train to get in," Blair said. "Apparently, the Liaison expressed the same concern about you being able to get home. The girl at the lake assured her that you would get home tonight." He paused, then added, "Vlad called too, but not about the weather."

A plow had come by recently, filling the entrance to the parking lot with a wall of snow. Blair revved the van's engine and rammed through the snow. The van lost traction for a moment, its tires spinning. Then it muscled through the rest of the white barricade and reached the road.

"Of course," Blair said dryly, "the girl at the lake didn't say getting home would be easy."

No, it wasn't easy, but most of the streets they needed were plowed to some extent, and the ones that weren't plowed had snow drifted in unnatural patterns that gave them one passable, if serpentine, lane.

Simon stayed quiet until they reached the Courtyard, letting Blair focus on driving. When they pulled in at the Utilities entrance, the gates were open enough for the van to squeeze through.

"That's not good security, leaving the gates open," Nathan growled.

"We're not going to get them closed until we shift some of that snow," Blair replied. He wasn't pleased about that.

"I don't think a potential intruder will get far," Simon said. It looked like someone had cleared the part of the Courtyard's main road that headed for the Green Complex. In the other direction, the road was completely hidden under fresh snow.

He twisted in his seat to look at Nathan and Marie. "Doesn't look like you'll get back to your own homes tonight."

"Julia's apartment is in the Green Complex. I can stay with her tonight," Marie said.

"Nathan?"

Before answering, Nathan glanced at Blair. "I guess I'll bed down in one of the apartments above the Liaison's Office?"

Blair nodded. "And I'll come back to the Utilities Complex and bed down there to keep an eye on things. The Crows will take care of the Corvine gate."

<Did something happen?> Simon demanded.

<Some things we can't discuss yet,> Blair replied.

A chill went through Simon as Blair slowly drove toward the Green Complex.

<Is Sam all right?>

Blair's lips twitched. <Sam is fine.>

He hesitated. <And Meg?>

<Not so fine.> A dark note in Blair's voice. <But nothing that can't be fixed.>

What did *that* mean? He was tired and frustrated and as worried as the rest of the *terra indigene* leaders over the unexplained aggression that had ended with so many dead in that western village. They had no answers, didn't even know where to begin looking for the enemy hiding somewhere in the human villages and cities scattered throughout Thaisia.

He knew the solution most of the Others would take if humans became too much of a threat. He'd make the same choice. But he wanted extermination to be the last choice, not the first.

He hadn't wanted to come home to trouble. He had hoped Meg and Sam . . .

But Blair said Sam was fine. So why wasn't Meg fine?

When the van pulled up at the entrance to the Green Complex, Blair reached into his coat pocket and pulled out a set of keys tied to a leather loop that would slip over a human head—or a Wolf's.

"Take the BOW as far as you can," he said, handing the keys to Nathan after pointing to the vehicle parked in the visitor's space. "You might make it all the way. Call Henry when you get to the apartment."

"Should I be on the lookout for anything in particular?" Nathan asked as he opened the van's side door.

"Same thing we always look for," Blair replied. "Intruders."

"I'll do a sweep from the Liaison's Office to the Corvine gate in the morning," Marie said, hefting her carryall. She followed Nathan out of the van.

Simon watched them trudge through several inches of snow. He wanted to shift, wanted to lash out at his enforcer, wanted to purge the uneasiness growing inside him. "We're alone. Now tell me."

"Sam is fine." Blair looked straight ahead. The only other sound was the rhythmic swish of the wipers. "I'm not easy about how she did it, but I'm sure she meant no harm, and I do like the results." He turned his head to look at Simon. "She got him out of the cage, and not just a few steps outside the apartment door to pee and poop. They've walked around the complex. He's gone to the office with her. He was with her this afternoon when she made some deliveries before the weather started to turn. Maybe he was ready to wake up, and she did things that were just strange enough to slip past his fear."

Simon looked away, confused by what he was feeling. Jealousy? Hurt? He'd spent two years trying to find a way to help Sam come back to them, and Meg had found the answer in a few days? He felt like a pair of jaws had closed over his throat, making it hard to breathe.

"How?" he finally asked.

"Something none of us would have considered," Blair said. "A harness and leash."

Shock. Fear. Fury. How dare *any* human try to restrain a Wolf?

"You let her do this?"

"First I knew of it, they were walking around the complex, and I wasn't going to take on Henry and Vlad in order to discipline her. And after seeing how the pup was *playing*, I thought it best not to interfere." Blair paused. "He's playing again, Simon. He's eating meat again. He's acting like a young Wolf again. For the most part. He still hasn't talked to any of us, but I think that will come if he's not scared back into that cage."

"Why would he be?" The pup was playing again? He wouldn't allow anything to interfere with that.

Blair went back to staring out the window. "Like I said, I'm not easy with how Meg got Sam out of the cage, but Henry and Vlad have been keeping an eye on them and have voiced no objections. Elliot, however, is a problem."

"Did he hurt Meg?" Simon asked, his voice stripped of emotion. Elliot didn't know about Meg. If he bit her, cut her . . .

"She's puking scared. I had the feeling there was something else, but Vlad wasn't interested in telling me. He did want me to remind you that while the

Sanguinati don't usually hunt other *terra indigene*, we are not exempt from being prey."

Simon couldn't believe what he was hearing. "The Sanguinati are going after Elliot?"

A long pause. Then Blair said quietly, "I guess that depends on whether you can talk Meg into staying."

"Well, she's not going anywhere tonight." Of course, someone who was puking scared might not consider the danger of trying to run when the roads were bad and the air too cold. Especially when that person had already run away once in exactly that kind of weather.

He unbuckled the seat belt. "Anything else that can't wait until morning?"

Another pause. "Nothing that can't wait. But if any monkeys dressed all in black try to enter the complex tonight, just kill them." A longer pause. "It's something Meg saw. Henry can tell you about it."

Simon shivered, and it wasn't because of the cold. Meg had cut herself while he was gone? How many times? What other scraps of information were going to be tossed at him?

"We're all going to meet tomorrow morning," he growled. "You, me, Tess, Henry, Vlad, Jester, and anyone else you think needs to be there."

"I'll call you in the morning to find out if we're meeting at the Business Association or the social room here at the complex," Blair said.

He nodded. Except for Blair, the rest of them lived in the Green Complex. They could meet early and then see about getting the stores and roads open.

Grabbing his carryall, Simon got out of the van and broke a trail to his apartment's front door. He reached for the door, then stepped back and looked around. Lights shining from the windows of every apartment except Meg's.

It wasn't that late, so it shouldn't have been strange to see all the residences lit up. But it seemed like there were too many lights, too much brightness, making that dark space too noticeable, almost ominous.

Why was Meg sitting in the dark?

His uneasiness became an itch under his human skin, making him anxious to shift to a more natural shape. As Wolf, he had the fangs and strength to deal with itchy problems.

He heard Sam howl—and Elliot's growl of reply. Opening his front door, he stepped into a tension that had him fighting not to shift and force both Wolves into submission.

Tossing the carryall toward the stairs, he stepped into the living room's archway, treading snow on the wood floor. Elliot whipped around to face him, teeth bared, the canines too long to pass as human. Sam gave Simon one accusing look, then sat in a corner of his cage, his back to both adults.

<Sam?> Simon said.

No answer. Not even a grumble.

Looking oddly uneasy, Elliot turned his head and snapped at the pup, "Stop this foolishness, and come out of that damn cage! You don't need to be in there!"

<In the kitchen,> Simon growled. Blood and anger. He could smell both.

"At least take off those snowy boots," Elliot said snippily. "You're tracking the wet all over the—"

Simon grabbed Elliot and pushed him against the hallway wall. "I'm not some human you can intimidate. And I'm not a pup anymore. You don't tell *me* what to do. *No one* tells me what to do."

He lengthened his fangs and waited.

Elliot stared at him for a moment. Then he closed his eyes and raised his head, exposing his throat to his leader.

Simon stepped back, not feeling sufficiently human or Wolf to decide how he should respond. Releasing Elliot, he walked into the kitchen, unlaced his boots, and put them on the mat by the back door.

Elliot fetched a couple of old towels and wiped up the floors. When he returned to the kitchen, Simon studied his sire.

"You stirred things up here," he finally said. "Why?"

"I'm not the one who—"

"You've angered the Sanguinati, and that's not going to help any of us right now."

"You don't know what's been going on here," Elliot snapped. "What that monkey-fuck female has done."

"She's not a monkey fuck, and she is not prey," Simon said, his voice a low, threatening rumble. "She is Meg."

"You don't know what she's done!"

"She gets mail and deliveries to the complexes on a regular basis. She has a routine with the deliverymen, so we get the merchandise we bought. And she got Sam out of that damn cage!"

"She put him on a leash, Simon. *On a leash!*"

"It's not a leash," a young, scratchy voice shouted. Or tried to shout. "It's a safety line. Adventure buddies use a safety line so they can help each other."

Elliot stared, frozen. Simon turned, barely breathing.

Small naked boy, wobbling on stick-thin legs. His hair was a gold mixed with Wolf gray that was rarer than a pure black or white Wolf. Gray eyes full of angry tears, and yet there was a dominance in that weak body that didn't match Simon's but was higher than Elliot's standing within the Lakeside pack. Or would be when Sam was an adult.

"Sam," Simon whispered.

Sam ignored him and glared at Elliot. "You made Meg cry, so I'm not sorry I bit you!"

Now Simon closed the distance between them and went down on one knee in front of the boy. "Sam." Fingers hesitantly touched those skinny, weak-muscled arms. A nose twitched at the odor of an unwashed body. "Hey. Sam."

Big eyes fixed on him now. He was the leader. He was supposed to make things better, make things right.

Just bite me, he thought. He understood *pup*. He wasn't sure what to do with *boy*.

<Elliot . . . > Simon glanced over his shoulder at his sire, who looked pale and shaken.

<Say whatever words will keep him with us,> Elliot said.

"This safety line for adventure buddies is a new thing you learned from Meg?" Simon asked.

Sam nodded.

"It's not something other Wolves have heard of. So Elliot thought the safety line was something else, something that might hurt you."

"Meg wouldn't hurt me," Sam protested. "She's my friend."

"I know that, Sam. I know." Another hesitant touch of fingers on the boy's shoulders. Compared to the human form of the other Wolf pups his age, Sam was small and too thin. But that would change if the boy didn't disappear again inside the Wolf.

"Is Meg going away?" Sam asked.

Simon shook his head. "No. She's not going away."

Elliot cleared his throat. "I will offer an apology tomorrow."

Sam swayed. His leg muscles trembled with the effort of keeping him upright. But the look he gave Simon, while shy, clearly had a focus.

"Simon?"

"Sam?"

"Can I have a cookie?"

He wasn't sure there was anything to eat besides Sam's kibble. He *was* sure of what he wouldn't find. "I'm sorry, Sam. We don't have any cookies."

"Meg does." Sam licked his lips. "They smelled really good, but she didn't know if Wolves could have chocolate, so we didn't eat any. But I could have one now."

Oh, chew a tail and spit out the fur. Sure, the *boy* could have one if the man was willing to knock on Meg's door and beg for it.

Right now, he would do a lot more than beg in order to get the cookie Sam wanted.

"I'll go ask her." He wrinkled his nose and smiled. "Maybe you should take a bath before you have a treat."

"I can help Sam," Elliot said quietly.

Simon rose and stepped back. "Then I'll get the cookie." And while he was there, he'd find out if Meg was planning to run away.

Thinking about her dark apartment and wondering whether any of the *terra indigene* would be welcome tonight, he took the spare set of keys for her apartment before going upstairs to the back hall door.

A quick knock. "Meg?" Another knock, louder. "Meg? It's Simon. Open the door." When he didn't get a response, he used the key, breathing a sigh of relief that she hadn't used the slide lock as well.

She was sitting at the kitchen table in the dark, her arms wrapped around herself.

"I don't want company," she said, not looking at him.

"Too bad." He reached for the ceiling light's pull string, then considered the brightness and flipped on the light over the sink. Going back to the table, he looked at her face and couldn't stop the snarl when he saw the bruise. That explained why Vlad was threatening to go after Elliot.

He leaned down, capturing her chin between thumb and forefinger in order to turn her head and get a better look. He leaned closer, breathing in the scent of her. The smell of sickness lingered on her clothes. Not sure what to do, he gave her cheek a gentle lick.

"Snow," he said, easing back. "Snow will help."

"What?"

Her eyes looked bruised. Not physically, which somehow made it worse. "Stay there." He found a kitchen towel, then went down the back stairs to the outside door. Leaning out enough to reach the snow, he packed a ball of it in the towel and brought it to her. "Put this on your face."

When she obeyed, he picked up the other kitchen chair and set it down so he could face her.

"I didn't mean to cause trouble," she whispered. Tears filled her eyes and rolled down her face. "I wasn't trying to hurt Sam."

"I know." Taking her free hand, he petted the soft skin, that delicate, strange skin that was the gateway to prophecy. "Elliot didn't understand, and he's sorry he hurt you. *I'm* sorry he hurt you."

"He said . . ." She shuddered.

Simon shook his head. "It doesn't matter what he said. You're safe here, Meg. You're safe with us. I'll make sure of that."

She lifted the towel away from her face. "The snow is melting."

He took the towel and dumped it in the sink. Then he turned to look at her. What was he supposed to do with her? What was *proper* to do with her? He knew how to deal with human females when they were customers in the store. He knew what to do when they wanted the heat of sex and he was in the mood to provide it. And he knew what to do with prey. But he didn't know what to do with Meg.

"Do you want food?" he asked, studying her back.

She shook her head.

"Tea?"

Another head shake.

He'd come here to get something for Sam, but that didn't feel right anymore. And yet how could he disappoint the boy?

Returning to the table, he sat in the chair. The bakery tin was right there in front of him, taunting him. Until she had shown up half frozen and changed some of the rules, it had been so much easier dealing with humans.

"Meg?" he asked softly. "Could I take a cookie for Sam?"

She blinked. Brushed away tears. Then she looked at the bakery tin and frowned. "Those are chocolate chip cookies. Can Wolves eat chocolate?"

It hadn't occurred to him to wonder. "He shifted, Meg. He's a boy." He couldn't meet her eyes, and he heard his own whine of confusion. "He hasn't shifted to human since his mother was killed. He hasn't talked to us in any way since the night Daphne died. He's been afraid to be outside, and he hurt himself a couple of times. That's why I had to get the cage. But you changed that. He couldn't have a cookie as a Wolf, so he shifted to a boy. I couldn't reach him, but you did—with a leash that isn't a leash and a cookie."

"You took care of him and you loved him and you kept him safe," she said. "Even if it didn't show, he *was* learning from you." She sniffed, then got up and rummaged in the cupboard until she found a small container. After placing a few cookies in the container, she gave him the bakery tin. "Do you have any milk to go with the cookies?"

"I don't know."

She opened her fridge and gave him an unopened quart.

The quick glance in her fridge didn't reassure him that *she* had enough to eat—especially if they were snowed in tomorrow.

Awkward, this sniffing around a female's personal life. Awkward, this no longer being sure how far he could push her when he hadn't hesitated to push before he'd left on that trip. Awkward, because somehow she was starting to matter to him the way his own people mattered.

He backed away. "Thank you."

"Don't let him eat all the cookies," she said. "Even as a boy, it would make him sick."

Nodding, he let himself out and fled back to his own apartment.

Sam was sitting at the kitchen table, explaining about safety lines to Elliot, who was listening as if every word was desperately important. The words dried up as soon as Simon put the bakery tin on the table.

"One," Simon said firmly. He poured a glass of milk for each of them and opened the tin.

Sam took small bites, savoring the taste while he eyed the bakery tin until Simon put the lid back on, confirming that one meant one.

"The Wolf cookies are good, but these are better," Sam said.

"Wolf cookies?" Elliot asked.

Sam nodded. "Meg got them special for me."

<What are Wolf cookies?> Elliot asked Simon.

He shrugged. Something else he needed to find out.

Sam yawned.

"Long day for all of us," Simon said.

Sam struggled to sit up. "I'm not tired. Meg would let me watch a movie."

<Is Meg going to be the stick he tries to use on us from now on?> Elliot asked.

<Only until I find out what Meg really allowed him to do,> Simon replied. "All right. Go pick out a movie."

Wobbling. Using the walls for support. But still holding on to a shape that had been a recent discovery before fear had frozen Sam into Wolf form.

Simon drained his glass, then finished off Sam's glass of milk. "Roads to the Wolfgard Complex aren't passable. You should stay here."

"All right." Elliot hesitated. "I'd rather not stay in this form."

He wanted to shed the human skin too. "We'll wait until Sam is asleep."

It didn't take long. Tucked on the couch, wrapped in a blanket to protect that small, shivering body, Sam was asleep five minutes into the movie. Simon checked the doors, turned off lights, and made sure everything was secure. By the time he returned to the living room, Elliot had already shifted.

Leaving the movie on, Simon stripped off his clothes. Then he shifted and settled beside Elliot on the living room floor. If the floor wasn't as warm or comfortable as the beds upstairs, the boy sleeping on the couch provided a different, and deeper, contentment.

"But I wanna go with Meg!"

As he toweled himself dry, Simon gave his nephew a hard stare and had a totally inappropriate wish that for one more day, he could chuck the puppy in the cage instead of dealing with a wobbly boy who was more stranger than family and was acting annoyingly human.

"You can't go with Meg today," he said firmly. He felt like he'd been saying the same words from the moment Sam woke up. "You're going to stay here with Elliot while I go to this meeting."

"But who's gonna be Meg's adventure buddy if I'm not there?"

"Someone else will have to be her adventure buddy." Preoccupied with the personal hygiene checklist he followed when he had to deal with humans, he didn't realize how badly he'd erred until Sam gave him a tear-filled, horrified look.

"But *I'm* her adventure buddy. She *said* I was!" Sam wailed.

Before Simon could reach for the boy, Sam stepped back from the bathroom doorway and darted out of Simon's bedroom.

Wobbly legs. Stairs.

Springing into the bedroom, Simon grabbed the jeans he'd laid out on the bed and ran into the hall. When he didn't see Sam on the stairs, he pulled on the jeans, then tried to zip and button while he rushed after the boy, expecting to find Sam hiding in the living room or in the kitchen, whining at Elliot about not being allowed to go with Meg.

But when Simon got down the stairs, the front door was open, Sam's clothes were strewn all over the floor, the damn leash was gone, and there was evidence in the foot-deep fresh snow of a bounding puppy making his escape.

Simon leaped out the door and snarled when his bare feet sank into snow. A few steps gave him a clear view of Meg's porch—and Sam standing on his hind legs, his forelegs shifted into furry arms that could reach the doorbell, and his front paws changed just enough to have fingers that could press the doorbell And press it and press it.

"Shit. Fuck. Damn damn *damn*." Swearwords were one of the best things humans had invented, Simon thought as he took the stairs in leaps. He was almost within reach when the door opened and Sam bolted inside, the red leash trailing after him.

Meg stood in the doorway, trying to scrunch herself into the bathrobe that didn't cover her lower legs. At another time, he would have given those legs a better look—just to check the visible skin for scars. Now, with Sam all furry and talking back at him and Meg looking like a bunny who had been dodging a Hawk, only to run smack into a Wolf, he did what he figured was the polite human thing to do and kept his eyes on her face.

Didn't stop him from grabbing her hand before she regained enough of her wits to shut the door in his face.

"Meg."

"Mr. Wolfgard, what . . . ?"

"Can you watch Sam for a while? I have a meeting this morning. I'll pick him up at lunchtime. But this morning, you can be adventure buddies."

"But . . . I was getting in the shower," Meg protested weakly. She shivered. "I have to go to work."

"Then the two of you can be adventure buddies at the office. Just don't get buried in the snow." A weak effort at humor, since that was a possibility.

<That's why we have the safety line!>

He was so startled to have Sam communicate with him in the *terra indigene* way after so long a silence, he squeezed Meg's hand hard enough to make her yip.

"Mr. Wolfgard," Meg said, pulling her hand out of his. "You're not dressed."

And neither was she. "Please, Meg. Just for the morning." He put some bite in the last words and looked past her to Sam.

Sam wagged his tail, not the least bit sorry—or worried—about how he got what he wanted.

When Meg didn't say anything, Simon nudged her back a couple of steps. "Get in the shower. It will warm you up."

Closing her door, he hurried down the stairs and back to his apartment. Elliot stood in the entryway, staring at the clothes on the floor and the open door.

"Blessed Thaisia, what is going on?"

Damn, his feet were cold, and the jeans were wet. "Meg's taking Sam with her for the morning. Put his clothes in a carry sack. I'll leave them with Meg when I go back out for the meeting. And call Nathan. See if the streets around the office and our stores have been plowed. There's no point having Meg try to get to work if there aren't going to be deliveries."

He headed upstairs, intending to take another hot shower and get fully dressed before he ventured outside.

"Simon?" Elliot called, stopping him at the top of the stairs. "Since I won't be watching Sam, I'd like to attend that meeting. If that's acceptable to you."

While there were specific individuals he wanted at this meeting, any leader of a gard or other group of *terra indigene* was allowed to sit in on the Business Association meetings. Today there were things to discuss about the past week in the Courtyard. There were also things they needed to consider about what happened in Jerzy, and Elliot should hear what was said about that.

And maybe Elliot should be told some things about Meg.

"All right. Check with Nathan first, then call Blair and tell him we'll be meeting in the Green social room."

He didn't wait for Elliot's reply. He went into his bathroom, stripped off the wet jeans, and stood in the shower long enough to warm up. While he got dressed, he considered the new challenge of weaning Sam away from his adventure buddy.

But first he would have to figure out a good reason why he would want to.

It didn't look like they were going anywhere.

Meg stared at the snowdrifts beyond the archway that led to the parking area and garages for the Green Complex. Paths had been cleared around the interior of the complex so that the residents could reach the laundry room, mail room, social room, and the apartments, but there was no way she was going to get her BOW out of the garage, let alone reach the road.

"Come on, Sam. We'll take a quick walk and go back inside." She shifted her grip on the carry sack that contained a complete set of boy's clothing and turned back toward her apartment, pondering how she would get to work. Businesses did open after snowstorms. Deliveries would be made. The mailman would bring the mail sack and pick up the mail deposited in the blue post box that was tucked against the wall of the consulate. People went about their business in the winter, even if it took them a little longer than usual.

As she and Sam walked toward the other end of the complex, she heard bells.

Sam lifted his muzzle and howled.

"Come on," Meg said, walking as quickly as she could.

They reached the road in time to see the sleigh pulled by two brown horses. One horse had a black mane and tail; the other's mane and tail were pale gold.

Tornado and Twister in their other equine forms.

And there, in the front seat, were Winter and Air, still looking like young women instead of girls. They wore no coats, no hats, no gloves. Their gowns were layers of fluttery material that looked like it had been woven from clouds that ranged in color from white to a dark, stormy gray.

"Are you playing today?" Winter asked once the sleigh stopped beside Meg.

"Not playing so much as not working," Meg replied. "I can't get my BOW out of the garage, so I'm not sure I'll be able to reach the office."

"Is reaching the office important?" Air asked.

"It is if we want our mail today or any of the packages that are on the delivery trucks."

Winter stared at the social room's second-story windows. Then she smiled. "We can get you to your office. It won't take long."

Meg looked over her shoulder, then back at the Elemental. "Are you sure you won't be late for the meeting? I think Mr. Wolfgard and some of the others are already there."

Winter gave her a smile that was chilling but, Meg was certain, was not meant to be malevolent.

"I won't be late for the part of the meeting that is of interest to me and my sisters," Winter said.

"Then, thank you. I appreciate the ride. And I've never ridden in a sleigh before." This one was longer than her BOW and had two bench seats.

She picked up Sam, grunting at the unexpected weight. Could he have gotten that much bigger in a week's time? She put him on the floor of the backseat, then scrambled up to sit behind Air. As she got herself settled, she saw Jester standing in his apartment doorway, watching them.

Winter lifted the reins. "Give the snow a spin, my lovely boys. Our Meg wants to get to work."

As Tornado and Twister trotted along at a speed that made Meg's eyes water from the wind and stinging cold, the snow in front of them spun into funnels, leaving enough snowpack on the road to provide a good surface for the sleigh's runners. She had to admit, they moved on the snow far better than her BOW, and Winter delivered her to the back door of the office sooner than she expected.

An area around the back of the Liaison's Office had been cleared, and there was a path to Howling Good Reads, A Little Bite, and Henry's yard. After thanking Winter and Air, Meg followed the path to the front of the building.

She didn't recognize the man wielding the shovel, but since he wasn't wearing anything over his flannel shirt, she figured he wasn't human. She was sure of it when he glanced her way and stiffened the moment he saw Sam and the red harness and leash.

For his part, Sam *arroooo*ed a greeting and leaped into the untouched snow.

The Wolf watched the pup for a moment before walking over to Meg and tipping his head in what might have been a greeting.

"I'm Nathan Wolfgard," he said, some growl under the words as he kept glancing at Sam. "Stayed above stairs last night."

She looked at the second story of the building. "There are apartments upstairs?" She'd noticed the staircase behind the building and the second-story door, but what was above the office wasn't any of her business. "You live there?"

He shook his head. "Stayed there. Blair wanted eyes on this part of the Courtyard."

Why? Not a question she could ask him, but her skin was suddenly prickling so much she wanted to dig her fingernails into it through all the layers of clothing.

"Got a path dug from street to door," Nathan said. "Not going to get vehicles in or out until our plow comes up from the Utility Complex, but the monkeys can reach the building if they've a mind to." He didn't look happy about that.

"Thank you for clearing paths to the doors," Meg said. "Come on, Sam. Shake off the snow. It's time for me to go to work."

Sam, now snow crusted and happily panting, gave himself a vigorous shake before following Meg back around the building. She got them both wiped down before she unlocked the front door and flipped the sign to OPEN. The snow along the wall of Henry's yard looked like a ramp, making her wonder if the snow was packed up the same way on the other side.

Five Crows settled on the wall. They didn't caw at the Wolf. After watching Nathan through the window, she decided nobody taunted a Wolf who was holding a snow shovel—or one who could pack a mean snowball and fire it at black-feathered targets if the targets became annoying.

She put fresh water in one of Sam's bowls, poured a little kibble in the other bowl, and made herself a cup of peppermint tea. Leaving Sam to gnaw on the last piece of stag stick, she took her tea and two editions of the Courtyard newsletter to the front counter. It was colder out there than in the sorting room, but she didn't have anything to sort yet and she wanted to keep an eye on the street.

She saw Nathan head for the back of the building, the shovel over his shoulder. A minute later, she heard the floor creak above her head. Then the quiet, steady sound of voices. Not conversation. After a moment, she concluded that Nathan must be listening to the television or radio while he, too, kept watch out a window.

Was there another reason Blair—and Simon?—wanted eyes on this part of the Courtyard, or was it simply a matter of having someone around if the stores didn't open today?

Since it wasn't likely that she would get an answer from any of the Wolves, Meg opened the first newsletter to find out what had been going on in the Courtyard.

"Got the Utilities gate dug out and closed," Blair said as he took a seat in the Green social room. "Got the plow out and starting on the business areas. Truck and bucket loader are following. We'll have to shift the snow to the mounding sites to clear some parking spaces in the lot and clear the area for the consulate and Liaison's Office. Nathan shoveled a path from street to office. He'll stay above stairs for a while, unless you want him elsewhere."

"Have him stay there," Simon said. Sam shifting to a boy last night and the ruckus this morning had kept his mind occupied. Now he wondered if Blair was being so cautious because of some vague threat that might come from humans or because he wanted to show other residents in the Courtyard that the Wolves were looking after the Liaison properly. Or was Blair trying to avoid any incident that would start a fight between the Wolves and the Sanguinati?

He didn't have to wonder for long. He just had to watch the Courtyard's enforcer when Vlad walked into the room and noticed Elliot.

So. The vampires were serious about killing a Wolf.

Jester and Henry walked in together. The Coyote looked a little too gleeful. The Grizzly just looked sleepy.

Tess walked in with her hair coiling and completely green. As soon as she spotted Elliot, broad red streaks appeared along with threads of black.

"There is a new danger to *terra indigene* and humans alike," Simon said. He waited until Tess took a seat before continuing. "So far, there have been no reports of strange killings in the eastern part of Thaisia, but there have been several odd deaths or queer attacks in the west. A pack of dogs attacked a pack of Wolves. The dogs were killed, but the Wolves then ran down several deer and savaged them without stopping to feed. In another village, a pack of human males attacked three females and two subordinate males with such violence, the police thought at first it was an animal attack. Three of the prey died during the attack. The other two died in the hospital. There have been more attacks—a double handful in all that occurred over several months. Since more of the attacks were human against human, there was no reason to think it was a sickness that was spreading from the humans to us."

"Until the deaths at Jerzy," Henry said quietly. "Until leaders among the *terra indigene* gathered to talk, and began to see a pattern."

Simon nodded. "Most of the attacks hardly touched us at all, except for the police sniffing around for some way to blame us. In a few cases, the sickness started in a village of humans that is enclosed by our territory, and no one can say how it reached one village when other villages on that same road were not touched. Sickness should have spread from village to village, leaving a trail, but that hasn't been true this time."

Vlad sat back and crossed one leg over the other. "The leaders from the Courtyards that were affected are satisfied that this sickness begins with the humans?"

"Yes. But the human leaders believe just as strongly that we're the cause."

"Doesn't matter what *they* believe," Jester growled.

"If the humans are spreading a new sickness to us, there is a way to fix the problem," Blair said, staring at Simon.

"That's not the answer," Henry said, shifting in his chair. "Not yet. First we or the humans must find the root of this sickness. Then we decide what needs to be killed."

"Agreed," Simon said. "Especially since there has been no sign of this sickness in the east." He sighed. "One thing ties each of these attacks to us: some Crows were killed near each of the villages a day or two before the attack took place. I'll talk to Jenni Crowgard. If Crows begin to die without reason, we need to take that as a warning that the sickness has reached Lakeside."

He waited a moment. "Now. What's been happening here?"

He wasn't sure if it was just timing or if Vlad had sent a signal, but as soon as he asked the question, the door opened and Winter walked into the room, followed by Erebus Sanguinati. After a moment of startled silence, two chairs were added to the circle.

Elliot was sitting close enough to him that Simon could smell his sire's fear. Bad enough to have Erebus come to this meeting, but one of the Elementals? They rarely concerned themselves with anything but their connection to Namid. And when they did, the results were unpredictable—and usually devastating.

"Meg had a prophecy while you were gone," Henry said, his abrupt words changing the direction of the discussion before it began.

Elliot gave Simon a startled look. "Prophecy?"

"Meg is a *cassandra sangue*," Simon replied.

Winter had no reaction. Erebus simply nodded.

"What do you know about blood prophets?" he asked Erebus.

"Very little. Meg is the first of her kind I have ever seen, so I did not know the *cassandra sangue* and the humans who have the sweet blood were the same," Erebus replied.

"What is the sweet blood?" Henry asked, his eyes narrowing in thought.

"They have adult bodies, but they retain the sweetness of a child's heart," Erebus said.

Simon thought about the old woman who had cut her face to see his future. A sweetness in her eyes, in her smile, despite her age. Not a feeb, like some of the adolescents had called her. No, there was nothing wrong with her mind. But perhaps that childlike innocence provided a veil against the terrible things the prophets sometimes saw in the visions.

"Not prey," Henry said, looking at Simon. "We've recognized something different about some humans without realizing what it was."

Simon nodded. "Meg."

"The Sanguinati do not feed on the young," Erebus said. "And we do not feed on the sweet blood, because they are both wondrous and terrible. That forbidding was done long ago, and it is still passed down from one Sanguinati to another, even though we had forgotten the reason for it."

"Why terrible?" Tess asked, leaning forward. Her hair was still colored, but it was relaxing into loose curls.

Erebus shrugged. "Prophecies swim in that blood. I do not think I would like to see such things if I drank from a *cassandra sangue*."

"Our Meg *is* going to stay, isn't she?" Winter asked, sliding a look at Elliot that chilled the air. "My sisters and I would be unhappy if someone made her leave."

How did she know about the argument between Meg and Elliot? More to the point, what would she do with that knowledge?

He didn't want to think about that, so he focused on Henry. "What prophecy?"

Tess, Vlad, Jester, and Blair already knew about Sam somehow being connected to men coming into the Courtyard with weapons. That explained Nathan being assigned to keep watch at the Liaison's Office and why Blair had spent the night keeping watch on the open Utilities gate. The men Meg had seen had come in during a storm.

"We have been vigilant," Henry said. "The pup has not been alone. Meg has not been alone. They have both grown stronger in the past few days."

Despite the potential threat seen in the prophecy, Simon relaxed a little as each member of the Business Association gave him a report. He even laughed during Blair's account of Boone's dealings with the Liaison and her request for special meat. There had been no clashes with humans in general or the police in particular while he'd been gone, no clashes among the *terra indigene* except for the misstep Elliot had made that angered the Sanguinati. But that wouldn't happen again. He'd banish Elliot from the Lakeside Courtyard before he let the other Wolf—or anyone else—harm Meg in any way.

And Meg. Making deliveries, making friends, making a life among them in such a short time.

Meg. One of Namid's creations, both terrible and wondrous.

That was something he was going to have to think about.

Dear Ms. Know-It-All,

The other night, I had a friend over for dinner and a walk on the wild side (if you know what I mean). Everything was going fine until the kissing and petting part. I got a little excited when he began to play push-away after I nipped him and, well, I ended up biting him on the thigh. It wasn't a big bite—didn't even need stitching—and despite what he claimed, it really wasn't all that close to his chew toy. Now he won't return my calls. What should I do?

Signed,

Puzzled

Dear Puzzled,

First, young terra indigene often get confused when food provides more than one kind of stimulation. But when you invite a human over for dinner, he expects to be served dinner, not be dinner. Second, even though humans claim to enjoy biting as foreplay, they only mean it when their partners don't have teeth of any significance. Third, no male, human or Other, feels easy when teeth get too close to the chew toy. So chalk this up to experience, and the next time you invite a human to take a walk on the wild side, stick to a jog in the park.

Trying to breathe and swallow at the same time, Meg spit peppermint tea all over the counter.

Ms. Know-It-All. The newsletter's dispenser of advice for interactions between humans and the *terra indigene.*

Gods above and below.

She wondered whether Lorne found the column humorous, or if knowing the Others thought this was sound advice for dealing with humans was the reason he preferred to keep a counter between himself and most of his customers at the Three Ps.

She was still wiping the tea off her counter when she spotted Harry walking up the narrow path from the street. She opened the go-through and reached the door at the same time he did. Pushing it open until he could brace it with his shoulder, she grabbed the top package and hurried back to the counter.

On second thought . . .

Putting the package on the handcart, she waited for him.

"Had a spill, Miz Meg?" Harry asked as he set the rest of the packages on the cart. There was an odd tone in his voice.

"Enough of one that the counter is still wet," she replied, looking over her shoulder, then back at him. "You go ahead. I'll fill out my notes as soon as I finish wiping the counter. I've seen cars slipping and sliding out there this morning, and you don't want your truck to get hit."

"That I don't. You keep warm now, you hear? And watch out for those spills."

"I will. Drive safe. See you Moonsday."

Harry waved at the Crows as he pushed open the door and headed for his truck. Meg finished wiping the counter, folded the newsletters, and put them in the paper-recycling bin in the back room.

When she went into the bathroom to wash her hands, she looked in the little mirror over the sink. Then she stood there, stunned.

Harry hadn't been commenting about the wet counter. He'd been staring at her face when he'd asked about a spill.

She'd forgotten about the bruise. She'd been so rushed to get ready for work, with Simon and Sam showing up and disrupting her routine, she hadn't looked in a mirror that morning, not even when she dragged a comb through her hair.

If Harry or one of the other deliverymen called the police and told them about the bruise . . .

She had to tell someone. Had to tell Simon. Just in case.

As she passed through the sorting room on her way to use the phone at the front counter, she glanced at Sam, who was still happily gnawing on his stag stick.

Meg's stomach did a funny little flip. While she waited for someone to answer HGR's phone, she promised herself that, from now on, she would make sure the stag sticks Boone was leaving for Sam really were made from deer.

Monty stood outside the Chestnut Street station, waiting for Kowalski to bring the patrol car around. Last night's storm provided a good excuse to make a courtesy call at the Courtyard without being too obvious that they were checking up on the Courtyard's leader—and hoping for some information about what happened in Jerzy.

"I could use some coffee this morning," Monty said after he got in the car. "Do you think the Courtyard stores will be open?"

"Hard to say," Kowalski replied, pulling into traffic. "The Others don't run their stores for profit. It's more of a hobby and experiment for them, and it's a way to get merchandise and services without going to human-run businesses."

No, they wouldn't need to be concerned about profit. When you were the landlord and an entire city was your rental property, any other business run by a Courtyard was an accommodation.

But when they reached the Courtyard, Monty saw the Others busily removing the snow from their parking lot, using a small bucket loader to scoop up the snow and dump it in the bed of a pickup truck. There were some lights on in A Little Bite and Howling Good Reads, but not enough to give an impression that the stores were open.

"Let's check the Liaison's Office," Monty said.

Meg Corbyn was open for business. Judging by the lights in the windows, so was the consulate. And this access to the Courtyard was already plowed.

"Wait here."

Entering the office, he walked up to the counter. The Wolf pup stood in the Private doorway, watching him.

"Good morning," Monty said. "Is Ms. Corbyn around?"

Since he didn't expect an answer, he stepped back, startled, when the pup suddenly shifted into a naked boy who shouted, "Meg! The police human is here!"

"Who . . . ?" Meg came into view and stared at the boy. "Ah . . . Sam? It's cold. You should put on some clothes."

The boy looked down at himself. Then he looked at Meg and grinned. "Don't need clothes. I have fur!"

And he did. He also had four legs and a tail when he darted past her and out of sight.

Meg looked a little wobbly when she approached the counter.

"A new development?" Monty asked, staring at the doorway. He'd seen one of them change from Wolf to child once before. Then, like now, seeing how fast they could shift made his heart race.

"Very new," Meg said. "I haven't sorted out the rules yet. Or even figured out if there are rules."

He looked at her face and felt a hard anger, but he kept his voice soft. "And that? Is that also a new development?"

She sighed. "It was a misunderstanding. It won't happen again."

"Are you sure?"

Simon Wolfgard stepped into the Private doorway. "*I'm* sure."

He didn't touch Meg, but he used his hips and shoulders to crowd her into stepping aside, ensuring he was the one standing directly in front of Monty.

"Mr. Wolfgard," Monty said. "I was hoping to have a word with you if you have a minute."

A long look. What did Wolfgard see? An enemy? A rival? Maybe an ally?

Noises coming from the next room, like someone jumping and huffing with the effort.

Meg started to turn to see what was going on, but Simon shook his head.

"HGR isn't open yet," Simon said. "But Tess just made some coffee." He looked at Meg. "Yours is on the sorting table, along with a cup of hot chocolate and some muffins." He raised his voice. "The muffins and hot chocolate can only be eaten by a boy wearing clothes."

A yip followed by the click of toenails on floor.

"Is there some kind of rule for when Sam should be a boy and when he's a Wolf?" Meg asked.

"A Wolf lifts his leg and yellows up snow. A boy has to use the toilet," Simon replied.

"And that will work?"

"Only if he needs to pee."

Monty coughed loudly to cover up the chuckle.

"Have your officer bring the car around to the back," Simon said. "We cleared a lot of the snow, but not having the car parked in front of Meg's office will make it easier for the delivery trucks. I'll wait for you at the back entrance to A Little Bite."

"Ms. Corbyn." Monty tipped his head and left. When he pushed the door open and looked back, Simon Wolfgard was staring at him—and there was nothing friendly in those amber eyes.

Hurrying to the patrol car, he instructed Kowalski to drive around back.

Thinking of that stare, he wondered if there would be another "misunderstanding" that would end with Meg Corbyn carrying another bruise.

As soon as Montgomery was out of sight, Simon turned on Meg. "Has that monkey been bothering you?"

Bunny eyes, all startled by the unexpected.

"No," Meg stammered.

"He makes you nervous." He smelled that on her.

"I—" She hesitated. "When I see the police, it's hard to remember that I can't be taken away, that they won't make me go back. . . ."

He snarled. Couldn't help himself. "They won't take you away. What else? He was angry. He has no right to be angry with you."

Another hesitation. Then she lifted a hand toward the left side of her face. "Does this make you angry?"

"Yes!"

"It made him angry too."

It took effort, but he took a step back. Montgomery was angry about the bruise? A reaction that matched his own. That was good. That was something he understood about the human.

"Lieutenant Montgomery is waiting for you," Meg said.

"You called the store. To talk to me."

"To tell you the deliverymen have seen the bruise and some of them might call the police to report it."

"Humans do that?"

"Sometimes."

And sometimes they didn't. That was the unspoken truth he saw in her gray eyes. He studied her face and the weird hair that had a line of black near the scalp.

"Mr. Wolfgard?"

A creak of the floor above him. <Nathan?>

<Here.>

<Keep watch.>

"I'll be back for Sam at lunchtime," he told Meg.

Then he left, passing Sam as he went to the back door. The boy's clothes weren't buttoned right, but he'd let Meg deal with that, since he and Sam would have something else to deal with once he got the pup back home.

As he walked up to A Little Bite's back door, he noticed how Officer Kowalski had parked the patrol car so that it was pointed out, and the police wouldn't lose any time turning around when they wanted to leave.

Montgomery watched him, a lot of things going unspoken behind those dark eyes. Seemed like a lot of things weren't being said today.

He led them into the shop. Tess's hair was still green, but now there were brown streaks showing, which meant she was getting calmer. She gave them all coffee and a plate of pastries that, even warmed up, tasted a little stale. Not that any of them commented on that. You either ate what Tess offered or you didn't.

He and Montgomery circled each other using polite words as they realized neither had much to tell the other. But listening to what was said under the spoken words, Simon understood that Montgomery had more interest in keeping the peace than he did. His only interest was in keeping his own kind safe by whatever means necessary.

And as they talked and circled, he understood that his own kind now included Meg.

Asia pulled her car into the delivery area in front of the Liaison's Office.

"Thanks for giving me a ride," Darrell Adams said. He fiddled with the door handle but didn't open the door. Instead he glanced toward the wall lined with Crows.

Freaking spies. She knew Darrell wanted to give her a kiss, knew he wanted to do a lot more. She'd had dinner with him a couple of times now. Didn't take much to prime his conversational pump, but despite working at the consulate, his well of information was pretty shallow. Okay, he *was* a human working for the *terra indigene,* so it figured they wouldn't tell him anything important. Still, he was a different way into the Courtyard. Problem was, if she was going to keep him interested and sufficiently agreeable to granting her a tiny little favor, she was going to have to give him sex. Not that she minded using sex as part of a job, but the men she'd slept with up until now had social clout. On the other hand, she needed to send her backers some fresh information soon.

But those black-feathered freaks were watching, and giving someone a ride on a snowy day wasn't as interesting to report as giving someone sloppy tongue.

"Guess I'd better go in," Darrell said.

"Guess so," Asia agreed. "You take care." She didn't offer to give him a ride home. She wasn't about to let him into her apartment, and she didn't want an awkward scene if he invited her up to his. Besides, as soon as he went inside, she wanted to pop in to see Meg—and hopefully get another look at that Wolf pup.

Before Darrell reached the consulate door and she shut off her car, a patrol car came out of the access way between the buildings, and she was right in its path. Her car wasn't unusual, but it was parked in the lot often enough that someone might notice it.

So she gave the men in the car a brilliant smile and a cheery wave before she headed for the exit. And she didn't breathe easy until she was driving away and was certain the police had turned in the other direction.

When Simon picked up Sam, his nephew was back to being furry. Blair had brought Meg's BOW to the office. Since she planned to shop in the Market Square during her midday break, he took the BOW and drove back to the Green Complex.

Parking in a visitor's space, he carried Sam across the road, then let the pup lift a leg before they went inside.

He closed the apartment door and locked it.

Being locked in fear for two years made a difference in a lot of ways, but for both their sakes, he couldn't let it make a difference in the most important ways. Not when Elliot had called to tell him Lakeside's mayor was still whining about the police's inability to apprehend the dangerous thief who looked like Meg Corbyn. Not when someone had brought an unknown sickness to the western part of Thaisia. Not when it was so vital to their own well-being that he remain the leader of this Courtyard.

Which meant nothing and no one could be allowed to challenge or undermine his leadership in any way.

It was the cocky way Sam held his head, so sure he was going to get anything he wanted from now on, that snapped Simon's temper. He was on the pup in a heartbeat, pushing him to the floor before rolling him on his back. One hand pressed down on Sam's chest while he leaned over the youngster, his fangs growing, his eyes fixed on the vulnerable throat.

<I am the leader, not you,> Simon snarled. <I give the orders, not you. I let you get away with disobeying me this morning, but not again. *Not again,* Sam. If you won't obey because you're living here, you'll have to live with Elliot in the Wolfgard Complex. If you still can't obey, you'll be sent to live with a pack beyond the Courtyard.>

Sam shifted to boy. Simon pressed harder on the chest and brought his fangs closer to that vulnerable throat.

"Why can't I stay with Meg?" Sam whined. "I wanna stay with Meg."

"You are a Wolf. Meg is human. There are many things you need to learn that she can't teach you. *And you don't get to choose.*" Simon waited, but the boy offered no defiance. "You need to be with other Wolves again. You need to learn again."

Tears filled Sam's eyes. "Meg?"

"Meg will be the reward for good behavior." He was pretty sure that would put him in the wrong with Meg, but he wasn't going to worry about that. Meg, too, needed to learn. She hadn't seen an adult Wolf. He would have to change that.

As soon as Simon released Sam, the boy shifted to pup and darted into his cage.

That, too, was going to change.

But as he heated up food for both of them, he wondered if he was trying to take away Sam's adventure buddy because he truly believed it was best for Sam and Meg, or if he was doing it because he felt excluded.

CHAPTER 15

On Watersday, Simon put the cash drawer in the register and opened HGR for business. He wasn't in the best frame of mind to deal with customers, but paperwork wouldn't have distracted him from thinking about what he was going to do when Meg closed the office for the midday break.

Yesterday had been sunny, and the city plows had cleared Lakeside's main roads as well as the residential streets. So today all the humans were out and about, as if Windsday night's storm had closed them in for a week instead of slowing them down for forty-eight hours at the most. The Courtyard's customer parking lot was full. There were humans working out at Run & Thump, including the Ruthie, who was Officer Kowalski's mate. Most of the tables at A Little Bite were full, and now that HGR was open, he anticipated many of those customers would be coming through the connecting door to shop or browse or just have a reason to be somewhere that wasn't home for a little while longer.

Cabin fever, humans called it. A phrase that made no sense to the *terra indigene*. When there was a storm, you slept or stayed quiet somewhere that was dry and warm. When the storm stopped, you went out to hunt and play. There was no need to be frantic about it. Wanting to do one and then the other was wisdom Namid imparted to all her creatures.

Most of her creatures anyway.

Not that he cared. The humans would end up buying a book or one of the limited number of magazines the store carried, and then they would be gone, out in the shock of the cold, heading for the next place where they would flock for a while before eventually returning to their roosts.

John approached the checkout counter, a worried look on his normally cheerful face. "Morning, Simon. I saw Sam at the Wolfgard Complex. Is everything all right?"

"He's playing with some of the other pups this morning."

"As a pup?"

Ah, that was the reason for the worry. The Wolves had been told that Sam had finally shifted to human, but most hadn't seen the boy, hadn't had a chance to identify by sight or scent who Sam was in his other skin.

"Probably," Simon replied, keeping his voice mild. "He was supposed to stay human for half the morning, but I think he wore out Elliot's patience by the time they were done with breakfast, and he received permission to shift." He couldn't blame Elliot for making that choice. Letting Sam shift back to Wolf was easier than listening to the continual *Meg did it this way* and *Meg doesn't do that*.

Meg was now the yardstick by which they were supposed to measure all things human. Of course, the boy had also campaigned for Meg to go with him to puppy school because there were things she *didn't* know.

Simon didn't think Meg really wanted to know how to eviscerate a rabbit. He could be wrong about that, but he just couldn't picture Meg pouncing on a bunny and ripping it open with her teeth.

Maybe if he tried harder to picture it?

"Looks like there's a gaggle of college girls next door," John said. "Do you want me to add more stock to the quick-buy table up here or shift and do security?"

He caught the scent of two other Wolves before he saw them. When they reached the front of the store, Nathan was in human form, and Ferus approached as a Wolf.

Simon watched Ferus take the corner spot that gave the Wolf on watch a clear view of the door and the whole front area of the store. Since he or Vlad were usually in the store when it was open, they typically didn't have more than one Wolf as added security. It was Ferus's turn to be the watch Wolf, so why was Nathan with him? "Is Blair expecting trouble?"

Nathan shook his head. "Henry said there should be a box of books here for our library. He wants to work with the wood this morning, and I wasn't doing anything particular, so I told him I'd pick up the box and take it over to the Market Square." He grinned at Simon. "Besides, tomorrow is Earthday, and I'm looking for some quiet. If I help with setting out the new books, I get first pick."

"You could always buy one," John said.

Nathan just laughed.

Since Nathan's presence gave him an extra enforcer in this part of the Courtyard, Simon didn't see any reason not to use the Wolf. "Before you pick up the box, step in at Run and Thump and the social center. Check the upstairs rooms; get a look at everyone who's there today. The Ruthie was there when I looked in the window. She's mated to one of the police. Keep an eye on her. We gave him—and her—a pass to shop in the Market Square. She knows the rules, but that doesn't mean someone won't try to slip in with her if she decides to shop before going home."

"I'll look in, let everyone see the Wolves are watching. Marie is keeping watch from above, but most humans don't think about the Hawks when they try to do something stupid."

Most humans didn't think about the Crows either, or how effectively they could sound an alarm that could travel all over the Courtyard faster than most humans could cause trouble.

Nathan walked out the front door. John went into the back room to fetch some books. And Simon watched the first customers enter HGR from A Little Bite. He tried not to snarl when he noticed Asia Crane among those customers. He didn't have the right temper to deal with Asia this morning and hoped she would buy a book and go away.

"Hello, handsome," she said as she sidled up to the counter. "Haven't seen you in a while. You been hiding from me?"

Another scent on her. Something familiar, but it was faint enough and not familiar enough to be instantly recognizable. He wanted to lean over the counter and get a better sniff, but she might mistake that for interest in her breasts, which was usually followed by an invitation to have sex. Since he wasn't interested in breasts or sex, he chose a different way of finding out what he wanted to know.

<Ferus. Come here and find out who she's been rubbing against.>

"Looking for something in particular, Asia?" Simon asked.

She leaned on the counter, giving him a clear view down her sweater. "Did you have something in mind?"

She let out a very satisfying squeal and almost leaped high enough to land on the counter when Ferus shoved his muzzle between her legs.

<The Darrell is on her coat but not in her sex place,> Ferus reported. Then he sneezed and went back to his spot in the corner.

"Freaking fuck!" Asia shouted. "What was that?"

Simon took his glasses out of their case and put them on. "Curiosity. At least he didn't find anything he wanted to bite." He bared his teeth in a smile and raised his voice. "Kind of crowded in here today. Lots of people looking to stock up on books in case we get another storm. Can my assistant help you find something?"

She looked like she wanted to tear his throat out, and at that moment, he had no trouble picturing *her* ripping a bunny apart.

"I don't want anything from *you*." She strode out of the store.

He hoped that was true. He hoped she'd have sex with Darrell and stop sniffing around him.

He stared at the gaggle of college girls who were standing nearby with their mouths open, watching the drama. "What about you? Are you interested in buying books?"

Many assurances that they were there to buy books. They fled to the shelves that would take them out of sight. He cocked his head, listening to John talk to the girls as he came back from the stockroom, catching the tone but not the words.

The girls had gotten what they came for. They would buy a few books as payment for being able to relate to their friends that they had seen, *for real*, a Wolf sniff a woman's crotch *in public*.

Sighing, he pulled the stack of book orders from beneath the counter. Before, he hadn't had enough to occupy his mind. Now he had too much.

Despite her blatant efforts to flirt with him, Asia was rubbing against Darrell, a human who worked at the consulate. Elliot had voiced no complaints about the man, which meant Darrell was a good worker, but he wasn't the kind of male Simon would have expected Asia to run after. He seemed too ordinary for a female who wanted to walk on the wild side.

Simon growled in frustration. He was missing something. He didn't think like a human, so he was missing something.

Unfortunately, he didn't trust any humans enough to ask one what it was about Asia's interest in Darrell that wasn't right.

Freaking Wolf! He used to let her flirt with him. Now he treated her like a rattlesnake he wanted to stomp under his boot. And now that she thought about it, Simon Wolfgard had started being mean to her around the same time the new Liaison showed up.

But he couldn't be humping that no-looks feeb! From what Darrell had told her—in confidence, of course—Simon Wolfgard hadn't entertained a female guest since his sister was killed. When Asia had learned that, his refusal to respond to her invitations made more sense. But the way he brought all the wrong kinds of attention to her now could turn into a professional fuckup. And, damn it, she didn't want to settle for Darrell because Meg was somehow screwing up her chances with Simon.

As Asia reached her car, she glanced toward the street and saw a white van drive by. And she smiled.

Meg looked at the empty dog bed, then looked away and told herself to focus on sorting the mail. She'd already had to go through a couple of stacks twice when she realized she had put some of the mail for the Chambers in with the mail for the Crowgard. If that mail had gone to the Corvine Complex, the odds of the Sanguinati getting it back unopened . . . Well, there really weren't odds sufficient for that.

Sam needed to socialize with his own kind, needed to spend time with the other Wolf pups. He'd already lost two years, and she had the impression that there weren't many youngsters his age in the Courtyard, regardless of species. So he needed to be with Wolves, and she was happy to work alone without interruptions.

Sure she was.

She hadn't known him a couple of weeks ago. How could she feel their—his!—absence when she'd known him for so short a time?

Pay attention, she scolded herself. *The ponies will be here soon, and they'll expect you to have mail for them to deliver.*

She focused on the work and tried to ignore the silence even the chatter on the radio couldn't hide.

Simon glanced at the wall clock behind the checkout counter and tried not to snap at Vlad for being late.

The Sanguinati studied the Wolf. "Something wrong?"

Simon shook his head. "Just have something that needs to be done."

Vlad looked around. "Are we providing shelter, or are the humans actually buying books?"

"Little of both. Sales have been pretty good today. Heather campaigned for some books that I normally wouldn't have in the store because it gives humans too many wrong ideas."

Vlad looked amused. "You mean the kinds of stories where the Wolf doesn't eat the female after he has sex with her?"

"After Asia and I snapped at each other this morning, and Ferus shoved his nose into her privates, we sold out all the Wolf-as-lover books. If you drink one of the customers pale, we should sell out the stack of vampire-as-lover stories."

"Heather should know better," Vlad muttered.

Simon slipped past Vlad and said nothing. There would be a spike in the number of girls who went out for a walk in the woods and were never heard from again. There always were when stories came out portraying the *terra indigene* as furry humans who just wanted to be loved.

Most of the *terra indigene* didn't want to love humans; they wanted to eat them. Why did humans have such a hard time understanding that?

"Are you going to come back?" Vlad asked.

He hesitated. "Not sure."

A lot was going to depend on how Meg responded to seeing a full-grown Wolf.

Almost time to close for the midday break. According to the grapevine—which, in the Courtyard, meant Jenni Crowgard and her sisters—the new library books would be available today. Since tomorrow was Earthday, Meg expected to have a lot of time on her hands, so she wanted to pick up a couple of books. Maybe she would also stop at Music and Movies for a movie. And she needed to pick up a few things at the grocery store on her way home. Maybe she would call Hot Crust and have a pizza delivered to the office before she left for the day.

Lots of things she could do tomorrow. Lots of things.

Meg turned off the radio and heard the quiet sounds coming from the back room.

"Merri Lee? Is that you?" She had been stopping in at A Little Bite for the past few days, but Tess might have sent someone over with her meal. "Julia?"

What pushed open the door and came into the sorting room wasn't a human or a Hawk.

The Wolf was a terrible kind of beauty, and so much more than the pictures she'd been shown of the animal, who paled in comparison to what the *terra indigene* had made of that form. Big and muscled, the Wolf approaching her had a dark coat shot with lighter gray hairs. Meg wasn't sure if it was the coat or something else about his nature that made him seem less substantial when he moved, made the eyes struggle to *see* him.

How many people had thought they were hallucinating right up until the moment they were attacked?

The amber eyes held a feral intelligence—and an annoyed frustration she recognized.

"Mr. Wolfgard?"

The Wolf cocked his head.

"Simon?"

He opened his mouth in a wolfish grin.

She recognized him. Points for her.

Then she looked at him again. Sam was going to grow up to look like that? "Wow."

He wagged his tail and looked pleased. Then he began sniffing his way around the room, making happy growls when he poked around in the corner that used to have a nest of mice. She stepped aside when he got to her part of the room, and she had the impression the passing sniff he gave her would have been much more thorough if she'd stood still. So she took another step back and didn't say anything when he poked his nose around Sam's bed.

He headed for the back room, his shoulder brushing her waist as he passed her.

She stayed where she was.

That was what was hiding inside the human skin? That strength, those *teeth?* No wonder the Wolves hadn't let her see them until she got used to living in the Courtyard. Sam running toward her for a pretend hunt had been scary enough. Being chased by a pack of grown Wolves . . .

People who entered the Courtyard without an invitation were just plain crazy! Wolves were big and scary and so fluffy, how could anyone resist hugging one just to feel all that fur?

"Ignore the fluffy," she muttered. "Remember the part about big and scary."

Then she heard sounds that had her rushing into the back room.

"What are you doing?" she yelped.

He had opened all the cupboards and found the puppy cookies. The ripped top of the box was in pieces on the floor. He grabbed one side of the box and shook his head, dumping a few cookies on the floor.

"Stop that!" Meg scolded. "Stop! You'll set a bad example for Sam."

She didn't think, didn't even consider the stupidity of what she was doing. She just grabbed the other side of the box and tried to pull it away from him.

Never play tug-of-war with a Wolf who weighs twice as much as you do, she thought as it became clear to her that her shoes had better traction, but he had more feet and more experience playing the game.

Before she could figure out how to gracefully end the contest, the box ripped and cookies went flying.

Simon dropped the box and dove for the cookies. Licked one off the floor—*crunch, crunch*—then swallowed before going after the next one.

"Don't eat off the floor!" Meg shoved him away from the cookies, surprising a growl out of him.

They stared at each other, him with his lips raised to show her an impressive set of teeth, and her realizing that it had probably been a lot of years since anyone had dared push him away from food he wanted.

She stepped back and tried to pretend she was dealing with a big version of Sam the puppy, since that felt safer than dealing with Simon the dominant Wolf . . . and her boss.

"Fine," she said. "Go ahead and stuff yourself with cookies. But *you're* going to be the one who explains why there aren't any left when Sam comes to visit."

Turning her back on him, she strode into the sorting room and kept going until she reached the counter in the front room, her legs shaking more and more with every step.

"Let him have the cookies," she muttered as she watched a white van pull into the delivery area. "Maybe they'll fill him up enough that he'll forget about wanting to eat the annoying female."

Pulling her clipboard from the shelf under the counter, she waited for the last delivery of the morning.

Henry stepped into his yard and reached back to shut the workroom door. The wood had stopped speaking to him a few minutes ago, so he had put his tools away and tidied up. He would get something to eat at Meat-n-Greens, then take care of the new library books—however many were left. Fortunately, there would be a list so he would know what books were supposed to be on the shelves.

The Crows on the wall were uneasy—and silent.

<What?> Henry asked.

<Stranger went inside with a box. He talks with the Meg.>

Nothing unusual about that. Now that they finally had a decent Liaison, they were getting more deliveries.

He breathed in cold, clean air—and breathed out hot anger as the scent from over the wall reached him. It belonged to the intruder who had broken in when Meg had first come to work for them and was living in the efficiency apartment.

An intruder who was now inside the office, talking to Meg.

<Simon?> he asked the Crows.

<Inside with the Meg,> Jake replied.

<Stay quiet.> He opened the workroom door, then pulled off his boots and socks. Putting them inside, he closed the door.

Between was not encouraged in the Courtyards. *Between* disturbed humans too much, stirred up too much fear. Right now, he didn't care. He shifted what he needed. His feet changed shape and acquired footpads, fur, and claws. His palms grew a pad, and his fingers changed to stubby, clawed digits.

The snow packed against the wall of his yard formed a ramp. He scrambled over the snow and down the other side of the wall, crouching beside the snow-pack while he studied the van. Then, staying low, he crossed the open area and reached the passenger's door.

A glance into the office. Meg talking to the intruder.

She didn't look like she wanted to talk to that monkey. But he did. Oh yes. He did.

Simon chased a cookie across the floor, enjoying the silly game.

Meg hadn't been upset when she saw him as Wolf. She had, in fact, been foolishly brave, daring to push the leader away from food. And they had *played*. He couldn't remember ever *playing* with a human.

Chasing one you were going to eat didn't count.

Did she play tug with Sam? What about throw? He didn't think she was strong enough to throw anything very far, but it could still be an enjoyable game. The three of them could play. They could . . .

Simon raised his head, growling softly but not yet sure what he was sensing that had him primed to attack.

He stepped into the sorting room, sniffed the air . . . and knew.

Meg wasn't just uneasy. Meg was *afraid*.

Her skin prickled so fiercely, it was everything she could do not to drop the clipboard and pen and pull out the razor to ease the awful feeling that had started as soon as the man walked into the office. Everything about him was *wrong*, but he hadn't actually done anything.

"Must get lonely, working here all by yourself," he said.

"Oh no. There are people coming and going all day." Not to mention the Crows who kept track of who came and went.

Trying to ignore the prickling, Meg frowned at the back of the van. Not enough information and far too many blanks. Who was this delivery service anyway?

Giving up on the van, she turned toward the package, sliding her eyes to get another look at the man. Big. Rough-looking. No name stitched on the shirt pocket. No company logo or identification on the jacket.

"There's no company name on this label," she said. The box was tall enough that she could see the label but not read it easily. Another black mark for this delivery service that their driver didn't think to tilt it for her. "Who sent this?"

He shrugged. "Couldn't say."

"It should be on your paperwork." Her voice turned sharp. There was something about the look in his eyes that reminded her of the Walking Names when one of the girls dared to ask a question that wasn't about a lesson. "Who is it for?"

"For one of *them*. What difference does it make?"

Something ugly in his voice now. But he was more frightening when he tried to go back to friendly, as if she couldn't hear the ugliness under the words.

"Sorry," he said. "Had a couple of rough deliveries earlier. Complaints about things I can't fix. You know?"

That was possible, although she suspected he deserved the complaints. Setting her pen and clipboard on the counter, she reached for the box, intending to turn it in the hopes she could at least make out which complex it should go to. If she couldn't read that much, she would refuse the delivery and write a memo to Simon and Vlad in case someone *was* looking for the package.

The man moved fast, clamping one hand on her wrist.

"Why don't you come with me?" he said, smiling when she couldn't break his grip. "We'll get something to eat and get acquainted."

"No." She twisted, trying to break free. "Let go of my wrist!"

"Whatcha gonna do? Bite my hand off?"

Simon exploded out of the sorting room. He didn't bother with the hand. His lunge took him over the counter far enough that his teeth just missed the man's face.

The man let her go and scrambled back toward the door. "You fucking bitch! I was just asking you out for a meal. You didn't have to sic your fucking dog on me!"

The "dog" snarled so savagely, the man bolted out of the office and scrambled into the van, his movements so violent the driver's-side tires actually lifted off the pavement for a moment. But there wasn't time to wonder about that, because Simon used his body to shove her into the sorting room.

He rose on his hind legs and shifted, but he didn't revert back to human completely before he grabbed her, and his fury, like the look of him when he was a queer blend of human and Wolf, was a chilling heat against her skin.

"Where is it?" He pulled her close and began sniffing her. "*Where is it?*"

She tried pushing him away, disturbed by the sensation of fur covering a human chest. "Where is what?" When he bent to sniff at her waist and hips, she squealed and struggled to get away.

"Where is the cut, Meg?" he snarled.

"I didn't cut!" She began fighting him. He was something out of nightmares now, and he terrified her. "Stop it, Simon! Let me go!"

She pulled away from him, smacking against the counter as a hand that wasn't quite a hand yanked on her sweater. She heard the sound of material ripping at the seams. And she heard his harsh breathing as he stared at the upper part of her left arm.

"I didn't cut," she said, trying not to cry. "I was in the back room with you, and then I was trying to deal with that deliveryman."

"But you knew he was bad," Simon argued. "*You knew.*"

"Not because I cut myself! Not because of a prophecy. Did you hear me describing a vision?"

"You don't have to say the words out loud!"

She didn't understand why he was so angry about the possibility of a cut. It was, after all, her choice now. But she realized there were things he didn't understand about the *cassandra sangue,* and judging by the way he kept looking at the scars, he knew they weren't right. He knew that much.

"Most people hear only about the euphoria, the ecstasy that blood prophets feel from a cut."

He cocked his head to show he was listening.

"And there is euphoria. There is ecstasy that is similar to prolonged sexual pleasure. But first, Mr. Wolfgard, there is pain. When the skin is first cut, in those moments before the prophet begins to speak, there is a lot of pain."

He didn't like that. She could judge how much he didn't like that by the red flickering in his amber eyes.

"Do you know how a girl like me is punished?" She raised her right hand and traced the diagonal scars on her left arm. "She is strapped to the chair, as always. Then she is gagged. And then the Controller sits in his chair while one of the Walking Names takes the razor and slices across old visions, old prophecies, and makes something terrible and new. All those images jumbled together with no reference point, no anchor. And because she is gagged, the girl can't speak. The words need to be heard, Mr. Wolfgard. When a prophecy isn't spoken, isn't shared, there is no euphoria. There is only pain."

He took a step closer to her, his eyes still on her arm. He raised a hand, but the fingers still ended in Wolf claws that hovered over her fragile skin.

"Why did they punish you?"

More than once. He could count the number of times she had tried to defy the Controller and Walking Names. One section of her arm was a crosshatch of scars. What she had seen and endured could have driven her insane. Instead, the images had come together in a pattern that had shown her how to escape.

"I lied," she said. "There was a man. A very bad man. He was a favorite client of the Controller who ran the compound where I was kept. This man did bad things to little girls. He traveled a lot for his business and he had found two girls he liked in different cities. One prophecy told him he could take one of the girls without anyone knowing. But if he took the other girl, he would be found and caught and he would die. He paid for another prophecy that would tell him which girl he could take and avoid being caught."

"You gave him the wrong images, the wrong place, led him to the wrong choice."

She nodded. "Before he could hurt the girl, the police found him and caught him—and killed him." She tried to cover the scars with her hand, but there were too many of them. "The Controller received a lot of money from this client, so he was very angry when the man died. I was strapped to the chair and punished several times because the client died." She swallowed a feeling of sickness. "The pain is terrible. I have no images that could convey to you how terrible it is. So I wouldn't have cut myself and kept silent, Mr. Wolfgard. Not without a good reason."

He looked less angry, but she didn't think he was convinced yet.

"If you didn't cut, how did you know the deliveryman was bad?"

Now she allowed herself a little of her own anger. "I pay attention, and he didn't behave like the other deliverymen who come here!" Because the feeling worried her enough that she wanted someone else to know about it, she added, "And that awful prickling started under my skin as soon as he walked into the office."

Simon cocked his head again. "Prickling?"

"I don't know how else to describe it. It's maddening! It used to be I felt this prickling only just before I was going to be cut. Now I feel it every day, and I want to cut and cut and cut to make it stop!"

He studied her. "Maybe this is natural for your kind when you're not caged. Maybe this prickling is your body's way of warning you that something is wrong. If I hear a rattling near a game trail, I don't have to get bitten to confirm there's a snake there. Maybe now that you're living outside the compound, your instincts are waking up. To a Wolf, that's a good thing."

She hadn't considered that.

"So what did your instincts tell you about that man?" Simon asked.

His face had shifted all the way back to human. Except the ears. They were smaller than they'd been a minute ago, but they were still furry Wolf ears, and it was hard to concentrate on words when the ears swiveled to catch sounds outside the room and then pricked toward her when she spoke. And something about the way he looked at her told her he wanted to test the soundness of her instincts.

"All the delivery trucks or vans have the company name on the side or on the back, and they park in a way that I can see the name before the driver comes into the office," she explained. "The men have their names sewn on their shirts or have a badge with their picture, and their jackets usually have a company name or logo. They *want* me to know who they are and where they work. That man didn't have a badge or even a logo on his uniform. There was no name on the van. The back license plate was packed with snow and couldn't be read. And the package!" Now that she was warming up to all the things that weren't right, her voice began to rise. "He couldn't tell me the company that had shipped it, couldn't tell me who it was for. The label didn't have a company name, and the writing was so bad, I couldn't tell who was supposed to receive it. No company who did business with the Courtyard would have sent a package like that!"

She thought about what she'd just said. "Simon," she whispered. "No company who does business with the Courtyard would have sent that package."

Simon didn't need to see her pale to know what she was thinking.

Bomb.

He leaped into the front room and vaulted over the counter. Grabbing the box, he ran to the door, shoving it open with a shoulder. Then he took a few steps away from the office to give himself some room and threw the box.

It flew over most of the delivery area and landed close to the street entrance. Skidding on the remaining layer of snow, the box finally came to a stop at the edge of the sidewalk, almost tipping into the street.

Pedestrians stumbled back. Drivers honked their car horns and swerved when they saw the box sliding into their path.

Then people caught sight of him and started screaming. Some simply turned and ran. Others bolted into traffic and narrowly avoided being hit.

The consulate door was flung open. Elliot, looking pale, shouted, "Simon! You're between forms!"

He didn't respond. Instead he lifted his head and howled a Song of Battle.

The Crows exploded off the stone wall, cawing their warnings.

He howled again. Answering howls came from the Market Square, from the Utility Complex, and, a few seconds later, from the Wolfgard Complex. Crows and Hawks and even some Owls were in flight, spreading the warning, sounding a call to battle.

And the Wolves continued to howl.

<Simon.> Elliot's voice sounded more controlled but still shocked.

<Call the police. Call Montgomery. Tell him to come here *now*.>

Elliot went inside the consulate.

Had to get control. Had to get out of sight and shift to one form or another.

He wanted to be Wolf. The Courtyard—and Meg—needed him to wear the human skin for a while. And he needed to find out what happened to that van and the intruder.

As he turned to go back inside, he noticed the Bear tracks.

<Henry?> he called.

<I have the intruder. I will deal with this. You take care of Meg.>

Only a foolish leader challenged an angry Grizzly without good reason.

He headed for the front door, then caught sight of Vlad in the access way that led to the Market Square and the rest of the Courtyard. Changing direction, he reached the Sanguinati and continued on to the back of the building.

"What happened?" Vlad asked. "I locked HGR's door and put Ferus on guard in front of it. No one is leaving until we have answers. Tess has locked everyone in too."

"A monkey touched Meg," Simon growled. "Tried to *take* Meg."

"Is she hurt?"

He didn't think she was hurt, but he knew something that needed to be done before anyone else saw her. "Wait. Tell Tess to meet us out here. The police are coming."

"Human law doesn't apply here," Vlad said coolly.

"No, it doesn't. But we're going to let the police deal with whatever is in the box the intruder brought into the office."

He went into the office through the back door, then stopped. Meg was still in the sorting room. In a few more minutes, there would be Crows and cops all over this part of the Courtyard. And there would be Sanguinati and Wolves. He hoped the girls at the lake would be content with a report from Jester.

It took effort to shift to fully human. Human wasn't as useful as Wolf.

He got back most of the way. He had a mantle of fur across his shoulders that ran down part of his back and chest, and he couldn't get his canines down to human size.

It would have to do. He pulled on his jeans and the lightweight sweater he'd been wearing when he first came in. Going to the back room's bins, he pulled out the gray sweatshirt he kept there and went into the sorting room.

Meg leaned against the counter, her arms wrapped around herself.

"Was it a bomb?" she asked.

"Don't know. The police will figure that out. Here." He held out the sweatshirt. "Going to be a lot of people around soon, and the police will want to talk to you." She looked pale, and it bothered him. "If you put this on, no one will see the scars."

She pulled off the sweater and put on the sweatshirt over the one-sleeved turtleneck.

The sweatshirt was big on her and she looked ridiculous. He liked it. And he liked that she was wearing something that carried his scent.

"Stay here," he said. "I'll be back in a few minutes."

She looked toward the back room. "I'm cold. I was going to make some peppermint tea."

He nodded. He was going to have his meeting outside anyway. "That's fine. Just stay in the building." Taking the sweater and the torn sleeve, he went into the back room. Pushing his feet into his boots, he stepped outside.

Vlad and Nyx were there. So was Tess, whose hair was coils of red with streaks of black.

"Meg is fine," Simon said.

Tess looked at the sweater he held in one hand and the torn-off sleeve in the other. "That doesn't look like she's fine."

"She is," he snarled.

"Why did this man try to take Meg?" Nyx asked.

"Henry will find out, and then we'll all know."

A dozen Crows sounded an alarm at the same time Simon heard sirens coming toward the Courtyard from several directions.

<Many monkeys,> Jake told him moments later. <Know some faces, but not all.>

"The police are here," he said.

"Might as well unlock HGR's door," Vlad said. "The customers aren't going to go far with this much excitement going on."

Tess sighed and held out a hand. "Give me that. I'll send Merri Lee to the Market Square to replace it."

His hands fisted in the material that held Meg's scent. "Merri Lee doesn't need this one to fetch another sweater."

Tess gave him a long look. Then she walked back to A Little Bite.

Nyx shifted to smoke below the waist and drifted up the access way. The Sanguinati were less concerned about being seen in a between form than the Wolves. Perhaps because humans didn't understand the danger and weren't sufficiently afraid.

"I'll look after the store," Vlad said after a moment.

"I'll deal with the police," Simon said.

"Montgomery isn't a fool. You called him, let him in that much. He'll ask questions."

Simon nodded. "He isn't a fool. Hopefully that means he'll know when to stop asking questions."

Monty's heart banged against his chest, and his mind wouldn't let go of the story of the Drowned City.

A possible bomb left in the Liaison's Office. An attack against the Others? Or against Meg Corbyn? Either way, the backlash could cripple the city if the Courtyard's leaders decided to punish all humans for the actions of one.

Police cars blocked the intersection of Crowfield Avenue and Main Street, redirecting traffic away from the Courtyard. The bomb squad was already there, along with a fire truck and an ambulance. Another half dozen police cars were parked haphazardly on Main Street. As Kowalski pulled up and parked, Monty spotted his other team, officers Debany and MacDonald.

Cops everywhere, but not one of them with so much as a toe inside the Courtyard.

"Gods above and below," Kowalski breathed. "What happened here?"

"That's what we're going to find out." Monty opened his door, then signaled for Debany and MacDonald to join him. "You two go around and talk to whoever is running A Little Bite and Howling Good Reads today. See if they know anything, and try to confirm that the human customers and employees are all accounted for." *And unharmed,* he added silently. That wasn't something he needed to tell his men.

Once they were on their way, Monty stepped up to the barricade erected by the bomb squad. "Louis?"

Louis Gresh, the squad's commander, spoke quietly to his men, then walked over to the barricade. "Monty." He nodded at Kowalski. "Not a bomb. Just a box full of rags and a telephone directory to give it some weight. I'll take it in and hand it over. Our people might find something useful."

Crows winged in. Some settled on rooftops. Others flew across the street to perch on streetlights. They cawed to one another and preened feathers—and noticed everything.

Louis watched them. "There are probably plenty of witnesses who could tell you what happened here, but I doubt you'll find one who will tell you anything."

Depends on how I ask the questions, Monty thought. "Appreciate the fast response."

"Any time." Louis looked at all the Crows watching the police, then looked up.

Following his gaze, Monty saw the Hawks soaring over the Courtyard. And deeper in the Courtyard, he heard Wolves howling.

"Good luck," Louis said before he walked away.

Taking a deep breath, Monty summoned the officers who had responded to the call. He gave them the task of checking the businesses across the street from the Courtyard. It was possible someone saw something and would be brave enough to admit it.

Slipping around the barricade, Monty stepped into the Courtyard, Kowalski beside him. "Karl, go see if there's anyone working at the consulate."

"Yes, sir."

He didn't look at the Crows gathered on the wall or the woman in the black dress standing next to the office. He just opened the door and walked up to the counter.

When Meg Corbyn stepped out of the other room, she looked pale and was wearing a gray sweatshirt that was too big for her.

"Are you all right, Ms. Corbyn?" Monty asked quietly. That's as far as he got before Simon Wolfgard appeared in the Private doorway. He would have preferred talking to her alone. He still had a question about that bruise on her face, and a woman wouldn't usually ask for help with the abuser listening to every word.

No, he reminded himself. *Wolfgard didn't put that bruise on her.*

"Shaken up, but I'm fine," Meg replied.

He studied her for a moment and decided that was close enough to truth, so he pulled out a notebook and pen. He'd ask anyone else to come to the station to make a statement. No point asking when he knew she wouldn't come, and if she did, he didn't want to consider who would be coming with her. "Can you tell me what happened?"

She told him about the white van and all the details that weren't there and should have been. She pushed up one sleeve and showed him the dark bruise on her wrist where the man had grabbed her, and then told him how the man had run back to the van when Simon appeared.

But she couldn't tell him where the van went, which way it turned when it left the Courtyard. She had been in the sorting room when the van drove off.

She didn't say it, but he'd be willing to bet she had been helped into the sorting room precisely so she couldn't see where the van went.

One glance at Simon Wolfgard was enough warning to ask about something besides the van.

The next question treaded close to danger, but he asked it anyway. "Do you need medical attention, Ms. Corbyn? Do you have any other bruises besides the one on your wrist?" He was looking at her face, but he didn't bring up *that* bruise. "There's an ambulance outside, and medical personnel. You don't appear to need a hospital—" He hesitated when Wolfgard started growling.

Meg shook her head. "I'm feeling a little stiff, but otherwise, I'm fine."

He had to accept her word for it.

"Is that all, Lieutenant?" she asked. "I'd like to sit down."

"That's all. Thank you. The information you provided will help us." He saw something in her face. "Anything else?"

The words weren't meant to alarm, but Simon immediately shifted to block the doorway, his amber eyes focused on Meg.

"Meg?" Simon said. "Is there something else?"

She sighed. "It's nothing. Foolish under the circumstances."

Human and Wolf just waited.

She sighed again. "I have this silly craving for pizza. Before this happened, I was going to call Hot Crust and order one, and now it's hard to think of anything else."

Hardly the expected response from someone who had just escaped an attempted abduction. Then again, the mind protected itself in all kinds of ways—including becoming focused on a treat—and maybe this was a typical way *cassandra sangue* reacted to frightening experiences.

"You're hungry?" Simon asked, some of the tension leaving his body as he studied her.

Meg nodded, then added hopefully, "They'll deliver to the Liaison's Office."

Not today, Monty thought. "Special circumstances. I'll call in the order for you and send a car to pick it up." When she started to protest, he lifted a hand. "I'll order a couple for the squad as well. Even policemen need to eat."

He saw a flash of something in Simon's eyes. Feral amusement? Or did the Wolf appreciate the courtesy he was showing to the Courtyard's Liaison?

"Pepperoni and mushrooms?" Monty asked. "Or would you prefer something else?"

"That's fine," Meg said. "Thank you."

Simon stepped aside and let her slip into the other room and out of sight.

"That's kind of you," Simon said.

"I'm here to help." When the Wolf didn't respond, Monty turned to go. Then he stopped and added, "A man who is running away might drop his wallet or even just a driver's license. Wouldn't notice if it fell in the snow. If we found where the man lived, we might find something that could tell us if he was working for someone—or with someone."

He didn't want the Others looking at every human as a potential threat, but the possibility of a partner meant Meg wasn't safe yet.

A thoughtful silence that held so much weight he could feel it settle on his shoulders.

"Something might have been dropped," Simon said. "And we can pick up the scent of something even if it's hidden in snow. If we find anything, I'll let you know."

Monty nodded. "I'll have one of my officers bring in that pizza."

"Better if it's a face we already know."

Another nod, and Monty walked out of the office. Kowalski fell into step with him.

"Anything?" Monty asked.

Kowalski shook his head. "First they were aware of trouble was when Simon Wolfgard sounded the alarm. After that, everyone went nuts."

"*Nuts* meaning 'primed for battle'?"

"That's how I read it."

As soon as he crossed the line that separated human land from the Courtyard, Monty stopped to assess the street. The bomb squad was gone, along with the fire truck, ambulance, and half the police cars. The intersection was still blocked, keeping traffic away from the Courtyard's entrance.

But the arrival of the shiny black car and the man leaning against it had occurred while he'd been talking with Meg and Simon.

As he walked over to where Captain Burke waited for him, Monty spotted the officers he had sent to canvas the businesses across from the Courtyard. He stopped and waited for them. "Anything?"

"Nobody remembers anything about the vehicles that were in and out of there today," Officer Hilborn said. "But *everyone* who had a window seat at the Stag and Hare saw the wolf man."

Monty frowned. "Wolf man?"

"Half man, half wolf. Or a furry man with a wolf's head. Until we all showed up, most thought it was a gimmick for a horror movie or some kind of stunt of the dumb and daredevil kind, being dressed like that and standing where the Others could see him. When they realized he was *real,* it scared the crap out of all of them."

Those images in horror stories and movies had to come from somewhere, Monty thought. "So, nobody saw a white van leave the Courtyard?"

Hilborn shook his head. "All they remember seeing is something a lot scarier than they thought lived in the Courtyard."

Too much fear makes people stupid.

Monty glanced at his captain. Burke was watching the Crows watch him. The man wouldn't stay patient for long, but there would be enough time to hear from Debany and MacDonald before he had to give his own report.

"Write up your report," he told Hilborn.

Hilborn tipped his head to indicate his partner and the other two officers who had been canvassing businesses. "Not sure how much good it will do. Everyone agreed on something that was a wolf and a man at the same time. After that . . . Well, pick your favorite scary movie."

"Understood." With a nod of dismissal, Monty turned to Debany and MacDonald.

"Nobody at A Little Bite knew there was trouble until Tess locked the front door and ran out the back, leaving the Hawk as guard and Ms. Lee to deal with customers," Debany said.

"Pretty much the same story at Howling Good Reads," MacDonald said. "Locked door, Wolf standing guard, no explanation." He looked at Kowalski. "Ruth was there. Apparently, humans who have been given a pass to the Market Square can be tagged as temporary employees. Or maybe she volunteered to help. That part wasn't clear. Either way, she ended up working the cash register and having an ongoing discussion with a Crow about the necessity of giving people correct change, even if that means giving them coins that are shiny."

After Debany and MacDonald had the pizza order and were on their way, Monty turned to Kowalski. "Take five minutes and have another look around HGR."

"Thank you, sir."

When he and Burke were the only ones left, Monty walked over to his captain.

"Any reason to keep the intersection blocked?" Burke asked.

"No, sir. I don't think there will be any more trouble here today."

"Today," Burke said heavily. "Seems that someone is still whispering in the governor's ear, and he's still leaning on the mayor to find that stolen property. You think this is connected?"

"Yes, sir."

"So do I. What have we got?"

Monty told him about the unmarked van and the suspicious behavior of the man posing as a deliveryman. Then he told him about the reports of a wolf man, and watched Burke pale.

"You've seen one of the Others like that?"

Burke nodded. "Early in my career, I worked in a village smack in the middle of wild country. Most of Thaisia is wild country, but we said it like that to indicate the village wasn't close to a bigger city. The Others who live in the wild places . . . Nobody knows if they can't shift into the human form well enough to pass for human or if they just don't want to. But you'll see those blends if you have to go out and visit their settlements, and they truly are the stuff of nightmares." He blew out a breath. "You think that van and driver left the Courtyard?"

"No, sir. But I'm hoping Simon Wolfgard will feel obliged to us enough to 'find' the man's wallet and hand it over."

Burke didn't say anything. Then he pushed away from the car and opened the door. "You're managing to keep things smooth, Lieutenant. Good work." He got in, started the car, and drove off.

And a handful of Crows went winging into the Courtyard to report.

Monty got into his car. While he waited for Kowalski, he took an envelope from the coat's inside pocket. The envelope was in Elayne's handwriting, and the pressure of pen on paper told him she had been cornered into sending it. The handmade card inside was from Lizzy, his darling girl. Hugs and kisses for her daddy.

He put the card away and closed his eyes. *Keep things smooth.* Besides all the lives at stake here in Lakeside, he had one very good reason for keeping things smooth.

With a little effort, Asia picked the lock on the apartment door and slipped inside. By the time she was done with this assignment, she would have some serious skills for her TV series. Asia Crane, Special Investigator, would be a native of Toland. . . . No. Most of the PIs currently on TV were from the East Coast's Big City. *She* would be a specialist brought in from the Cel-Romano Alliance of Nations to uncover corporate intrigue in Thaisia, or unmask a threat to the human government, or even deal with problems between humans and the *terra indigene.* Maybe her character could have an ongoing romance with an officer on the ship that routinely traveled across the Atlantik, providing transport between Cel-Romano and Thaisia. Maybe she could have a tame Wolf as an assistant, who could sniff out information other investigators wouldn't be able to find. Wouldn't *that* be a kick in Simon Wolfgard's ass?

One way or another, this assignment was going to make her a very hot property who could write her own ticket—and name her own price.

Thank the gods she'd parked on a side street when she returned to the Courtyard. She had wanted to be around when Simon Wolfgard realized Meg the feeb was missing. Instead, she'd found cop cars all over the place, the intersection blocked, and all kinds of talk about someone *trying* to do something suspicious at the Liaison's Office. Something to do with a box or a van or . . . something.

Everyone who had a mobile phone was chattering nonsense, but it was enough to tell her that White Van had failed big-time.

The idiot not only bungled the snatch; he got caught. She wasn't worried about him coming back here and finding her searching his apartment. Even if he managed to get out of the Courtyard, he was gone, gone, *gone.* But she had left a couple of printed notes under the van's windshield wiper, providing information about Meg's routine. A pro would have disposed of the notes.

A pro wouldn't have gotten caught.

As research for her upcoming role, she'd followed White Van one night to find out where he lived. His location had been a tidbit of information for her backers and not of much interest. However, she figured it would come in handy if she needed to point the cops toward a convincing suspect. But the fool had done that himself. Worse, he'd thrown himself to the Wolves, and the gods only knew what he would tell them before they killed him.

So she was here, doing a fast search to make sure the police—or someone worse—wouldn't find anything that would come back and bite *her.*

Nothing.

She found the magazines under the mattress and rolled her eyes. But she flipped through them, hoping pages wouldn't be stuck together, and found a slip of paper with a phone number.

Not a local number. And considering what White Van had been trying to do, that number could be lucrative.

Asia pocketed the slip of paper, put the magazines back under the mattress, and left the apartment.

Late afternoon. Debany and MacDonald had delivered the pizza, and it had eased something in Simon's chest when Meg showed enthusiasm and appetite for the food.

Not really hurt. Not if she was eating with such obvious pleasure. No longer afraid because an intruder entered the office. And not afraid of him, not when she was willing to tease him about being too full of cookies to want pizza.

Happy Meg made him calmer.

Happy Meg was willing to share food. She even tore off the top of the pizza box, put two pieces on it, and took it outside for the Crows.

He knew enough to insist she put the pieces behind the office instead of out front, where humans could see. Humans had already seen enough of between forms. It was better if they didn't see Crows with little hands at the ends of their wings, pulling food apart.

While the Crows were distracted, he took his pieces of pizza and ate at the front counter, watching the street.

Merri Lee had brought new sweaters for Meg and persuaded her to see Elizabeth Bennefeld for a massage to relax. So Meg was in the Market Square, being pampered, by the time Simon finally locked up the Liaison's Office. When he stepped out the back door, he noticed Blair leaning against the garage, waiting for him.

"Henry is very angry," Blair said quietly. "He shifted and wants to be left alone until tomorrow."

"Did he say anything before shifting?" Simon asked.

"Someone hired the intruder to take Meg away from us. They gave him a number to call but nothing else. He also said someone left him messages, telling him where Meg lived and when she was in the office. He didn't know who was helping him."

"Someone who knows where Meg lives." She was protected in the Green Complex, but in the office? "Someone stays with her from now on. More than Crows keeping watch. More than someone upstairs who might not reach her before she's hurt."

Blair hesitated.

"She saw me as Wolf, and she wasn't afraid. So there will be one of the Wolfgard in the office when she's working."

Blair nodded. "Boone wants to know if he should put out the sign and let everyone know we have special meat."

Simon almost agreed. Then he thought about the police. He had let them in, and Montgomery was going to come sniffing around for a while. And he thought about Meg asking for meat for Sam, and he thought about the Ruthie shopping in the Market Square. Sooner or later, both females would see the sign and have to accept what it meant. But this time it would be too obvious where the meat came from.

"No sign," he said. "Pass the word that there is meat available for whoever wants it. And make sure at least some of the blood is offered to Erebus."

"That part was already done. Nyx came by and collected it."

Yes. Erebus would want blood from the man who tried to take Meg, who *touched* Meg.

"You want us to save any meat for you?" Blair asked.

He wasn't human. Would never be human. "I want the heart. I'll come by for it later."

When Meg was asleep.

By the time Meg woke up the next morning, the sun was shining and the sky was a clean blue. Poking her nose out her front door convinced her that, despite the blue sky and sunshine, it was still wicked cold. Since there was nothing she had to do and nowhere she had to go, she warmed up the last piece of pizza and ate it for breakfast while she read a few more chapters of the book she'd borrowed from the Courtyard library.

The last two Earthdays in the Courtyard had been full of turmoil of one kind or another, but just by looking out her window, Meg sensed a difference. Today the Green Complex, maybe even the whole Courtyard, felt quieter.

When she got tired of reading, she dusted the furniture, swept the floors, and ran the sweeper over the carpets. By the time she took a shower and wiped down the bathroom, she was also tired of domesticity, and feeling a little uneasy about the lack of company.

Was she the only one in the complex? Was everyone else off doing something in another part of the Courtyard?

You're safe here, she thought. *No one is going to come this far into the Courtyard, looking for you.*

Even so, by the time she'd eaten the stew Meat-n-Greens had sent home with her yesterday, she wanted to get out of the apartment, despite the cold. So she gathered up her clothes and towels, then bundled herself up for the short walk to the laundry room. Once she had the washers going, she went upstairs to the social room.

Henry looked up and smiled when she entered.

"Didn't expect to see you up and about today," he said.

She shifted her feet, suddenly wishing she'd stayed downstairs. "Humans aren't *that* fragile. I was scared yesterday, and my wrist got bruised. It's not like I fell off a cliff or something."

He laughed, a warm sound. "You are the first human to live among us here, so there is much for us to learn."

She came closer to the table where he was sitting. "But you have those apartments that you let people use. And you have people working for you and shopping at the Market Square."

"We have those things," he agreed, "but that's not the same as living among us the way you do now."

She didn't know what to say, so she focused on the colored bits and pieces on the table. "A puzzle?"

"A pleasant diversion on a winter afternoon." He gestured to the other chair. "Sit and join me if you wish."

She sat and picked up several pieces, one after another.

"You have never put together a puzzle?" Henry asked.

Meg shook her head. "I've seen pictures of games, including puzzles like this, but there was no need for us to play them in order to recognize them in a vision."

"Then it's time for you to experience the world instead of just identifying its pieces."

She watched him work for a minute before she began to look for connecting pieces. There was an easiness to the silence between them. In fact, they didn't speak until she returned from the laundry room, having put the clothes and towels in the dryers.

"Are we the only ones in the complex?" she asked when she took her seat at the table.

Henry nodded. "Most are spending the day with their kin in the other complexes. The Coyote is enjoying a run."

"And Tess?" Meg put four puzzle pieces together before picking up her thought. "I've seen her only in her human form."

"None of us have seen her other form. We know she is *terra indigene*. We know how to read her warning signs. But what she is when she sheds her human skin—that is something known only to Namid."

Deciding she'd asked enough questions, Meg worked on the puzzle with Henry until her laundry was dry. She packed up her laundry bag, bundled herself for the quick walk, and headed back to her apartment.

Halfway there, she saw the Wolf rushing toward her in the fading afternoon light.

"Sam! No!" Simon's voice.

The pup ran past her instead of leaping on her, then turned back and tried to grab a corner of the laundry bag.

"If you rip the bag and I have to wash all these clothes again, I'll wash you with them," Meg warned.

His head cocked. His tail wagged. And she wondered if she had just put a very bad idea in a puppy's head. But he wouldn't actually try to climb into a washer. Would he?

Sam spun around and rushed toward Simon, who was standing near his own apartment door. The pup leaped up, barely giving Simon enough time to catch him before leaping down and running back to Meg.

Once she was close enough that he was bouncing between them, he began talking at her.

Smiling, she shook her head. "I don't speak Wolf."

"No shifting out here," Simon said firmly. "It's *cold.*"

Sam talked back at his uncle.

As a reply, Simon opened his apartment door. "Go inside, and I'll ask her."

Sam bounded into the apartment, sliding as his wet feet hit the bare floor. Shaking his head, Simon closed the door and looked at her.

"Everything all right today?" he asked.

"It was quiet," she replied. "Peaceful."

He shifted his feet and looked uncertain. In fact, he seemed reluctant to look directly at her.

"Mr. Wolfgard?"

"After Sam has his bath, we're going to watch a movie, and he was wondering—*we* were wondering—if you would like to join us."

Emotions were harder to define on a real face than on a labeled picture, so she wasn't sure which message she was supposed to reply to. He had invited her to join them, but . . . "You would prefer if I found a reason to decline?"

"No." The word was snapped out. Then he took a step back, and she heard the soft, frustrated whine.

Simon must have gone to school at some point, must have received the kind of education that enabled him to run a business and a Courtyard, but she suddenly understood what Henry meant about the difference between *dealing* with humans and having one live among them. Having one they treated as a friend.

He wanted her to come over and watch the movie, but something was making him unhappy about it.

"I spend a lot of time in this skin on the other days." Simon thumped his chest and looked at the snow piled in the center of the complex's courtyard. "Earthdays are the days I can be Wolf. But I want to encourage Sam to shift, and that means wearing the human skin for a while every day now."

She took the words apart, as if they were images that would be put back together to make a prophecy—and understood. "You'd like to spend the evening in your other form."

"Yes."

"Well, after you make the popcorn and put the movie on, why can't you do that?"

Now he looked at her. "You wouldn't mind?"

"No, I wouldn't mind."

"Seven o'clock?"

She smiled. "I'll see you at seven."

She felt Simon watching her as she climbed the stairs to her apartment. She heard Sam howl. And she wondered how many residents of the Courtyard knew she was going over to her neighbor's place to watch a movie.

Simon washed the dishes and swallowed impatience. He couldn't wait to get out of this skin, this shape. It had a few advantages over the pure Wolf form, but it wasn't *natural*, and having to remain in that skin after it began to scrape on the heart and mind could push a *terra indigene* into a crazed rage.

Not all that different from what had happened out west, except the crazed rage had occurred while the Others were in animal forms.

Not something a leader who had to look human so much of the time wanted to consider might happen to him.

He shook his head, as if that would send the thoughts flying.

Meg said she was all right with him being Wolf while she watched the movie with Sam. He didn't think she was lying.

He went upstairs and got Sam out of the bath, half listening to the grand plans the boy thought would fit into the couple of hours before bedtime. He let Sam dither over which movie to watch while he went into the kitchen and made the popcorn. Even in this form, the stuff didn't have any particular appeal for him, but it was a traditional human treat when watching movies, so he made a big bowl of it for Meg and Sam to share.

He had just finished pouring the melted butter over the popcorn when someone knocked on the front door. Sam let out a sound that was part boy squeal and part Wolf howl as he rushed to the door and pulled it open.

The boy's words tumbled over one another so fast, they made little sense except to convey happy excitement. Then Meg's voice, still close to the door.

Simon cocked an ear. Why was she still close to the door? Had she changed her mind about spending time with them?

No, he realized as he heard her voice in the living room now. She had stopped to take off boots and coat. Why hadn't she used the back door? Was front door a different message than back door?

He'd worked hard to learn the rules of doing business with humans, but there could be a whole other set of rules for personal interactions.

Frustrated now—and suspecting he was making a simple thing complicated—Simon brought the popcorn into the living room. He went back to the kitchen for two large mugs of water. Placing everything on the table in front of the sofa, he greeted Meg and retreated to the kitchen to shed the clothes and shift.

He crept toward the living room, silent and waiting. Sam and Meg put the movie disc in the player and got it started. He listened to the bits and pieces about other movies, listened to boy and woman settling down on the sofa. He waited a couple of minutes longer, then slipped into the living room.

They were tucked at one end of the sofa, the bowl of popcorn on Meg's lap, their eyes focused on the television.

A dart behind the sofa to come around the other side.

A moment's tension. A moment's fear. Then Meg patted the cushion and said, "I think we left enough room for you."

He climbed up on the sofa, filling the remaining space.

"Popcorn?" Meg asked, tipping the bowl toward him.

As an answer, he turned away from the bowl, lightly pressing his muzzle and forehead against her upper arm. More tension, but when he did nothing, she slowly relaxed and began eating the popcorn.

Simon closed his eyes. Keeping his head against her arm, he breathed in the scents that were Meg. The hair was still stinky, but not so much now, and the rest of her smelled good. Pleasing. Comforting.

After a few minutes, he nudged her arm until his head rested on her thigh. Another moment of tension. Then, making no protest, she shifted the popcorn so she wouldn't keep bopping him with the bowl.

A few minutes after that, he felt her fingers shyly burrowing into his fur.

The first time she sucked in a breath, he almost sprang up, thinking she'd heard something outside. Then he began to understand the rhythm of her touch and Sam's comments about the story. Dozing, he could follow the story through Meg's fingers and breathing, only half listening to the boy's "This is a scary part, but they'll be all right," and "Watch what happens now!"

Pleasure. Comfort. Contentment.

Except for the hair, she really did smell good.

Simon came fully awake when Sam said, "We can watch another one."

"You can, maybe," Meg replied. "But I have to work tomorrow, so it's time for me to go home."

"But—"

<Enough, pup,> Simon said. <Brush your teeth as I showed you. I will see Meg home and check the ground around our den. Then I will come back and read you a story.>

<Meg could read me a story.>

Simon raised his head and looked at the boy.

Sam slid off the couch. He gave Meg a shy smile and Simon a wary glance.

"I can come to work with you tomorrow," Sam said.

"You have school tomorrow," Meg replied, smiling. "And I'm not going to agree to something without talking to your uncle first. So good night, Sam."

He poked out his lower lip, as if trying to see what kind of reaction he would get. When Meg and Simon both stared at him, he sighed, said good night, and went upstairs.

Meg set the bowl on the table, then looked at her hand. "Guess I should have gotten some napkins at some point."

He stretched his neck and swiped a tongue over her palm. When she didn't pull away, he took another lick, and kept licking until he cleaned the salt and butter off her skin.

She smelled good. She tasted even better.

"That's good. Thanks," she said. She picked up the bowl and mugs, pushed to her feet, and walked out of the room.

Getting off the sofa, he yawned and stretched, then followed her into the kitchen.

"I'm not sure if popcorn goes in with the compost or in the incinerator bag," Meg said. "So I'll leave that for you."

Retracing her steps, she put on her coat and boots.

It was hard not to crowd her, hard not to jump, hard not to invite her to play. But it was almost time to sleep, and he didn't want Meg to get riled up or worried about being around a big Wolf. He could go for walks with her and Sam if she wasn't afraid of the Wolf.

He went out with her and walked her up to her own door. He waited until she was inside, then took a thorough sniff around her porch before going down and checking the rest of the complex.

As he reached the road, Allison hooted a greeting and glided past him on her way home. Lights were on in Vlad's apartment, which meant the vampire had returned from his evening in the Chambers.

No unfamiliar scents. No sign of danger.

For tonight anyway, they were all safe.

Satisfied, Simon trotted back to his apartment and the boy who was waiting for a story.

"Hello?"

"The messenger you hired to retrieve your property got careless. The Wolves got him before the police did."

"Who is this?"

"Someone who has a better chance of helping you reacquire your property—for the right fee."

"How did you get this number?"

"Like I said, your messenger was careless." A pause. "And I thought it might be inconvenient if the police found this number when they searched the man's apartment."

"There are several messengers looking for my property. Which one got careless?"

"The one in Lakeside."

"Are you sure you've found my property? Describe her."

A hesitation. "Short, delicate, has gray eyes."

Silence. Then, "How long will it take you to retrieve her?"

"A few weeks."

"Unacceptable. Too much profit will be lost in that amount of time."

"Your property is stashed in a very inconvenient place."

"I can help with that by providing some muscle and accessories."

"I prefer to rely on my own accessories, but the muscle will come in handy."

Another silence. "I'll give you a week to come up with some useful information that will assist me in reacquiring my property. If you prove to be a valid source, we'll discuss fees and bonuses."

Click.

Asia listened to empty air for a few seconds, then hung up the phone and watched her hands shake. She'd pulled it off, made the contact, sounded like a pro who reacquired property every day. Sounded like someone who wouldn't flinch about reacquiring living property when it was necessary.

So no-looks Meg wasn't just the thief; she was the *stolen property*? Someone worth enough that several people had been hired to find the feeb?

"If Asia Crane, SI, had this information, what would she think?" Asia muttered.

She picked up the phone and called Bigwig. "What kind of person could be stolen property?" she asked as soon as he answered the phone.

A crackling excitement filled the phone line. "We've picked up a couple of whispers that a blood prophet wandered off," he said. "Men have been searching the Northeast Region for some sign of her. You think you've found her?"

Asia's thoughts spun so fast, she could barely think at all. Meg was a *cassandra sangue*? No wonder White Van had tried to grab her. No wonder someone had pressured the Lakeside government to help find her. That skin must be worth thousands and thousands of dollars. Maybe even a million!

And it was surrounded by fangs, claws, and beaks that could render it useless.

"Do you think you've found her?" Bigwig asked again.

"I don't know. Maybe." Asia hesitated, trying to figure out who would give her the best offer for her help. "Someone tried to abduct the Courtyard's Liaison today, so I'm going to have to be careful about asking questions."

"You think she's there? In the Courtyard?" A pause. "Yes. Yes, that makes sense. The mayor has been quite frustrated by the lack of progress the police have made with regard to the thief I told you about. So the prophet and thief are one and the same."

Have to decide now, Asia thought. *Gamble on someone who might make good on his offer, or stick with the men who can guarantee I'll have a show that lasts enough seasons to make me a very rich woman?* "Yes, I think they are."

"Even if we can't find the original owner, there are others who—"

"I already found him." There was a weight to the silence that followed her words, so she pushed on. "I did some investigating and searched the apartment of the would-be abductor. I found a phone number. I got off the phone with the interested party just before I called you. He's sending in his own people, but we'll receive a finder's fee and some compensation for continued assistance."

"I guess you do want to star in your own TV show."

She grinned. "I guess I really do." After promising to give him daily updates, she hung up and moved around her apartment, unable to relax.

Something in his tone of voice. A lack of confidence that hadn't been there until she told him she'd already made contact with the man she assumed was Meg's Controller.

Had Bigwig hoped to sell Meg to the highest bidder? Or had he hoped to tuck the feeb away somewhere, to be used exclusively by his chosen few?

Didn't matter now. The hired muscle was heading for Lakeside. Time to change her focus. And that meant Darrell was going to get lucky after all.

And her luck was changing too. Bigwig and the other backers might be unhappy about a blood prophet slipping through their fingers, but she would bring them something even better: a small, furry bargaining chip.

CHAPTER 17

When Meg stepped into the office's front room on Moonsday morning, she found a Wolf staring at her from the other side of the counter. A glance at the go-through confirmed the slide locks were still in place. That didn't instill any feeling of safety, especially when the Wolf stood on his hind legs and plopped his forelegs on the counter in much the same way a man would rest his forearms.

Backing through the Private doorway, she eased the door closed, turned the lock, and bolted for the telephone in the sorting room. Her hands shook, making it harder to dial, but she got through to Howling Good Reads.

"There's a Wolf in the Liaison's Office!" she shouted.

Bewildered silence filled the phone line before John Wolfgard said, "Isn't there supposed to be?"

"Not a furry one! Where's Simon? I need to talk to Simon!"

More silence. Then, warily, "He's there, at the office."

"No, he's not. I know what Simon looks like as a Wolf, and *that's not Simon!*"

"That's Nathan," Simon said, walking in from the back room. "He's on duty this morning."

Meg hung up the phone, then picked up the receiver, said, "Good-bye, John," to the dial tone, and put the receiver back on its cradle.

"Did you open the front door?" Simon asked, fishing in a drawer for the office keys. Finding them on the counter next to the phone, he picked them up and took a step toward the Private door.

"No, I didn't open the door. There was a Wolf in the way!"

He stopped and studied her. Gave the air a little sniff. "You're acting strange. Is it that time of the month?"

She shrieked. His human ears flattened in a way human ears shouldn't, and he backed away from her.

In the front room, the Wolf howled.

Then Simon seemed to remember who was the leader. He stopped backing away, and his amber eyes suddenly had that glint of predator.

"You weren't afraid of me when I was Wolf," he said. "Why are you afraid of Nathan?"

"He's got big feet!" Which was true, but beside the point. It was just the first thing that popped into her head.

"What?"

An insulted-sounding *arrrroooo* came from the other side of the door, a reminder that Wolves also had big ears.

Meg closed her eyes, then took a deep breath and let it out. Took another one. She wasn't going to get anywhere with either one of them if she kept sounding like a ninny. And she was having some trouble explaining to herself why she had that moment of panic. "A strange Wolf is scarier than a familiar Wolf, especially when you're not expecting any Wolf at all."

Simon waved a hand, dismissing what she thought was a perfectly logical point. "That's Nathan. He's staying. As the Courtyard's leader, I made that decision."

"As the Liaison, I should have been informed *before* a change was made to this office."

Simon took a step toward her. She took a step toward him.

"Arrrooooo?" queried Nathan.

"Someone paid that man to take you away, Meg," Simon growled. "Someone tried to hurt you. So a Wolf will be on guard when the office is open. Nathan is an enforcer for the Courtyard. He's one of our best in a fight."

"But—"

"It's decided."

She wasn't going to win, wasn't even going to sway him enough to have Nathan stay out of sight. She glanced at the Private door and lowered her voice. "What happens if he bites a deliveryman?"

"That'll depend on whether he's hungry."

She wanted to say, *Ha, ha. Very funny.* But she was pretty sure he wasn't joking.

And she was sure he was right about the man who grabbed her. Sometimes dealing with the Others filled up her head so much, she forgot about the Controller.

"I should have been consulted." She tried that tack one last time.

His only answer was to open the Private door, then unlock the front door and flip the sign to OPEN.

At least he had to use the go-through, since there was a Wolf clogging up the counter. When he came back into the sorting room, he tossed the keys in the drawer—and tossed her a look that made her want to slug him.

"Mr. Wolfgard . . ."

He turned on her, baring teeth that lengthened as she watched.

"If you say another word about this, I will eat you, and I won't leave so much as an ear for *him*." He jerked his head toward the front room.

Then he was gone. She flinched when the back door slammed.

She peered into the front room. Nathan was no longer hanging over the counter. He was lying on the floor, staring at the Crow perched on the wooden sculpture outside. As soon as she stepped into the front room, he looked at her.

She tried a smile. "Good morning, Nathan. Sorry about the confusion."

He lifted a lip to show her some teeth, then pointedly turned his head and went back to staring at the Crow.

Yep, Meg thought. *He's insulted, and I'm not going to be forgiven anytime soon.*

Retreating to the sorting room, she flipped through the Pet Palace catalog to see if there was anything she could order that would change that.

"Harry, Nathan. Nathan, Harry."

The deliveryman looked at the Wolf and paled. The Wolf looked at the deliveryman and licked his chops.

Meg figured the morning was going to go downhill from there. But Harry surprised her.

"Heard on the news that there was some trouble here," Harry said. "No details, but there never are about such things when it involves the Courtyard." He studied her. "That trouble was here, in this office?"

For answer, she pushed up her sleeve enough to show him the bruise on her wrist. "A man pretending to make a delivery grabbed me. Mr. Wolfgard showed up before he could do anything else."

Harry pursed his lips and made a peculiar sound with his teeth. Then he huffed out a breath. "The Crows out there are good for warning you about trouble, but they don't have the muscle to take care of trouble once it gets through the door." He rapped his knuckles on the counter. "You take care, Miz Meg."

He left, giving Nathan a brisk nod on his way out.

The rest of the morning went along much the same way. There was a knee-jerk reaction when a deliveryman walked in and spotted Nathan. Most said something along the lines of, "You got a new helper? What happened to the Crow?" Meg took this to mean that dealing with a Crow might be peculiar, but it was much preferred to dealing with something that weighed as much as you did and growled at you.

Only one deliveryman refused to come inside once he spotted Nathan, and that was the man who had paid too much attention to Sam and the harness the pup was wearing. She ended up calling Lorne at the Three Ps to run over from his shop and take the packages, because Nathan blocked the door, preventing her from going outside while that particular man was there.

After the mail was delivered, Meg checked her list against the previous week's. She looked at Nathan, who was sniffing around the front room in a way that made her hope he knew the difference between a counter and a tree.

"That's the last of the regular morning deliveries," she said, hoping she sounded bright rather than demented. "I'm going to be working in the sorting room for a while. You want to go outside for a few minutes and stretch your legs?"

He didn't respond, so she went into the sorting room to deal with the mail and other deliveries. A minute later, she heard the Crows. When she peeked through the doorway, she saw Nathan outside, moving back and forth in the delivery area, nose to the ground. Then he raised his head and howled.

"Well, that will help traffic," she muttered as answering howls penetrated the building from several directions.

We are here.

That was always the message. But she had the feeling people wouldn't have to go into Howling Good Reads anymore to catch sight of a Wolf.

<Nathan?> Simon called. He looked out his office window while he listened to the Wolves who responded to Nathan's howl. <Where are you?> That first howl hadn't been muffled by enough walls or glass.

<Outside.>

<You're supposed to be inside, guarding Meg.>

<The Meg said to go outside.>

<You don't take orders from Meg.>

<She'll feel easier about me being in the office if she thinks I do.>

Nathan had a point. Meg's peculiar reaction to seeing a Wolf in the office kept scratching at him. Most humans who had seen one Wolf didn't get upset about seeing another one, as long as it wasn't attacking someone. At least, that was true of the customers who came into Howling Good Reads. To them, a Wolf was a Wolf was a Wolf. On the other hand, he liked that he wasn't interchangeable with the rest of the Wolfgard and that Meg knew him on sight, even the first time she'd seen him as Wolf.

He spotted Nathan when the other Wolf rounded a corner to sniff around the back of the office.

<Anything?> Simon asked.

<No scents that shouldn't be here,> Nathan replied, lifting a leg to yellow up some snow.

It took a little too much effort to stop himself from running over to the office and marking his territory. Not that he should consider the Liaison's Office as being more *his* territory than the rest of the Courtyard.

He shifted his feet and whined softly.

Have to stay human and do my own work—and trust Nathan to do his.

He heard the Crows, watched Nathan head for the back door and slip inside the office.

<Delivery?> he asked the Crows.

<A female,> was the reply. <We know her face.>

A familiar female who would go into the office to talk to Meg. Someone who wasn't *terra indigene.* The Crows would have said if the female was Other. That narrowed the possibilities. But Heather was downstairs, shelving stock. Merri Lee wasn't scheduled to work at A Little Bite until lunchtime. The Ruthie? Maybe, but he didn't remember seeing her around the store in the mornings, and she usually spent time at Run & Thump later in the day. Which left Asia Crane.

Simon pictured Asia alone with Meg—and snarled. No reason. Asia hadn't done anything except be too pushy about wanting the Liaison's job and wanting him to take her for a walk on the wild side. But she didn't seem that interested in either of those things anymore.

And if she was, she wasn't saying anything to him.

<Nathan? Stay close to Meg.>

He didn't get a response and didn't expect one. Going back to his desk, Simon looked at the telephone. With Elliot at the consulate, there were five Wolves in this part of the Courtyard, but only two were in Wolf form—Nathan and Ferus, who was on duty at HGR. It wouldn't hurt to have a couple more Wolves close by, especially because he'd promised Sam that the pup could spend the afternoon with Meg.

Maybe he should mention that to Meg?

He picked up the phone, but he didn't call Meg. Instead, he called Blair and arranged for an increase in the Wolfgard presence in the Liaison's part of the Courtyard.

Asia strolled up to the Liaison's Office, hot chocolate in hand. On previous dates with Darrell, she had hinted that Simon might be a wee bit jealous about the time she was spending with another man. Now that plans had changed, she wanted everyone in the Courtyard to know she was Darrell's girlfriend.

She didn't think Simon would give a damn one way or the other, but she hoped he would lower his guard some if she no longer paid attention to him and didn't have much time for Meg.

"There you are!" Asia said when Meg stepped up to the counter. "I was whittling my way down to nothing with worry, but this was the first chance I had to check on you." A quick look over Meg's shoulder. She didn't see the Wolf pup, which was a disappointment, but she did see the box of sugar lumps on the big table. Confirmation enough that Meg brought out the sugar on Moonsday.

"Check on me?" Meg said.

"I heard the police were here and there was some big commotion. And then I heard you were injured, maybe even in the hospital, so I just had to see for myself that you were all right. Here. I brought you some hot chocolate." Darrell hadn't actually said anything about Meg. He'd just mentioned the ambulance being on the scene—and he told her some freaky story about a wolf man standing right out where everyone could see a lot more than they wanted to see.

"Thanks." Meg took a sip and set the cup on the counter. "I'm fine. Someone brought in a suspicious box, that's all."

Not by a long shot, Asia thought. *That little incident had the whole Courtyard buzzing right along with the cops.* "Well, I'm glad to hear you didn't take any harm." Now she made a show of looking past Meg. "Say. Where is that adorable puppy that was with you the other day? He was just the cutest thing."

"He's not here today."

Before Asia could push to find out where the puppy was when he wasn't at the office, a full-grown Wolf appeared in the doorway, startling her into taking a couple steps back. Despite their size, the damn things were so *quiet*. After that Wolf rammed his nose into her crotch, she was a lot less interested in being around any of them unless she could pick them up and carry them away.

Meg looked at the Wolf, then said to Asia, "I have a different office buddy now."

"All the time?" Asia asked.

Meg hesitated. "The incident on Watersday . . . It was alarming at the time, and with so many police officers responding, it caused a lot of fuss. So Mr. Wolfgard decided to add some security in the office during business hours—the same kind he has at the bookstore."

She hadn't appreciated how badly White Van had bungled the snatch, but this just confirmed how pointless it would be to continue hanging around Meg. Anything she said from now on would be reported to Simon.

A chorus of neighs gave her an excuse to leave.

"More friends?" she asked.

"The ponies are here for the mail."

"And the sugar."

"That too. Thanks for the hot chocolate."

"I'd still like to go out to lunch one of these days," Asia said. "You let me know when we might be able to do that."

Not that it's going to happen, she thought as she left the office. She looked toward the consulate, spotted Darrell in one of the upstairs windows, and blew him a kiss. *I am going to be all kinds of distracted with my new boyfriend.*

She sauntered to HGR and stayed long enough to make sure she'd been spotted. Then she picked a book at random, relieved that it wasn't Simon manning the register when she went up to pay for it.

As soon as she returned to her car, she called Darrell. He was thrilled to have the opportunity to invite her out on another date.

Meg didn't know where Nathan had gone when she went to A Little Bite for lunch and then walked over to the Market Square to browse in the library for a while, but he was waiting for her at the back door when she returned for the office's afternoon hours. She wondered if he was making an effort not to startle her again, since his appearance that morning made it obvious that he could get into the building by himself.

She opened the doors and spread the *Lakeside News* on the sorting table to skim the paper for whatever might be of interest to the Others. Nathan was in the front room, sniffing everything.

When the Crows started fussing, she went to the counter, tensing when she saw an unscheduled delivery truck. Then it turned enough for her to read the Everywhere Delivery name.

"It's Harry," she said to Nathan as she hurried to open the door for the deliveryman.

"Was asked to make a special afternoon delivery," Harry said when he put the box on the handcart. "Got the other piece to bring in, but you might want to make sure the floor is dry wherever you want to put it."

"Good idea." Meg hurried into the back room and fetched a towel. While Nathan paced, clearly not sure of where he should be, she wiped down the floor where he'd been lying that morning. "Right over here, Harry." Since his boots were snowy, she took the bulky stuffed fabric from him and positioned it herself.

"Need your signature, Miz Meg," Harry said.

She signed his slip, made her own notation on her clipboard, and waited until Harry drove off before she smiled at Nathan. "Go ahead. Take a look."

He moved forward cautiously. He circled it, sniffed it, whapped it with a paw. Then he found the product tag and stared at it for a moment. Turning toward her, he lifted a lip in something that might have been a sneer.

"I know it says it's a dog bed, but I'm sure a Wolf can use it," Meg said.

Nothing but grumbly sounds from the Wolf.

"Fine. If you want to lie on a cold, hard floor instead of something comfy and warm just because *Wolf* is spelled d-o-g, you go right ahead." She went into the sorting room and shut the door. Then she remembered the other box and opened the receiving door long enough to pull the handcart into the sorting room. If he was going to be so churlish about her trying to do something nice for him, she sure wasn't going to leave six defenseless boxes of dog cookies alone with him.

She tucked the boxes—three boxes for puppies and three for large dogs—in the cupboards under her sorting table. Then she went back to reading the paper until the Crows announced the next delivery truck.

Simon walked into the front room of the Liaison's Office and stared at the Wolf curled up on . . .

"What is that?" he asked, stomping snow off his boots as he stepped toward Nathan.

<Mine,> Nathan replied.

"How did it get to be yours?"

<I am guarding, so it is mine.> Giving Simon a smug look, Nathan added, <I got cookies too.>

Ignoring the warning growl, Simon ran a hand over the fabric, squeezed the stuffing, and looked at the tag.

"Where did you find this?" Not only did it look comfortable; it would look neater than the pile of old blankets he now had in his office for the times when he wanted to shift to Wolf and nap for a while.

<Meg found it.> Nathan put his head on his paws and watched Simon.

The leader always had first choice of food, of females, of anything that came to his attention. A leader who always took what another had was a leader who ended up constantly fighting to retain the leadership.

"This one stays here for whoever is on guard. I'll ask Meg to order another one for me." He glanced at the closed door and wondered why Meg hadn't come out, since even human ears should have heard him talking to Nathan. <Any trouble?>

<No, but a Hawk told me the Darrell asked Elliot for permission to use one of the above stairs places. I think he found a female for sex.>

He had a good idea which female Darrell had found.

The first time Asia came in to Howling Good Reads and indicated she'd like to have sex with him, he'd tried to imagine being with her. Something about her interest hadn't felt right, and all he could picture was a trap with steel teeth hidden under leaves and twigs. But that was his reaction to her, and, to be honest, he was relieved she'd turned her attention to a human male and would leave him alone now.

He didn't like her, so he didn't trust her. He didn't care if that was fair or not. Just like he didn't care if it was fair to wonder if the Others should continue to trust Darrell once he began having sex with Asia. After all, males did plenty of foolish things when they wanted sex.

He didn't say anything to Nathan. His new reservations about Darrell were a discussion to have with Henry and Vlad. But right now, he had to face another discussion.

Using the go-through, he went behind the counter, studied the closed door, debated a moment, then knocked before opening it just enough to say, "Meg?"

No answer. Walking into the room, he didn't find a woman. Before he had a chance to howl about her being gone, he heard the toilet flush. Her whereabouts discovered, he opened cupboards until he found the cookies. He had his hand in the box when Meg walked into the room.

He stuffed a couple of cookies into his coat pocket, then closed the box and put it back where he'd found it.

"Where did you get the bed for Nathan?" he asked.

She sighed. "Does it really matter that the tag says *dog* instead of *Wolf*?"

It would if they decided to send some into the settlements, but he could ignore the words here in the Courtyard. "I wondered because I would like to get one for my office. And maybe a couple of extras to put in our general store."

"I ordered it from the Pet Palace."

He winced, thinking of what Elliot would say about purchasing anything from such a place. Well, he just wouldn't tell Elliot where the beds came from.

"Order more."

"All right." She gave him a puzzled look. "How did you know about the bed?"

"I didn't. I came over to see if Sam can stay with you for the rest of the afternoon. I'll fetch him from school. He can go with you on your deliveries, or you can leave him with Henry."

"All right." Now she looked uneasy. "Simon? Asia asked about Sam. She saw him while you were out of town, when he was here with me."

"What did you tell her?"

"I told her he wasn't here today. Then she saw Nathan. She and I talked for a couple of minutes, and she left. Sam is cute, and humans do like cuddling puppies and kittens." She shrugged. "I don't think she meant any harm by asking, but I thought you should know."

"Good." He nodded. "It's good you told me. I'll take your BOW and go get Sam now."

He went out the back door. As he crossed the space to the garage, he looked back at the stairs that led to the two small apartments over the Liaison's Office. A meeting place. An overnight place. A sex place for those among the *terra indigene* whose status in the human world required more privacy than was available in the rooms above the social center.

A trap with steel teeth. He needed to figure out what he didn't understand about Asia being with Darrell before that trap snapped shut.

CHAPTER 18

With Sam beside him in the front seat, Simon drove away from the Courtyard's school and headed for the Liaison's Office. The school was tucked near the center of the Courtyard, well hidden from prying human eyes.

It wasn't safe for *terra indigene* youngsters to go to school with human children, so Courtyards provided their residents with an education similar to what humans received. A human couldn't cheat a Wolf who could add and subtract like anyone else. Two plus two equaled four, no matter what species you belonged to.

Thaisia's history, on the other hand, was a different matter altogether. Humans and Others held very different opinions about *that* subject.

But that day's report of arithmetic, reading, and writing had been covered in the first two minutes of the drive. Now Sam was back to a more important topic.

"But Nathan isn't *doing* anything," Sam said. "*Why* can't he play with me?"

"He is doing something," Simon replied. "He's on guard, so he can play only during the midday break when Meg isn't in the office."

"How come Meg needs a guard now? Nathan wasn't guarding when I was with Meg before."

He didn't want to tell the boy about the intruder, but if he didn't say something, the pup would keep on pestering him and Nathan about why the Wolf on guard couldn't play.

"A man came into the office. He was mean to Meg. We didn't like that, so Nathan is there to make sure nobody else is mean to her."

Sam looked out the window. Then he asked in a small voice, "Is he the man who hurt Mom?"

"No. Those men ran away. We'll find them one day, Sam. We will. But the man who came into the office wasn't one of them."

"I want to be Wolf when I'm at the office."

Simon glanced at the boy. "Meg can't communicate the way the *terra indigene* do. You won't be able to tell her what you learned in school today if you're Wolf."

"I can tell her when we get home. I can't wear the harness in this form, so I have to hold the safety line in my hand, and sometimes I forget and drop it."

"You don't have to wear the harness anymore." He wished the boy wasn't so focused on that harness and leash. It made the other Wolves uneasy. Well, it wouldn't bother any of them much longer. The pup had grown sufficiently in just a few days' time that the harness wouldn't fit him in another week.

Sam gave him an incredulous look. "If I don't wear the harness, how am I supposed to pull Meg out of a snowbank when she falls in?"

Simon kept his eyes on the road. The boy had said *when*, not *if*. Just how often did Meg fall into a snowbank? Was she clumsy, or was it play? Or did she end up in the snow after getting tripped by a puppy?

"And Meg isn't a good digger," Sam continued. "As Wolf, I'm lots better at digging."

"Is that why you were the one digging out the BOW when it got stuck in the snow yesterday?" Simon asked mildly.

Sam scooted down in his seat and mumbled, "You weren't supposed to know about that."

"Uh-huh." He had fielded a dozen calls from Hawks, Owls, Crows, and a couple of Wolves who had watched that piece of idiocy and couldn't wait to tell him about it. He found it interesting that none of them had offered to help. In fact, the Wolves told him they had deliberately stayed out of sight, letting Meg and Sam work it out for themselves. And they had. Between them, they had gotten the BOW unstuck and continued with the deliveries.

It also explained why, when he'd returned from an hour's run with Blair and a few other Wolves, he'd found the television on and pup and prophet sound asleep on the living room floor.

Since she was spooned around Sam to keep him warm, Simon had figured it was only sensible to stay as Wolf and tuck himself against her back to keep *her* warm.

The fact that tucking up against her made him feel content had nothing to do with that decision. Nothing at all.

When they arrived at Meg's office, Simon helped Sam fold his clothes and place them in one of the back room's storage bins, then opened the door to the sorting room after the boy shifted to Wolf. The pup gave Meg an exuberant greeting, *arroooe*d at Nathan, then began sniffing around the room for the cookies Meg had hidden.

"You have anything you want me to walk over to the consulate?" he asked.

"No, thanks," Meg replied. "Darrell came by and picked up the mail." She paused, looking puzzled.

He caught a whiff of uneasiness in her scent and took a step toward her. "Something wrong with him coming by?"

She shook her head. "Just that no one from the consul has come for the mail before this week."

He debated about whether to tell her about Darrell's scheduled monkey fuck, but he didn't say anything because she suddenly yelped.

"Your nose is cold!" she said, looking down at Sam. "And don't think I'm buying that 'I was just checking for cookies' look as an excuse to stick a cold nose against my ankle!"

Sam talked back at her, sounding quite pleased with himself, then trotted around the sorting table to resume his quest for cookies.

Grinning, Simon left the office and walked over to the consulate.

Darrell was at a desk, looking like he'd already caught the scent of a female in heat and was about to lose his brains over it. Giving the human a nod, Simon went up the stairs to Elliot's office.

"You wanted to see me?" he asked when his sire looked up.

"Yes."

Elliot gestured to the visitor's chair, and Simon wondered which politician he was mimicking. He also wondered why the other Wolf looked uncomfortable.

"Everything still going well with Ms. Corbyn?" Elliot finally asked.

"Some reason it shouldn't be?"

"I saw Nathan and Sam chasing her yesterday afternoon behind the office. They seemed . . . serious . . . in their pursuit."

Ah. "Henry talked Meg into playing deer hunt, claiming that Sam needed to work on his skills in chasing game. I think he was mostly making sure that she got some exercise. Meg is convincing in her role as designated prey, which is why Henry wanted to keep them in sight—in case Nathan became too enthusiastic or another Wolf mistook the game for a real hunt. In the end, it will build up Meg's muscles and stamina, and build up Sam's muscles and stamina, and Nathan will have a good time romping with them as a reward for guard duty."

Of course, listening to John whine yesterday about not being allowed to go out and play hadn't done anything for his own eroding self-discipline—especially because he could tell just by watching that Meg really did make a good squeaky toy.

Elliot smiled. Then he chuckled. "It's good to see the pup playing again. Now, if we can just get him out of that harness."

"He says he needs it to pull Meg out of snowbanks," Simon replied, his voice bland.

Elliot laughed. As the laughter faded, he sobered. "I'm sorry I struck her. Her instincts are odd but from the heart, I think."

Simon nodded. It was a little annoying to have Sam quoting Meg about human things when she actually knew less about the regular human world than every member of the Business Association, but her lack of knowledge about the Others was working to their advantage. What other human would accept the label of *prey* in order for a little Wolf to chase her?

"Darrell is having his assignation this evening," Elliot said.

"We agreed to let him use one of the rooms above the Liaison's Office," Simon said.

"He also wants permission to bring his companion to the Meat-n-Greens for dinner."

"Why? It's not a fancy place, if you want to impress a woman. You go to a human-run restaurant for that."

"But it is in the Market Square, a place very few are allowed to see. Some women become quite stimulated by the thrill of the forbidden."

"Do you know who he wants to bring in?"

"It's the female who was sniffing around you. At least, Ferus said he smelled Darrell on her."

Simon nodded. "Asia Crane." Forbidden thrill. That explained why youngsters from the university or the business and technical college were always sniffing around HGR and A Little Bite, or spending an evening in the social center in the hopes of rubbing up against the *terra indigene*. But he'd had the impression Asia had been sniffing around for something more. Did humans gain some status among their own kind if they were allowed in the Courtyard's Market Square? Maybe he would ask the Ruthie the next time she came into HGR. She was proving to be quite reliable for a human.

"Give him a guest pass for the Market Square," Simon said. "Tell Darrell he can take his female into any stores that are open. But make sure he knows it's a one-time pass."

"I'll tell him."

Simon pushed out of the chair. "I have to go. Vlad is handling the store today, but I promised to deal with some of the paperwork."

He walked back to HGR, detouring at A Little Bite for coffee and a fruit tart that he'd sniffed earlier in the day. Taking his treat up to the bookstore's office, he growled his way through some paperwork—and tried to shake the uneasiness he felt about giving Asia Crane any kind of access to the Courtyard.

Meg kept her eyes on the road as she followed the familiar route to the Chambers. "Today you are *not* going to jump on me and scare me into driving into a snowbank because you saw a deer and wanted to get out and chase it. Right? Because we do not need to get stuck two days in a row."

She had really, really, really hoped that Simon—and Blair—hadn't heard about the snowbank. Finding a short-handled shovel in the back of the BOW next to the snow brush and ice scraper had been proof enough that one—or both—knew about yesterday's adventure.

Sam grinned at her and wagged his tail.

No help there.

Of course, she had never seen real deer before, and seeing a handful in what looked like a snow corral had been the other reason she hadn't focused on the road those few seconds too long.

Not that she was going to admit that.

As she drove past Erebus Sanguinati's marble home, she glanced to the left. Then she stopped and stared at one of the interior roads. Most weren't plowed with any consistency, and the few that were led to buildings that had no designation. Since she didn't need to drive along those roads to make her deliveries and didn't think the BOW could muscle its way down them anyway, she stuck to the outer ring and the interior roads that provided access to all the complexes, as well as the Pony Barn and the girls at the lake.

Maybe in the spring, when those unmarked roads were accessible again, she would drive around the interior of the Courtyard and find her own little spot where she could go when she wanted some solitude.

But as she looked at that narrow, snow-covered road again, the skin just below the newest scars—the ones that had shown her where her life would end—began prickling so fiercely she wanted to scream. If Simon was right and this was some kind of instinctive defense the *cassandra sangue* possessed, then that road represented some kind of danger.

When she drove past the road, the prickling didn't fade. In fact, it got worse, becoming more concentrated under the skin below those new scars.

She turned on the BOW's headlights, wondering how she could have forgotten that she needed lights to drive at night.

Except it wasn't night. She and Sam were making the afternoon deliveries, and she didn't need the lights to see the road.

Shaking, Meg stopped the BOW and put it in park, ignoring Sam's whining as he tried to climb into her lap and lick her face.

The prickling turned into a harsh buzzing under her skin.

It had been more than a week since her last cut, and that one had been a paper cut, an accident. Maybe that's why she felt so edgy, so desperate to relieve the prickling.

Maybe that's why she had just slipped into something that wasn't quite a vision. Or wasn't a vision in the same way she had been trained to see them.

This was new, unknown, frightening. This was worse than being distracted by a deer for a few seconds. If she hadn't remembered *when* she was driving, would that weird vision have continued until she crashed the BOW?

She'd been driving alone. At night. So whatever this was, it was personal. It was about her. And there was only one way she was going to find out more.

This wasn't about a physical craving. There wasn't going to be any euphoria. But she *had* to find out why she'd reacted so strongly to a road that she'd experienced inside a vision for a few seconds.

Have to wait, she thought, gritting her teeth as she put the BOW in gear. *Have to wait until I finish the deliveries and get Sam home.*

"Not many packages today," she told Sam as she drove to the last section of the Chambers. She left him in the BOW while she tucked a couple of items in the delivery boxes outside the fence, but she clipped his leash to the harness when she reached the Hawkgard Complex and let him come with her to the mail room.

Two packages to the Wolfgard Complex, then four boxes of another building-block toy for the Corvine social room. She had no idea what the Crows were building, but based on the comments made by Jenni and Crystal when she saw them in the Market Square, the Crows gathered each evening to work on these constructions and were having a great time.

By the time she reached the Green Complex and parked her BOW in the garage, her emotional need to make the cut was as fierce as her need to relieve the prickling in her skin. She tried to sound and act normal, but Sam's anxious whines told her plainly enough that the pup knew something was wrong.

And if Sam sensed it before she did anything, she was going to have to avoid Simon until the cut scabbed over. She just didn't know how to do that when he would be here soon to fetch the puppy.

When they were inside her apartment, she hung up her coat, took off her boots, and smiled at Sam. "I have to use the bathroom. Do you want to change while I'm doing that?"

It didn't surprise her that he followed her to the bathroom and tried to go in with her instead of going into her bedroom to shift and put on the clothes she had ready for him.

She locked him out, then stripped off her sweater and turtleneck. Taking the razor out of her jeans pocket, she opened it and laid the blade flat on her arm, its back against the previous scar. Then she turned her hand, bringing the honed edge against virgin skin—and pressed down lightly.

The sensation of skin parting, as if it were fleeing from the steel.

Lifting the blade, she placed the razor on the sink and braced for the pain. It flowed up from some dark place inside her while the blood flowed from the wound.

That interior road, just past Erebus's home. Not much snow on the pavement, but snow falling, heavy and fast. Dark outside, but she couldn't tell if it was early evening or late night. A sound like a motor mated to hornets. Driving alone in the dark at a reckless speed, no lights to give away her position. That sound closing around her. And behind her, Sam howling in terror.

But safe. This time, he was safe.

Coming out of the prophecy, Meg braced herself against the sink and swallowed the need to scream from the pain. So much worse than that little cut on her finger. Maybe even worse than the cuts that had shown her the Courtyard and Simon Wolfgard.

At least the prickling under her skin had stopped. She had gotten that much relief from the cut.

Gasping and crying, she washed the cut before putting on antiseptic cream and taping a thick pad over it, hoping to hide the smell of blood. Then she cleaned the razor and made sure she wiped the sink. As a last step, she used the toilet, not sure how long scents could be picked up by a Wolf nose.

She put on the turtleneck, careful not to pull the bandage, then the sweater, and left the bathroom. She expected to find Sam dressed, more or less, and waiting for her in the kitchen with his list of desired snacks. She found him still in Wolf form, huddled by her front door. He looked at her and whined but wouldn't come to her, wouldn't move away from the door.

Uneasy, she didn't push him. She brought him a couple of puppy cookies, which he refused to eat. He just huddled by the door, shivering.

She knew the moment Simon started up the stairs to her front door. Sam alternated howling and clawing at her door.

"Get out of the way, Sam," she said. "I can't open the door with you standing there."

As soon as the door was open, he bolted out of her apartment and down the stairs, racing past Simon.

"He's upset," she said. She tried to shut the door in Simon's face, but she wasn't fast enough. He didn't force his way in, didn't make any demands, but she was sure that the flickers of red in his eyes and the way he sniffed the air meant he knew exactly why Sam was upset.

Returning to the kitchen, she poured a glass of orange juice. Then she sat at the table and waited for whatever Simon was going to do.

He had washed the cage and put it in one of the basement storage bins. He was willing to look the other way about the harness and leash for a while longer, especially now that he knew why Sam wanted to keep wearing it, but he couldn't tolerate looking at that cage anymore.

And yet, when he opened the door to their apartment, Sam ran for that spot and huddled where the back corner of the cage used to be.

Simon removed his boots, went into the living room, and knelt beside the shivering pup.

<Sam? What's wrong?> *Besides the smell of blood on Meg.*

Whining, Sam climbed into Simon's arms.

<Did something happen when you and Meg were making deliveries?>

<Don't know.> Barely a whisper, but at least Sam was responding. <The bad happened after.>

<Where did you go after?>

<Meg's den.> Whining and shivering. Then, <I remember that smell. When Mom . . . Something in the bathroom hurt Meg, and there was that smell.>

Stupid bitch, Simon thought as he cuddled Sam. *Why slice herself when the pup was still with her? Why couldn't she wait until he'd gone home and wouldn't pick up the scent of fresh blood?*

Why indeed?

As the scent of her blood faded, replaced by the familiar scents of his own den, Simon's anger also faded.

No euphoria if the words of a prophecy weren't spoken. Only pain.

There were other reasons for a blood scent, especially in a female's bathroom. Could have been an accidental nick. Could be a different kind of blood that a pup wouldn't know about yet.

No. *That* kind of blood wasn't mixed with a medicine smell.

He didn't realize he was growling until Sam began licking his chin and making anxious sounds.

He'd been wrong the last time he accused her of cutting herself. He wouldn't make that mistake again.

<Henry?> Simon called.

<Here.>

<I need guidance.>

<I am almost home. Meet me there.>

Relief washed through him. Maybe his own memories of finding Daphne and Sam that terrible night made it hard for him to be rational about Meg being hurt. Maybe he was just as vulnerable as Sam in that way.

"Sam? I need to talk to Henry. Can you stay by yourself, or do you want me to ask . . . Elliot or Nathan to stay with you?" It told him how much she had become one of them that Meg was his first choice to stay with the pup.

Sam shifted. Simon enclosed the naked boy in his coat, letting his own heat warm cold skin.

"Can I watch a movie?" Sam asked.

"You can watch a movie."

"Can I have a snack?"

"You can have a snack that I will make for you."

Worried gray eyes looked into his. "Simon? Is Meg going to die and leave us?"

Simon shook his head. "If Meg was badly hurt, she would tell us. And she didn't look hurt, Sam." Actually, she did. Her face, her eyes, still showed signs of pain when she answered the door and tried to pretend everything was fine. "I'll check on her after I talk to Henry."

He couldn't do more than that for boy or woman, so he made a snack for Sam and put in the movie before he went over to Henry's. The Grizzly had returned and was making tea when Simon walked into the Beargard's kitchen.

He waited until they were seated at the table, the tea steaming in cups, before he told Henry about Sam and the scent of blood.

"Did she look wounded?" Henry asked.

"She's not wounded," Simon snapped. "She cut herself. You know it and I know it. But I don't know what to do about it."

"It's not your decision."

"I'm the leader. It *is* my decision."

Henry sipped his tea and said nothing for a minute. Simon struggled to keep his canines the proper human size while he waited, understanding that Henry was making him wait.

"How many humans do you trust?" Henry finally asked.

"Not many. Hardly any."

"I think our Meg trusts even less than you. In her own way, she is even more private than *terra indigene*, and I think she has been allowed so little privacy. Will you be like the human who used her and thought he owned her, or will you be a friend she can trust?"

Simon bared his teeth and snarled at Henry. Then the snarl faded because the Beargard had revealed the trap. If Meg cut herself, she saw a prophecy. If he forced her to tell him what she saw, she might believe she had traded one kind of controller for another. She might run again.

He sighed, a sound full of frustrated acceptance. "If she averages one cut a week for fifty-two weeks, how many years can she survive at that rate?"

"I don't know," Henry replied quietly. "The question to ask is, Where do you want her to spend those years?"

"With us. I want her to spend them with us." He pushed away from the table. "Thanks for the tea."

On the way back to his apartment, he climbed the stairs and knocked on Meg's door. She answered so promptly, he suspected she'd been waiting for him.

"Sam thought you weren't feeling well," Simon said. "That's why he was upset."

"I'm fine."

She didn't sound fine, and she looked tired. He didn't like her being alone when she looked that tired.

Wasn't his place to push or demand. He didn't like that either.

"Anything you want to tell me?" he asked.

She hesitated, then shook her head.

"All right. See you tomorrow."

He went down the stairs, alert for the slightest sound from her, the softest call to come back.

All he heard was the gentle closing of the door.

Asia closed her eyes and thought of elegant dining, polished hotel rooms, and men who knew more about sex than that widget A was supposed to go into slot B. That most of the people she'd seen eating at Meat-n-Greens were actually enjoying the food was reason enough to call in exterminators—the kind that had the hardware to eliminate all manner of pests. She'd had no complaints with her fillet until she made the mistake of asking what kind of beef it was, and learned it was horse.

Except for the picture it put in her head, horse wasn't as bad—or gamy—as Darrell's fillet of moose. Apparently, one description fit any meat.

And the apartments the Courtyard's upper echelon used for intimate entertaining! She couldn't imagine women wanting to spend an hour here for anything but bragging rights—or a lucrative ulterior goal.

As for the sex, the less she thought about it the better, especially when she was going to have to accept another invitation from Darrell. She'd seen just enough tonight to have a plan, had been risqué enough to have Darrell panting for more without coming across as *too* knowledgeable. That alone should be worth a bonus—and prove the caliber of her acting skills.

Asia Crane, Special Investigator. She could imagine Darrell in a couple of years, bragging about having slept with Asia, superstar of a hit TV series.

She sighed, kissed Darrell's chest, and started to wiggle out of bed.

"Where are you going?" he asked, trying to draw her back to him.

"Honey, it's late. I have to go."

"I thought we were going to spend the night together."

"Oh no. I can't do that. Not the first time. It wouldn't be right. And my car's in the Courtyard parking lot. What if someone notices it was there overnight?"

Darrell frowned. "Are you still worried about Simon Wolfgard being jealous? Because he knows about us. He gave his approval for the guest pass I got for you."

Sure, she'd wanted people around the Courtyard to know Darrell was her boyfriend, but it hadn't occurred to her that Simon would know she was the woman up here with Darrell tonight. But Asia Crane, SI, would have expected Simon to know about this romp and figured out a way to use it.

Yes. Simon knowing she was here tonight was good. Better than good, because now he wouldn't have any reason to question her scent being somewhere he might not expect.

She gave Darrell's chest a quick kiss. "No, honey. I'm not worried about Simon Wolfgard in any way. I made it clear the other day that I'm looking for a *real* man, not a Wolf pretending to be something he's not and never can be." Okay, she hadn't said it in those words when she took that last shot at flirting with Simon, but she didn't think Darrell would ask the Wolf, so no one would know.

She felt a change in Darrell, felt the possessive way his hands now stroked her body.

"Then what's the problem?" he asked.

"I already told you. I might not be able to resist being passionate with someone special, but I'm not the kind of girl who has dinner *and* breakfast on the first big date." She stroked his chest. "Besides, I didn't bring anything with me for overnight." She pressed a finger against his lips before he could argue. "Don't spoil it. Please. Just tell me how soon I can pack that overnight bag."

"Just as soon as I can arrange to have the room again." He rolled, pinning her. "But we have time for one more. Don't we?"

"Oh yes." She wrapped her arms around his neck as he settled between her legs. "We surely do."

"Hello?"

"Did you get my present? The items were selected just for you."

"A special messenger delivered it, even though I never gave you my address."

"Information can be acquired if one knows who to ask."

"Well, I love my present. I can use a number of these items on my date tomorrow evening."

"Would you like some company? That special messenger has a variety of skills. In fact, two dozen messengers from that company are now in the city. They're trained to handle delicate or volatile packages."

A light laugh. "No, thanks. I'll do just fine on my own. And I expect to find a little bit of something to send back as a thank-you."

"In that case, I'll look forward to our next conversation."

Asia hung up the phone and put on the thin gloves used in a hospital's contagious ward. As she examined each vial in the carefully packed box sent by Meg Corbyn's owner, she silently thanked Bigwig for all the information she'd been given about various drugs and the penalties for possessing them. At the time, she'd thought of it as useful information for her TV role. Now it was vital information for real life.

Some of the items in the box were easy enough to come by, because there were few, if any, aftereffects on the person who was dosed. Some were worth several years in one of the rough prisons just for possessing the stuff, and a life sentence if you were caught using it. One item was something she'd never heard of, something called gone over wolf. Until she found out what it did, she wouldn't ignore the warning to use it sparingly.

Asia lifted the last vial, read the label, and put it back very carefully.

And some items would earn a person a one-way trip into the wild country. No prison. Nothing so kind. Just a long ride into the Others' territory, and then you were set loose with no food, no water, no shoes.

There was no record of anyone surviving that particular punishment.

Her new benefactor, as she'd begun to think of Meg's owner, might be able to pull enough strings to keep himself safe from the penalties for having any of these items, but she was under no illusion that he would be that protective of her. And she had no doubt Bigwig and his group of backers would distance themselves from her if she was caught with any of the prison-worthy drugs, let alone the one that carried an automatic death penalty. So it was in her own best interest to use that last vial as soon as possible.

And she knew just how it would do her the most good.

"You know what I would really like to do?" Asia said to Darrell as she drove down the access way and parked her car behind the Liaison's Office. There it was protected from potential thieves and out of sight of patrol cars who might take too much notice of a car left in the Courtyard parking lot overnight. On Sunday, the car being in the lot had been her excuse to leave. Tonight, having it tucked away meant Darrell was the only one who knew for sure she had come back to the Courtyard with him.

"I've got a pretty good idea," Darrell replied with a grin that looked a tiny bit off, just a little mean.

"Before *that*." She turned off the car's headlights and could barely make out the shape of the man in the other seat.

If any of the Courtyard businesses had outdoor lights by their back doors, no one had remembered to turn them on—not even the one she knew was at the top of the stairs she would be climbing shortly. Was a light too much courtesy to show a human, or had the Others assumed Darrell would take care of it?

That thought made her wonder if there would be clean sheets on the bed, and if anyone else had used the room yesterday.

"What do you want to do?" Darrell asked, that hint of mean gone as if it had never been there.

She leaned toward him, found the zipper on his trousers, and tugged it down an inch. "Take a little drive."

"A drive?" His voice rose, almost cracking as she pulled the zipper down another inch. "Where?"

"To the Green Complex and back."

His hand clamped over hers. She didn't think his panting was solely due to lust.

"Asia, are you crazy?"

"Humans are allowed in the Green area."

"Only if they have a pass! And even then it's risky once you're away from the Market Square."

"But you do have a pass," she said, putting a heavy dose of honey in the words while her fingers worked his zipper down another inch. She had slipped a few flakes of gone over wolf into his last drink at the Saucy Plate, just to see what would happen. And so far, the answer was nothing at all. Maybe she had used it a little *too* sparingly. "And I *want* to be the kind of woman who is brave enough to do something a little risky. Like spend the whole night with a man," she finished as she tried to move her hand away from his zipper.

His hand tightened on hers almost painfully before he let her go. Withdrawing her hand, she sat primly, her eyes looking straight ahead.

"I just thought we could have a little adventure before . . ." She moved her body to convey embarrassment. "I wanted to do something special for you tonight. Something like that girl was doing in the movie we watched the last time. That you wanted me to do but I couldn't. I even bought a book. You know. One of those manuals. Went to a bookstore clear across the city to buy it. But I guess you don't want . . ."

He gulped air, and she knew she had him.

"We aren't getting out of the car," he said, a tremor in his voice.

"Oh, no," she agreed. "That would be *too* risky."

"We can't take your car," he said after a moment. "They don't use cars like this inside the Courtyard. We'd be spotted a minute after we got past the Market Square. But *anyone* could be driving a BOW up to the Green Complex for a visit."

Good to know, Asia thought. "Then what should we do?"

"Wait here. I need to get a key from the consulate."

After Darrell left the car, she counted to twenty before she opened her door and got out. She unbuttoned her coat and reached for the camera she had hidden in an interior pocket. Then she looked around. No point trying to get photos of this area. Even the camera's flash wouldn't give her anything useful.

Darrell returned, puffing as if he'd run a marathon. Or had been running from a pack of Wolves.

"I'm not sure which BOW might be available, but the key fits any of them," he said.

Also good to know, Asia thought as she watched him open and close the door of an empty garage slot.

"Here's one." He waved at her to join him.

She took her keys and locked her car. Her overnight case—and the special accessories—were in the trunk. She wasn't planning to wear any of the clothes, so it didn't matter if they were stiff from cold. And the powders in the vials wouldn't freeze.

Hurrying across the snowy pavement, she slipped into the BOW's passenger's seat. She wondered whether the thing had a motor and hoped it had a heater.

It had both, more or less.

She clenched her teeth while Darrell backed out of the garage, then spent time closing the garage door.

"If an Owl spots the open door, it will sound the alarm," Darrell said as he drove out of the Courtyard's business district.

"Oh. I'm glad you thought of that." They were still in sight of the business district when she spotted a yellow tube of light next to the road. "What's that?"

"Solar light," Darrell replied. "The Others put them at forks in the roads. The Green Complex is on the outer ring."

"Where does the left-hand fork lead?"

"The interior of the Courtyard. Or maybe it goes to the Corvine gate. I don't know."

He sounded too nervous, so she stopped asking questions.

There were no streetlights, so there was damn little to see and no landmarks she could describe to someone else. As far as she could tell, there was a whole lot of nothing in the Courtyard until they reached the Green Complex, where

Simon Wolfgard lived. When Darrell backed into one of the visitor's parking spaces across the road from the complex, Asia swallowed her disappointment. It was just a U-shaped apartment building that didn't even have symmetry to give it a finished look. This is where the members of the Business Association, the movers and shakers among the *terra indigene*, lived?

Plenty of lights here. Plenty of Others at home?

"Humans are so much better at this stuff," Asia said.

"What stuff?"

"Buildings and cars and *everything*."

Nodding, Darrell made a disparaging sound. "*They* think they're living fancy because they have running water and central heating and don't have to take a shit in the woods if they don't want to."

Such language from Darrell? Asia studied him with more interest. Where had that spark of anger come from? "I thought you liked working at the consulate."

"Working for a consulate looks good on a résumé," he replied. "And with the credit at the Market Square that employees get on top of the wages, I'm paid almost twice as much by working for the consulate as I would receive from an equivalent position in human government. But this is just a stepping-stone, a way to something better."

Which was the real Darrell Adams: the sexually inept milquetoast she had slept with the other night, or this angry man who probably spent his evenings fantasizing about putting a bullet through Elliot Wolfgard's brain?

"You hate them, don't you?" she asked.

Just as Darrell was about to reply, Vladimir Sanguinati stepped out of one of the apartments. The vampire glanced their way and paused, then seemed to focus on them too much for her liking.

"Have you seen enough?" Darrell asked, his bravado deflating as the vampire walked toward them. He put the BOW in gear and drove away, spinning the tires in his effort to put some distance between them and the Green Complex before Vlad got close enough to identify them.

She hadn't seen enough. She still didn't know which apartment belonged to Meg Corbyn and which belonged to Simon Wolfgard. But at least she had some of the information the special messenger would need.

And she needed to think about how a substance called gone over wolf had changed milquetoast to angry man, even if the change had lasted only a minute or two. A lot of things could be achieved in a minute or two if they were the right minutes. It might be worth another experiment, depending on whether she had to accept another date.

For now, she needed to finish this evening's plans. So when they got back to the room, she was going to give Darrell the kind of sex he didn't have balls enough to even dream about.

Asia watched Darrell for another minute before she slipped out of bed. There had been just enough gone over wolf left in his system to make him interesting once he got aroused, but twice was more than enough. The knockout drops would keep him under for at least an hour, and that was plenty of time.

She put on Darrell's trousers, cinching them with a belt she had bought yesterday so that the scents of all the other people who had touched it in the store would still be fairly fresh. She put on his shirt, even his socks. She put on his winter coat. Pulling the wool cap out of one pocket, she tucked her hair under it. She transferred her camera and a small flashlight from her coat to his, then put on her own boots, because she didn't want to risk a fall.

Her hand hovered above her overnight case. There were all kinds of ways this could go wrong. But when she succeeded, the payoff was going to be sweet enough to make her the hottest star in Sparkletown.

She selected a vial and slipped it into the coat pocket. Taking the keys off the bedside table, she let herself out of the room and made her way to the back door of the Liaison's Office.

Three keys on the ring. One was for the room they were using. One was for the other abovestairs room. And the third . . .

Yes! Asia thought as she opened the office's back door. She removed the boots, then twisted her feet to press Darrell's scent into the floor. She took out the flashlight, turned it on, and looked around.

Typical back room of an office. A table and two chairs, the pseudokitchen with its mini fridge and counters. A washroom, and a storage area full of bins of clothes, some clean and some just this side of ripe.

Nothing in the fridge that was useful to her plans. But in the cupboard under the counter, she found what she was looking for: a partially used box of sugar lumps.

Wishing she could turn on a light, Asia put the flashlight on the floor and took the vial out of her pocket. The crystals didn't look any different from sugar crystals, and from what she'd learned about this stuff, it didn't taste much different either, which is why it was so effective and the penalties for using it were so high. She tapped crystals over the top layer of sugar lumps, then gently shook the box to coat more of the lumps. She continued doing that until she poured the last crystals over the sugar.

Putting the empty vial back in the coat pocket, she replaced the box of sugar, picked up her flashlight, and went into the next room.

Not much to look at. Who could stand working in such a boring room day after day? There wasn't even a stack of mail that would give her a few names she didn't know from the bookstore and coffee shop.

She opened a cupboard and found boxes of dog cookies. For a moment, she regretted using all those crystals on the sugar, then realized it was just as well she hadn't been able to give in to impulse. If anything happened to a Wolf, it could be seen as an act of war. But she had never heard of Others named Ponygard, which meant the stupid ponies were just animals. They would be a distraction, a way to stir things up, nothing but collateral damage in the overall scheme.

Opening a drawer under the counter, she stared at a sheet of paper for a long moment. Then her heart bumped with excitement. She had found a map of the Courtyard. Gates, roads, buildings—everything the extraction team would need.

Payday!

Pulling Darrell's shirt over her hand, Asia picked up the map with two fingers and put it on the big table. Then she took out her camera . . . and swore under her breath.

A flashlight and the flash on the camera weren't going to do it. If she wanted pictures that would be useful, she was going to have to turn on the lights, just for a minute.

No curtains on the window. Nothing she could use quickly to block the light.

Stop stalling, she thought as she waved the flashlight over the walls until she found the light switch. *The faster you take the pictures, the faster you can get out of here.*

Flipping on the lights, she hurried back to the table and took several shots of the map as the full page, then several more in zoom mode to provide more details. She put the camera in the coat pocket and the map in the drawer, flipped off the lights—and heard an Owl hoot.

Damn, fuck, shit. Was one of *them* perched on the wall next to the office? Or, worse, perched on the railing of the stairs she needed to climb?

She crept to the back room, put on her boots, opened the outside door, and listened hard. No feathers rustling overhead, no more hooting.

Slipping out the door, she locked it, then turned off the flashlight. Her foot was on the first stair when she thought about the empty vial in her pocket. According to Bigwig, the police presence and the speed in which they responded to anything involving the Others were unusual. That meant an empty vial could be as good as a confession if they found it on her.

Taking the vial out of the coat pocket, she walked a few feet from the stairs and shoved the vial into a snowbank as far as she could. Then she pushed the snow around to cover the hole, brushed off the coat sleeve, and hurried up the stairs.

Stripping out of Darrell's clothes, she took the clothes she'd worn that evening into the bathroom, along with her overnight case. She had taken a shower with Darrell as part of the foreplay, using the soap and shampoo the Others insisted their employees use. Now she gave her clothes and body a light spritz of the floral scent the Others associated with Asia Crane because she *always* wore that scent when she went into Howling Good Reads or A Little Bite.

And that scent wasn't in the Liaison's Office.

She put everything away and slipped into bed, grateful for the trapped body heat. Darrell was still in a heavy sleep and didn't do more than grunt and turn away from her when she tried to ease her cold body closer to his warm one.

An hour passed. Then two. She thought about that vial hidden in the snow, where it would hopefully remain until spring. She thought about the camera and the incriminating photos on the camera's storage card. She thought about how to sever her relationship with Darrell.

She thought about what Asia Crane, SI, would do.

She slipped back out of bed, got dressed, gathered her things, and left. She didn't give her car enough time to warm up, and she didn't brush enough snow off the back window before she drove out of the Courtyard. It was late, and there was hardly any traffic. That didn't mean a cop wouldn't tag her.

She drove another block before she pulled over and properly cleaned off all the windows. Then she dug her mobile phone out of her overnight case and made a call, but it wasn't to Bigwig.

"Hello?"

"I need one of your special messengers. Someone who can print some pictures and can also take more personal instructions."

"He can be at your residence in thirty minutes."

"I should be back by then."

Asia ended the call, tucked the phone back in the overnight case, and drove to her apartment. She had chosen the university district because it was close enough to the Courtyard but not one of the neighborhoods that rubbed against the land controlled by the Others. It wasn't likely that any of them had seen her, except when she visited the stores, so they wouldn't know where she lived.

It was now very important that they didn't know where she lived.

When she got home, she barely had time to turn on a couple of lights before there was a soft knock at the door.

The same special messenger who had delivered her present.

"You have something for me?" he asked after he closed the door.

She shucked off her coat and took the camera out of the interior pocket. "I have pictures that can't be seen by anyone working in a photo shop."

He waggled the black case he was carrying. "And I have a private way of printing photos." He walked over to her dining table and began setting up.

She watched him hook up a miniature printing center. "I've never seen anything like this. Must cost a bundle."

"Costs an arm—literally—if it's lost or damaged, but the benefactor who finances these assignments believes in giving his people the highest-quality equipment, since there are rarely second chances."

"How can something like this be manufactured without the Others knowing about it?" Asia asked.

He gave her a feral grin. "You can hide all kinds of things from them if you know how. Now. Give me that storage card, and let's see if what you've got is worth that late-night phone call."

Stung by the implied criticism that she had annoyed an important man for a pittance of information, she popped the storage card out of the camera and handed it to the messenger. He slipped it into one of his little boxes, then clicked on the program that would open the pictures.

He studied them for a minute. Then he whistled softly. "I stand corrected. These are worth a late-night call." He looked at her with new interest. "Where did you find this?"

"In the Liaison's Office."

"How fast do they respond to threats?"

"Fast. And the police respond almost as fast."

"Damn. They usually drag their heels when a call is about a Courtyard."

"Not here." She hesitated. This whole assignment was a lot riskier than anything else she'd done for her backers, and doing work for this benefactor *and* her backers had its own kinds of risk. But, damn, it was exciting and just the kind of thing Asia Crane, SI, would do.

"I think some distractions, some false alarms, would be smart," she said, slipping into the role of her alter ego. "Give the police a reason to slow their response time. Create distractions that are nothing but annoyances."

He began printing the pictures, studying the overall map of the Courtyard while the enlarged images printed. "Small distractions and annoyances close to the gates." He moved a finger around the area that contained the shops, consulate, and Liaison's Office. "Activity mostly during the day?"

"And early evening. They don't keep regular hours like a human business, but most of the businesses are closed by nine p.m."

"What about this place? The Utilities Complex."

Asia shook her head. "Don't know. I'd guess more activity during the day, but I'm not sure if humans are allowed in there."

"We can find out," he said absently while he continued to study the map. "Distractions. We can keep them stirred up so they don't recognize the real threat when it comes."

"But nothing until after Moonsday."

He turned his head and studied her. "Why is that?"

"Because I already put the first distraction in motion. And I figure it will happen on Moonsday."

He finished printing the pictures, even printed out one extra of the overall map for her to keep. After putting his equipment back in its case and sliding the pictures into a manila envelope, he gave her a thorough look—and smiled. "I was told you also needed something more personal."

"Not that," she said. "I don't want anyone's scent there except the man I was with tonight."

"Then what are you looking for?"

"Rough me up. Not enough to need a hospital or report it to the police, but enough that other women would understand me wanting to break up with this man—and not come around where he might see me. I need a reason not to be around the Courtyard on Moonsday."

He narrowed his eyes. "You setting him up?"

"Let's say he's going to act as insurance for all of us."

The messenger gave her body a coldly professional study while he pulled on a pair of thin leather gloves. "Then let's get started."

CHAPTER 20

"Are you sure?" Simon asked, after closing his office door and returning to the desk.

"I'm sure," Vlad replied. "I followed them from the Green Complex. And this morning, Blair confirmed that the BOW should have been fully charged, since he connected it to the energy source yesterday afternoon, and it isn't."

"Then why didn't you take care of it last night?"

"Why didn't you take care of it this morning after Nathan told you he'd found Darrell's scent in the back room and sorting room?" Vlad countered.

Simon glanced at the comfy Wolf bed in the corner of his office—an item several of the Wolves now had in their work spaces—and knew he and Vlad had the same reason for not killing Darrell right away.

He didn't care what the police or the human government or the whole damn city of Lakeside thought about him tearing out the throat of a human who broke trust with the *terra indigene*. But there had been the possibility that Meg had asked Darrell to deliver something to her at the Green Complex, and he'd gotten scared when he saw Vlad because he'd allowed Asia Crane to come with him. And there *was* the slightest possibility that Meg had asked Darrell to help her with something in the back room or in the sorting room. The Business Association wasn't as strict about keeping known humans out of those rooms since Meg started working for them, mostly because she needed human company to be happy, and the Others wanted her to be happy so she would stay.

Couldn't eat Darrell if the man really had been doing something for Meg.

"We can't allow a monkey to break our rules," Vlad said.

"No, we can't. But Darrell works for Elliot. Since the man didn't do more than drive to the Green Complex without permission, I'll let Elliot decide how to deal with him." Simon thought for a moment. "After I talk to Elliot, I'll call Chris Fallacaro and have him change the locks at the consulate and on the Liaison's Office."

"What about that Asia Crane?" Vlad asked.

"She was with Darrell and she never left the vehicle. I'm not sure we can call that trespassing," Simon said. Especially since Vlad let her leave the Courtyard last night. "She's banned from the Courtyard, starting now. And that includes the stores, even HGR and A Little Bite." The relief that he had a reason to keep her far away from Meg was so sharp, it almost hurt.

If Meg got mad at him for banning Asia, he would accept it. He would. For a little while, anyway.

"All right," Vlad said. "I'll inform Grandfather of the Wolfgard's decision. You talk to Elliot."

When Vlad left, Simon stretched his neck and shoulders, feeling the pop of tight muscles loosening. That done, he called Elliot, then sat down and worked out the wording for the flyers Lorne would make for him as soon as the Three Ps opened.

Vlad flowed under the door of Elliot's office, a patch of smoke moving over the carpet, keeping close to the wall. He didn't care that Elliot saw him enter and knew he was going to listen to the Wolf deal with the human. He just didn't want Darrell to notice he was there.

While there was no doubt that the human would be dismissed from his job at the consulate, there was no certainty he would get out of the Courtyard, despite the short distance between the consulate's door and the delivery area's street entrance.

No matter how fast a human could run, the Sanguinati could move faster. And per Erebus's orders, unless Vlad was convinced that Darrell had done nothing more than act foolishly because of a woman, the man wouldn't get past Nyx when he bolted for the presumed safety of the human-controlled land.

"Mr. Wolfgard?" Darrell said as he fiddled with the knot in his tie. "You wanted to see me?"

"Yes," Elliot replied, his voice smoothing into a sound that gave nothing away. "Do you know why?"

"No, sir. But . . . someone emptied my desk and put some of my personal items in a box."

"No, we put *all* of your *personal* items in the box. The rest of the items in the desk actually belong to the consulate. Now you'll hand over the keys you were given, as well as your pass to the Market Square."

"But . . . why?"

"You're being dismissed for a breach of trust."

Rapid breathing. Pulse spiking. Face turning pale. And even with all those acknowledgments, the fool still tried to deny what the Others knew.

"I didn't," Darrell said.

"I hope for your sake that the breach begins and ends with you taking that female to the Green Complex. I hope you understand what will happen if you become indiscreet about what you've seen or heard in the consulate."

"Sir, I think I've done a good job here," Darrell began.

"You did. I was pleased with your work. But you broke the trust we had given you, and now you have to go. However, before I let you leave this room, I need one answer: What were you looking for in the Liaison's Office?"

"I wasn't in the office," Darrell protested. "I was in the abovestairs room I was told I could use last night. I was with my . . . friend . . . until I woke up this morning."

"So you were never in the office?" Elliot asked, his voice still smooth.

"Sure, I was in the office. Went to pick up the consulate mail a few times."

"Why?"

"Why?"

"Yes," Elliot said patiently. "Why? You've never done that before."

Darrell squirmed in the chair. "I wasn't comfortable being around the other Liaisons. But Meg is a pleasant girl, and she always has the mail bundled in an orderly manner. I just thought picking it up would be a friendly gesture."

And a way to set up Meg as the next potential friend if Asia Crane didn't work out? Vlad wondered.

"Whose idea was it to go to the Green Complex?" Elliot asked. "Your pass doesn't extend beyond our business district without permission, and your guest didn't have permission to go anywhere last night except the designated room for your . . . social interaction."

"She wanted to see it, as an adventure."

"See what? It was late. It was dark."

"I think she wanted to see where Simon Wolfgard lives." Darrell hung his head and talked to his tie. "She said she wasn't interested in him anymore, but I think she is. I think she pretended . . ."

<That's enough, Elliot,> Vlad said. <I'll inform Grandfather that this monkey tried to impress the female and is nothing worse than a fool. Since that Asia is being banned from the Courtyard, the explanation will satisfy him.>

Leaving Elliot to finish the dismissal, Vlad flowed under the door, shifting to human form when he was in the hallway. When he got outside, he stopped long enough to tell Nyx that Darrell was allowed to leave the Courtyard intact. Then he walked down the access way between the buildings and stopped behind the Liaison's Office.

The truck from Fallacaro Lock & Key was already there, and Chris Fallacaro was working on the office's back door. Blair was watching him, which was probably why it was taking the human so long to change a lock. Having youngsters watching in order to learn was one thing. Having the Courtyard's primary enforcer watching was something else altogether.

And there was Meg, pulling up and looking confused because the truck and Blair's BOW effectively blocked her ability to park her own vehicle.

They hadn't discussed what they were going to tell Meg, and he didn't want to push Simon—especially when they weren't on opposite sides. He would have preferred a more permanent solution to ridding themselves of Asia Crane, and he should have taken care of it last night. Since he'd made the wrong choice, he thought Simon should be the one to take the direct approach now—and provide them all with some blood and meat in the bargain.

But what would they have said to their Liaison? *It's like this, Meg. We didn't like that Asia Crane, so we ate her.*

When dealing with humans, honesty isn't always the best policy, Vlad thought as he walked over to the BOW and opened Meg's door.

"What's going on?" Meg asked as she got out of the BOW.

"Let's go inside. It's cold out here." He cupped her elbow as they walked to the back door.

Blair said something to Chris. The man jumped, whipped his head around in a way that must have made a few muscles twang, then pulled the door open wider for Meg to slip inside.

She swapped boots for shoes, hung up her coat, and went through to the other rooms to open up the office. Vlad followed her, then stood in the Private doorway while she leaned against the counter.

"What happened?" she asked.

"A breach of trust. Darrell broke one of the rules," he replied, wanting to be blunt and direct as he would be with one of his own kind. But he suddenly wondered how much blood prophets in general, and Meg in particular, knew about sex and felt the need for caution when explaining why the human was upstairs last night. "He's been dismissed. Since he had a key to the consulate as well as keys to this building, we're getting the locks changed."

"Do you do that every time an employee leaves?"

"Not every time."

She paled, which alarmed him.

"Is Sam in danger?" she asked.

Interesting question. "I don't think so."

Of course, Nathan chose that moment to open the front door. He paused when one of the Crows cawed at him, then raised an arm in invitation. The Crow flew over, and the two of them came inside. The Wolf shot one look at the bed, then stomped the snow off his boots and approached the counter. The Crow hopped from arm to counter, sliding a little.

Meg looked at the two of them. "Good morning, Nathan. Good morning, Jake." She slanted a look at Vlad. "Are you all going to stick around here?"

"Until the locks are fixed. Once the locks are changed, Blair will meet Chris at the Utilities Complex to make all the sets of keys. Front door lock will be changed too."

"All this because Darrell broke a rule?" Meg asked.

"It was an important rule," Vlad replied smoothly, trying to balance Nathan's growl.

The crunch of tires on snow made all of them look toward the delivery area.

Meg pulled her clipboard from under the counter and accepted the pen Jake offered. "Try not to scare the deliverymen, all right?"

"*Caw,*" Jake said.

Vlad stepped into the sorting room, where he would be out of sight. It didn't escape his notice that Jake was the only one of them to offer her any assurance about that.

He didn't think it had escaped Meg's notice either.

After giving her approach a good deal of thought, Asia walked into Howling Good Reads, satisfied that she had hit the right balance: makeup just a little too heavy, as if she were trying to cover up something; hair styled but not as well as usual; a cowl-neck sweater that would show off the bruises on her shoulders when she moved in certain ways, but didn't shout that she wanted them seen.

The special messenger had done a good job pretending to be a milquetoast who suddenly turned rough. But if a Wolf shoved his nose where it had no business being, all he would smell was Darrell.

The girl at the register looked at her and paled. Asia thought it was because Heather had glimpsed the bruises. Then she caught her own name in big letters on some kind of flyer next to the register.

She took a step toward the register. The next thing she knew, Simon Wolfgard was blocking her, snarling in a way that destroyed any pretense of his being human.

"Asia Crane, you are banned from the Courtyard," he said in a voice filled with authority and anger. "That includes all the stores within the Courtyard." He took a step toward her, forcing her to take a step back. "That includes this one. You can leave this time, but if we see you on our land again, we'll kill you."

The customers at the front of the store froze.

Asia lifted her chin, switching her performance from rough-sex victim to defender of humankind. "You can't ban me from a store. That's discrimination. None of you would be able to buy any of your precious junk if human stores discriminated against *you*."

"They discriminate against us plenty. That's not the point. The point is, you went sniffing around where you don't belong, and we caught you, but we're going to let you and Darrell walk away this one time. Yes, we banned him too. As for the rest of you," he said, addressing the other customers, "if you want to shop at other stores because we banned the two people who broke our rules instead of banning all of you, that's your choice." He turned back to Asia. "And you're out of time. Get out now or die."

He grabbed one of the flyers and slapped it against her chest. "Take this with you so you don't forget."

She took the flyer, crumpling it in her hand. She considered making a parting comment, but she realized he was looking for an excuse to kill her right there, right now. He would splash her blood over half the store and count the loss of merchandise as worth it.

"What did I ever do to you?" she whispered, pleased with the natural quiver in her voice.

He leaned toward her, and his voice was just as low. "When I find out, I'll come hunting for you."

She walked out of the store, her mind racing. She'd always paid in cash for anything she'd bought at HGR or A Little Bite. Hadn't she? She was Margaret A. Crane on all the ID her backers had provided for her, and that was a common enough name. So she wouldn't be easy to find. Even Darrell hadn't known where she lived.

As she got in her car, a patrol car pulled into the Courtyard parking lot. The officer who got out and headed for HGR was one of the cops who dropped by daily.

Asia's stomach did a funny little flip. Was that Wolf going to hand out those flyers to the cops?

She was getting way too much attention, and all the wrong kind. If the special messenger got wind of this and informed his benefactor, it could be the end of a very lucrative arrangement. Even her backers now wanted her working in tandem with this benefactor's men and would be keenly unhappy if her actions blew the whole operation by making the Others too antagonistic against humans.

But the benefactor's special messenger had known what she was going to do today. After all, he'd helped her with this charade. So all she had to do was convince him that getting banned from the Courtyard had been part of her plan all along.

CHAPTER 21

On Moonsday morning, Meg opened the office, prepared her clipboard, and breathed a sigh of relief. After Darrell's dismissal and Asia's public banning, all the humans who worked for the Others had been edgy, especially the humans who worked in the Market Square and would have a harder time escaping if the *terra indigene* turned savage. But with the exception of more patrol cars driving past the Courtyard, Firesday and Watersday were ordinary workdays. Earthday had been an enjoyable balance of chores and a long, fun romp in the snow with Simon and Sam in their Wolf forms. The romp had tired her out so much, she fell asleep while they all watched a movie that evening.

And Simon didn't say a word about her using him as a furry pillow.

She still wasn't sure why Darrell wasn't supposed to visit the Green Complex. He had worked for the consulate, after all. Surely there was more sensitive material in that office than whatever could be observed in the dark about the outside of buildings.

Except Darrell had brought Asia, who really wasn't allowed to be there.

Meg gave her arms a brisk rub, relieved when the prickling under her skin subsided. Going out at night to look at the Green Complex was odd, but she'd seen plenty of training images of someone sitting in a dark car, watching a building. Obsessed ex-lovers. Stalkers. Police. Asia didn't fit any of those labels, but Meg thought the other woman was impulsive enough to jump at a chance to see any part of the Courtyard. And since Asia had been so curious about Sam, maybe she'd hoped to get another look at the puppy.

Did Asia know Sam lived with Simon at the Green Complex? Meg shook her head, unable to remember. Well, it didn't matter anymore. Asia was gone and Darrell was gone, and neither of them had been part of her vision about men dressed in black.

Giving her arms a final rub, she dismissed thoughts of Asia and Darrell and went about her day. She chatted with Harry when he came in with his deliveries, laughing at his jokes even when she didn't understand them. She spent several minutes trying to convince Nathan that he couldn't have entire boxes of dog cookies and had to choose which kind of cookie he wanted for a snack. When he insistently pointed a big paw at each box, she ended up giving him two cookies of each flavor, which he took back to his Wolf bed to crunch.

Around midmorning, she got tangled in a bizarre game of tug between Nathan and Jake. She didn't know which of them had brought in the length of rope as a toy, but the Wolf, still lying on the bed, had his teeth in one end of it, and the Crow had his feet clenched around the other and was madly flapping his wings. Her mistake was thinking she could break up the game by grabbing the rope right in front of Jake's feet. Suddenly Nathan was on his feet, wagging his tail while he growled at her, and Jake's caws sounded suspiciously gleeful. Because the floor was a little snow-slick and her shoes didn't have enough traction, she was pulled from one end of the room to the other and couldn't figure out how to let go of the rope without falling on her butt.

She got out of the game only because Dan walked in with a delivery and started laughing so hard, he almost dropped the packages. After signing for the delivery, she retreated to the sorting room and pondered what game the Wolf and Crow really had been playing: tug the rope or trick Meg into playing with them.

It said something about human resilience that a week after Nathan had been assigned as the office's watch Wolf, most of the deliverymen were accepting of his presence, if still justifiably wary. A few tossed a "Hi, how's it going?" in Nathan's direction before they took care of business with her. Only one company had a new driver coming to the Courtyard, replacing the man who had refused to enter the office the first time he saw Nathan.

Once the mail was sorted and packages going out to *terra indigene* settlements were properly tagged for the earth-native trucks, Meg peeked into the front room. Jake was on the counter, fluffed up and dozing. Nathan was on his back, paws in the air, also snoozing. At that moment, they didn't look like much security, but she knew they'd be awake the instant they heard footsteps or tires in the delivery area.

Leaving them to their morning nap, she headed for the back room. The ponies would be here in half an hour, and she wanted to be ready.

When she stepped into the room, a sickening rush of images filled her mind. Old hands, young hands, male hands, female hands, dark hands, pale hands. All reaching for something and . . . Shrieks of pain. Cries of anguish.

Meg stumbled out of the back room, shaking. Was she sick? Was she going insane? Was this what happened to *cassandra sangue* when they didn't live in the compounds? Was this *why* they had originally been brought to live in such isolation? Maybe this was the reason the girls were allowed so little personal experience, why their lives were so sterile.

She rubbed at her arms, at her legs, at her belly, at her scalp, wanting to dig and scratch and claw until the painful prickling went away. It had *never* been this bad, and she had never seen actual images *before* a cut.

But there had been that moment on the road the other day when she had slipped into a vision without cutting.

Bracing her arms on the sorting table, Meg fought to think.

Sensitive skin. She had overheard the Walking Names once when they were reviewing the value of the girls. They said prophecies from her were the most expensive because her skin was so sensitive, it became attuned to the visions even before she was cut. She just had to be around something connected to the prophecy.

And Simon had speculated that this prickling was a sign her instincts were waking up because she was living and doing and experiencing for herself instead of seeing the world as labeled images.

Was the prickling under her skin not only a warning but also a measuring stick? A little tingle that was annoying but faded quickly indicated a small choice that wouldn't have major significance, while the harsher, painful buzz . . .

Meg returned to the back room, staggering as the images flooded her mind again. But she couldn't figure out what was causing the reaction.

"Something there," she whispered, fleeing to the sorting room. "Have to do it. Have to cut out this vision hiding in my skin."

But she needed a listener this time, because whatever was struggling to break through was too big for her to endure alone. And she was scared that she wouldn't be able to sort out the images of the prophecy, wouldn't be able to recognize the warning or put the pieces together.

Who to call? Not Simon. He'd be angry that she didn't call him, but he'd be angry about the cut too, and she felt certain that they didn't have time to argue.

She tiptoed to the Private door. Jake and Nathan were still napping. She closed that door as quietly as possible and turned the lock. Then she called A Little Bite, hoping that whatever guardian spirit looked after prophets would guide Tess's hand to answer the phone.

"A Little Bite," Tess said. She sounded cheerfully annoyed, which meant the coffee shop was busy.

"Tess? It's Meg."

Silence. "Is something wrong?" Tess's voice was no longer cheerful or annoyed. Now there was something in it that made Meg shiver.

"Yes," Meg said. "I need your help. It's urgent. Can you come now? Just you."

Tess hung up. Meg hoped that was a positive response. Going into the bathroom, she thought about what she would need and what Tess would need. She almost reconsidered, almost called Henry. But she didn't call him for the same reason she didn't call Simon: it just wasn't smart to be in a room with a carnivore when she slit her skin and spilled her own blood.

"I have to go," Tess told Merri Lee. "Call Julia. Tell her to come in as soon as she can. Tell Simon you need Heather to help you until Julia arrives."

"He'll want to know why," Merri Lee said. "What do I tell him?"

"When I know why, I'll tell him," Tess replied. She pulled on her coat and left by the back door, striding toward the Liaison's Office.

Why didn't you call Simon, Meg? Why call me? Do the prophets have any idea what I am? Did you call me out of knowledge or ignorance?

"Thanks for coming," Meg said, locking the back door as soon as Tess slipped inside the office.

"Why didn't you call Simon?" Tess asked.

"I thought this would be too dangerous with a predator in the same room."

Ignorance, then, Tess thought. If Meg was trying to avoid predators, she wouldn't have knowingly called one most of the *terra indigene* feared.

"I need to cut," Meg said, her words tripping over one another. "Something terrible is going to happen, and there is something in this room that is a part of it."

"But you don't know what it is?"

Meg shook her head.

"What do you need from me?"

"I need someone to listen to the prophecy, to write down what I say."

"All right. Where?"

"In the bathroom. It's private there."

"What will I need?"

Meg pointed at the items on the small table. Her hand shook, telling Tess how much effort it was taking for Meg to hold on and not slash herself indiscriminately. "The tablet of paper and the pen. When a cut is made, the images come as they come. Write them down. Then someone will have to figure out how they fit together in order to understand what they mean."

Tess tipped her head toward the front of the office. "What did you tell Nathan?"

"He and Jake are sleeping."

The Wolf wouldn't be sleeping much longer. Their breed of earth native had keen senses, and the lack of sounds in the sorting room would alert Nathan just as much as an unfamiliar one. Once the Wolf realized Meg was locked out of reach, he'd call the enforcer and call his leader, and there was no telling who else would respond.

"Let's get this done," Tess said. She shrugged out of her coat, hung it on a peg, removed her boots, and followed Meg into the bathroom.

Meg's hands hovered over the button and zipper on her jeans. "I think this needs a bigger cut. I think the skin on my legs will work best. I need to remove my jeans."

"Arrroooo?" A query. Not loud, since Nathan was in the front room and they were in the back, and there were several closed doors between them. But it meant the Wolf was awake and aware.

Tess flushed the toilet. "That will buy us a little time. But the next time

Nathan doesn't get an answer, he's going to call Simon and Blair." No need to mention that Henry and Vlad would also be looking for answers if the watch Wolf started making a fuss.

Meg stripped off the jeans and dropped them in a corner of the bathroom floor. On the toilet seat, neatly laid out, were the razor, ointment, butterfly bandages, a package of gauze, and medical tape. On the floor was a hand towel. Color stained her cheeks when she sat on the floor and examined the scars on her legs.

"How do you choose the place to cut?" Tess asked, sitting back on her heels so she was facing Meg and could watch the girl's body and the expressions on her face as well as listen to the words.

"The Controller chose, based on how much the client was willing to pay for the prophecy." Meg stared at her own skin. "Until I ran away, I didn't make my own cuts. I don't really know how to choose."

"Yes, you do," Tess said quietly. "It's part of who you are." She picked up the razor, opened it, and handed it to Meg. "You know where to find this prophecy."

Meg took the razor and closed her eyes. Her free hand moved over her left leg, upper and lower, front and back. Her hand moved to her right leg. Her fingers stuttered just below the knee. Opening her eyes, she laid the razor on the right side of the shin bone, turned her hand, and cut.

Tess watched Meg's hand shake with the effort to set the razor down with the blade turned away. She watched the girl pale, saw pain in those gray eyes that she found arousing, but there was also trust in those eyes instead of fear. She couldn't, *wouldn't*, kill trust.

"Speak," Tess said, her voice rough with the effort to deny her own nature. "Speak, prophet, and I will listen."

Box of sugar lumps. A hand withdrawing. A man's hand wearing a thin leather glove. A woman's hand, the nails polished a pretty rose color. A dark winter coat that had nothing distinctive. The sleeve of a woman's sweater, the color a bright, unfamiliar blue. The ponies rolling on the ground near the barn, screaming and screaming as black snakes burst out of their bellies. Skull and crossbones. Sugar full of black snakes. The ponies screaming. A skeleton in a hooded robe, passing out sweets to children. A skull laughing while children screamed and screamed as the black snakes ripped their way out of those young bellies.

"Hands," Meg whispered, her strength visibly fading. "Skull and crossbones. Black snakes in the sugar."

"Your words have been heard, prophet," Tess whispered. "Rest, now. Rest."

With a moan that was wantonly sexual, Meg laid back on the floor. Her eyes glazed and her body suddenly had the scent of a different, and enticing, kind of arousal.

"Arrrrooooo!"

Out of time, Tess thought, springing to her feet. She looked at Meg, at the hand towel soaking up blood that continued to flow from the cut. She wasn't sure how much blood was too much, but she knew what she had to deal with first.

As she pulled open the bathroom door, she caught a glimpse of herself in the mirror over the sink. Hair the color of blood turning black as the grave. She strode into the back room at the same moment Simon unlocked the outside door, leaping in ahead of Henry and Blair. Nathan squeezed between Henry and Simon, everything in him focused on the blood scent.

"Get out," Tess snarled. "All of you, get out of this room. *Now!*"

"Don't you dare give orders *to me*!" Simon snarled in reply. His head began changing to Wolf to accommodate the jaws and fangs that would serve him better as weapons.

"Stay out!" Tess said again. Something in her voice must have gotten through to Henry, because he grabbed Nathan by the scruff just as the Wolf launched himself toward the bathroom.

Nathan snapped and snarled, but he couldn't break Henry's hold.

"You all have to leave. That goes for you too, vampire," Tess said as smoke flowed through the open door. If a fight broke out now, someone would die. If one of these males died, the rest would realize what she was, and she would have to leave. She didn't want to leave. It was rare for her kind to find acceptance, let alone cautious friendship, even among other *terra indigene*. "Simon, there are things you all need to know, but it's dangerous for you to be in this room right now. Meg needs tending. Let me help her."

His eyes were red with flickers of gold, a sign he was insanely furious.

"You can do this?" Henry asked, his voice a quiet rumble.

Tess nodded. "She asked me to come and hear the prophecy. She asked for my help. Let me finish helping her."

"There must be something we can do," Henry said.

She started to deny it, then realized it was an order—and she realized why. Simon was snarling, almost vibrating with rage. Maybe it was the scent of blood pushing the Wolf, maybe it was because he, too, valued friendship. One of his pack was hurt, and because Meg wasn't a Wolf, he didn't know what to do.

"Fetch a pillow and a couple of blankets," she said. "And not ones that stink of those other humans." She wasn't sure if Asia's scent would matter to Meg, but it mattered to her. "There's a wheelchair in the bodywalker's office. Fetch that too. And someone call Jester. He needs to be part of this discussion."

<Why?> Simon asked.

He couldn't vocalize as a human despite his head having shifted back to looking human? Not good.

"You can call Jester, or you can call the girl at the lake. One of them needs to hear this."

All the males flinched.

"I have to take care of Meg. I've left her long enough. We'll meet in the sorting room in ten minutes."

None of them liked it, but they all filed out of the room. Simon, of course, was the last one out. He looked at her hair.

"I'll take care of her, Simon Wolfgard," Tess said softly. "You don't know yet how much we owe her, but I do."

He left, closing the door behind him.

Blowing out a breath, Tess hurried back to the bathroom. Meg was still on the floor, but she turned her head and looked at Tess.

"Did you get an answer?" Meg asked.

"I got one." She filled the sink with warm water and found a couple more hand towels. "We're going to have to think about what you need in this bathroom if this is typical of what happens when you cut. No, stay down. I'm not sure how much blood you lost, and you've already upset the Wolves, the Grizzly, and the vampire. You can't afford to get dizzy and fall down."

After soaking one towel in warm water, she carefully washed the blood off Meg's leg, then bent closer to examine the cut. "Looks like it's starting to clot now. Do you usually cut this deep?"

"It has to be deep enough to scar," Meg replied. "Although *cassandra sangue* skin does tend to scar easily."

Did Simon realize that? Or hadn't it occurred to him that Meg could be injured while romping with Wolves, even if the Wolves didn't mean to hurt her?

After patting the leg dry, Tess applied the antiseptic ointment, used the butterfly bandages to close the wound, then covered everything with gauze and medical tape. She rolled the bloodiest towel in the other two and put them all in the wastebasket.

"I'll help you up so you can sit on the toilet," Tess said, doing exactly that. "What usually happens after a cut?"

"We're given a little food, then taken back to our cell to rest to make sure the cut closes properly." Meg hesitated. "Tess? Am I going to have to talk to Simon?"

"Yes, but not until you rest."

"Could you hand me my jeans? I should get dressed now."

Tess looked at the bandage she'd wrapped around Meg's leg and considered the jeans. She shook her head. "You need something looser, so we can keep checking the cut. Stay there." Not much time left before the rest of them returned.

Taking the last hand towel, she went to the cupboards and rummaged until she found a small, clean jar. Using the towel to avoid touching the box of sugar lumps, she dumped some of them into the jar. She left the box on the floor with the towel, sealed the jar, and put it in her coat pocket. Then she helped Meg into the loose fleece pants she found in the storage bins. They were too big for the girl, but they had the advantage of being easy to push up past the knee.

She tore off the pages that held the prophecy, folded them, and stuffed them into her back pocket. Leaving the tablet and pen on the little table, she walked into the sorting room. As she opened the outside doors, she realized they had one other problem: where to put Meg while they had this meeting. She didn't want to leave the girl in the back room with the box of sugar, and she didn't think Meg would want to be around Simon and the others who took an interest in her until they knew why she had made the cut. The front room was too exposed, but they could lock the door and refuse deliveries.

The abovestairs room that Darrell *hadn't* used was a possibility, but what else might be up there that the Others hadn't sensed?

A BOW pulled up to the sorting room's outside door. Blair and Simon got out. Neither looked friendly—or forgiving.

"Meg needs to rest," Tess began, "but we shouldn't use the back room yet."

For answer, Simon pulled a Wolf bed out of the BOW while Blair pulled out the wheelchair. Henry had pillows and blankets. Vlad had one of the food carriers she used for deliveries. Jester was there, looking concerned as he noted what the others were carrying. And Nathan, still in Wolf form, just looked at her and growled.

They all marched past her. Simon raised an arm to sweep all the stacks of mail off the table. Yipping, Jester hurriedly put the stacks on the counter so that Simon could put the Wolf bed on the table. Henry laid one blanket over it and set the other one aside with the pillows. Blair opened the wheelchair. Vlad set the food on the counter, avoiding the mail only because Jester reminded the vampire that *Meg* had sorted that mail, and ruining her work was an insult.

"Now," Simon growled. "Meg."

"She's in the bathroom," Tess said. "I'll bring her in."

"I'll get her," Vlad said.

"She's one of Namid's creations, both wondrous and terrible," Tess said. She nodded when they all froze. "No one should go sniffing around the towels I used for her. And no one should go sniffing around the box of sugar."

Simon turned on his heel and went into the back room.

"What's going on?" Jester asked.

"You need to handle the mail today," Tess said. "Tell the ponies there isn't a treat."

"It's Moonsday," Jester protested. "There's always sugar on Moonsday, and they *all* come up to see Meg. Even old Hurricane."

"Not today," Tess repeated.

Simon came back in, carrying Meg. Her cheeks were a blaze of color. His cheeks had fur forming and receding as he struggled to hold the shape he needed instead of the one he wanted. His fingers had Wolf claws instead of fingernails, but Tess noted how carefully he set Meg on the makeshift bed they had made for her.

"Would you like something to eat?" Tess asked.

"No," Meg replied. "I'd just like to rest."

Meg's voice sounded pale, and Tess struggled with her own urge to respond. The death color had faded from her hair, but that pale sound brought strands of black back into the red.

Simon adjusted a pillow under Meg's head and covered her with the other blanket. Then he leaned close. "Nathan is here to guard. Don't lock him out again."

A grumpy *arrrooo* from Nathan before the Wolf sat next to the table.

"Close those outer doors," Tess said. "We still have a few minutes before the ponies arrive, and Meg should stay warm." She flipped the lock on the Private door, then opened the go-through and kept going. She turned the sign on the front door to CLOSED and turned that lock.

They gathered in a corner of the room, far enough that Meg probably wouldn't hear them, especially with the Private door mostly closed to keep the room warm.

"Something in the back room disturbed Meg enough that cutting her skin for a prophecy was needed," Tess said. "She asked for my help." She pulled the papers out of her pocket and handed them to Simon. "These are the images she saw."

Henry and Blair leaned over his shoulders to read.

"Makes no sense," Blair muttered.

"Pieces of a puzzle," Henry replied. "We need to put the pieces together to find the answer."

"The answer is poison," Tess said quietly. "Skull and crossbones is a human symbol for poison. That is what Meg was trying to tell us. Someone poisoned the sugar in order to kill the ponies."

Jester whined. Vlad took the papers from Simon to read the words for himself.

"This skeleton in the hooded robe and the children," Vlad said. "That's not about us."

"Maybe this poison was used before or is about to be used elsewhere," Tess countered. "Maybe these images are the only way the prophet can help someone identify this particular kind of death."

"That means calling the police," Henry said.

Simon nodded. "Montgomery."

"Do we let him into the back room?" Vlad asked.

"No," Simon replied. "But we'll give him the box of sugar, let his people figure out the poison." Now he looked at Tess. "What can we do for Meg?"

"She says she was given food and rest when she was cut before," Tess said. "The back room and bathroom need to be cleaned and all the rags burned, along with anything that has Meg's blood on it. I'll do the cleaning. Merri Lee will help me."

"After the police are gone," Simon said. "After the poison is gone."

Jester looked at Simon. "After the ponies have the mail, I'll tell Winter. But I think she's going to want to talk to you."

Simon nodded. Then he looked around. "Where is Jake?"

"Probably informing the entire Crowgard that something happened to Meg," Blair said sourly.

"Vlad, get a shipping box and packing tape from Lorne," Simon said. "We'll put the box of sugar lumps in that. I'll call Montgomery and have him come here. And I'll take care of any deliveries that come until the office closes for the midday break."

Vlad opened the front door and flipped the sign back to OPEN as he walked out. Jester slipped back into the sorting room and returned with the stacks of mail, which he laid out on the front counter before going outside to wait for the ponies.

"Let the Crows spread the word that the Liaison will not be making any deliveries this afternoon," Henry said before he left.

Blair walked out without a word to anyone, leaving Tess and Simon.

"I'm not sure the euphoria is worth the pain that comes before it," Tess said softly. "She didn't make that cut for herself, Simon. She did it for us. Remember that before you snarl at her."

She walked out of the office, then hesitated before she headed for the sidewalk instead of staying within the Courtyard. She'd forgotten her coat, would have to fetch it later. As she walked the short distance to A Little Bite, her coiling hair turned red and black in equal measure, and she allowed the smallest glimpse of her true nature to show through the human skin.

And everyone who looked upon her died just a little.

Simon walked into the sorting room, looked at Nathan, and jerked a thumb over his shoulder. <Out.>

Nathan showed his teeth. <I'm guarding.>

<I want to talk to her. Go in the other room. Come back when I'm done.>

The Wolf wasn't happy about it, but he went into the front room.

When he was alone with the troublesome female who kept him confused, Simon leaned close enough to feel her breath on his face, to breathe in her scent.

She smelled of pain and a strange kind of arousal that made him want to sniff between her legs. And she smelled of blood and the medicine Tess had put on the cut. He wanted to sniff that too, wanted to get rid of the human medicine and clean the wound as a Wolf would.

But Meg was human, so human medicine was best for her.

"I know you're not sleeping," he whispered. "You can't fool someone who has listened to you sleep."

"Are you saying I snore?" she asked, her eyes still closed.

"No." He considered. "I don't think so. But I know when you sleep."

She swallowed. Such a bitable throat, so soft yet firm.

No, he thought, pressing his forehead against her arm. *Meg is not bitable.* He raised his head and studied the gray eyes that now looked back at him. "I'm the leader. You should have called me. Even if you wanted Tess to be there instead of a Wolf, you should have told me first."

"I knew there was something wrong. Didn't want anything bad to happen while I was arguing with you."

It was a valid point. Not that he would tell her that.

He touched her hair. Still weird in color and funnier-looking with the black roots. When it grew out, he might actually miss the orange hair.

He wasn't going to tell her that either.

"I'll watch for deliveries," he said. "You rest. There is food. You want to eat?"

"Not yet." Her eyes closed, then fluttered open again. "Is Nathan angry with me?"

"Yes. If you lock him out again, he'll bite you."

The briefest smile. "Bet he won't if I tell him he can have all the cookies."

He watched her, listened to her, and knew she was truly asleep. He kissed her forehead and found the act pleasing for its own sake. And, he admitted as he licked his lips, it was enjoyable for other reasons. Meg wasn't bitable, but he really did like the taste of her.

He traded places with Nathan. While he watched Jester fill the mail baskets and explain to the ponies why there wasn't a treat, he dialed the number that would bring Crispin James Montgomery back to the Courtyard.

Monty realized Kowalski had been talking to him only when silence suddenly filled the patrol car.

"I'm sorry, Karl. I wasn't listening. Have some things on my mind."

"Like why we're being called this time?" Kowalski asked. "Kind of strange to be told something is urgent and then be given a specific time to show up."

"That's part of it." Another part was Captain Burke informing him that the mayor was grumbling about how many resources were being used on behalf of the Others when they didn't feel inclined to return any favors. Burke suspected His Honor was floating the idea of Humans First and Last as his potential campaign platform.

Let me worry about the mayor, Lieutenant. You just remember that all roads travel into the woods.

In other words, remaining on good terms with the *terra indigene* was more important than human politics.

They pulled into the delivery area for the Liaison's Office. Monty drew in a breath. Closed sign on the door, but he could see someone at the counter.

Someone who wasn't Meg Corbyn.

"Come in with me, Karl." Not his usual request, but this time he wanted backup with him instead of waiting in the car.

As they walked up to the door, Simon Wolfgard approached from the other side. He turned the lock and opened the door.

"Is Ms. Corbyn taking the day off?" Monty asked as they all walked up to the front counter.

"Midday break," Simon replied. "She'll be back for the afternoon deliveries." He didn't sound happy about that.

The door into the next room was wide-open. The room itself didn't interest Monty, but the wheelchair parked next to a big table did.

"Ms. Corbyn seems to be accident prone all of a sudden," he said softly. Would Meg be there for the afternoon deliveries, or would the Others have a different excuse for her absence?

Simon turned, looked at the wheelchair, and snarled. "She hurt her leg this morning. She *says* she doesn't need the wheelchair, but that's what is used when humans are injured. Isn't it?"

Monty wasn't sure if that was a question or a demand to confirm the answer the Wolf wanted. "Wheelchairs aren't used for minor injuries, unless a person can't walk for some reason."

"Well, we don't want her to walk on that leg today." Then Wolfgard seemed to pull back, as if the admission that the Others were actually trying to take care of a human revealed too much. "That's not why I called you. Meg . . . *We* suspect there is something wrong with the sugar lumps that were in the back room. The Liaison usually gives the ponies sugar on Moonsday as a treat, but she had a feeling something was wrong. Some of us believe the sugar was poisoned, but we don't have a way of testing it."

Monty put the pieces together and filled in the unspoken piece: Meg, the *cassandra sangue,* had cut herself and saw poison in the sugar. Simon wasn't going to acknowledge that his Liaison was a blood prophet, but that explained his over-the-top solution to dealing with what should be a minor injury.

"Where are the sugar lumps now?" he asked.

"In the back room. We packed the box in another box," Simon replied. "You can bring your car around to the back door so you don't have to carry it far."

What did she see besides poison that made you this wary? Monty wondered. He looked at Kowalski. "Bring the car around to the back door."

"Yes, sir."

He turned back to Simon. "Do you have any idea who might have done this?" He'd received one of the flyers banning a woman named Asia Crane from the whole Courtyard, including the stores. And he'd heard the whisper that an employee had been fired for breach of trust, whatever that meant.

Simon hesitated. "No. No one had a reason to hurt the ponies." He shifted from one foot to the other. "Lieutenant . . ." A deep breath before words tumbled out. "Skull and crossbones. A skeleton in a hooded robe. Screaming children with black snakes pushing out of their bellies."

"What?" Monty braced his hands on the counter. Was that a threat?

"We think that poison was used to kill some human children. Or it will be used."

"Here? In Lakeside?"

"Don't know where. Don't know when. Maybe it already happened. Maybe it's something that can be stopped." Simon took a step back from the counter. "I'll open the back door for your man."

Staggered, Monty stayed at the counter until Kowalski drove back to the delivery entrance. Simon Wolfgard didn't come back to the front room, so Monty left.

"Back to the station?" Kowalski asked.

"Yes. Where is the box?"

"In the trunk. Figured that was better than having it in a closed car with us."

Monty nodded. Keeping his face turned to the passenger's-side window, he said, "Karl? Do you remember hearing about children being poisoned by someone dressed up like a skeleton or a death's head in a hooded robe?"

Kowalski hit the brakes, then fishtailed the car before he regained control. "Sir?"

"We might have a line on another crime."

"Gods above and below," Kowalski muttered.

Neither of them spoke again until they reached the station. With Kowalski starting a search for a crime that matched those clues, Monty reported to Captain Burke.

Burke's eyes turned a fiercer blue while his face paled. "That's all he gave you?"

"I think he gave me all they had," Monty replied. "He didn't have to say anything."

"Most of them wouldn't have." Burke sighed. "All right. We have only one lab in Lakeside set up to handle and identify poisons. Have Kowalski drive over and deliver the box personally. I'll put in a call and see what I can do to bump our request to the top of the queue. You see what you can find out about children being poisoned. And as sad as it would be to find it, let's hope you do find a report. If it already happened, we know where and when, and maybe even what kind of poison."

"If it hasn't happened, how do we warn the rest of the cities in Thaisia?" Monty asked.

"I'll have to think about that. It may surprise you, Lieutenant, but not everyone likes me. And not everyone who does like me likes my stand with regard to the Others. We didn't empty the precinct's coffers to buy a prophecy, and anyone who has heard one will recognize that clues like that tend to come from a prophecy. If we admit it was a footnote in a prophecy done for the Lakeside Courtyard, we're telling a whole lot of people that the Others have a resident blood prophet."

"Putting a target on Meg Corbyn, with no certainty we're doing our own people any good."

Burke nodded. "I'll make some calls and spread the word as best I can—after you run the search to find out if this already happened and was, may the gods be merciful, a tragic reference rather than a future possibility."

"Yes, sir."

Monty sent Kowalski to the lab and took over the search. How old were the children? And where were the children?

Lizzy, he thought, looking at the picture of his daughter that sat on his desk. *Be safe, Lizzy.*

When it started snowing in Simon's office, he yanked off his sweater and shirt to cover the computer. Vlad knew more about the things than he did, but he did know that snow and anything that plugged into an electrical outlet weren't a good combination. Hearing footsteps in the hall, he leaped for the doorway before Winter and her fury actually entered the room.

His torso and arms furred as a defense against the cold that surrounded her. Her gown fluttered despite an absence of wind. As bits of it flaked off, it became snow that rapidly covered the floor around her.

"Who tried to poison our ponies?" Her voice added an icy glaze to the frosted glass on his door and rose to the volume of a storm. "Who dared raise a hand against our companions and steeds? *Who?*"

"I don't know," Simon replied quietly, looking into her eyes. "Meg saw enough to protect them and to warn us, but she didn't see who poisoned the sugar."

An awful silence. The Elementals were dangerous enough when they gave passive guidance to Namid's weather and seasons. When they were capricious and cruel, they could cleanse a piece of the world of everything but themselves.

"Should I ask Meg to try again?" Simon asked.

Winter touched the green scarf around her neck. "No," she said, her voice quieting. "No. Jester says our Meg bled to protect the ponies. He says there was pain."

"Yes."

"She has done enough." Winter started to turn away. Then she stopped and didn't quite look at him. "Her leg. It will be difficult to walk over snow-rough. It might cause pain."

"It might," he agreed, not sure where she was headed with this.

"I will ask my sister if she would wake for a few days and soften the air. It will be easier for our Meg to walk if the pavement is free of snow."

"She would appreciate that. And I appreciate that."

Winter walked away, the train of her fluttering gown trailing behind her.

Simon rushed back to the desk and removed his shirt and sweater. Overall, not too many flakes fell in the office or on the desk. Since the computer was still running and didn't explode when he touched a key, he figured it would be all right. Using the clothes, he had everything on the desk wiped down by the time Vlad came upstairs.

"She sounded angry," Vlad said. He disappeared for a moment, then returned with a couple of towels from their restroom and helped Simon wipe down the furniture.

"But still in control enough not to create a blizzard inside the store." He considered how she would have entered. "Did the books in the stockroom get snowed on?"

"No, just the floor. John is mopping that up now. I'll get a broom. We can sweep up the snow in the hallway and on the stairs." Vlad looked around, then extended a hand. "Give me the shirt and sweater. I'll use the dryer at the social center. It's closest, and your things will be dry by the time you need to take Meg back to the office for the afternoon deliveries." He paused, then asked, "What are you going to do with Sam?"

"Blair is taking him. Nathan and I are having a hard enough time leaving the bandage on Meg's leg alone. I don't think a puppy could stop himself from worrying at it, and he could hurt her. She'll stay with us this evening, and Sam can cuddle with her in human form."

When they had the snow swept up, Simon receded the fur, put on a spare flannel shirt he kept in a bottom desk drawer, and got back to work.

Pausing at an intersection, Meg rolled down the driver's-side window and breathed in air that held the warmth of spring. Oh, winter was still beneath that warmth, but the roads were clear of snow and ice, she was on her midday break, and she was alone for the first time since she made the cut two days ago.

Even friendship could feel smothering, especially when your friends were large and furry and liked a lot of physical contact. She came to realize that despite taking a human form, the Others' understanding of human anatomy was mostly limited to what parts of that anatomy they liked to eat. They had responded to the cut on her leg with the intensity usually reserved for an amputation.

Yesterday she had appealed to Merri Lee, Heather, Ruth, and Elizabeth Bennefeld to explain that a simple cut that was healing well didn't require a wheelchair, a driver, or a guard constantly watching her in case she keeled over. Simon didn't want to accept it, but they hadn't given him any wiggle room.

And that was why she was driving the BOW by herself on this fine Windsday afternoon, looking for a spot where she would stop and eat the box lunch Tess had made. Interior roads were clear for the first time since her arrival in the Courtyard, so she turned the BOW inward, following whatever road appealed to her.

Trees and open spaces. She saw a Hawk on a tree stump. She didn't look closely enough to determine what he was eating for lunch.

Stopping at one intersection, she watched all the ponies canter past her, clearly enjoying a chance to run. She turned in the direction they had come, only to discover *they* had turned and were now following her, slowing when she slowed, lengthening their strides when she sped up a little, staying with her as she turned onto one road after another. They left her when she turned toward the little houses that belonged to the girls at the lake. She pulled up next to one of the houses, then got out to walk along the wide path that circled the lake.

Winter was skating, a mature woman now with hair that streamed down to her waist and was as white as the snow that floated in the air around her. Seeing Meg, she waved and said, "Stay there." Her voice didn't carry, exactly. It seemed to rise from the banks of snow.

The Elemental flowed up effortlessly from the lake, leaving no footsteps in the snow. She smiled at Meg. "Where are your companions?"

"I'm enjoying a wander without them," Meg replied, returning the smile.

"Are you also enjoying the gift from me and my sister?" Winter asked.

It seemed an insult not to know what was meant by a gift. And, really, when Meg looked around, the meaning was clear enough. "Soft weather. Clear roads. The sun coming through a window to create a beam of warmth." She looked at Winter. "You did this for me?"

"You like to be out on the land, like to touch it. We wanted to make it easier for you to walk and enjoy without hurting your leg." Winter looked away. "The ponies are dear to us. What was intended for them is not something we will forget. But you saved them. That is also something we will not forget." She looked at Meg and smiled. "Spring would like to meet you. She is down by the creek."

"Then I'll walk down and say hello."

Meg continued around the lake to the road that ran between the lake and the creek. A girl stood on the rocks that formed a natural retaining wall, watching two ducks paddle around in open water no larger than the circle Meg could make with her arms. There were other dark patches at the edge where land and water met—a sign of melting ice.

The girl turned. Seeing Meg, she ran up a path between snowbanks. Her hair was a mix of browns, and her dress . . .

Meg wasn't sure if her dress was made to resemble flowers or if it was made of the flowers that would be the first to bloom when the snow melted. She could match tulips, hyacinths, and crocuses with their images, but there were others, blue and delicate, that looked as if they would never bloom in any place that wasn't wild.

The girl took Meg's hand in her own, and her joyous laugh made a few of those delicate wildflowers bloom at her feet.

"You are our Meg," she said. "I am Spring. I usually wake for a few days while Winter still reigns, although not quite this early. But we wanted to give you something as thanks for saving the ponies, and it's not appropriate for Summer or Autumn to rise yet, so I'm here." Her laughter sparkled in the air.

"I'm glad I was able to help." *And I've wondered whether someone tried to poison them because I was here.* "You're visiting for a few days?"

Spring nodded. "In another day or two, I'll sleep again. Not so deep as before, but I'll sleep most of the time for a few more weeks. Winter has kept a list of the new books that have come to our library since I danced in the Courtyard, and she says if I make a list of the ones I want to read, you'll deliver them. This is true?"

How could she resist the girl and that smile? "Yes, it's true."

More laughter. More flowers blooming around them.

Then Spring turned serious. "The warmth awakens, but it also weakens. Beware, our Meg." She pointed to the creek. "Do you see? The ice has yielded in some places. In other places, it is solid but weak. Not a place to walk or skate now. It will harden again in a few days, although maybe not all the way."

"Why will it harden?" Meg asked.

"A storm is coming from our brothers and sisters in the north. By Watersday, it will cross Lake Etu. I will return to my bed, and Winter, Air, and Water will rule for a while longer." Spring smiled at her. "I'm glad to have met you. I look forward to seeing you again."

I hope I do see you again. "I'd better get going. If I'm late getting back, Mr. Wolfgard will send the whole pack out looking for me."

She had meant it as a joke, but Spring's reply was serious.

"Of course he would," Spring said. "Namid has given you to us, and we value the world's gifts." Giving Meg one more smile, she ran and hopped and skipped down the road.

Meg returned to her BOW and drove back to the office. She ate her lunch in the spotlessly clean back room while reading a chapter of the latest book she'd borrowed from the library.

If I'm late getting back, Mr. Wolfgard will send the whole pack out looking for me.

Namid has given you to us, and we value the world's gifts.

And for the rest of the afternoon, she ignored the words that had produced a light prickling under her skin.

Asia sat in the Stag and Hare, watching the traffic and the Courtyard's delivery entrance while she waited for the special messenger. She had gone to an upscale salon yesterday and changed her natural blond to a rich cinnamon. A change in foundation garments softened her breasts instead of emphasizing them, and a couple of new, looser sweaters completed her superficial transformation. It wasn't a bad look for her, and she decided to think of this as a test run for a disguise that Asia Crane, SI, might use for an undercover assignment.

The messenger arrived, looked around, then beamed a smile in her direction. When he reached the table, he bent toward her, as if about to give her a kiss. Then he hesitated and touched her hand instead.

He's something of an actor too, Asia thought. He'd given the hostess the perfect impression of a man who wasn't yet a lover but wanted to be.

"Anything interesting?" he asked as he draped his short winter coat over the back of the chair.

"Nothing." She tried to keep the frustration out of her voice. There should have been an uproar in the Courtyard on Moonsday after the ponies ate the sugar, but there had been nothing then and nothing since.

"Nothing easily seen." He opened his menu, skimmed the insert for the day's specials, and placed his order as soon as the waiter arrived.

Asia ordered the soup and sandwich special and worked on being polite. She had altered her voice from syrupy to friendly but crisp. That, along with the difference in hair and cleavage, was a sufficient change to make the staff just uncertain enough about having seen her before.

When they were alone again, the messenger leaned forward, looking as if he were doing nothing more than flirting with a pretty woman.

"Someone became uneasy about the sugar and didn't give it to the ponies," he said. "The police have it now and will test it for poison."

"That's not good," Asia muttered.

"It's not significant. Our benefactor made a call and took care of it. The bottom line is humans before Others, so the tests on the sugar have been bumped way down in the lab's queue. We'll be gone before anyone gets around to fulfilling that particular request."

"So it didn't do anything for us."

"Oh, but it did. It confirmed that our benefactor's property is hiding in the Courtyard and using up a valuable asset to help the beasts. Knowing that, we take our preparations to the next stage."

The waiter brought their meals and topped off their water glasses. The first glass and top off was part of the meal in restaurants like this one. After that, with the water tax being what it was, a glass of water cost as much as a glass of wine.

"The story I've spun for the locals is that two dozen men, friends of mine from our university days, have come to Lakeside for a winter vacation—snowmobiling, cross-country skiing, and so forth. There are good trails in the park, and there is an inn nearby that caters to visitors who enjoy winter sports. It even has a parking area just for snowmobiles. This thaw has soured things somewhat for winter sports, but we're exploring the area and enjoying a chance to catch up with old friends. We aren't complaining to the proprietors about the unseasonably mild weather, and that makes us good customers." After giving her another smile, he took a big bite out of his sandwich.

"Two dozen men amount to a lot of expense to retrieve one item." Asia swallowed a spoonful of soup. She hadn't believed the benefactor would send that many men for this job. Her backers would want a large chunk of the finder's fee that she'd been promised, but even so, her cut would be substantial. And that was just from helping the benefactor reacquire Meg. The *real* money would come from the acquisition of the Wolf pup.

"According to the weather reports, there's a storm coming in on Watersday." The messenger wiped his mouth with a napkin. "We'll use it to cover our tracks and reacquire the property."

"Wouldn't it be better to get in and out before the storm hits?" Asia asked. "No," she continued, answering her own question. "Those damn Crows are always watching."

He nodded. "My men scouted the neighborhood, including the area of the park nearest the Courtyard. Some of the Crows spotted the snowmobiles and followed two of them halfway across the park. The birds need to be grounded by a storm so we can work without being spied on."

"You're taking a chance if the city closes some of the roads."

"The storm is coming down from the north, and we'll be headed out on the roads running east or south. We'll stay ahead of it, and even if we have to hole up for a few hours, we'll get far enough away that anyone trying to follow us will lose our trail. In the meantime, we're going to cause some mischief."

"Like what?" Having more appetite now than she'd had at the start of the meal, Asia tasted her sandwich.

"A few college boys with good throwing arms, a van with a side door, and a few dozen eggs to make a mess. Firecrackers thrown over the fence by a team on a snowmobile. Setting rags and paper on fire at one of the Courtyard entrances. We'll be pulling the same pranks on neighborhood streets in the area." He gave Asia a big smile. "Besides keeping the police busy, we'll have a chance to observe how the Others respond—how many head for the problem, how many head for whatever places they think need defending, and what areas are left vulnerable that we can exploit."

"The business area of the Courtyard is usually deserted once their stores close," Asia said.

He nodded. "And the door in the parking lot's back wall is wood with a simple lock. Their security is pitiful. Makes you wonder how they've managed to stay in control of this continent."

"When does this mischief begin?" Asia asked. Then she almost dove to the floor in response to a rapid series of loud bangs.

The messenger grinned. "Right about now."

"Is this typical spring fever?" Monty asked as Kowalski drove them to the next case of reported mischief. They'd already had three calls from the Courtyard. Simon Wolfgard had been annoyed about the first set of firecrackers that had been tossed in the Liaison's Office delivery area and the Courtyard's customer parking lot. And he hadn't been amused by the eggs that had been thrown at the windows of Howling Good Reads and A Little Bite. But he'd been seriously pissed off about the second set of firecrackers tossed in the delivery area, because the dumb-ass teenagers had lingered on the sidewalk, taunting Nathan, who slammed out of the office in challenge. Then Meg ran after Nathan. She tripped and might have hurt herself if she hadn't landed right on the Wolf, effectively stopping him from getting too close to the firecrackers.

Louis Gresh had answered that call, and Monty was waiting to hear from the bomb squad's commander whether there was anything hidden among the firecrackers that could have injured woman or Wolf.

"Typical?" Kowalski shook his head. "Most kids aren't going to risk getting smacked for using the week's ration of eggs, so this egging windows is new."

"They could be buying the eggs on their own," Monty said.

"Eggs cost twice as much without the household ration coupon," Kowalski countered. "High school and college boys coming in to buy eggs and paying that price are going to get noticed. And if they buy from a store in their own neighborhood, we'll hear about it or their parents will."

Monty pinched the bridge of his nose. "I don't like this, Karl. It feels like we're being set up."

"By whom?"

He lowered his hand and sighed. "I don't know."

They pulled up to the curb and got out. Looking at the egg-splattered front window, they didn't need to ask the irate owner what the problem was.

"Storm is coming in on Watersday," Kowalski said. "That should put an end to this."

Monty took out his notebook and pen. "I hope you're right, Karl. I truly do hope you're right."

CHAPTER 23

With exaggerated care, Captain Burke set the phone's receiver in its cradle. Then he looked at Monty and said, "We're being stonewalled, Lieutenant. The lab just informed me that they have to deal with evidence that pertains to actual crimes first. Our request is for a crime that was *almost* committed. My guess is we'll see summer before we see a report."

"Humans First and Last," Monty said, thinking about the mayor's potential reelection platform.

Burke nodded. "That's how I'm reading it. Now. What are you going to tell Simon Wolfgard?" He gave Monty his fierce smile. "There's not much that goes on in this station that I don't know about, so I know Wolfgard has called once already this morning looking for an answer."

"I'll tell him the truth. The lab will do the tests as soon as they can."

"You think he'll believe that?"

Monty didn't bother to respond.

"Wolfgard will know the lab is trying to screw him without buying him dinner first," Burke said quietly. "Let's hope he continues to believe in *your* sincerity."

When Vlad, Henry, and Tess came into HGR's office, Simon didn't waste time. "The monkeys aren't going to help us. Montgomery gave me excuses, but the end result is we aren't going to know if the sugar was poisoned."

"The lieutenant had seemed honest in his dealings with us," Henry said, sounding disappointed.

Relenting a little, Simon pushed back his own anger. "He sounded frustrated, even a little angry. The police lab doesn't want to help us, and they aren't interested in helping him either."

Vlad shrugged. "A strike against the monkeys, and something that won't be forgotten."

"No, it won't be forgotten." Especially after Elliot's report earlier this morning about the mayor's efforts to court supporters of a humans-only policy for Lakeside.

Fools had tried that before in other parts of Thaisia. The wild country was still reclaiming the last town that had such leaders, so it wasn't all that many years ago.

Tess stirred. Or, more to the point, Tess's *hair* stirred, curling as it changed from brown to red.

"There is another way to find out if the sugar was poisoned," she said.

"How?" Simon asked. As he studied her, he realized that Tess wouldn't look any of them in the eyes when she was angry.

"Get Darrell Adams's home address for me. Elliot should have it in the consulate's employee files."

Tess waited until evening before she walked to a bus stop a couple of blocks away from the Courtyard. As part of the agreement with Lakeside, the *terra indigene* could ride any public transportation in the city for free. But using that bus pass would bring attention she didn't want, so she paid the fare, putting in her coins like the humans before taking a seat a few rows from the front. She kept her hair bundled under the wool cap, but she loosened the scarf she'd wrapped around her neck and mouth.

She transferred to another bus, finally getting off at a stop a few blocks from the apartment complex where Darrell Adams lived. She walked briskly, fighting her own nature with each step. She wanted to shift closer to her natural form, but it was important to remain recognizably human. No one who looked upon her true form could survive. Since she was here to test someone else's weapon and send a warning to the police, an apartment building full of corpses would be overkill.

When she reached Darrell's apartment, she heard the television through the closed door. Were the neighbors annoyed by the volume? She cocked her head as music suddenly drifted out from another apartment. Or did they all turn up the sound to hear their own choice and drown out the competition?

She knocked on Darrell's door, then knocked again loudly enough that the door across the hall opened and an old woman peered out. Tess ignored the woman and knocked again.

Darrell finally answered, the television program now blaring into the hallway almost muting the sound of the door across the hall being vigorously shut.

"What do you want?" Darrell asked when he recognized her.

Tess let the tiniest bit of her true form show in her eyes as she looked right at him. "We have something to discuss."

He staggered back from the door, and she followed him inside, catching him by the arm and leading him to the recliner that was clearly his preferred place to sit.

Only a momentary heart flutter, only a temporary weakening of the limbs from that brief glimpse of her. He needed to be in good health for the test.

She pulled off the wool cap. Her hair—black with threads of red—tumbled around her shoulders, coiling and moving. She removed the small jar from a zippered inner pocket of her coat, unscrewed the top, and held the jar out to Darrell.

"Take two," she said. "Eat them."

"Why?"

"You can choose between the sugar or this." Looking into his eyes again, she let the human mask fade from her face a little more.

Darrell wet himself.

She shook the jar. "Two."

He took two sugar lumps, popped them in his mouth, chewed a couple of times, and then swallowed. She brought her face back to the image her customers and the *terra indigene* were used to seeing, but her hair remained the death color with those few threads of red.

As she watched him, she tapped two sugar lumps onto the floor near Darrell's chair. She didn't have to wait long. Twice she turned up the volume on the television to drown out his screams, and twice those screams eclipsed the sound.

Someone began pounding on the door, shouting, "What's going on in there? We've called the police!"

Busybody, Tess thought, annoyed. And because she was annoyed, she stuffed her wool cap in her coat pocket and walked out of the apartment, leaving the door open. She kept her eyes averted, but her true form was close to the surface and her coiling hair drew the eyes of those she passed. She savored the little bit of death that touched every person who looked at her.

She walked and walked, her hair still black but starting to relax. She still kept her eyes averted, although it was doubtful any of the people in the cars even glanced her way, and there were very few people on foot.

A man lounging in a doorway spotted her and stepped in her path. She didn't know if he intended to rob her or rape her. She didn't care. With him, she could slake her hunger.

She looked him in the eyes and held his gaze while he collapsed. She stepped around him and kept going. Eventually, when the cold had more bite than her anger, she tucked her hair under the wool cap, walked to the nearest bus stop, and took the next bus home.

On Firesday afternoon, Monty was at his desk, enjoying a cup of hot tea while he chipped away at reports. By yesterday evening, the egging had stopped—mostly because the grocery stores were out of eggs and the little neighborhood markets were keeping the eggs in the stockroom and only bringing them out for known adult customers. The firecrackers were still going off here and there, and someone had set fire to a section of junipers that the Others had planted as a privacy screen between the Courtyard and Parkside Avenue. A handful of men riding snowmobiles in Lakeside Park claimed they saw two people drive off in a pickup truck just before one of the riders spotted flames.

Fire engulfed the bushes, mostly because none of the snowmobilers had remembered to bring a mobile phone with them, and no one in the passing cars had thought to report seeing flames. By the time the fire department arrived, there was nothing for them to do because something had ripped up the bushes and dumped them, a section of the Courtyard's wrought-iron fence, and more than two feet of snow across the northbound lanes of Parkside Avenue, bringing traffic to a skidding halt.

The damage was consistent with a tornado, although every meteorologist

Monty called that morning swore there had been no indication of a weather pattern like that, and even if they *had* seen something, a selective strike was simply not natural.

He thought using a tornado to put out a fire was over the top, but it was a grim reminder that the humans didn't know half of what lived in the Courtyard and watched them.

The break in the fence bothered him because it was another point of entry, along with the hole caused by a pickup jumping the curb late last night and punching a hole in the fence that ran along Main Street. Two different pickups and two random acts? Or the same people?

Monty shivered. There had been too many random acts lately. And that made him wonder whether someone was trying to cause trouble.

I guess I'm not the only one thinking along those lines, he thought when Captain Burke, dressed for the outdoors, approached his desk. Burke stopped, not looking at Monty while he pulled on his gloves.

"Get your coat, Lieutenant," Burke said so quietly that Monty was sure no one else could hear. "We're going for a walk. I'll meet you outside."

Even more uneasy now, Monty complied and met Burke outside the station.

"Let's walk a bit," Burke said, heading up the block.

"Anywhere particular?" Monty asked.

"Just away. Do you have your mobile phone?"

"Yes, sir."

"Good. Now turn it off."

Oh, gods.

They walked two blocks, then three blocks before Burke spoke again.

"I got a call from Captain Zajac a few minutes ago. You remember Darrell Adams?"

Monty nodded. "He worked for the consulate and was fired a few days ago."

"He died last night. It appears he ate some poisoned sugar, since two sugar lumps were found near the chair where he collapsed."

They walked another block before Monty was able to speak. "We didn't help them, so the Others did their own test on the person they believed responsible?"

"I don't think Mr. Adams would have gotten out of the Courtyard alive if the Others had believed he was the one who attempted to poison some of them. But he wasn't chosen at random either."

"Will the lab put a rush on the results for this death?" Monty asked.

"Now, now, Lieutenant. Don't sound bitter," Burke said lightly. "They have good reason to put a rush on it. The officers who responded walked in thinking they were confirming a suspicious death. After what else was found, Zajac is scared down to his toes, because he doesn't know how many more deaths may follow."

Monty frowned. "I don't understand."

"We're assuming Adams ate some of the sugar. He's dead. But there's one of the neighbors who says he pounded on the door, and when he looked at the woman who walked out of Adams's apartment, his left arm and shoulder went numb. He was taken to the hospital. No injury, no wound, but the muscles in the arm and shoulder are dead. Another neighbor, an old lady who claimed to see the woman arrive and peered out her door in time to see the woman leave, has a dead eye. No sign of injury, no explanation. Shortly after that, people began showing up at hospital emergency rooms, claiming shortness of breath or dizzy spells or chest pains or a sudden weakness in their limbs. By this morning, most of them have recovered without any explanation for what caused the physical symptoms. The only thing they have in common is they were near Adams's apartment last night, all around the same time."

"How are the officers who responded?" Despite the cold, Monty realized he was sweating.

"They're fine." Burke paused while they waited for a traffic light to change. Once they crossed the street, he continued. "So are the man and boy who came in just as the woman was leaving. The man says he caught a glimpse of her and immediately turned his back, putting himself between her and his son. He also held a hand over the boy's eyes. He told the officers, 'We didn't look at her. I remembered the myths, and we didn't look.' The man wouldn't tell the officers anything more, and Zajac is understandably reluctant to do more probing."

"Wouldn't he want to know?" Myths? Would the university have someone on the faculty who could find the source of the myth?

"No, he doesn't want to know. And neither do we." Burke's stare warned Monty that he meant it.

"You know how some people say 'If looks could kill'?" Burke asked after a moment. "Well, it seems there is something among the *terra indigene* that has the ability to do exactly that."

"... travel advisory in effect until six a.m. tomorrow. WZAS is recommending no unnecessary travel. Figured we'd say it before you hear an official announcement from city hall. So get your milk and toilet paper and head on home, folks. We've got several inches of snow already clogging up the streets, and there's more coming. Current projections say the entire city of Lakeside could get up to two feet before this lake-effect storm blows itself out, and we're not even going to think about measuring the drifts. Wind chill could dip to minus twenty by this evening. We'll have a full list of closings on the half hour and hour. This is Ann Hergott bringing you the news and weather reports, whether you like it or not. And now, from last year's blockbuster movie, let's listen to the hit single 'If Summer Never Comes.'"

Monty turned off the radio and pulled on his coat and boots. He wasn't on duty today, but everyone was on call. He'd seen a few bad storms during the years he'd lived in Toland. There had even been a few times when the Big City had closed down for a day. But listening to Kowalski, Debany, and MacDonald yesterday—men who had lived in Lakeside all their lives—he realized he hadn't seen the kind of storm *they* considered bad. And they were all gearing up for *bad*.

Checking to be sure he had his keys, he went outside.

Black clouds were piled up like huge boulders waiting to fall on the world. As he stood there, his skin stinging from the cold, the snow came down faster and harder. A plow had gone by earlier, but the street was filled in again. And that made him wonder if anything was going to be able to get in or out of his street in another hour or two.

Returning to his apartment, he called Kowalski.

"What's your opinion of this storm?" he asked when Karl answered.

"It's coming in faster than expected," Karl replied. "I just heard on the radio that everything downtown is closing, and all social events for tonight have been canceled. Traffic is already starting to snarl because of the amount of snow on the roads, and it will get worse."

"The plows?"

"Will do what they can to keep the main drags open, but there's only so much they *can* do until this storm blows over."

Monty thought for a moment. "In that case, I'm going to pack an overnight bag and catch a cab down to the station while I can still get there. What about you?"

"You'll have a better chance of getting a cab if you tell the driver you'll meet him at the corner, since you live off one of the main streets. I don't think a cabby will try to drive down any residential street at this point. Too much chance of getting stuck. Me and a few other guys helped dig out a couple neighbors who had to report to work. Medical personnel, emergency aid, and firefighters are being called in." A hesitation. "Actually, I thought you were calling to tell me to come in."

Why would that be a problem? Monty wondered, hearing something under the words. More than the weather. He was getting the impression that Kowalski would resist leaving home for as long as possible.

"I tried calling the inns and hotels closest to Lakeside Park, but I guess some of the phone lines have already gone down, because I didn't get an answer."

Monty gentled his voice in response to the worry in Karl's. "That's a concern, but is it an immediate problem?"

"A group of men are in town for some kind of reunion. They have snowmobiles. I figured it wouldn't hurt to locate them and see if they might do some volunteer work."

"What aren't you saying, Karl?"

"We didn't think the storm was going to hit quite this fast, so Ruthie went to Run and Thump to work out and then was going to stop at the Market Square grocery store to pick up a few things." Kowalski hesitated. "Nobody is answering at Howling Good Reads or A Little Bite, and I haven't gotten through to

Ruthie's mobile. We're only a few blocks from the Courtyard, but I'm not sure Ruthie can get home at this point."

Monty watched a car slowly making its way down the street. "Karl? I have to go. Keep looking for those snowmobiles. I'll have my mobile phone with me, so let me know when you've made contact with Ruth."

"Will do." Kowalski hung up.

Monty quickly packed a bag, called for a cab to meet him at the end of his street, and headed out into the storm.

Asia rammed her rental car into the snow clogging the Courtyard parking lot, determined to create a path for her escape once she acquired the Wolf pup. She would have preferred parking across the street, but all the spaces near the Stag and Hare were filled, and when she passed the city lot that was available to the customers of all the businesses within that block, it was obvious that only the last car that managed to jam itself in was going to get out, and even that was doubtful.

She gunned the engine until the tires spun, then took her foot off the gas and put the car in reverse to back up enough to take another run at getting into the lot. Ignoring the blare of a horn from the car that just missed her rear bumper when she reversed, she put the gearshift in drive and gunned the engine again. The car slewed and ended up stuck, completely blocking the other cars in the lot.

Swearing vigorously, Asia slammed out of the car. Piece of shit. She had *told* the rental company she needed a car that could handle snow, and they had assured her this one could under most conditions.

Most conditions, my ass, she thought as she reached in for the pack of supplies on the backseat. After pulling out the hammer axe, she slipped the pack's straps over her shoulders, then made her way to the back wall of the parking lot.

She tried the wooden door in the wall first, hoping the Others hadn't bothered to lock it. No such luck. But there was mounded snow that rose to the top of the wall. That would be easy to climb.

Using the hammer axe, she hauled herself up the mound, then got a leg over the wall and lowered herself to the snow piled on the other side. This side of the parking lot hadn't been cleared all day, and the cars in it weren't going anywhere for a while. She was going to leave a trail, but she couldn't worry about that.

She studied the padlock that secured the wooden door that provided access between the two lots, and swore. Had to find the key for the padlock. She wasn't getting out the way she got in, not with that pup in tow.

She slipped one arm out of the pack as she considered the one-story brick building that formed the parking lot's right-hand boundary. A garage door and a regular door. She tried the regular door first. When it opened, she slipped into a garage full of snow-removal equipment and gardening tools. Basically, a groundskeeper's shed.

Closing the door most of the way in case any of the Others *were* out in this weather, Asia pulled a small flashlight out of her coat pocket and swung the light along the wall next to the door. She grinned fiercely when she spotted the key rack. The last key in the row was on a loop of string and had the word PADLOCK written above it.

Taking the key, she hurried out and opened the padlock, then tossed it over the wall to ensure a quick exit. She put the key back in its spot, then checked the other keys. One was labeled BOW.

Yes! she thought as she pocketed the key. Darrell had said one key fit all the BOWs, so all she had to do was find one of those little vehicles.

The opposite wall of the maintenance garage had a reverse setup of doors. She made her way to the other regular door, then turned off the flashlight and opened the door just enough to peer out and confirm that these were the garages she'd seen when she'd spent the night with Darrell.

The messenger had moved up the timetable when it became clear the storm was worse than anticipated and had hit the city faster than originally reported. The only problem with the new timetable was that Meg hadn't closed the office yet. When the messenger and his men created the distractions that would pull Simon Wolfgard and the rest of the Others to various parts of the Courtyard, Meg had to be tucked into her apartment at the Green Complex, all safe and snug and easy to grab.

Pushing up the sleeves of her parka and sweater the necessary inch, Asia checked the luminous dial of her watch. Only three thirty in the afternoon, but it was already dark because of the storm. That would work to their advantage.

She jerked back, shutting the door almost all the way as the back door of Howling Good Reads opened and she heard Simon say, "Tell her to wait. I'll be back in a minute."

She watched him stride toward the Liaison's Office, and she saw him stop as something caught his attention. He remained still for a moment, then continued to the office's back door.

Checking her watch again, Asia settled down to wait.

As soon as Simon walked into the office's back room, he could feel Nathan's restless energy and hear Meg's voice. She was talking to someone, but he didn't think it was the Wolf.

<Nathan?> he called.

<I want to go home,> Nathan said, sounding edgy. <We should go home.>

<You might not get as far as the Wolfgard Complex, but we are leaving this part of the Courtyard.>

<Good. We need to den.>

They certainly did need to get home and settle in. He had closed HGR half an hour ago, and Tess had done the same at A Little Bite, but he was still chewing over what to do with their human employees, especially the ones Meg considered friends. He couldn't just chuck them out the door to find their way home. Not when he could look out HGR's windows and see the traffic gridlock that had already formed and was going to get worse.

A couple months ago, he would have closed the store and not given Merri Lee and Heather another thought. They were humans who were not edible because they were useful, and that's all they were to the *terra indigene*. But somehow they had become Meg's human pack, so now they were borderline members of the Courtyard and, therefore, under his protection.

He didn't like thinking of humans like that. He didn't like it at all.

Well, he would deal with Merri Lee and Heather. But first he had to deal with Meg. And that meant dealing with Nathan.

<What's wrong with you?> he asked as he walked through the sorting room. Meg was at the front counter with her back to him. Nathan had his forelegs on the counter and looked grumpy, which wasn't a good way for a guard to look when there wasn't anything nearby he could catch and eat.

<Her!> Nathan replied. <She is restless and keeps rubbing her skin like she has fleas. I tried to sniff her for blood, and *she smacked me.*> Growling softly, he looked at Meg and lifted a paw.

"That's not a problem," Meg said to someone on the phone, absently pushing

Nathan away when he tried to slap the phone to disconnect the call. "Delivery on Moonsday will be fine. You be careful driving out there. Thanks. You too." She hung up and shook a finger at the watch Wolf. Then she noticed Simon and blushed.

<Do you see?> Nathan demanded. <Make her go home.>

Meg was restless and rubbing her skin? Was she feeling the prickling that indicated a potential vision, or was the storm making her uneasy, like the rest of them? He didn't care why she was restless. He was getting her away from this part of the Courtyard.

"You're closing up now," Simon said, blocking the Private doorway and not giving her room to maneuver.

"I'm trying to do exactly that. It would be easier if I didn't have as much help," Meg replied, sounding like she was ready to bite someone.

Nathan whined and gave Simon a pleading look.

It was embarrassing to hear one of the Courtyard's best enforcers whine like a puppy.

"I checked with all the delivery services who usually come by on Watersday afternoon," Meg said. "Most of them didn't have any deliveries for the Courtyard today, and the ones that did, I told them delivery on Moonsday is fine. Besides, Harry from Everywhere Delivery called a couple of minutes ago to tell me a driving ban has just been issued for the entire city. No unnecessary travel. So I'm almost ready to go."

"But . . . ?" He could read her well enough now to know there was something more.

She took a deep breath and blew it out. "Two things. The BOW's charge was low when I got back from lunch. I'm not sure it has enough charge for the drive home, and I'm not sure I can drive in snow this deep."

"You're not driving. Jester should be here with a pony in a few minutes."

Meg brightened. "We're riding in the sleigh?"

He shook his head. "Only the Elementals drive the sleigh. Jester is bringing the sled. It's big enough to fit you and Nathan. I'll take the BOW back to the Green Complex. If it doesn't make it, I'll shift and go the rest of the way home in Wolf form." No protest from her. Probably because she wanted to ride in the sled. "What's the other thing?"

Now she looked uneasy, as if she were about to stomp on his tail. "Merri Lee takes a bus to work." She turned enough to look at the snow falling and falling and falling.

Simon relaxed, pleased that he'd anticipated this. "She's not going home. Neither is Heather. They can pick up some food at Meat-n-Greens or the grocery store, and they'll stay in the efficiency apartments tonight. I'm going to talk to Lorne and see if he wants to stay. Marie Hawkgard is staying to keep watch, and Julia will also be in the efficiencies."

She opened her mouth, and he expected her to say she would stay with her friends in the too-exposed part of the Courtyard. But as she looked at him, all the color bled out of her face.

"I need to get home," she said quietly. "Tonight I need to get home."

"That's why Jester is coming with the pony sled." Simon studied her face. Why did she look so pale, so scared? "Meg?"

She shook her head. "I need to go to the toilet."

Worried about what she might do in that room, he snarled, *"Meg?"*

"I can't just lift a leg like you do, so I have to pee before going out in the cold," she snapped at him.

He took a step back, letting her pass. But he also gave her a quick sniff. Nathan was right; there wasn't any fresh blood scent on her.

He opened the go-through for Nathan. "Wait for her by the back door. I'll lock up."

He fetched the keys from the drawer in the sorting room and used the go-through. Nathan had told him that Meg usually wiped the floor after the last delivery because it got slippery from the snow brought in on the deliverymen's boots. She hadn't done that, which made vaulting over the counter a good way to slip and break a leg or, at best, take a bad fall.

As he flipped the sign to CLOSED, a hooded figure in a green and white parka hurried up to the door. He considered ignoring the human and locking up, but he'd seen that same parka walking out of the Courtyard a few minutes ago.

Pulling the door open, he growled, "What?" before he recognized the Ruthie, who looked like she was trying not to cry.

"Mr. Wolfgard," she said, sounding breathless. "I'm glad I caught you before everything closed up. My car is in your parking lot."

"That's sensible." It would be out of the way, and the adolescent Wolves could have fun digging it out tomorrow.

"But there is a car stuck in the parking lot's entrance. The driver isn't in the vehicle, and I can't get around it."

He followed the trail of her words and realized he had come to a different conclusion than she had. "You're staying. Go around to the back door of Howling Good Reads. I'll meet you in a couple of minutes."

"But . . ."

"Go to the back door," he snapped. "It's time to find shelter, not go running in the snow."

After a hesitation, she nodded. "Thank you."

He watched until he was sure she was headed toward the back of the building instead of being foolish and plunging into the storm. Like Meg had done the first night she came to the Courtyard. What was wrong with human females that they didn't have sense to find shelter?

Of course, if Meg had taken shelter somewhere else instead of stumbling along until she came to the Courtyard, she might not have found them, and he might never have known her. So maybe Namid was wise to make human females do foolish things.

<We are gone,> Nathan said. <Jester is taking Meg to her den. I will wait for you there.>

That much settled, Simon finished locking up the office. He poked his head into the Three Ps long enough to tell Lorne to close up and come to HGR. Then he trotted to the bookstore's back door. Nudging the Ruthie inside, he found the stockroom full of confused, anxious people. And there was Tess, who looked amused.

"Cars are stuck in the parking lot, so you two aren't getting out," he said, pointing at Ruthie and Heather. Then he pointed at Merri Lee. "And taking a bus tonight is foolish. So you're staying. We'll open the efficiency apartments and bring food for you. You'll have shelter. Marie and Julia Hawkgard will also stay here tonight."

"I have a box of chocolates and a couple of movies," the Ruthie said. "I figured this would be a good movie night."

"What about other people who might be stranded?" Merri Lee asked.

He shook his head. "Someone is trying to hurt the *terra indigene*. Let strangers find shelter elsewhere. They won't be safe here."

While Tess went up to Simon's office to fetch the keys for the efficiency apartments, John drew Simon aside.

"I can stay too," he said. "Having the Hawks stay is good, but having a Wolf guarding the door will be better."

"All right. Take the delivery sled and go to Meat-n-Greens. Get enough food for everyone for tonight." When the back door opened, Simon added, "And take Lorne with you."

That much settled, he bounded up the stairs and reached his office doorway at the same moment Tess was leaving.

"I'll be heading out in a BOW in a few minutes," he said. "Do you want a ride?"

Her brown hair kept twisting into corkscrew curls then relaxing, a sign of indecision. Finally, she shook her head. "I'm going to keep an eye on this part of the Courtyard."

"I don't want us scattered." He didn't think she would willingly share a room with anyone overnight, and even though they were in sight, the rooms above the Liaison's Office felt too far from company or help. He didn't want any of his people isolated.

"I'll be fine," she replied. "I have a change of clothes at the shop. I had planned to take a couple of books from our library and indulge in a snow day reading feast, but I'll just pull a couple of books from HGR's shelves instead. I might even bake a batch of cookies and join the girls for a movie."

It all sounded normal and reasonable, which was why he didn't believe her. This was Tess, and she was rarely interested in things that were normal and reasonable.

"All right," Simon said. "I can—"

"Stop sounding like a pack nurse trying to keep the pups in one place. Go home and work on keeping your own brainless pup from romping outside in a blizzard."

If she was going to put it *that* way . . .

"I'll walk the humans over to the apartments," he said, his hackles raised a little about being called the pack nurse. He held out his hand. She dropped the key ring into it.

When he got back downstairs, Heather and the Ruthie were returning from the front of the store.

"I finally got ahold of Karl," the Ruthie said, smiling at all of them. "He appreciates your letting me stay here."

Simon couldn't think of an appropriate response, so he led his gaggle of chatty humans to the efficiency apartments. He'd opened up some of the Courtyard stores in order to study humans more closely, to *watch* them just as Elliot kept watch over the ones who were the city's government. Looking after some of them made it all so . . . personal. Humans and *terra indigene* weren't supposed to be *friends.* It wasn't done.

But, somehow, it seemed he had done exactly that.

Meg wanted to savor her first ride in a pony sled, but the wind had picked up, driving the snow and making it hard to enjoy anything but the prospect of reaching a warm, dry place. So she huddled in the back of the sled with Nathan while Jester sat on the seat, so bundled up she had barely recognized him. The only one of them who seemed to be enjoying himself was Twister, whose harness bells jingled and whose clumpy pony feet spun the snow all around him as he trotted down the road.

He might be removing enough snow off the road that someone could drive a BOW all the way to the Green Complex, Meg thought. *As long as that someone didn't wait too long.*

Would it make a difference? How would it make a difference? She'd felt edgy, itchy, ever since the snow had started falling, driving Nathan nuts because he picked up the mood but didn't understand the source. Edgy and itchy, but the real prickling under her skin didn't start until she saw Simon.

"We're here," Jester said, twisting on the seat.

Nathan scrambled off the sled, then waited for her to pick up the carry bags containing the food she'd bought during her midday break. He went ahead of her, breaking a trail, for which she was grateful. She wasn't quite as grateful when he stopped at her stairs, shifted into that weird and disturbing half-man / half-Wolf shape, grabbed one of the carry sacks, and bounded up the stairs with it.

The stairs were buried under snow, and it would have been hard for her to haul both bags because she couldn't see where to put her feet, and he *had* been trying to help. Still, she avoided looking directly at him—and at the parts that weren't adequately covered with fur—while she opened her front door, stomped off what snow she could, and stepped inside.

Shoving the carry bag into her hand, he immediately shifted back to pure Wolf.

"Do you want to come in?" she asked.

His answer was to choose a spot on the latticework side of her porch where he had some protection from the snow and wind—and where anyone coming up the stairs wouldn't see him before he saw them.

He lay down and gave her an "Idiot, aren't you going to close the door?" look. So she closed the door, shrugged out of her wet winter clothes, and hung them in the bathroom to drip.

She put the food in the refrigerator and cupboards, and wondered if anyone would think to check for edibles before they all spoiled.

The prophecies and visions didn't work the same in the outside world as they had in the compound. Her own experiences, her own memories provided context. That was why, when she saw Simon standing in the Private doorway, she had slipped into that weird kind of vision that didn't require cutting.

Fur. And teeth. And terrible cold. Then flashes of the remembered images from the visions she had seen about the Courtyard. A storm. Men dressed in black. A sound like motors and hornets. The interior road near Erebus Sanguinati's home. Sam howling in terror. A white room with that narrow bed. And Simon Wolfgard.

She shifted the images this way and that like puzzle pieces, changing the sequence and searching for clues. She could save Sam. If she followed one sequence of images, she could do that much. After that? She wasn't going to give in. She wasn't going to hand over her body like it was someone else's property. She would fight as hard as she could for as long as she could. The only thing she would gain from fighting was her own sense of being a person instead of a thing, because the end would be the same.

This was the beginning of the prophecy she'd seen about herself.

This was the night she was going to die.

CHAPTER 25

S*low and steady,* Monty thought as the cab did a crawl and slide down Whitetail Road. *Slow and steady.*

Every time they reached a traffic light, he listened to the *zzzzzeeeeeeeee* of tires spinning as the cars tried to get enough traction to move through the intersection and keep going. When they finally reached the Chestnut Street intersection and it was clear they were going to wait through several changes of the traffic light before the cab would be able to make the turn, Monty said, "I'll get out here," and paid the driver.

"I think we'll get through this storm all right," the cabby said as Monty got out. "It looks like the snow is letting up."

Asia listened to the *putt putt brrmmm* of a BOW growling its way through snow. Then she called the special messenger.

"Simon Wolfgard is headed for the Green Complex. Your benefactor's property should be there already. Looks like some employees are staying overnight in the apartments above the shops, but there's no one in the business part of the Courtyard who will interfere with you."

"We're all in position. The Stag and Hare is still open and crowded. You can blend in there. As soon as we've reacquired the property, we'll be heading out of the city. I'll call you."

Maybe he would call her. She had a feeling she might be conveniently left behind. That was fine. The messenger and his men were just the diversion she needed to acquire the pup and get out of the Courtyard before the Others knew what happened.

She waited another minute, then left the maintenance garage and hurried to the garage that held the BOW Darrell had driven last week.

That space was empty, but when she opened the next door, that garage contained a BOW. She unhooked the vehicle from its power source and got in. The BOW grumbled when she turned the key, but the engine turned over. She located the controls for the lights and wipers. When she turned on the lights, she noticed the power bar showed a thirty-percent charge.

She couldn't remember how much charge the BOW had used the night Darrell had driven to the Green Complex, and that annoyed her. Asia Crane, SI, would remember that kind of detail from just a glance at the dashboard.

It'll be enough to get me there and back, Asia thought as she turned off the lights and backed out of the garage. *After all, I'm not the one breaking the trail.*

Muscling the BOW into the tracks left by Simon's vehicle, Asia headed for the Green Complex and the bit of fur that was going to make Bigwig and the other backers piles of money and make her a very famous woman.

A gust of wind playfully pushed the BOW. Simon growled, not sure if that gust was simply weather or if it was Air amusing herself. Either way, the direction had shifted, which meant the storm was curling around the city instead of continuing to slam through it. That softening had to be Winter's doing, with help from Air. It was still a good day to get home and stay home, and with tomorrow being Earthday, clearing the delivery area and the parking lot could be done leisurely. And he liked the idea of Wolves digging out the cars stuck in their lot. That would be more fun than being in human form and shoveling.

Maybe they could let the ponies . . . ? No, he wasn't ready to encourage the ponies to reveal their true nature and abilities by clearing the snow in the places where humans could see them. But inside the Courtyard was another matter. Tornado, Cyclone, and Twister were not small forces, but they could work smaller for play. He could tell by the way the road had been cleared that Jester had hitched one of them to the pony sled so that Meg would be able to get home. And Blair had noticed short snow funnels that moved along the Courtyard's interior roads at the speed of a trotting pony. The three ponies were pleased because they didn't get to use their natures often in this part of Thaisia, and Blair was pleased because he wasn't using time or fuel to plow the roads.

And Meg could drive anywhere she wanted within the Courtyard without getting stuck in the snow, which pleased all of them.

It took more time than usual, but he reached the visitor's parking at the Green Complex and slowed to consider. The lane leading back to the garages hadn't been cleared at all, and any vehicles that were back there weren't going anywhere for a day or two. That left the spots across the road from the complex.

Someone with large, powerful limbs had swiped most of the snow from the guest spots. Simon wasn't sure two BOWs could fit into the cleared space and have room for the drivers to get out, but there was plenty of room for him, and nobody else would be using a vehicle to get home. In his smoke form, Vlad could travel faster in this weather than any other *terra indigene* except the Elementals.

He studied the snow next to the cleared space. Then he turned off the BOW's lights and let his eyes adjust. With the lights on, it appeared that what stood beside the parking space was a swirl of snow. But in the dark, that swirl became a shape.

Henry Beargard was a large man and a massive Grizzly. But when Henry took the spirit bear form, he was even bigger. And standing on his hind legs, as he was now, he looked like he could pluck the stars from the sky.

<Henry?> Simon asked.

<Thaisia is restless. I am restless. A different kind of storm is coming.> Henry paused. <The first time Meg shared a prophecy with us, she saw a storm.>

He growled. She had shared those words with Henry, the spirit guide for their Courtyard. And the Grizzly was restless.

Henry dropped to all fours and moved off. <The storm is speaking. I must listen.>

Simon watched him go, his form visible only because the Wolf knew what to look for. He parked the BOW and hurried across the road, wondering if he'd find Sam at his apartment or at Meg's. Then he stopped, listened.

<Tess?> he called. <Did you change your mind about staying around A Little Bite to wait out the storm?>

<No,> she replied. <Why?>

<I heard another BOW heading this way.> Nothing out there now, but he *had* heard it.

<I'll check the garages and get back to you,> she said.

He hurried to his apartment. As he put his key in the lock, Nathan said, <Sam is up here with Meg.>

Simon finished unlocking his door, but went up the stairs to Meg's porch. Nathan's fur had a light coating of snow, making the watch Wolf nearly invisible in his chosen spot.

Nathan cocked his head. <Simon?>

He didn't have a chance to respond before Tess called, <Simon!>

<Report,> he said.

<Another BOW was taken from the business garages. Whoever took it didn't bother to close the door.>

<Blair will chew someone's tail about that.> A thought occurred to him that formed a bone in his throat. <Where are the humans we allowed to stay in the apartments?>

<They're in the apartments, making snacks and choosing movies to watch.> Tess paused. <I found tracks, mostly filled in now, coming from the direction of our customer parking lot. An intruder may have climbed a snowbank and come into the Courtyard—and maybe took the BOW as well.>

A BOW wouldn't do anyone any good on the city's streets, especially in this weather, but someone could get fairly deep into the Courtyard before finding roads the ponies hadn't cleared at all.

Simon went back down the stairs. Nathan followed him. They stood perfectly still—and listened.

Jester looked at his charges, then at the big flakes of snow that would have been prettier if there hadn't been so many of them.

Twelve little ponies all snug in their stalls, he thought. *And one Coyote who was going to snuggle into the straw with them.*

No point going to the Green Complex. He had everything he needed right here. And he wanted to keep an eye on the ponies, especially old Hurricane, who wasn't having an easy time making his way through the snow. That was something he needed to mention to Winter. The Elementals' steeds were slow to age, but even their time in the world came to an end, and their place was taken by youngsters who filled the same niche. Still, it was never easy when a pony reached his time, and Hurricane was a favorite of Air and Water.

He started to close the door all the way when he heard a sound and stepped outside to pinpoint the direction. A motor, yes, but not a BOW or any other vehicle used in the Courtyard.

Baring his teeth, Jester shifted his ears to their Coyote form to catch the sounds better. More than one vehicle with a buzzy motor.

Hadn't Meg said something about buzzy motors? And now that he heard them in a slightly different way, he realized he *had* heard this sound around the Courtyard over the past few days. *But not inside.*

<Intruders!> he shouted.

His own warning was eclipsed by an explosion coming from the direction of the Utilities Complex.

Simon heard the explosion, pinpointed the direction, and shouted, <Blair!> while Nathan howled a warning.

<We're being attacked!> The incredulity in Blair's voice swiftly changed to fury. <I'll deal with these intruders.>

<They might have guns!>

No response. None was needed. Anyone coming in to blow up a part of the Courtyard would have guns.

Another explosion, the sound fainter and coming from the western side of the Courtyard—the side closest to Lakeside Park, the side where there was a gap in the fence because of the fire a few days ago.

Howls in the west from the Wolves responding to that threat. Nathan beside him, growling and restless, wanting to rush off and help the same way *he* wanted to meet the enemy and destroy them.

As Simon spun around to tell Meg he had to leave, Crows were screaming about attackers. And then he heard Jester's fear-filled and angry shout, <The Pony Barn is on fire!>

Jester listened as the Crowgard raised a call to battle, listened as that buzzy motor sound came closer and closer to the Pony Barn. He watched as smoke filled the winter sky above the Utilities Complex and thought, <Blair is going to rip out someone's belly for this.>

What else had Meg told them about the buzzy motors? Men dressed in black.

Men with guns. Sam howling. But Sam wasn't howling. Plenty of other Wolves, but not the pup, so . . .

Hurricane bolted out of his stall in the back of the barn and cantered toward the open door where Jester stood, followed by Cyclone and Fog. A moment later, one stall window shattered, then another. And a moment after that . . .

"Out!" Jester shouted at the ponies as fire suddenly roared up from the deep beds of straw in two of the stalls. "All of you, get out!" Then he added in a shout to anyone who could hear him, <The Pony Barn is on fire!>

Hurricane bolted out the door.

Buzzy motors. A gunshot. Blood spraying the snow as Hurricane went down.

Jester howled in fury and ran to the pony. Another shot as he dove for cover, Hurricane's dying body shielding him from the bullet.

The rest of the ponies shifted as they surged out of the barn. While they looked like horses, they were now the Elementals' steeds, and the screams of rage that rose from deep within the Courtyard as Hurricane died came from Earth, Air, Fire, Water . . . and Winter.

Cyclone and Fog were the next steeds out the door. As Fog ran, he instantly veiled the land all around the Pony Barn, while Cyclone whipped up the fallen snow into a smothering, stinging weapon. They chased the buzzy motors, no longer bound to flesh that would stumble in deep snow or be stopped by bullets.

Quicksand and Twister raced after Fog and Cyclone, while Tornado and Tidal Wave raced for the Utilities Complex, the snow spinning into a funnel around the hooves of one and rising in a growing wave behind the other. Avalanche kicked up the snow around the barn, smashing through the barn wall and sending a river of snow into the stalls to smother the fire.

Earthshaker and Mist galloped off, heading for the trouble in the western part of the Courtyard. Thunder and Lightning were the last two who leaped out of the barn, cracking the sky with savage light and a rumble that shook the ground.

"Wait!" Jester shouted at them.

They turned back, snorting and stomping.

He didn't know what to tell them. He took care of them as his service to the Courtyard, and they listened to him up to a point. But they weren't his to command.

Then he didn't need to decide what to tell them. In a voice filled with fury, Winter said, <Coyote, bring the sleigh to the lake.>

Simon rushed up the stairs and almost knocked Meg over when he bounded into her apartment. He grabbed her arms, aware of Sam running out of the kitchen. The boy's eyes were bright, but Simon didn't have time to consider if that brightness came from excitement or fear.

"Meg, I have to go. The Courtyard is under attack. You and Sam stay here until I get back. Do you understand me? *Stay here.*"

"Go," she said. "We'll be all right."

He raced down the stairs, and he and Nathan trotted toward the BOW. Then he stopped. Three entrances into the Courtyard could accommodate vehicles when the roads were clear. Someone must have come in through the Utilities Complex gate to cause that explosion. But there were also those two breaks in the fence where someone could sneak in. Someone had come in through the one on Parkside Avenue to cause the explosion in the western part of the Courtyard. The other one . . .

Growling, Simon turned to Nathan. "The hole in the Main Street fence is between our stores and the Green Complex."

<Deep snow,> Nathan said. <Hard to break a trail.>

"They have runners they can put on their feet. Skis," he corrected, thinking of the human word. "And those sleds with motors." Buzzy, annoying things, but maybe useful. "I'll find Blair. You check that hole in the fence and make sure none of those monkeys invading our land are trying to come *here*." He looked back at Meg's apartment.

Nathan took off. Simon ran to the BOW and headed for the Utilities Complex at a reckless speed.

Meg rubbed her sweaty hands on her jeans, then held one out to the boy. "Come on, Sam. We're going to stay at your house until Simon returns."

"But I wanna stay here," Sam protested.

She shook her head, unable to explain, even to herself, why she wanted to be in a place where the door opened to ground instead of stairs.

He whined quietly as she led him out the kitchen door to the second-floor entrance in Simon's apartment. When they reached the living room, she knelt in front of him, that gray-eyed boy who made her wonder if she had any younger brothers. She had never heard of a male *cassandra sangue,* and lately had begun to wonder what happened to the male children who were born to the girls who were bred. Were they abandoned? Killed? Fostered somewhere for some other use? She would never know. But for a little while, there had been someone in her life who could have been her little brother, and she loved him.

"Listen to me, Sam," she said quietly. "Some bad people have come into the Courtyard, and they're causing trouble." She could feel him shrinking into himself. When she took his hands, they were furry and no longer shaped like a human's. "You need to mind me and do exactly what I say. All right?"

He nodded. She wasn't sure he could speak anymore.

"I want you to shift to Wolf form. You're stronger and faster as a Wolf."

He struggled to form words. "Safety line?"

"No." She shook her head. "Not this time. Don't let *anyone* put you in a harness or attach a safety line to you. If anyone tries to do that, you bite them as hard as you can and you run. You understand?"

"Bite and run."

"Yes."

She helped him out of his shoes, sweater, and shirt. "You shift now."

Sam went behind the couch to finish pulling off his clothes. Meg sat back on her heels. Might not come to anything. Maybe she was being foolish or had misunderstood. Prophecies could change. A different choice in a string of choices could change everything. She and Sam were here, in the apartment, not out there where there was fear and pain and death. Why would they need to leave here until Simon and Nathan returned?

The prickling under her skin suddenly returned, and in the quiet that surrounded the Green Complex, she heard the sound of a BOW.

Vlad, Nyx, and a handful of their kin flowed over the snow like segments of a black serpent as they headed for the Utilities Complex. Other Sanguinati were headed for the western breach to help the Hawks and Wolves fight the intruders.

He and Nyx hadn't questioned Erebus's command to destroy whatever dared touch the *terra indigene*. Would these monkeys have started a war with the Others if Meg hadn't come to the Courtyard? Maybe not. But someone the monkeys wanted back so much was someone the *terra indigene* were determined to keep.

Besides, he liked Meg, and her diligence in delivering Erebus's movies gave Grandfather an untarnished pleasure the Sanguinati patriarch hadn't experienced in many years.

<Vlad, look,> Nyx said.

A funnel of snow racing toward the buildings in the Utilities Complex. Beside it, moving just as fast, was a rising wave of snow.

Gunshots. A scream of pain. And the buzzy sound of snowmobiles.

Vlad and his kin flowed past the charred wing of a Hawk but didn't see the rest of the body. As they rounded one corner of the main building, he saw a handful of intruders on snowmobiles. He saw Ferus trying to crawl away from the part of the building that was blown out and burning—and he saw one of the intruders raise a gun and shoot the already wounded Wolf.

Vlad shifted partway, catching the gunman's attention. Distracted by smoke starting to take human shape, the man didn't see Blair, who was in the between form, until the Wolf knocked him off the snowmobile and tore out his throat.

The rest of the intruders are going to get away, Vlad thought savagely. Their machines would get them out of the Courtyard, and they would use the storm to hide among the rest of the monkeys.

Then he realized the funnel of snow was heading straight for the Utilities gate and would reach it before the intruders could. As for the wave of snow . . .

<Get Ferus,> he told Nyx, seeing the tidal wave of snow crest and understanding what was about to happen. <I'll get Blair.>

Nyx shifted to her human form from the waist up, grabbed Ferus around the middle, and flowed over the snow, half carrying, half dragging the wounded Wolf. Vlad shifted all the way to human, grabbed Blair's shoulders as the enforcer continued to tear at the enemy, and almost had his face ripped open when the Wolf turned on him and lashed out.

"Come with me!" Vlad shouted. "Now, Blair!"

A glance behind him was enough. Blair ran, and Vlad, shifting back to the safety of smoke, flowed after him as Tidal Wave released the snow and sent it crashing down, catching the three monkeys who had tried to evade Tornado. One man, jettisoned from Tornado's funnel, flew over their heads and landed in a circle of smoke that grew hands and mouths and fangs.

Ignoring the feast, Vlad headed for the spot where Nyx waited with Ferus.

"Tornado left the Courtyard," Blair said, shifting all the way back to human as he trotted up to them. "There's going to be some damage to the monkeys' part of the city."

"Do we care?" Vlad asked.

Blair looked at Ferus, who was turning the snow red. "No. We don't care." He studied the ground and buildings around them. "Come on. I think we can muscle one of the BOWs out of the garage and get Ferus to the Wolfgard bodywalker."

A frantic knocking on Simon's front door.

"Meg? Meg! Are you in there?"

Meg looked back at Sam, whose furry face peered at her from behind the couch. Then she went to the door, pulled it open, and just stared at the blue sweater showing under Asia's white parka.

"Meg . . ." Asia began.

"I don't know that color blue," Meg said, feeling cold inside as Asia stepped into the apartment.

"I know I'm not supposed to be here," Asia said in a rush. "But, Meg, you have to listen to me. Some men are coming for you. All the other things that are happening now are just a diversion. And the other things that happened over the past few days? Those men were studying how the Wolves react. I have a BOW. It's right outside. I'll help you get away."

"I don't know that color."

"What difference does *that* make?" Asia shouted.

"I saw that blue in the vision, with the sugar and the skull and crossbones," Meg said, her voice so rough it produced an answering growl from Sam. "*You* tried to poison the ponies."

Something in Asia's face shifted, erasing all pretense of concern. "It was just a means to an end, like this is."

"Like what is?"

"I meant what I said. They're coming for you, Meg, but I'm not interested in *you*. Just give me the pup. I'll be on my way, and you can run. You might even make it out of the Courtyard and find another place to hide for a while longer. Maybe forever."

Stalling for time, Meg realized. All the talk was just a way to stall for time. But there was one thing she needed to know. "Why do you want Sam?"

Asia smirked. "I know some men who would love to have some leverage over a Courtyard leader. They're powerful men who could get a lot of concessions for us humans. A couple of them might even enjoy having an exotic pet for a while."

He's not property, Meg thought as the cold inside her gave way to a furious heat. Giving Asia a hard shove, she shouted, "Run, Sam!"

Asia returned the shove, knocking Meg into a wall. Sam exploded from behind the couch. He had filled out a lot in the past three weeks, making up for the lack of growth during the years he'd been frozen by his mother's death. His teeth didn't sink into anything but Asia's parka sleeve, but his weight and the way he swung his own body to bring down his prey was enough to throw her to her hands and knees.

Meg pushed off the wall, shouted "Sam!" and ran out the door. She wasn't dressed for outside—no coat, no boots; nothing but jeans, her heaviest sweater, and shoes. But she ran to the BOW Asia had driven and yanked the door open. Sam jumped in and scrambled out of her way as she got in, turned the key, and put the BOW in gear before she closed her door. She was driving away from the apartments by the time Asia reached the road.

Glancing in her rearview mirror, she saw staggered lights approaching the Green Complex. Those must be the men Asia said were after her.

"You did good, Sam." She'd heard the explosion and knew there was a problem up ahead, so she made the first left-hand turn she could, pushing for speed on a road oddly stripped of snow. "You did good." Then she added silently, *Now it's my turn.*

At first, it didn't look like there was much wrong with the Utilities Complex. Then Simon spotted Blair kneeling beside Ferus and saw the bloody snow. He pulled up close to them, put the BOW in park, and jumped out.

"How bad?" he asked Blair, adding a silent call to Vlad, who immediately stopped his efforts to shift the snow around the garage doors and strode toward them.

"One of the Hawks is dead, and Ferus took a couple of bullets," Blair replied. "Not sure how bad he's hurt inside, but he's bleeding plenty. We need to get him to the Wolfgard bodywalker."

Simon sprang up and opened the BOW's back door. In the winter, most BOWs carried some basics: two blankets, a short-handled shovel, a snow brush, and an ice scraper. He grabbed the blankets and laid them out in the snow next to Ferus. He and Blair lifted the wounded Wolf onto the blankets, wrapped him, and eased him into the back compartment. Blair went around to the passenger's seat, but Simon waited for Vlad.

"Something?" he asked, stepping away from the BOW.

"Nyx says there is a broken feast," Vlad reported. "Three of the intruders are dead and already growing cold, but the other two . . . The hearts still beat, and the blood is still hot."

"Then don't waste them."

"Big hole in the back of the building. The wave of snow smothered the fire. I don't know if we'll find any of our own in there."

Simon bit back impatience. Ferus was bleeding. He didn't have time for this.

The Sanguinati did not always consider such things, but he knew Vlad well enough to know this wasn't idle talk.

"The Elementals' steeds are running with no hands on the reins," Vlad said.

He wasn't sure that was true, but he shrugged. "That isn't up to us."

"What do we do if Winter unleashes her fury?"

He knew the answer to *that*. As he opened the BOW's door, he said, "We do our best to survive."

Six snowmobiles roared up to the Green Complex. The special messenger pointed to three of his men and said, "Go after her. I'll catch up."

They raced after the BOW.

Pushing up his goggles, he gave Asia a cold stare. "You couldn't follow orders, could you?"

"You want Meg Corbyn. I just want the Wolf pup." When the stare didn't change, Asia added, "She was going to bolt. I held her up as long as I could."

He turned his head and said to one man, "Take her back to her car."

"My car is stuck in the parking lot," Asia protested.

"Then you'd better get it unstuck before these creatures notice you," he said harshly. "You can take the ride or walk." He put his goggles back on, then drove off with one member of his team. The other man waited, watching her.

She hesitated, tried to think it through. Then she realized he was about to leave her and hurried to mount behind him. She pressed against his back, shielding her face as best she could while they raced back to the business part of the Courtyard.

She needed time to think. The special messenger would have cut her out of the deal, would have made some excuse so his benefactor wouldn't have to give her or her backers any payment for their help in finding Meg Corbyn. And that would probably sour the TV deal she'd been promised. But the messenger didn't have Meg yet, and if she telephoned her backers fast, she could spin the story any way that would give her the best paycheck.

The team that set fire to the Pony Barn raced toward the Corvine gate. The leader looked over his shoulder and bared his teeth in a grin. Stupid fucking animals. If you left a gate open, that was an invitation to come on in, wasn't it?

The Crows winging a few feet above the snow, following them, would have made good target practice, but his orders were to get out of the Courtyard as soon as the assignment was complete.

Shooting one of those ponies hadn't taken extra time and was a bonus distraction. Besides, what did the Others use ponies for anyway? Transportation? Food?

Then fog suddenly surrounded him and his team, so thick he could barely see the headlights on the other snowmobiles.

"Halt!" he shouted, hoping his men wouldn't run over him. How could fog roll in so fast? And where the fuck was the road that would take them to the gate? And what was that sound?

A gust of wind pushed the snowmobile forward, and heavy rain drenched him.

Rain? When it was *this* cold? What the . . . ?

The last man in line screamed as spinning winds and punishing rain turned snow into an ice field. The snowmobiles slid away from one another, lost in the thick fog that should have been blown away with the wind—and wasn't.

Gasping for breath, the leader tried to see something, anything. "Report!" he shouted.

"Here!" a member of his team answered.

The leader didn't have time to shout a warning before a funnel of snow appeared out of the fog, snatched the man off the snowmobile, and turned away in a move that didn't belong to any natural storm.

Another shout. The lights of a snowmobile headed right for him. He revved the engine of his own machine, then realized with a shock that the runners were frozen to the snow. The other man veered at the last minute, clipping the leader's machine enough to break it out of the ice before the other machine suddenly pitched forward, tossing the rider over the handles.

The fog lifted as quickly as it had arrived, giving the team leader a clear view of one of his men struggling and thrashing and screaming and *sinking into the snow.*

And he suddenly had a clear view of a horse the color of sand standing beside the odd snow, watching him.

Snow acting like quicksand. Gods above and below, what kind of place is a Courtyard anyway that snow can turn into quicksand?

Seconds later, only silence. A snowmobile, its nose buried. Unmarred snow that gave no indication that a man had just died beneath it. And a horse staring at him with hate-filled eyes.

He raced away, ignoring the twisted machines and twisted bodies, intent on outrunning the horse that raced after him.

The right side of the snowmobile sank, pitching him off. He rolled, then tried to get to his feet, but the snow sucked his legs down. Unbalanced, he fell back, and his arms sank to his elbows, pinning him.

"Help me!" he shouted. "Help!"

The Crows winged in, and the horse ran off. Before he could free an arm, they were on him, shifting into three naked females and one male. They yanked off his goggles, ripped off his ski mask, tore open his parka.

"What do we do with him, Jenni?" the male asked.

The one named Jenni cocked her head to one side, then the other. "He killed a pony. And he's one of the monkeys who were trying to take our Meg. So I say one for me." Her head shifted from human female to black-feathered Crow. She grabbed his head in strong hands and plucked out one eye with her beak. Tipping her head back, she swallowed the eye, then shifted back to a human female with a few black feathers still mixed with her hair. "And one for you."

The male's head changed. The Crow plucked out the man's other eye.

Ignoring his screams, they were gone in a flutter of wings, leaving him blinded and bleeding and half buried in the snow.

Meg slowed the BOW to a crawl as she drove over Ripple Bridge. The sky was a dark gray that made it hard to see without headlights, but the headlights would have made *her* easier to see.

Once they crossed the bridge, she rolled down her window and listened, then looked at Sam. "Do you hear the bad men?"

He whined, which she took for an affirmative answer.

Rolling up the window, she drove as fast as she could to the Chambers. She had to get this much done. She had to.

The interior roads weren't clear of snow, and the BOW slipped and slid and a couple of times almost got stuck. Finally reaching the gate in front of Erebus's home, Meg jumped out and held the door open for Sam. Before he could dash off, she picked him up and staggered to the gate.

"Mr. Erebus! Mr. Erebus! We need help!"

The door opened, and Erebus glided over the snow-covered walkway.

"Why is our Meg out in such weather when an enemy is among us?"

She tried to lift Sam above the gate, but couldn't do it. "Those men," she panted. "They're after Sam. I *know* they're after Sam. Please take him, Mr. Erebus. Simon is protecting the Courtyard, and there's no one else who can keep those men away from Sam except you. I know it's against the rules for anyone to enter the Chambers, but he needs your help. He needs you."

Sam began to squirm and struggle, but she held on to the pup while her eyes stayed fixed on the old vampire. "Please help us."

Erebus pulled open the gate. "Come in. Both of you will be safe here."

She heard snowmobiles approaching from two directions. They didn't need to stay on the roads, so they must have split up in the hopes of trapping her. And that meant she had run out of time.

She shoved Sam into Erebus's arms and stepped back. "I'll lead the men away from here."

"No," Erebus said. "You come in too."

"Sam won't be safe if I stay." She cut off his objections by adding, "I know this."

She got back in the BOW and took off, shivering from cold and blinking back tears as she drove recklessly down the interior road that would take her to her fate.

An explosion, Monty thought as he hung up the phone. *In the Courtyard. Oh, gods.* He grabbed his coat and headed out to commandeer whatever car was available.

When his mobile phone rang, he almost ignored it, but Debany and MacDonald were already on patrol, and they might be calling to report. "Montgomery."

"Kowalski, here. Ruthie just called. There was an explosion in the Courtyard, maybe more than one, but not near the shops. I'm heading there now. Thought you should know."

Then the Utilities Complex was probably the target of one of those explosions. "How can you get there?"

"I do some cross-country skiing. I can make it to the Courtyard."

He understood why Kowalski wanted to get to Ruth, but how were the Others going to respond to *any* human right now, especially an armed man? "You take care, Karl, and stay in touch."

"Yes, sir."

When Monty stepped outside, Louis Gresh was waiting for him.

"I heard," Louis said. "You're going to need help. And you're going to need someone driving who can handle this snow."

"Thanks," Monty said as they got in Louis's car.

"Just doing my part to keep us alive," Louis replied.

As they reached the intersection of Parkside and Chestnut, they saw the flashing lights of patrol cars and emergency vehicles. Louis shook his head and continued on Chestnut. "We'll go up Main Street. We'll have the best chance of getting through that way."

Monty just nodded—and hoped they got through in time.

The special messenger and his fourth man caught up to the three he'd sent to chase down the benefactor's property. They were idling in front of a black wrought-iron fence.

According to the information he'd been given, the damn female was supposed to be physically weak and without the practical knowledge needed to operate machines or drive vehicles. Unless they were following a decoy, which he didn't believe, the benefactor's information was out of date.

"Where?" he snapped.

"She left the pup with the old man who lives in that little building," one man reported. "We saw her turn onto the road up there." He pointed. "We'll have no trouble catching her."

Maybe not, he thought. But there were things happening now that hadn't shown up during their testing forays—like those snow funnels that appeared out of nowhere and disappeared just as fast. In addition to that, the team that had set fire to the barn wasn't answering their radios anymore, and the men who came in through the western breach in the fence were talking about the ground shaking and water twisting up into frozen walls, blocking their escape. They were heading for the exit around where the Crows roosted or whatever the fuck Crows did. Trouble was, according to the map Asia Crane had provided, the Wolves were between the western breach and the Corvine gate.

Maybe he should have wondered why the money had been so good for this assignment, but he hadn't, and none of them would get anything if the property wasn't reacquired.

He wagged a finger at two of the men. At least Asia Crane's fumbling had supplied them with a bonus acquisition. "You two get the pup from the old man. We'll reacquire the property, and then we'll all get out of here."

That said, the messenger raced up the road the property had taken.

Simon and Blair carried Ferus into the bodywalker's den in the Wolfgard Complex and laid him in the bed of straw she had prepared.

"Bullets," she growled as she unwrapped the blankets. "Are the monkeys with the guns still alive?"

"No," Blair replied.

She nodded in satisfaction, then said, "Go. I will do what I can, and Namid will decide if he is to remain with us or become a part of Thaisia."

They backed out and looked at each other, not sure where they were most needed—until Simon heard Sam's panicked *<Arroooo! Arroooooo! Meg's gone! Meg's gone!>*

<Sam!> Simon called. <Where are you?>

The pup didn't answer him, but Vlad did.

The Sanguinati gathered around Erebus's home, all smoke and shadows as the two men pushed open the gate and stepped into the Chambers. Sam had stopped trying to escape from Erebus's arms and now howled and howled as if his puppy heart was broken.

Erebus stood on the threshold, smiling at the prey who were so obliging to bring themselves to the feast.

"Give us the pup, old man," one of the monkeys said.

"Eh?" Erebus replied, turning his head as if to hear the words better. As if he couldn't hear a heartbeat anywhere within Sanguinati land.

"Give us the pup if you know what's good for you."

"Come, little one," Erebus whispered, taking a step back. "This is not for you to see."

"Hey!" one monkey shouted as the two men rushed toward the closing door.

<They are more than prey,> Erebus said, his words rolling through all the Sanguinati. <They are enemies of our Meg, and they are enemies of the Sanguinati. Take them away and punish them.>

Vlad was so startled by the words, his smoke form condensed into a partial human shape. Punishment was a death that took days and broke the mind before it destroyed the body. Only the most hated enemies were condemned in that way, and the words told him the depth of Erebus's hatred for these particular humans. So Grandfather's next words didn't surprise him.

<Vlad. Find our Meg. Keep her safe.>

As his kin surrounded the two intruders, he sent a message to Simon. <Sam is with Grandfather.> Then he shifted fully to smoke and pursued the men who were pursuing Meg.

Asia picked herself up, still not sure what happened. They hit something. Or something hit them. But she'd heard the sound of bone breaking before the driver went flying and the snowmobile went up a snowbank at a bad angle and tipped over. Lucky for her, she bailed out before it tipped, but . . .

Had she really seen a giant bear made out of snow just before the accident? Impossible!

Asia glanced at the dead man and swallowed hard. Then again, *something* had swiped off the man's face.

A howl rose from behind her. She didn't know squat about the supposed tonal qualities of Wolf howls, but that particular Wolf sounded pissed off, and she didn't want to run into him.

She took a step toward the snowmobile, thinking she could right it and drive out of the Courtyard, maybe all the way back to her apartment, where she would pack and be ready to leave town as soon as the driving ban lifted.

Something nearby growled.

Stepping away from the snowmobile, she began walking toward the Market Square and the parking lot. She didn't give a damn about the driving ban. She'd just get her car unstuck and get out of town.

Nothing growled as she continued walking, but another howl was flung to the night sky—and was answered.

Asia broke into a jog.

Meg braked too hard and did a 360-degree spin before regaining control and stomping on the power pedal. She'd be scared later about what she'd just done. Right now, she had to get to the lake. She wasn't sure if Winter would be there, but Spring would be. Maybe Air and Water too. She hadn't met Earth or Fire, the other two cousins, but she'd filled a couple of library requests for each of them in the past week. If they were around, they would help her. Wouldn't they?

A yellow triangle next to the power bar warned her that the BOW wasn't going to run much longer. Behind her, she glimpsed lights. Those men, the enemy, were still after her.

Almost to the Courtyard Creek Bridge. And once she crossed the bridge, she would be in the Elementals' part of the Courtyard.

Simon stripped off his clothes, shifted to Wolf, and burst out of the Wolfgard Complex, followed by Blair and Elliot. <Meg!>

<She's headed for the lake,> Vlad reported. <There are three intruders behind her, and I'm behind them.>

The lake. Not too far from the Wolfgard land, then. Not far from him.

He took off, running, loping, bounding into and through drifts in the road, moving steadily toward the lake and Meg.

As Thunder and Lightning galloped toward the lake, Jester hung on to the front seat of the sleigh. Every time the horses' hooves slammed into the ground, the potential for another storm grew in intensity. It could fade; the storms did sometimes. But Jester doubted this one would fade.

Humans often said payback was a bitch. Well, *Winter* was looking for payback.

Having survived the results when Winter was in full temper, he almost felt sorry for the humans.

Almost.

The yellow warning triangle was replaced by a blinking lightning bolt—the "charge me" symbol. A few seconds later, the BOW rolled to a stop within sight of the bridge. Meg got out, poised to run across the bridge. But the snowmobiles roared into sight, the headlights blinding her.

She knew what it felt like to be free, to have friends, to have a *life*. To have people she loved. She wasn't going to let anyone take that away from her.

She bolted down the bank that led to the frozen creek. Harder to catch her, harder to disappear with her if she could reach the creek where she would be in the open and the Others could see her.

Her feet went out from under her, and she slid to the edge of the constructed retaining wall next to the bridge. As soon as she lowered herself to the creek, she screamed "Help!" and began shuffling across the ice.

"Stop!" a man shouted behind her. "Stop, you stupid bitch!"

Meg kept moving toward the other bank, slipping and sliding while men shouted for her to stop.

"Winter!" she yelled. "*Winter!*"

"Meg?" The voice seemed to come from everywhere—from the snow and from a coldness that was so bitter, Meg felt like she was breathing ice.

"Stop!" a man shouted.

The crack of gunshot. Something hit the ice near Meg's right foot. Shards struck her, and she jerked to her left, still moving toward the bank.

Cracking sounds under her feet. Remembering Spring's warning, Meg veered toward the right. Another shot sprayed shards of ice that had her turning back toward the weakened ice.

Winter suddenly appeared on the bank.

"They have guns!" Meg shouted. She tried to hurry and get off the ice before her friend was noticed by the men with guns. *Just another step,* she thought. *Just another step.*

"Meg, no!" Winter screamed.

As she took the last step, her hands reaching for the stones that acted as a natural containment wall on this side of the creek, the ice shattered beneath her feet, and Meg went under.

CHAPTER 27

The special messenger swore when the property fell through the ice. Still had a chance to retrieve her. If he could drive off the bitch standing on the bank, his men could cross the bridge and . . .

Two more women suddenly appeared. One of the women leaped from the bank, smashing through the ice while black smoke flowed across the creek toward the hole. The white-haired woman who was dressed like something out of a creepy novel *screamed,* and then the one standing next to her *screamed.* And then he couldn't see anything because it was snowing so hard, and that snow was whipped by such a savage wind, he couldn't even see his own hand. As he fought his way back up the incline to his snowmobile, he heard tree limbs snapping around him.

What were those bitches?

No chance to recover the property now. Good thing the benefactor had made a subsidiary deal for the Wolf pup with the Sparkletown bigwig who had hired Asia Crane.

Had Asia tried to double-cross all of them when she went after the pup by herself? He didn't know and, at this point, he didn't care. He just hoped the pup's acquisition would be profitable enough to make this job worthwhile.

He crawled the remaining distance toward the barely visible lights of two snowmobiles.

"Report!" he yelled, fighting to gain his feet.

He tripped over one man whose head was almost twisted off the shoulders. Where was the other member of his team? Fucking coward must have run off.

Or was taken?

Lightning tore the sky, closely followed by thunder that shook the ground.

When he reached his snowmobile, he took a moment to recall where he needed to go in order to escape from this place. Then he roared across the bridge.

Fuck this assignment and this fucking city. As soon as he handed over the pup and got paid, he was getting back to civilization. And he hoped his balls fell off if he *ever* took another assignment that involved the fucking Others.

Cold. So cold. Already impossible to breathe.

Suddenly, Meg's hands felt the sting of bitter cold air. She tried to grab for something, anything. She thought she felt fur, but she couldn't hold on.

Cold. So cold.

She slipped back into the dark.

<Meg!>

Simon clamped his teeth around her forearm firmly enough to hold her. When Vlad flung her toward the surface, Simon felt her fingers in his fur as she tried to grab him. But she hadn't been strong enough to hold on.

The ground rumbled beneath him, shaking him off his slippery perch just enough that Meg's head went under the water again. He hauled on her arm, pulling her back up while Blair grabbed for anything he could without ripping her skin with his teeth and claws.

Vlad was doing his best to keep her where they could reach her, but as smoke he couldn't help her, and in human form he risked being swept under the ice. Even Water was trying to get Meg to safety, but she didn't know how—*none* of them knew how—to help a human.

Shifting to a between form that kept the Wolf head and teeth but gave him the fur-covered body of a man, he finally got his fingers through a belt loop in her jeans and pulled her up the bank.

<Meg!> Smelling blood, he noticed the gash in her chin. He licked off the blood, licked and licked to clean the wound. <Meg!>

Lightning flashed. Thunder rumbled.

<We don't know human medicine,> Blair said. <How do we fix her?>

<We take her to a human bodywalker. Hospital,> Simon replied. She was so cold. If she were a Wolf, he would know what to do. But she wasn't a Wolf, she was Meg, and he didn't know what to do except take her to the humans who could fix her.

He squinted at the blinding snow, hunching over Meg to give her some protection. How were they supposed to reach a hospital?

Jester was suddenly in front of him, holding out blankets. Then Winter placed a freezing hand on his shoulder and said, "I'll drive you to the human place."

Wrapping Meg in one blanket, he carried her to the sleigh and climbed into the backseat. He settled on one side of her while Jester pressed against her on the other side, tucking the second blanket around all of them as best he could.

Simon stared at Blair, his enforcer, and Vlad, who was Erebus Sanguinati's most trusted weapon. <The Elementals gave the intruders a backhanded slap, and that storm will slow their attempt to escape. Find them. Don't let *any* of our enemies get out of the Courtyard.>

Blair howled the Song of Battle and took off. Vlad gave him a nod, shifted to smoke, and followed his own trail.

Air leaped into the front seat beside Winter, who looked back at Simon. Despite his own fury, it took all the courage he had not to whimper at what he saw in her eyes.

"Run, my boys. Run!" Winter shouted to Thunder and Lightning. "Run for our Meg. AND LET THE STORM FLY!"

She screamed, and Air screamed.

Simon held on to Meg, licking the leaking wound on her chin as the Elementals unleashed their rage on the city of Lakeside. And he wondered if the hospital with its human healers would still be there by the time the sleigh arrived.

Monty and Louis were a couple of blocks from the intersection of Chestnut and Main when the new storm came out of nowhere and hit Lakeside with an insane fury.

Fog rolled so thick through the streets, they couldn't see anything but the taillights of the car ahead of them—and half the time they couldn't even see those. Mist followed fog, creating a thin glaze of ice on the street, and what fell on the windows defied the wipers' ability to keep the glass clear. Snow fell heavy and fast, and the traffic that had been making slow but steady progress was instantly bogged down. Tires spun on the ice, and the wind was a battering force that slammed some of smaller cars into other vehicles as funnels appeared and disappeared, ripping a door off a car and flinging it through the window of a nearby building. Postal boxes were torn off their concrete platforms, becoming another hazard for motorists and pedestrians alike. Even people, knocked off their feet by the wind, were flung into the fog-filled streets, invisible to drivers. Lightning flashes came so fast, they reminded Monty of strobe lights, and the thunder that followed each flash rattled buildings and shattered windows.

"Turn on the radio," Louis said. "Don't know what good it will do, but I'd like to know what we're in for."

Monty turned on the radio.

". . . blew in out of nowhere. They're calling it the storm of the century. We've had a foot of snow in the past fifteen minutes, and there is no sign of it letting up. Lightning strikes have taken out some power nodes, and several areas of Lakeside are without electricity. Telephones are erratic. Ice is coating the lines, and they're snapping under the weight. So are tree limbs. Being outside isn't just hazardous, it's suicidal. We're WZAS, but we're not being a wiseass now, folks. This is big and it's bad. Get off the streets. Get to some kind of shelter. This is Ann—"

Static. Monty shut off the radio.

A storm that hit the city with insane fury. The radio station might be saying it came out of nowhere, but Monty figured that by now everyone in Lakeside realized *where* this storm came from. But how many had heard about an explosion in the Courtyard and could even guess why this vengeance was pounding the city?

When it was done, how many of these people would be left to bury their dead and rebuild their lives? How many would try to pick up the pieces without ever knowing why this storm tried to destroy them?

<Tess.>

<Henry?>

<That Asia Crane is one of the humans who came to harm Meg. Nathan is driving the prey back to the Market Square. Don't let her escape.>

The special messenger raced toward the Corvine entrance. The fucking Crows wouldn't be out in this storm. The wind would snap off their wings. Gods below, *nothing* should be out in this storm.

But something was standing there. Two of them. In his way.

Female forms caught by the snowmobile's headlight. One of them was brown, but the other had red hair tipped with yellow and blue. They swung out of his way before he ran them down, but as he passed them, the brown one stomped her foot.

The earth lifted under him, under all that snow, tossing him and the snowmobile into the air. He felt the machine tipping and couldn't regain the balance. As he came down, he threw himself off the snowmobile to avoid being trapped.

He hit snow that melted under him so fast, he found himself at the bottom of a crater filled with several inches of steaming water. Then the red-haired female leaped into the crater, grabbed his shoulders, mashed her lips against his, and breathed into his mouth.

Fire burned his throat and seared his lungs. Burn holes appeared where the yellow and blue ends of her hair brushed against his parka. Struggling to breathe, he reached for his gun, tried to defend himself. She grabbed his hands, and fire burned through the gloves, turning his hands into torches.

She held on and *laughed*. Then she released him, sprang out of the crater, and disappeared.

Have to get out. Have to get away.

He was still struggling to draw air into his damaged lungs and pull himself out of the crater when the Wolves found him. And he was still alive when they began to feed.

Asia rubbed at the snow crusting her eyelashes and looked again.

She'd made it. She'd reached the Market Square. From bits she'd heard, the Others didn't always lock their doors. She might find something open, might be able to get out of this storm for a little while.

A howl came from somewhere behind her. That freaking Wolf. Why didn't it have the sense to hole up somewhere?

An answering howl came from somewhere ahead of her.

Gods above and below, *another one*?

She turned her back to the wind to give herself a chance to take a few full breaths. She couldn't take shelter in the Market Square. If the Wolves found her there, they would kill her. She had to get to her car. Or maybe she would leave the freaking car and just go to the Stag and Hare to wait out the storm.

With luck, the special messenger had stashed Meg somewhere. And the Wolf pup too. Maybe she wouldn't get as much money as she'd hoped, but the experience would be invaluable for her TV series and give her an "I've seen the real thing" edge no other actress could match.

As soon as she could get out of this city, she would head back to Sparkletown. She would meet with Bigwig, who would be her producer, and then she would spend a couple of days on a beach, baking in the sun until her bones finally thawed.

But before she could do any of that, she had to get out of the Courtyard.

Staying close to the buildings, Asia trudged the length of the employee parking lot to the wall that separated that lot from customer parking. Gasping for breath, she leaned against the wooden door that provided access between the two lots.

Almost out. Almost safe. She could make it.

She kicked snow away from the door in order to pull it open enough to squeeze through. Then she waded through thigh-high snow—and bumped into one of the other cars that was buried in the lot. Fighting her way to the lump of snow that was closest to the street, she let out a giddy laugh as she brushed the snow off the driver's-side door. She needed to get out of the storm for a few minutes before fighting her way up the street to the Stag and Hare.

"Keys," she said, pulling off a glove in order to unzip the pocket that held the car keys. With keys in hand, she went to the back of the car and kicked the snow away from the tailpipe to give the exhaust a way to escape. Then she hurried back to the door and opened it. "Going to get out of here. Going to get warm."

"No. You're not," Tess said.

Asia turned and felt something break inside her mind when she looked at the black hair that coiled and moved, looked at the face Tess usually hid behind the human mask. She tried to look away, but she couldn't make her eyes work, couldn't do anything but stare at something she didn't want to see.

She sagged and would have slid to the ground if Tess hadn't grabbed her arm to keep her upright.

She couldn't feel that arm, and her legs weren't working right. And beads of sweat trickled down the inside of her skull. She could feel them trickling and tickling inside of the bone.

That wasn't right.

Tess eased her into the driver's seat, lifting her legs and positioning them so that all she had to do was shift her foot to the gas pedal. Her hands were gently placed in her lap. Leaning in, Tess tossed the keys onto the passenger's seat. Asia could see them out of the corner of her eye, but she couldn't turn her head to look at them, couldn't lift her hand to reach for them. Couldn't do anything except feel the relentless, terrible thing that was happening inside her body.

It was raining inside her skull.

"Wha . . ."

Fingers turned her head so she could look at that terrible face with its terrible smile.

"Wha . . . are . . . you?"

Tess stared at her, then breathed in deep and sighed as if she'd just tasted something wonderful. "You monkeys have no word for what I am."

Her face was turned again so her eyes stared out the windshield that showed her nothing but snow. The car door closed.

Asia's mind continued to break. Her body continued to break. Nerves finally screamed their warnings of pain, but she couldn't move, couldn't speak.

And inside her skull, it continued to rain.

Tess squeezed through the door at the back of the parking lot, then pushed it closed.

In ancient times, there had been a name for her kind. But the naming attracted the named, so the word was said to be cursed. As races and languages changed, the symbol of the word, still recognized in the primal part of the human mind, was never translated into newer languages. Which was why, beyond a few whispered myths, even the rest of the *terra indigene* no longer knew about Namid's most ferocious predator.

Long ago, there *had* been a word for her kind. Then, as now, it meant "harvester of life."

CHAPTER 28

A car was stuck in the intersection, blocking traffic in every direction.

"No," Louis said as a man got out of that car and walked away. "No. You can't do that."

Monty watched the man and instinctively braced himself. "Louis, *he's trying to run from something.*"

Lightning struck the intersection, thunder shook everything on the street, and a gust of wind *shoved* the car out of the intersection as a sleigh raced by, heading for the hospital.

"Follow the sleigh." Monty's heart slammed against his chest. He could think of one person in the Courtyard who, if injured, would need human help. And if Meg Corbyn *was* in that sleigh, everyone in the hospital was at risk if the *terra indigene* reacted badly.

As if the blizzard wasn't a bad enough reaction.

Louis didn't ask questions. He turned right on Main Street and went after the sleigh, driving down a street that was suddenly cleared of all obstacles.

As they approached Lakeside Hospital, Monty pointed and said, "There."

Nodding, Louis started to make the turn into the emergency-care entrance.

The sleigh was parked right in front of the emergency-care doors. The horses—one black and one white—tossed their heads and stamped their feet. Lightning cracked the sky while thunder shook the car right off the pavement. It ended up packed against the snow mounded beside the emergency-care entrance.

"Damn it," Louis said softly, looking at the wall of snow against the driver's side of the car. "You need backup?"

Monty pushed his door open. "Don't know. You get the car out of the way of the ambulances first."

"Right."

Monty struggled to walk up the slight incline to the emergency-care doors, keeping his head down in an effort to see—and breathe. Whiteout conditions. Killer wind chill. And there, suddenly standing between him and the doors, were two females.

Not human, he thought as they watched him approach. *Not Other in the way the shifters and vampires were Other. Elementals.* He swallowed fear and refused to think about which ones he was dealing with.

"I'm Lieutenant Montgomery. I'm a friend of Ms. Corbyn." Maybe that was stretching the truth, but right now he'd stretch the truth until it broke if it got him inside so he could find out what happened.

"Our Meg is inside," the white-haired one said.

"She's hurt?"

"Yes."

He heard the rage in her voice, her hatred for the human race.

"I would like to help."

She stared at him with those inhuman eyes. Then she stepped aside. "Tell the monkeys that this storm will not end until Simon Wolfgard says our Meg will get well."

Monty bolted inside, intending to grab anyone who might know where Meg Corbyn could be found. Seeing a nurse, he reached for his badge. Before he could say anything, he heard a yip, a startled yell, and an enraged voice roaring, "She needs human medicine, so we brought her here. *Now fix her!*"

Monty ran toward the commotion. He slammed into a fur-covered but otherwise naked Simon Wolfgard, breaking the Wolf's clawed hold on a pale but angry doctor.

"Mr. Wolfgard!" Monty shouted. "Simon!"

Something wrong with the eyes, Monty thought. More than being neither human nor Wolf in form.

Someone whimpered nearby. He glanced at another *terra indigene* who was crouched on the floor, cradling a blanket-wrapped Meg Corbyn.

"Mr. Wolfgard, let me talk to the doctor. Let me help," he said firmly when Simon snarled at him. The Wolf didn't lunge at any of them, so Monty took the doctor by the arm and led him a few steps away.

"I'm Lieutenant C. J. Montgomery, Lakeside Police Department."

"Dr. Dominick Lorenzo. Look, Lieutenant, we've got ambulances fighting to get here with *people* who need our help. We can't be indulging *them* just because—"

"Sir, I understand your feelings. But she's human, and she's their Liaison. They came *here* for help. Unless she gets the very best care you can provide, this city will never see another spring. I'm sorry to place this burden on you, but the lives of everyone in Lakeside are now in your hands."

Lorenzo glanced toward the entrance. "You can't know the storm won't end."

"Yes, sir, I can, because the fury driving this storm was standing outside this hospital a minute ago and told me flat-out that our lives depend on their Liaison getting well."

"Gods above and below," Lorenzo muttered. Squaring his shoulders, he strode back to where Simon Wolfgard stood trembling with rage.

"Do you know what happened to your friend?" he asked.

"She fell through the ice when she was running from the enemy," Simon snarled.

"Most likely hypothermia, but we'll make sure nothing else is going on," Lorenzo said. "Let's get her into the exam room at the end."

Snatching Meg from the other *terra indigene* male, Simon followed Dr. Lorenzo. Monty followed them, and the other male trailed after him.

Monty half listened to Lorenzo's rapid instructions to the nurses who were getting Meg out of her wet clothes. Before the doctor could close the exam-room door, Simon muscled in, leaving Monty with little choice except to go in with him and hold him away from the doctor and nurses.

Turning his face to give Meg that much privacy, he whispered to Simon, "What's wrong with you? Are you sick?"

The question brought back some of the thinking intelligence in Wolfgard's eyes. "I feel . . . *angry*."

"Did you take anything before you started feeling angry?" *Any drugs?* Not likely, but it *was* possible Simon had ingested something without realizing it.

Simon shook his head, his eyes fixed on the people touching Meg.

Then a nurse sucked in a breath. Turning his head, Monty looked at Meg Corbyn's bare arms and saw the evenly spaced scars—and the crosshatch of scars on her left arm. Answering the unspoken question in Lorenzo's eyes, he said, "Yes, she's a *cassandra sangue*."

"Get more blankets and a heating pad," Lorenzo said. When one of the nurses bolted, he tipped his head to indicate he wanted to talk to them out of the room.

"How long was she in the water?" he asked Simon.

"Not long. We heard Winter scream when Meg fell through the ice. We pulled her out."

"And before that? Did you remove her coat before you brought her to the hospital?"

Simon shook his head. "No coat. No boots. She was running from the enemy."

"How did you get here?"

"We came in the sleigh."

Lorenzo didn't look happy. "All right. We'll start with external treatment; see if we get enough indication that we can bring her around that way. Now. That gash in her chin. I can close it without stitches, but only if you can leave the bandages alone. If you can't, I'll have to use stitches to make sure the gash stays closed and heals properly. But stitches puncture the skin, and that might cause her some mental distress, even in her present condition. Also, if I use stitches, the whole chin would no longer be viable for cutting."

Simon's eyes blazed red. He snarled, "Do you think we care about her because of her *skin*? She's not property to us. She's *Meg*."

Monty held on to the Wolf, pushing him back from Lorenzo. "He has to tell you that, Simon. You're standing in for Meg's family, and it's his duty to tell you so that you can decide what is best for her."

Simon panted with the effort to control himself. "Fix her."

"It would be best if you stayed out of the room while I tend to her."

Feeling the objection in the way the Wolf's muscles bunched, Monty said quickly, "If you give me your word that you'll wait right here, I'll go in and stand guard for you."

He thought Lorenzo might object, but the doctor just waited with him for Simon's answer.

A sharp nod. Wolfgard was panting and growling, so a nod was the best he could do to give permission.

The nurse arrived with blankets and a heating pad. Lorenzo and Monty followed her into the room. When Lorenzo closed the door, they all jumped at the howl that rose from the other side of the door.

"Can you keep him from doing that?" Lorenzo asked as he cleaned and closed the gash in Meg's chin. "Scaring everyone in the emergency room isn't going to help."

"Let him stay in here with her. I think he'll be calmer that way." Monty glanced at the bed, then looked away. "You've dealt with blood prophets before?"

"I saw a few of them during my residency. Anytime the skin is punctured, it opens the girl to prophecy."

"So if Ms. Corbyn needs stitches . . . ?"

"Only the gods know what she's seeing right now because of the gash," Lorenzo replied grimly. "Every stitch would only add to it."

Monty leaned against the wall, feeling sick. He didn't speak again until Lorenzo finished and the supplies were properly stowed away.

"Let him in," Lorenzo said.

Simon leaped into the room the moment Monty opened the door. He stared at Meg. "She's cold. She's shivering!"

"That's a good thing," Lorenzo replied. "We'll use the heating pad to warm up the blankets. We'll keep her warm, keep watch on her heart rate and breathing."

"Not so different from a Wolf," Simon said quietly.

"I'm calling in my men," Monty said, knowing he wouldn't have anyone but Louis for backup until the storm ended. "One of them will be on guard at all times."

"Is that necessary?" Lorenzo asked.

"Yes, sir, it is."

Simon blinked. "Winter is outside." He walked out of the room.

"I have to take care of other patients," Lorenzo said. He looked toward the two nurses.

"I'll keep an eye on Ms. Corbyn," Monty said. "Your people are needed elsewhere."

When Lorenzo and the nurses left, Monty noticed the Other who crouched against the wall outside the room. "I'm Lieutenant Montgomery. Can you tell me what happened in the Courtyard?"

"I know who you are," the male replied wearily, pushing to his feet. "I'm Jester." He walked into the exam room and closed the door. "I can tell you some of it."

When Jester finished, Monty stepped out of the room and called his men. He couldn't reach Kowalski, who had been trying to ski to the Courtyard, and hoped the man had found shelter somewhere. Debany and MacDonald were a few blocks from the hospital and were bringing in some injured citizens. When he reached Burke and gave a summary of what had happened, the captain agreed with the necessity for guards while the Liaison was in the hospital and an abduction attempt was still a possibility.

Sending Jester to fetch one of the plastic chairs from the waiting room, Monty stood by the bed. Was Meg's breathing labored? Was she too pale?

He leaned down and said quietly, "Ms. Corbyn? You're safe now. We're going to keep you safe. But you have to help us. We all need you to get well."

Her eyes fluttered open.

"Meg?"

"Cold." Her voice was barely audible. "Cold."

"We'll get you warm."

Her eyes closed.

A minute later, he heard Jester set down a chair by the door—and Simon Wolfgard returned, snow melting off the fur covering the mostly human body.

"She woke up for a moment," Monty said.

Simon rushed to the side of the bed. "Meg? Meg!"

"I'll let Dr. Lorenzo know she came around that much." Leaving Simon and Jester to stand watch, Monty found the doctor and reported. Then he found Louis, who was trying to reach his own team. Finally, he found a vending machine, got a cup of coffee, and returned to the exam room to begin his shift of guard duty.

Still in human form, his clothes spattered with Hurricane's blood, Jester curled up in a corner of the exam room, his head pressed to his knees. He whined softly for a few minutes, then drifted off to sleep.

Simon stood by the bed, watching Meg. He felt so confused, so . . . *angry*. He had a reason to be angry. The enemy had invaded the Courtyard, had destroyed buildings, had *killed* some of the *terra indigene*. And they had threatened Sam and tried to take Meg. Even so, this *angry* didn't feel right, and the closer he was to human, the more he felt not right.

"Did you take anything before you started feeling angry?" Monty had asked. The possible answer to the question made him uneasy, so he wasn't going to think about it. Not now.

He glanced at the closed door. Meg was cold, shivering. The blankets weren't helping. He knew what he would do for a member of his pack. He carefully got onto the narrow hospital bed, grumbling because it was barely wide enough for a single human. After fixing the covers over him and Meg, he shifted to Wolf and curled his tail over her feet.

Much better.

<Meg?> She couldn't hear him, couldn't answer, but he called anyway. <Meg?>

He stretched his neck, sniffing at the bandages that covered the gash in her chin. He didn't like them. They shouldn't be there. He wanted to pull them off and lick the wound. Lick and lick until it healed.

He drew back his head. He had promised to leave the bandages alone. He'd brought her here for human healing, so he mustn't undo what the doctor had done.

Not so angry now. Not feeling so alone now with his body touching hers.

Winter outside in the sleigh, those cold, rage-filled eyes fixed on him when he came out to talk to her.

<They are taking care of Meg,> he'd said. <They will make her well.>

Winter nodded. Then she and Air drove off. And as he turned to go back inside, the wind died down and the snow stopped falling.

The door opened. Simon turned his head and bared his teeth, ready to spring up and attack. But it was Dr. Lorenzo, so he stayed where he was.

"I came in to check on Ms. Corbyn," the doctor said. "I'll check her pulse, then use a stethoscope to listen to her heart and lungs." He touched her wrist and looked at his watch. Then he put the metal disk on her chest and appeared to be listening.

Could Lorenzo hear the little rattle in her lungs that Simon could hear without the disk?

"Pneumonia's a concern," Lorenzo said quietly. "But she might avoid any problems." He glanced at the Wolf body under the covers. "The main thing now is to keep her warm."

When Lorenzo left, Simon stretched out his neck again, still wanting to get rid of those bandages and the medicine smell under them. With a quiet grumble, he licked her arm instead.

Her fingers flexed, burrowed into his fur.

<Meg?>

"Don't tell Simon about spinning the BOW," she mumbled.

He lifted his head. *<Meg?>*

But she was asleep again.

Nowhere to go. Nothing he could do while she was here. Settling his head on her shoulder, he closed his eyes and slept.

CHAPTER 29

Vlad studied the ash that drifted off the two bodies. The last two enemies had been in sight of the Corvine entrance, had almost escaped. Riding their machines, they might have gotten out if they'd met up with anyone but Fire.

Suddenly aware that the swooshing sound he'd been hearing for the past minute had stopped, he looked toward the open gate. The figure hesitated, then came forward, moving slowly on skis.

"Mr. Sanguinati? It's Officer Kowalski. I work with Lieutenant Montgomery."

He recognized the voice, but he still felt suspicious. "Do humans ski during storms?"

"No, sir, not by choice. But I heard about the explosion in the Courtyard and was coming to see if I could help when I got caught in the blizzard. My mobile phone is still working, and I got a call through to the station. The lieutenant's teams are heading for the hospital. Protection for Ms. Corbyn while she's there."

Still trying to work out if there was another message under the words, Vlad looked toward the Wolfgard part of the Courtyard as howls filled the air.

"Problem?" Kowalski asked.

"One of the Wolves died."

"In the storm?"

"He was shot by the intruders."

"I'm sorry."

And Kowalski was genuinely sorry, Vlad realized. He looked at the two snowmobiles that Fire had left untouched. "Do you know how to work these machines?"

"I've ridden on them a few times, so I know enough to drive one."

"Then you will show me, and we'll use the machines to reach the hospital."

Picking up the steaming mug of tea, Henry walked over to the windows of his studio. Nothing he wanted to see out there. Not tonight. *Terra indigene* had died today, and some humans had died in the storm that was the Elementals' response to those deaths—and to the harm done to Meg.

The intruders had also died, and that was good.

Now they would see if the humans would resume their wary peace with the *terra indigene* or if there would be war. He hoped the humans would show some sense. It had been many years since the *terra indigene* had crushed a human city. If it came to that here, he would regret the deaths of some of these people.

Shaking his head, Henry sipped his tea. No point stirring up the bees if you weren't looking for honey.

On his way back to this part of the Courtyard, he'd found Nathan, exhausted and half frozen, still trying to chase after that Asia. But Tess had dealt with Asia Crane, so Henry shifted from spirit bear to Grizzly and broke the trail for the Wolf right up to the back door of the efficiency apartments. The girls had put Nathan's paws in warm water to melt the ice clumped between his pads, had patted him dry with towels, and given him food and water. Now Nathan and John were curled up in the apartment, asleep, while the girls were at A Little Bite, making food and hot drinks. And Lorne, with Henry's permission, was in the social center, letting the stranded use the toilets and rest in a warm place for a while.

Last winter they would have stood behind their locked doors and watched the humans die. But things had changed around the Lakeside Courtyard, and those changes held promise for all of Namid's children. So he hoped the human government would be wise enough not to choose war.

Meg woke slowly, feeling a rattle and burn in her chest.

White room. The hated and feared bed. And a figure at the end of the bed.

"No," she moaned. Had it been a dream, a delusion?

"Meg?" The figure leaped toward her, his weird-shaped hands coming down on either side of her head. "Stay awake, Meg. Stay awake!"

A face out of nightmares, out of visions of dark water and terrible cold. Then the fur receded and she recognized him. "S-Simon?"

Red flickered in his amber eyes and he snarled at her. "If you *ever* scare me like this again, *I will eat you*!" Then he pressed his forehead against her arm and whined.

Not a dream? She had reached the Courtyard, had been building the life that had swum through the dark dreams? "Where are we?"

"Hospital." He raised his head and snarled again. "You stupid female. You fell through the ice and cut your chin!"

He paced, he panted, he snarled and whined. He threatened to eat her a half dozen times. But when he howled, all kinds of people ran into the room.

Terror filled her when she saw the man in the white coat—the same kind of coat that had been worn by the Walking Names—but Lieutenant Montgomery was the next person into the room, followed by Vladimir Sanguinati.

"Ms. Corbyn, I'm Dr. Lorenzo," the white coat said. "You're awake, and that's welcome news." He slanted a glance at Simon. "Although hospitals are supposed to be quiet zones, even when there is good news."

Simon just growled at the doctor.

"I want to leave," Meg said, desperate to get away from the bed and the room that felt too much like the compound, like a cage.

Dr. Lorenzo shook his head. "Considering the condition of the streets, none of us are going anywhere until morning. Besides, you need warmth and rest. Which is why Lieutenant Montgomery, Mr. Sanguinati, and I were talking about moving you to a private room on another floor. It will be quieter, and, frankly, we need the exam rooms down here in emergency."

"I agree with Dr. Lorenzo," Vlad said. "A private room will be less stressful for everyone."

"But I want to leave," Meg said, looking at Simon. Would he understand why she was afraid to be here?

Simon hesitated, then shook his head. "Your lungs rattle. I can hear them. We'll stay here until your lungs don't rattle."

So they bundled her up, plunked her in a wheelchair, and took her up to another room, where they tucked her into another bed, gave her warm drinks and a bowl of soup, and then left her with the vampire and the Wolf.

"Sam?" she asked.

"He's fine," Simon said.

"He's a little hoarse from howling for so long," Vlad said. "But otherwise, he's fine. After we sent news to the Courtyard that you would be all right, he settled down. He's still with Grandfather Erebus. They're watching movies."

"Kept him safe," she whispered.

"You should have stayed with Erebus too," Simon growled. "Stupid female. And I do not want to know about you spinning the BOW, because I'm sure I would have to bite you."

She blinked at him. *Oh. That wasn't a dream either?*

Vlad chuckled, an earthy sound. "Let it go, Simon. It's probably best if we don't know too much about how our Meg ended up in the creek."

"Asia," Meg said. "She came to the apartments. She tried to take Sam. Did she get away?"

They both shrugged, but she saw the look they exchanged. And she wondered how much special meat was going to be available to the Courtyard's residents over the next few days.

CHAPTER 30

Throughout the night, Monty, Louis, and Kowalski stood shifts outside Meg Corbyn's hospital room, while Debany and MacDonald ferried medicines to people who needed them and could be reached. At one point, Jester had ridden back to the Courtyard with Vlad, who returned with clothes for Simon and Meg, two more snowmobiles that the Others offered to MacDonald and Debany for their use . . . and Jake Crowgard.

Monty didn't ask about the location of the previous owners of the snowmobiles. Maybe they would be filling out DLU forms for those men; maybe not.

By dawn, news began filtering in.

Lakeside was cut off for the time being, not only by a record snowfall but by the "glaciers" that blocked every road out of the city. Monty wondered if spot melting to clear a road or two was possible—if anyone dared to approach the Courtyard and ask politely.

An hour earlier, Officer Debany called to tell him Asia Crane had been found dead in her car. Monty hoped he never heard that much controlled terror in a man's voice again.

The shifters and the vampires are the buffer between us and the rest of what lives in the Courtyards, Monty thought. *We were given a glimpse yesterday. Let's hope we're smart enough to heed the warning.*

He pushed to his feet when he saw Douglas Burke walk toward him, then walk past him a few steps—just far enough so they wouldn't be directly outside Meg Corbyn's room.

"Captain."

"Lieutenant." Burke hesitated. "Thought you should know. Our mayor died in the blizzard." There was a peculiar, almost fearful note in his voice.

"He was out in it?" Monty asked.

"He was in his bedroom, with the door locked and the windows shut. When they found him this morning, the room was filled with snow, floor to ceiling. Medical examiner will have to determine if he froze to death or smothered—or died of some other cause, since there are some suspicious wounds around major arteries and an insufficient amount of blood around the body." He paused. "The acting mayor wants it known that he will do his utmost to maintain a cordial relationship with the *terra indigene*." Another pause. Burke lowered his voice even more and added, "Between you and me, I think the *terra indigene* connected His Honor's interest in apprehending Meg Corbyn with the attack on the Courtyard and the abduction attempt. And that's why they killed him."

"But the governor was the one who had pushed for it, sending the orders down the line." Monty studied his captain's face and felt chilled. "What else happened?"

"The governor of the Northeast Region also died last night."

"But the governor lives in Hubbney." The actual name was Hubb NE. A small town that was the hub of government for the Northeast, it was an hour's train ride north of Toland, and it was hundreds of miles away from Lakeside. "How did he die?" *Heart attack?* Monty hoped. *Or a traffic accident?*

"He froze to death in his bathtub." Burke's smile held no humor. "Not only did the water freeze around him so fast he wasn't able to escape, but it somehow forced its way down his throat and then froze in his lungs. A hideous way to die, I should think."

"Not too dissimilar to what might have happened to a woman if she fell through the ice while being pursued by unknown assailants," Monty said, shuddering.

"Not too dissimilar," Burke agreed.

So the Others had decided the governor was also to blame for the attack and had reached across hundreds of miles to eliminate another enemy.

"Well," Burke said. "I'm guessing the hospital has provided a place for their staff and law enforcement to crash, so why don't you take a couple of hours?"

Monty tipped his head toward the door. "It's my shift."

"I'm taking your shift, Lieutenant. Get some rest. You've earned it."

He was swaying on his feet, so he didn't argue. But he did wonder which one would be the first to poke his head out the door to get a look at the unfamiliar police officer: the Wolf, the vampire, or the Crow.

On the Thaisday after the storm, Monty walked into Howling Good Reads and nodded to Heather as he scanned the front of the store. Then he walked up to the counter, giving her a warm smile.

"I noticed the Open sign," he said. He and his men had driven by several times a day once the roads were cleared, checking for that sign. "No customers today?"

"Not yet," Heather replied with forced brightness. Then she pointed to the stacks of paper on the counter and the full cart of books. "But there are plenty of orders to bundle up for shipping."

You're not sure the human customers will come back, Monty thought. He had wondered the same thing. Just like he'd wondered if the Others would open any of these stores to humans again. The Lakeside Courtyard was the most progressive Courtyard in the whole of Thaisia, with its human employees and human customers. Granted, humans still had limited access, but it was a positive start that could ripple through the continent and ease a little of the ever-present tension between humans and Others in cities and towns across Thaisia. But the Lakeside mayor and Northeast Region governor aiding and abetting someone the *terra indigene* considered an enemy could also ripple through the continent, and the storm in Lakeside and the slaughter in Jerzy were grim reminders of how the Others took care of difficulties caused by humans.

And yet there had been a bright note, and that's what had brought him to HGR as soon as the store reopened.

"I'd like a word with Mr. Wolfgard if he's in," Monty said.

"I'll see if he's available." Heather picked up the phone and dialed an extension. "Mr. Wolfgard? Lieutenant Montgomery would like to speak with you." A pause. "Okay, I'll tell him." She smiled at Monty. "He says to go back to the stockroom."

"Thanks." As he walked to the back of the store, he realized this meeting would also have significant ripples, and the next few minutes would determine if those ripples would be good or bad.

"Lieutenant." Simon glanced at him, then checked a list and pulled more books off the stockroom shelves.

"Mr. Wolfgard. No watch Wolf today?"

"They come and go. That was always true, although Ferus and Nathan were the ones who spent the most time on guard at HGR. Ferus is in the Ash Grove now, and Nathan thinks our Liaison is more entertaining than the customers."

"Ms. Corbyn has returned to work?" He'd seen the lights on in the Liaison's Office when he and Kowalski had driven past, and that, too, had been a good sign.

Simon nodded. "She should stay in the den until next week, but she *snarled* at me when I suggested it."

Monty wasn't sure if the Wolf was offended or pleased, so he didn't reply. But he thought, *Good for you, Meg.*

"Something on your mind, Lieutenant?" Simon asked.

Many things, but he'd start with the one least likely to offend. "I understand you've set aside one of the efficiency apartments for my officers' use. Thank you."

Simon looked uncomfortable. Then he shrugged. "We had the space. We set two of the apartments aside for our human employees so they don't have to go out in a storm. And Henry still has the one he prefers when he wants to stay close to his studio. Letting your officers use the last apartment was sensible."

And it would add another layer of defense to the Courtyard.

"I heard you removed the water tax on the Chestnut Street Police Station and the hospital that took care of Meg."

"So?" Simon disappeared for a minute, then returned with an armload of books that he put on the cart.

"It's appreciated." Now they'd come to the next layer of discussion. "And to show his own appreciation, Dr. Lorenzo would like to set up a small office here and provide medical treatment for your human employees."

No reason to mention that part of Lorenzo's interest was the *cassandra sangue* living among the Others. Having the opportunity to gain some understanding of Meg Corbyn's race was not something the good doctor would pass up.

"We don't have room for . . ." Simon stopped.

Monty held his breath.

"Maybe," Simon said. "But allowing this doesn't change the fact that most of you are still just meat."

No, it doesn't change that, Monty thought. *But* most of us *is a long step from* all of us, *and if you can learn to trust some of us, all of us have a better chance of surviving.*

"I'll discuss this with the Business Association," Simon said. "Maybe Dr. Lorenzo can come and talk to us about an office—and check on Meg while he's here."

"I'll tell him to call Howling Good Reads and set up a time with you."

He could read body language well enough to recognize Simon was feeling closed in by all this talk about more humans in the Courtyard, even if he was the one allowing them access. So this conversation wasn't going to last much longer.

"I have work to do," Simon said, a growl of warning under the words.

"Then I'll be brief," Monty replied. "Your anger at the hospital was excessive even under the circumstances. I think you know that. Do you have any idea what caused that enhanced aggression?"

"No."

Flat. Cold. The voice of a leader who will allow no challenge.

And a lie.

"All right," Monty said, taking a step back. "I'm willing to help. Please remember that."

Red flickered in the Wolf's amber eyes.

The sound of a door closing. A moment later, Jester approached them.

Giving the Coyote a nod, Monty walked out of the stockroom. He stayed in the store a minute longer, scanning the display of mysteries and making a selection.

Humans have courage and resilience and they endure, Monty thought as he paid for the book and left Howling Good Reads. Roads would be opened, buildings repaired, and life would go on.

And the humans who had contact with the Courtyard would do their best to help everyone survive.

Simon stared at the Coyote while Montgomery's words circled around him, closing in.

"Your anger at the hospital was excessive even under the circumstances."

"How much did you hear?" Simon asked.

"I like it here," Jester said. "I want to stay."

Montgomery's words seemed to echo in the room.

"Do you have any idea what caused that enhanced aggression?"

"How much did you hear?" Simon snarled.

"I won't tell," Jester said. "I'll never tell."

Quick-thinking Coyote who sometimes saw too much, heard too much. But unlike many of his kind, Jester wouldn't break his word.

"You can stay." Of course, what wasn't said was if he couldn't trust Jester to stay, he also couldn't allow the Coyote to leave. But he figured Jester knew that already.

"Thanks, Simon." Jester backed away. "I'll go check with Meg and see if she wants the ponies to come up today."

Then he was gone, and a moment later, Simon heard HGR's back door closing.

"Do you have any idea what caused that enhanced aggression?"

Oh yes. He'd had plenty of time to think about it while they'd waited to take Meg home, and he had a very good idea what had caused that strange anger. Even the Sanguinati wouldn't drink the sweet blood of the *cassandra sangue*, and he'd licked up plenty of it from the gash in Meg's chin.

Winter and Air hadn't paid attention to him on the race to the hospital, but Jester had been with him. And Blair and Vlad had been with him at the creek when they pulled Meg out of the water. Give either of them enough bits of information, and they would figure it out too.

He would keep his suspicions to himself for a few more days. Then he would talk to Henry before deciding who else needed to know what he suspected: that the blood of *cassandra sangues* was the source of the sickness that was touching humans and Others in the West.

But that was for another day, and Henry already carried the weight of another secret.

Simon had been at the hospital guarding Meg when Asia Crane was found. He hadn't seen her, but Henry had. And all Henry said to him was, "I know what Tess is. We will never speak of this."

Dangerous to be the only one who looked at a body and understood a truth about the predator who did the killing. Or maybe wise to be the only one to carry that burden. Either way, Tess was still running A Little Bite and baking chocolate chip cookies for Meg and Sam.

"Enough," he growled. "You have a business to run." And until he pulled these books so Heather could fill the orders, he had to stay here instead of going over to the Liaison's Office to play with Meg for a few minutes.

Checking the list, he pulled more books off the shelves in the stockroom and thought about Meg, because thinking about Meg made him feel calmer, happier.

She had been released from the hospital on Moonsday, but he'd used Sam's need to stay close to her as a way to keep her home for a few more days. And he'd also pointed out that most of Lakeside was still shut down, so the stores *couldn't* send out any deliveries. Even then, she'd been stubborn about staying indoors.

Well, he could be stubborn too, especially when dressing Meg had turned into a game. He and Vlad and Jenni had raided the Market Square stores for clothes to keep Meg warm. They made fingerless gloves for her, and then demanded that she wear mittens over them if she so much as stuck her nose outdoors. If she actually went outside for even a minute, she had to wear an undershirt, a turtleneck, a sweater, and a down vest zipped up all the way so her chest would stay warm. Plus her winter coat and a scarf and wool cap. And two pairs of socks with her boots.

None of them had given the colors of the clothes any thought until Merri Lee came back from visiting Meg on Windsday afternoon and grumbled about her friend being dressed like a paint-store explosion.

Shortly after that, he'd overheard Merri Lee, Heather, and Ruthie ordering clothes that, they said, would work with what Meg already had, so he figured the clothes game had run its course.

But there was still the hat game.

He scanned the shelves again when he didn't find two of the books he wanted.

"We're out of that one too?" he muttered as he added another caught-in-a-storm thriller to his list of reorders. Despite the lack of customers today, he'd been on the move since he unlocked the door, and he'd done nothing but pull stock to fill orders going to *terra indigene* settlements!

He refused to consider why the Elementals had put in a request for a handful of the caught-in-a-storm titles.

He stopped and let a shudder run through him. Even among the *terra indigene*, it took a little time to stop feeling afraid when the Elementals lashed out in rage.

But even Winter was calmer now that Meg was home.

Elliot's meeting with the acting mayor had also helped calm everyone. The man had been quick to assure the Courtyard consul that all the wanted posters that had provoked such a tragic case of mistaken identity had been destroyed, and the police would do their utmost to apprehend anyone who caused Ms. Corbyn any distress in the future.

All the Others living in Courtyards throughout Thaisia would be watching to see if the human government in Lakeside would keep its word.

The man who sent the enemy into the Courtyard, the man who had given Meg a designation instead of a name, was still out there. Her skin was still worth too much profit for him to stop trying to get her back.

That Controller was still looking for her, and now the *terra indigene* were looking for him. The governor hadn't known much, but he'd told the Elementals who came visiting his house in Hubbney everything he knew about Meg's enemy. Sooner or later, the Others would find the man, and a human piece of Thaisia would be reclaimed by the wild country.

Simon looked at his hands, which had grown furry. He snarled when he couldn't get them back to looking human, a sign that he was too agitated to wear this skin. Since he didn't want to scare off Heather, he did the sensible thing.

He stripped off his clothes, shifted to Wolf, and went to the Liaison's Office to have a few minutes of playtime with Meg.

Meg put in a music disc and turned on the player. She didn't want to listen to the radio anymore. She didn't want to hear about the people who died in the storm or the damage the city had sustained. Maybe she should feel bad about not wanting to listen to the news, but what happened wasn't her fault. If she had let those men take her, the Elementals still would have savaged Lakeside for the death of old Hurricane, if for nothing else. She could argue that, being the reason the storm ended, she had saved more people than she had harmed by being here.

Didn't make her feel any less sorry for the people who had been hurt. And it made her wonder whether Lieutenant Montgomery felt the same way.

She had expected to die in the Courtyard, had seen the images from the prophecies come to pass. But the outcome had been different. Not only had she survived, but she had also prevented Asia Crane and those men from taking Sam.

She would always be short, but she wasn't helpless and she wasn't small. Not anymore.

She glanced at the clock. Bracing for the sound, she set the mail on the sorting table a moment before Nathan howled. Apparently, he intended to do that on the hour, every hour, while the office was open.

The Meg Report. *Meg is here. Meg is fine.*

She hoped he would grow bored with this particular game very soon.

Hearing a sound from the back room, Meg picked up a stack of mail and barely glanced up when Simon trotted into the sorting room.

Something had changed between them while she was in the hospital. She wasn't sure if Simon considered her a friend, a playmate, or a valued toy, but he seemed to enjoy playing games with her.

Speaking of games . . .

Standing on his hind legs, Simon rested one forepaw on the table and extended the other to touch her nose. She suspected the name of this game was Plop the Hat on Meg. If her nose wasn't warm enough according to whatever criteria he was using at that moment, he would fetch the floppy fleece hat he had bought for her and make her put it on.

But she was no longer helpless or small. If she was going to be a squeaky toy for big, furry playmates, she was also going to have some say in the games. Starting now, with the choice of game.

She pulled back her head and glared at him. "If you try to touch my nose again today, I won't give you any cookies."

Simon withdrew the paw, seemed to consider that for a moment, then reached out again as if testing her.

"I mean it, Simon. No cookies for the *whole day*."

Nose or cookies. Hard choice. But in the end, the cookies won.